Pick 6

by

Francis Zita

First published by Dog Ear Publishing
4011 Vincennes Rd
Indianapolis, IN 46268
www.dogearpublishing.net

ISBN: 978-1-4575-4461-3

This book is printed on acid-free paper.

This book is a work of fiction. Places, events, and situations in this book are purely fictional and any resemblance to actual persons, living or dead, is coincidental.

Printed in the United States of America

For GDP, mi amor.
The best and the beautiful.

"All animals are equal, but some animals are more equal than others."

—George Orwell, *Animal Farm*

CHAPTER

1

Meetings, trainings, and spreadsheets. Corporate team building. Godforsaken conference calls. James cursed them all as he smacked the pillow and rolled over yet again, sighing. He tore off the covers and dangled a leg from the side of the bed, cringing at the bright red numbers of the alarm clock. Every minute of restlessness meant rising for the dreaded work day loomed that much closer.

Three hours trickled by since his body woke him up, informing the middle-aged man he needed to empty his bladder once again. The nightly occurrence tormented James for the last several months and getting the condition checked out by a doctor was atop his to-do list in the immediate future. But he knew it wouldn't happen. Over two years had passed since his last routine physical.

The bathroom disruption propelled his unsettled mind onto full alert, generating a keen awareness of how much sleep he was losing. A half-hour felt like an hour and an hour equaled an eternity, compounding the stress that plagued him over his everyday monetary issues. Did he pay the car insurance on time? When were their property taxes due? Would there be any raises at work? Were the rumors of downsizing true? He tried fantasizing about golfing on the PGA tour and traveling back in time to his youth, but nothing could penetrate his thick wall of worry. The only remedy to his angst ridden situation was a change of scenery.

He slid off the bed and placed his feet on the fake hardwood floor, crouching down, searching for his gray tattered sweat pants and a T-shirt.

Quietly, gingerly, mindful to not wake Dee, he tiptoed from the bedroom down a dark hallway and into a small corner office. He flicked on a table lamp before falling into a desk chair to fire up his laptop.

As the computer booted up James rubbed his belly and grimaced. The leftover nachos he selected for his late night snack were regretted. He crunched on a chalky antacid and connected online, engaging in his newfound hobby of chess. After getting destroyed three times in a row by an opponent from Sri Lanka he declined the invite for a rematch, logging onto his email account instead. That move didn't prove any better. All twelve new messages were nothing but spam, marketing everything from sweepstakes scams to penis enlargement to international brides.

He surfed the internet searching for a website of acceptable intrigue. The usual porn sites he frequented offered little hope as James wasn't horny and had no interest in masturbating despite its reliability as a sleep aid. He read a sports blog, checked the weather, and watched a video clip of *Saturday Night Live*. Completing the entire Home Depot customer feedback survey took only five minutes; the one from Lowe's even less. The monotony of nomadic clicking eventually led him to the celebrity gossip section of his favorite New York newspaper.

James scrolled along the page and was in the midst of a scandalous story set in a Manhattan night club when an advertisement for a lottery game flashed on the side of the screen. It was bright and distracting and he closed it out twice but it reappeared anyway. He paused, recalling his family trip to upstate New York just two weeks beforehand. Regardless of their insufficient funds, the Hortons ventured northward for his godparents' fiftieth anniversary party and to commemorate the special event he'd purchased a lottery ticket. But a combination of too much booze and too little sleep had clouded his memory. He'd forgotten all about it.

He slid open the filing cabinet and dug through a pile of paperwork long overdue to be shredded. The motel receipt for their New York getaway was halfway down, stuck to a high interest pre-approved credit card offer. He noted the date of the party and entered the lottery website, staring at the dusty screen with the kids' fingerprint smudges all over it. With nothing else to do at three in the morning on a work night James leaned back, reminiscing about the fifty year celebration of his Aunt Helen and Uncle Stewart.

A VFW Post in a rustic suburb of Buffalo served as the party venue and his uncle gave a long winded toast that made people cry. With the help of some cousins he never met before, James slammed multiple shots of Jäger-meister at the open bar. Big glasses of draft beer were involved and somehow, over the course of four hours, Dee convinced the self-proclaimed world's worst dancer to step out onto the dance floor. Once there he wouldn't leave and proceeded to cut the carpet with the rhythmless moves of the white boy shuffle. He winced at the disturbing images his dancing conjured up and preferred to have that section of the night permanently blocked from his memory.

The party began midafternoon and wrapped up early for the majority of the old timer crowd. Anybody under the age of ninety with their wits about them was just getting warmed up, resulting in an after party back at the motel. On the way over James took an essential detour to a liquor store loading up on spirits. He asked the cashier for a quick pick lottery ticket and jammed it into his pocket. He promised to remember the night forever but the rest of the evening was a peppered blur of meaningless conversations about religion, sports, politics, and what city deserved bragging rights for the best chicken wings in the world.

James sat up in the chair, crunching another antacid, rubbing his stomach some more. He had more fun at the party than initially remembered and with a large chunk of it accounted for he couldn't help but think about the ticket. *Where could I have put that little fucker?* he asked himself. Intrigued, the task of attempting to locate the tiny piece of paper he'd purchased over a thousand miles away preoccupied his brain as the prospect of returning to sleep faded away.

The first place he checked was his wallet. He cracked open the pleather money holder given as a Father's Day gift and saw nothing more than twenty-seven dollars that needed to be stretched for both gas and lunches along with a two-for-one golf coupon. He contemplated sneaking back in the bedroom to rummage through his nightstand but given the time, thought better of it. He looked through the desk, the filing cabinet, and behind the bookcase. James searched every inch of the 100 square foot room with no success.

He knew the ticket was probably lost into a forgetful black hole never to be seen again, but he ignored the obvious and forged ahead. He rummaged through a stack of take-out menus in the kitchen junk drawer, removed the garbage can liner, and flipped over the cushions of the couch. Finding his son's old retainer and a DVD two weeks overdue at the library was a bonus to be sure, but the hunt appeared to be bleak.

A picture of the Twin Towers hung unevenly near the front door and as James passed it he caught his reflection in the glass. The chin under his chin was birthing a new chin and the lightly etched wrinkles that once skimmed his forehead had burrowed into deep trenches. He shuddered while straightening the frame and touched his face, poking and pulling the skin of a stranger.

A loud tapping sound on the window was a welcomed distraction. Giant bugs and hungry moths were drawn to the light, repeatedly slamming the glass. One bug resembled the creature from *Aliens*. Past them to the right, three feet away in a layer of crushed stone, bubbled a sprinkler head that shouldn't be bubbling. James stepped outside to ensure the system was completely turned off, not wasting a drop, not wasting a penny, and added a new spigot on the household list of items to replace.

The warm tropical air engulfed him like a hot wet blanket and after living in Florida for over twenty years as a northern transplant he never adjusted his body or mind to cope with the stifling heat. He walked towards the driveway and keyed into his beige Corolla parked next to the minivan. The search continued.

He plopped down in the passenger's seat, opened the glove box, and sifted through the cornucopia of items inside. After removing the car manual, a pair of broken sunglasses, and a bundle of McDonald's napkins, he came across an envelope printed with stationary from their motel stay in Buffalo. He tore it open and a small note was scribbled onto the inside flap. It appeared to be written in half-legible fluid drunkenese, which James could understand. He held it up to the interior car light, squinting. It read, "KEEP ME DUDE! GIANTS LOST. YOU OWE COUSIN HARRY 50 BUCKS."

Two crooked arrows bookended the note pointing towards the bottom. He reached inside and extracted the lucky find. The prize was wrinkled and frayed with a large grease spot on the corner. James laughed aloud. He hadn't a clue how the ticket got sealed in an envelope, placed in the car, and hidden inside the glove box with a note to boot. He shook his head exiting the car and smiled. The scavenger hunt was complete.

The ceiling fan swirled overhead, wobbling, while he compared the numbers on the lottery website to the ones held in his hand. The first number up was 2: check. The second number came up as 7, the third number 16. Check and check. He scratched the side of his head and circled the numbers in pen. *At least I got my dollar investment back.* The fourth number on the ticket was 23: check. He wiggled to the edge of the chair and nibbled his lower lip, his face close to the screen. The fifth number on the ticket was 40, also a check. His heart pumped like a thoroughbred galloping down the homestretch and he shifted his wide eyes one space to the right, begging for the last number to shine upon him, begging for the glory of it all and....

He saw nothing. The screen went blank, then gray, and then blank again. The laptop made a harsh grinding sound before shutting down. He hit a few keys, hit Ctrl-Alt-Delete, and then hit the computer itself. The deep freeze had taken over. James threw his arms above his head and stood up, forcing the chair to slide into the wall. He released a low pitched, "Holy shit," that bounced around the office but was within an acceptable decibel range of not waking anybody up. The ticket was a definite winner of some sort, but for how much?

James wanted to kick himself for the technical malfunction, thinking of the afternoon he spent computer shopping the previous year.

"Nah, this one's too much," he said to the overzealous sales associate, his arms folded across his chest. "Actually, all of these seem kind of pricy. Don't you have anything cheaper? I only need it for the basics. Getting on the internet. Checking my email. That kind of stuff."

The associate led him to an area in the back of the store with dim lighting and grimy shelves where a hand written sign hung overhead stating REFURBISHED. It was a death row of motherboards and hard drives, CPUs and RAM; everything mis-matched together for one last gasp of computing life. James was thrilled. With the money he saved the kids were treated to summer long passes at the water park. One week after the store's limited warranty expired the computer began freezing up and blacking out. Three months later, the company went out of business.

James unplugged the frozen laptop from behind his desk and removed the battery. At least forty-five minutes were needed before it would boot up again. He had no idea why.

He left the house under controlled excitement and dashed into the garage, moving around several old paint cans amidst a pile of clutter. Lying on his stomach, he reached for the pack of hidden cigarettes stashed away when once, maybe twice a month, he snuck out to light up a smoke.

Two summers earlier, while vacationing at Cocoa Beach, the nasty habit he enjoyed so thoroughly was kyboshed under the duress of Dee threatening to withhold her highly prized vagiola if the practice continued. The monastic repercussions were certainly not to be had for the married man, but considering what was at stake for the Hortons' future, he rationalized that this particular moment in time transcended all the rules.

A flawless smoke ring floated towards the ceiling. He straddled a five-gallon bucket of house paint wondering how much money hitting five out of six numbers would get him. Depending on how many people played, how many people won, and the size of the jackpot; the payout could be as miniscule as a few grand or as large as a $100,000. Maybe more. It wasn't life altering money or the kind where you quit your job and move to Hawaii, but it would definitely serve as a pressure relief valve. Until that night, winning $300 on a scratch-off was the most he'd ever won.

But what if? He paused, stamping out the cigarette after maximizing to the edge of the filter, allowing his mind to speculate the infinite possibilities of attaining the sixth number and the power it would unleash.

His hands were clammy and his mouth was dry as he paced about the garage contemplating the *what if* factor of financial freedom. James wanted it so bad it was painful. Questions of all kinds sprang to his head. *What would I buy? Who would we help out? What's the fair amount to donate to charity? Should it be kept a secret? Whose face would I rub in it?* He peeled back the top of the cigarette pack and saw it was empty. Five butts and an hour had passed him by.

He looked around the garage before leaving and felt scared, perhaps even terrified. Terrified for knowing deep in his core that without divine intervention or some other miracle, the realistic possibility of achieving anything great in his life was too far removed. He didn't have the natural ability or aptitude to be an entrepreneur, inventor, intellect, or successful businessman. Planning for his future with great promise never got past the planning stage. It all went so fast. James Horton was capped out in a mediocre career with a hefty mortgage, two kids, unrelenting bills, and the limited prospect of earning more money. That's all there was and all there would be until his death. He knew it. He saw it once before, witnessing his father fight to go to work while dying because he needed the money. His old man was quagmired in debt with nothing to show for it. At forty-eight years old, James desperately didn't want that nightmare to be his destiny. He wished for nothing more than to escape the haunting fear that grew in reality with each passing day.

Both knees cracked as they hit the concrete slab. He hung his head and pressed his palms together, praying to God for the first time since Christmas, struggling to remember every word of the Lord's Prayer. He assured his almighty savior of the genuine good intentions he had for the money. Fulfilling his church tithing as instructed by the priests would be honored to the fullest. As a Catholic part-timer, he hedged his bets the best way he knew how.

He washed up in the kitchen for his post-cigarette scrub down and popped in a breath mint. The computer booted up slowly as he stretched his back, still sore from cleaning the attic. He took a long deep breath and then quickly, as if ripping off a Band-Aid, looked at the screen. His legs bounced in unison. His teeth were clenched. The final number displayed on the website was the most important of his life: 56. He blinked several times, rubbed his stubble chin, and second guessed if his eyes and brain were working in proper alignment. He checked the numbers again. And again. And again. He checked all six numbers at least ten times, frontwards and backwards, inside and out, upside and down. Each time the results were the same. James Horton had done it. He'd won the New York State lottery.

His body tingled and he felt dizzy. Breathing became difficult. He didn't know if he was overwhelmed by euphoria or having a panic attack. On the cusp of hyperventilating, he placed his head between his knees, steadying himself, hoping not to faint. Strange thoughts pushed to the surface, questioning his reality. *Maybe I'm asleep. Is this a dream? An acid flashback? My parents warned me not to do drugs. Am I dead? Is this heaven? Could I really be this lucky?* Never one to believe in the metaphysical, time slowed to a crawl, and he bordered on the verge of an out of body experience.

Ten minutes passed before he mustered enough strength to move his limbs and regain his composure. He slid open the desk drawer, not knowing why, but searching for a sign, searching for an answer. The latest mortgage statement waiting to be paid rested on top of his check book. He viewed it, noticing the outstanding balance they owed to the bank along with the horrifying monthly payment due in five days. The simple act was like a backhand across the face.

He launched himself out of the chair and jumped two inches off the ground, yelling a thunderous, "Yes!" Screaming an unintelligible arrangement of blissful cusswords, he bolted into the bedroom and leapt next to his wife, shaking her. "Honey get up! We're rich! You hear me? We're rich."

She shot straight up as if stung by a bee. Startled and disoriented, his wife looked around in a panic. "Are the kids alright? Is the house on fire? What's going on?" she said, ready to fight or flee.

"Dee, listen. Get up. We hit the lotto. I got all six numbers. We won the lottery!"

"What are you talking about?" she said, falling back onto the pillow. "You scared me to death. It's five o'clock in the morning."

"You won't ever have to worry about getting up early again. We just hit the lotto. Do you understand what I'm saying? The lottery Dee!"

"You can't be serious," she said, turning on the lamp and pulling herself up against the headboard. Her eyelids were puffy and dried saliva occupied the corners of her mouth.

"Remember last month when we were up in Buffalo for the anniversary party? I bought a quick pick at that liquor store we stopped at. I forgot about it until tonight when I was messing around on the computer because I couldn't sleep. Dee, we won ten million freaking dollars. You've got to see this."

She reached for a glass of water on the nightstand and her eyebrows lifted. "Are you sure it's not some kind of mistake?"

"I'm sure. Here's the ticket. Come check it on the computer yourself."

He grabbed her hand, yanking her from bed. They ran to the office and as James did earlier, she checked the ticket repeatedly searching for an error. She couldn't find one.

At first Dee was unable to speak, but then she started to cry. She turned facing James, collapsing into his chest and squeezing as the tears grew bigger, faster. Her crying triggered him to break down and the married couple kissed, exchanging, "I love you," between heavy sobs. The special moment was a combination of super joy, utter disbelief, and the understanding of what a vast sum of money could do for their lives, and more importantly, the lives of their children. They held each other in one long beautiful wet and snotty embrace.

Their tears of joy soon transformed into jubilation. They held hands, sang, and jumped around. Dee danced in a circle as James attempted to moonwalk. Before too long both of their children stood outside the office door with blank expressions. They watched their parents grope one another and act the part of escaped mental patients.

"Mom. Dad. Are you guys okay? What's going on?" asked their fifteen year old son Cole.

"Yeah," their twelve year old daughter Samantha said. "You guys totally woke us up."

Without hesitation James grabbed the kids, incorporating them into a giant group hug. Dee explained the fantastic news through her tears in a quivering voice. Pure pandemonium overtook the Horton household as each family member wore a plastered smile on their face. A sense of invincibility permeated the air. James' prayer had been answered.

A forceful knock at the front door interrupted their joy.

"At this hour?" said Dee.

"Probably somebody from the homeowners association," said James. "I swear those people never sleep. I must've left the garbage cans on the curb a minute too long or the lawn is an eighth of an inch too high. We won't have to worry about that nonsense anymore."

He peered through the peephole and to his surprise, saw two policemen. He opened the door, asking if there was a problem.

"You tell me sir," the younger officer replied, a bit brash. "We're responding to a call from one of your neighbors. They heard a series of loud noises and thought there may be a disturbance. Is everything alright in there?"

James smiled. "Everything is more than alright. We got some amazing news and were celebrating. That's all. Sorry if we got a little too loud. We'll tone it down. Thanks for coming out. You can tell the widow Myers we're perfectly safe over here. Have a good night."

"Sir, we still need to come in and check out the house for a minute. It's protocol."

"Sure, have a look around."

The Hortons laughed at the disruption and went right back to celebrating, only in a much quieter fashion. James then came up with a brilliant idea, announcing to the family, "Kids, Dee, go get dressed. We should officially celebrate our good fortune. We're going to get pancakes." And with that proclamation, in the early morning hours of Monday, September 8th, 2008, they piled in the minivan and headed on out to the Orange Blossom Diner.

CHAPTER

3

Passionate moans rang through the master bedroom as James and Dee had morning sex for the first time in almost a year. The newly crowned millionaires slept barely a wink and lay in bed naked, their bodies entwined. They made love not as a husband and wife toiling through a predictable routine in the missionary position, but fucked with the ferocity of two hormone charged college students displaying the magnetic attraction of animalistic desire. They were carefree and sweaty. They felt young again. He couldn't remember the last time they French kissed like they meant it.

Dee arose from the crumpled stained sheets and walked to the bathroom for a shower. He admired the sway of her sweet full ass the entire way. *That's the girl I remember marrying. That's my girl.* He plugged in the laptop, clicked on the weather, and searched into next day flights bound for his boyhood state.

James Horton was a big man, standing six four, and after a lifetime of wrestling his large frame into the small seats of coach he'd be traveling first class all the way. There'd be no battling strangers for real estate on the armrest or the awkwardness of touching their legs. He had no intention of scouring the internet for discount airlines, hoping for a bargain priced special, and looked forward to sipping an ice cold beverage in the spacious comfort of the VIP section. He even envisioned a tour of the cockpit.

Choosing an airline that suited every conceivable need, James purchased four first class tickets one way out of Florida for the next day at noon. He tackled the process with a sense of authority, playing the part of the man he longed

11

to be. Feeling strong and virile, he wasn't taking any more of the crap life had to offer. A newborn James Horton roamed the planet.

"Dee," he yelled across the bedroom upon completion of his first task in charge. "Are you going to give your office a two week notice?"

She swung open the bathroom door and emerged topless in a pair of white panties, her wet brown hair wrapped in a towel. "Honey, come on. What do you think?"

"I don't know. I know how you are sometimes. Maybe?"

"Good Lord no," she said. "I'm out of there like yesterday. I'll call Karen and tell her what happened, politely and politically correct of course. I will say, in the nicest possible way, that I won't be coming into the office to perform my paralegal duties at her firm anytime soon." She darted towards the bed, launched herself on his lap, and kissed his neck before massaging his ear with her tongue. If he'd been a tad younger or had a Viagra handy, round number three of their sexathon would have continued.

He peeled her away. "That's what I thought. But I wanted to make sure. Hun, I'm about to do something I've wanted for a long time, but was always too scared. It's what most people want. This, my dear, is going to be fun."

"Do what you have to do," she said. "I know how much you hated that job. Thankfully, my situation was different. My co-workers and boss weren't that bad. They were actually very nice."

"You sound like you're going to miss them or something."

"Will I miss them at all? Hmm. Let me think. The pay stunk and the job was boring as hell. No, I'm pretty sure I won't miss any of it. Well, maybe the free pizza we got every Friday." She removed her hand from his face and abandoned the attempt of seduction. "Make sure you call the lottery office to confirm their address. I'll finish getting dressed and then you can take your wife out for the most expensive lunch we've ever had. We're going to remember this day forever." She messed up his hair and left the room.

That's the plan baby. That's the plan.

He pecked away at the computer and selected the words with precision for maximum effect. James never imagined witnessing his true dreams come to fruition. His youthful aspirations of playing pro ball and dating a Hollywood starlet had long been abandoned. He had no delusions of becoming the next Mick Jagger. After four years of on again-off again community college, earning him a generic degree in communications, his career path ascended slowly: bouncer, security guard, grocery store clerk, assistant deli manager, assistant customer service manager, customer service manager, customer service liaison, and his latest gig as junior corporate trainer for newly hired phone reps at Snake Hill Hot Sauce Company. Decades flew by working in the trenches, keeping his head down, clawing to the next rung of the ladder the best he could. He chased it, always chased it, and no matter how hard he worked, he was never going to catch it. The elusive carrot would remain elusive. It didn't really exist. James understood that. He accepted it. That's what *his* kind of people did. But now, with a boatload of cash to back him, he'd finally reclaim his dignity and make a once lost dream come true.

Each letter he pressed on the keyboard streamed waves of pleasure through his body. He addressed the email to his boss, his boss' boss, and his boss' boss' boss. Two other people who'd given him a hard time over the years were copied in as well for fun.

His infamous email, that was to eventually backfire yet become industry lore, began, "Hola Don the douche." James proceeded to make accusations of backstabbing and the unfairness of how people got promoted. He mentioned people's bad breath, their repetitive wardrobe, their comb-overs, the non-stop brown nosing, and their myopic view of the future. He gushed with negativity like a dam that had been breached and thinking his days as a proletariat were a thing of the past, held nothing back. The conclusion of his brash manifesto read, "Have fun working sixty hours a week and stressing about how to increase market share. I will never have to be on a conference call ever ever again. Can you say that? Instead I'll be on the golf course ladies and gents. The private ones!"

He hesitated before hitting send, correcting his grammar with spell check. He read it and reread it, feeling somewhat embarrassed. Was it too far, too cruel? His finger hovered above the delete button. Perhaps it was wiser to disappear without creating any noise.

"You ready hun?" said Dee, her face radiating with the afterglow of good sex. "I'm starving and the kids are waiting in the car."

"Be there in a minute." James stared at the four long paragraphs. *Was it all that bad? The Christmas parties were nice.* And then he remembered the incident of Tom Dufford, his boss' boss, the parasite with the limp gait and horrible mustache, who through some technical mix up on a phone call training session, he overheard say, "Did you see Horton training that new guy yesterday? He towered over him like Lurch. You can't tell me he isn't related to Bigfoot. I wouldn't be surprised if *National Geographic* does an investigation and profiles him as a fucking Neanderthal. Is it too much to ask one of you idiots to hire a pretty girl once in a while?"

"Screw it," he said out loud. He put a red exclamation on the email, indicating it was urgent, and pressed send. The powers that be would talk about what a giant buffoon James Horton was for a long time to come.

The Horton family spent the rest of the day lounging about the house digesting their epicurean feast, talkative and excited. The kids utilized every mode of communication short of the telegraph to spread the word of their good fortune. Not far behind them was Dee as James continued arranging the details of their trip. When the address books ran dry and their boasting was forced to an end, everyone gathered in the living room with paper in hand, creating long lists of things they wanted to buy, constantly updating and amending them.

James stretched out on the couch reading a golf magazine and listened to their requests no matter how outrageous they may be. He felt proud to be the man of the house. For the first time in life he could provide for his family at the level they deserved. Samantha talked about getting a dog, tickets to a Hannah Montana concert, and a shopping spree at the mall. Cole had his heart set on a new Ford Mustang for his sixteenth birthday along with an iPod, iPhone, Xbox, and as many video games that would fit in his closet. Dee made elaborate plans to Europe and beyond.

"James, you're awfully quiet over there," she said. "What are you going to splurge on?"

"I'm good hun. Getting my windows tinted on the Corolla and a new set of golf clubs would be a good start. You know, I've always wanted to try some Kobe beef. Maybe we could throw some steaks on the grill."

"Daddy," said Samantha, "You can get anything in the whole wide world you want. Anything."

"Come on dad," said Cole. "No new sports car? No Lamborghini or Maserati?"

"My car works perfectly fine, thank you very much. And besides, I don't know how to drive a stick."

The three of them mocked his lack of imagination and called him a boring old man. He loved it. But the middle-aged man had already been given the greatest gift there was: no debt, no stress, and no financial worries.

He never desired to own a McMansion or have five luxury automobiles parked in the driveway. The pragmatic nature of his upbringing wouldn't allow it. Questions such as, "Do you know how much it would cost to cool the house?" or "Do you know how much car insurance I would need for that fleet in the garage?" would ruin the enjoyment. He didn't covet extravagant jewelry, designer clothes, or an army of servants tending to every whimsical fancy. He simply wanted to stop worrying about the day in and day out lack of money that adversely affected their lives. And money, as always, was never far removed from his mind. It was blazed into his consciousness on a daily basis: the mortgage, car payments, homeowners insurance, auto insurance, health insurance, life insurance, food, gas, credit cards, HOA fees, taxes, home maintenance, car maintenance, yard maintenance, utilities, cable, the internet, cell phones, retirement, the kids' college fund, clothes, entertainment, vacation, the holidays, school costs, and the multiple other items to fall on a list that had no end. His view of the world was shaped by his finances.

But winning the lottery instantly erased a future full of worry. It afforded him the rare luxury of placing his head on the pillow at night with a clear unburdened mindset, thinking the thoughts of an economically liberated man. Financial freedom was a basic notion to be enjoyed every hour of every day for the rest of his life and it couldn't be tagged with a price or sold in a store. To James Horton's inner being, he yearned for nothing more.

CHAPTER

4

Their flight was delayed ninety minutes for a maintenance issue and while the other passengers became exasperated and hovered around the gate complaining, the Hortons sauntered back to the various gift shops and cafes without a care in the world. Time had become relative. When they did finally board the plane well ahead of anybody else, James felt bad for his former comrades standing in the long line of coach, waiting for the cattle call to be seated. But a quality scotch on the rocks nestled in his hand soon erased any pangs of guilt.

They cruised along at 36,000 feet enjoying the roominess and amenities first class offered, including the extra pillows and warm hand towels. James closed his eyes, listening, but didn't hear it. He didn't hear the screech of a crying baby or the wailing of fussy toddlers that always seemed to plague his flights. He never knew flying could be such a pleasurable experience.

He reached over and rubbed Dee's thigh. "I've been thinking hun. You know, about how to take the money."

"Good, me too."

"I think taking the lump sum is the way to go. That way we have it. Nobody can take it away and nothing weird could happen. I called Teddy this morning to tell him the good news. He said if we invest the money safely we should make even more than taking the payments. You know, because of the interest. It made pretty good sense to me. What do you think?"

"And how would Teddy know about this kind of thing?" she said, sipping a cup of chardonnay. "Isn't he still doing landscaping?"

"Yeah. He's running his own little business and doing okay. But he has a friend of a friend that's a stockbroker."

Dee put down her magazine and shifted to face him. Her brown eyes were lively and the burgundy lipstick popped against her yellow blouse. "I don't know James. That's a lot of money for us to try and budget at one time. Neither of us are going to pass for Warren Buffet when it comes to investing. Think about it. We've been married for sixteen years. Have we ever owned a single stock, CD, mutual fund, or anything at all financially related? The only interest we've ever known is the bad kind. The kind when you're on the wrong side of the loan. We even managed to lose that savings bond my grandfather gave us as a wedding gift." She took his hand. "Maybe our smartest move here is to take the payments. It would be less confusing and give us some kind of structure. That way, we know we have a certain amount of money coming in every year. It'll put us on a budget. Even we can't really screw that up. Plus, we get more money in the long run."

He fluffed his pillow and adjusted the air vent, raising his hand to make sure the temperature was cooling.

"James? Are you listening?"

He hesitated. "Yeah, I know. I guess I see your point. But what if something happens? Something unforeseen and out of our control. The economy is in a recession right now. What if things got worse? What if things got real bad? What if the state of New York went bankrupt?"

"But that's not going to happen. They'd get money somehow."

"Maybe. But what if some strange event occurred where the lottery money was taken away by the government because they needed it for something else? What if the fund dried up? What if they hired a covert assassination team and had all the lottery winners secretly disappear so they didn't have to pay them? Or they poisoned them? Didn't Stephen King write a book about that?"

She laughed. "When was the last time you read a book? The tenth grade. Now you're citing authors?"

"Fair enough. But how about this? What if the plane crashed and we all died? Where would the money go then?"

"I thought you stopped doing drugs when Cole was born." She let go of his hand and picked back up the magazine. "Are you listening to yourself? You sound insane."

"All I'm saying is stuff happens sometimes in life that we have no control over. Why risk it?"

"You really need to take a break from watching so many movies. There's no conspiracy theory and the sky isn't going to fall. Trust me. The payments make sense."

"I know hun," he said, rubbing her thigh again. "And I don't mean to sound like a nut. Really, I don't. You, I trust. But the government is a different story. Remember a few years ago when they sent us the wrong amount for our tax refund? We had to call them nonstop to get it corrected and it took like three freaking months before they sent us the rest of the money. Picture that on a much larger scale. We should take the money while we can and dump it in the private sector. That's the safest play. That's what Teddy says anyway."

"Well, it's not Teddy's money, is it?"

He took a sip of scotch, swirled an ice cube around his mouth, and spit it back in the glass. "I know it's not Teddy's money. He's only trying to help, that's all. His buddy, those guys that work on Wall Street, they really know what they're doing. They're all rich for a reason. Why should the government earn interest off our money?" He kicked off his shoes and closed the shade. "How about we sleep on it? We'll figure everything out in the morning."

"It's a ton of money either way," she said, flipping the page. "More than we could ever have imagined or hoped for. A week ago we were stressing over where to get the money for Samantha's braces and how to fix the air conditioning unit. Now we're debating how to receive millions of dollars. These are the kind of problems I like having."

"I'll drink to that," he said, tapping his cup against Dee's wine.

"You're lucky I love you James because sometimes your ideas are totally crazy. It's kind of scary."

"That's what you said when we were broke. Now, as a millionaire, I'm simply eccentric."

"Whatever. You're nuts then, okay?"

"Maybe a little. But you married me. And now you're stuck."

"We all have regrets in life," she said. "And a divorce would be too costly for us both." They laughed and leaned inward for a long intimate kiss.

Their plane landed in the historic state capital of Albany and the Hortons rented a jet black Land Rover. They drove around shopping, eating, and then shopping some more before exhaustion set in and everyone grated on each other's nerves. They checked into the most expensive hotel in town and James booked the kids their own separate room providing unlimited video game rentals. With the allure of hotel sex beckoning, he had romantically dirty plans for his wife.

Two bottles of champagne, a box of chocolates, and dozens of assorted flowers were delivered to their honeymoon suite. James surprised his wife with the tennis bracelet she'd wanted for years. They watched a soft porn movie for a full ten minutes while Dee modeled her new lingerie before he tore it off, and she tied him up. Act two of their lustfest surpassed the first as they traded orgasms like sparring partners and although he debated about buying it, James was glad he'd purchased the updated version of the *Kama Sutra* when they'd strolled through the aisles of the book store. He actually felt sore, a good sore.

"Dee, you up?" he asked, caressing her shoulder as it approached well after midnight.

She lay there like an unmovable log breathing softly. He watched her stomach rise and fall against the satin sheets and spooned her briefly until his arm cramped up and started going numb.

He stared at the ceiling, counting the seconds between blinks of green light from the carbon monoxide detector. It was twenty. Up next, he focused on the steady orange light of the smoke detector, followed by the bright yellow light of the TV power button. The red glow of the alarm clock completed the Christmas tree feel of the room.

James threw a forearm over his head and waited, wondering when his bladder would come calling again. He crossed, uncrossed, and re-crossed his feet. A train whistle blew far off in the distance as the seconds turned into minutes and on into hours. His thoughts were his only companion and for the second straight night they were pleasant and comforting. It was a nice surprise. It would take some getting used to.

The next morning, despite limited sleep, James was full of energy and the first one up. He woke the kids and dragged them to the suite, ordering far too much room service for everyone to eat. After triple checking the directions to the lottery office he showered, repeatedly singing the chorus to the "We're in the Money" song, butchering the lyrics with a tone deaf ear.

Dee ironed his favorite gray suit from Sears used for every special occasion and although he sucked in his gut, zipping up the pants required an extra effort. He finished dressing and when his wife sashayed from the bedroom in a flower print sundress he clapped and if he could whistle, he would have. Her toenails and fingertips matched in color and she wore a cute little hat he'd heard about for hours.

"Hun, you look beautiful."

She twirled then curtsied, blowing him a kiss. He caught it and reciprocated.

The kids watched their parents, or the two aliens inhabiting their parent's bodies, and stuck a finger in their mouths.

"Go get dressed," James said to them. "I want to be the first ones there."

"Dad, we are dressed," said Cole. "This is the stuff we got yesterday."

The kids attempted to get away with designer blue jeans and overpriced T-shirts, but following a ten minute argument with zero chance of winning, they acquiesced into something more presentable. The Horton clan looked clean cut and polished when they left the hotel, masking their middle class insecurities.

The lottery office was located in the neighboring small city of Schenectady adjacent to the famed Proctors Theater. The tall brick building had few windows and a ridiculously large parking lot. Upon entering the customer service center on the main floor they were greeted by an employee whose coffee hadn't kicked in yet.

"Who are you here to see?" asked the receptionist, his eyes glued to a computer screen. He tore off a chunk of bagel and dipped it in cream cheese, holding up a finger when the phone rang. "Lottery office," he said in a mumbled voice.

James turned to Dee, shrugged, and folded his hands. The receptionist still had the phone to his ear, an ear studded with three earrings near a tribal tattoo, when he repeated with an attitude, "Sir, who are you here to see?"

"Oh, I thought you were still talking on the phone," said James. "Sorry. I mean, we have a ticket to cash in. We just got in from—"

"Down the hall on the second right. The small conference room. Wait there."

"Thank you," said Dee. "Could you—"

"Lottery office," the receptionist said into the phone. "Who do you need to talk to?"

James clutched the winning ticket in his large sweaty palm and tried not to grip too tight, wrinkling it further. The room had a broken thermostat, releasing a cool arctic draft reserved for the height of summer, and the kids left their jackets on as James wrapped his arm around Dee. His legs bounced up and down spastically and she grabbed them twice asking him to stop. When their ticket was finally swept away to be verified he bit his thumbnail down to the nub.

Twenty agonizing minutes later a man roughly the same age as James entered the room. He didn't smile or grin or say hello. He'd worked at the lottery department for eighteen years and had eighteen more until retirement. His job demanded he assist everyday people in becoming millionaires while realizing his chances of attaining anything close to that were impossible. The most he could hope for was a three percent cost of living adjustment and an extra week's vacation.

He joined the Hortons around an oval shaped table and patted his head with a handkerchief. The bald man, whose eyebrows had merged into one, skipped the formality of congratulations. He leaned forward in his seat and hunched over, sorting through a deep stack of papers, scribbling notes. James observed the worker bee in action and couldn't help feel a certain degree of pity for the man, a certain bond, knowing he was that miserable kind of guy only days beforehand. But the man's bad attitude didn't matter. Nothing short of a nuclear holocaust could ruin their day.

The lottery agent eventually acknowledged their anxious faces and addressed them.

"Mr. and Mrs. Horton, we have reviewed your lottery claim and your ticket is valid. You are entitled to the sum of ten million dollars, minus taxes of course. Please sign at the bottom of the page indicating I have gone over this information. Now there are two ways to receive the money. The first option, the one we highly recommend, spreads out the money for your convenience over the course of twenty years and—"

James watched the man lick his finger, remove another paper from the pile, and continue talking. He didn't hear a word the bald bastard said. His legs bounced harder than before, lightly shaking the table, and he was unable to contain himself.

"I think we know what we're going to do," he said, cutting the man off mid-sentence. "We're going to take the money. The lump sum."

Dee whipped her head around, her long hair following, and her eyes narrowed as he pulled out his check book and slid it across the desk. "Here is my checking account information along with the routing number at Trustworth Bank and Savings in Florida."

"Thank you for your efficiency Mr. Horton," said the agent. "But you do understand the stiff penalties for taking the money up front rather than spreading it out. It's something you may wish to consider."

"Excuse me," said Dee. "You'll have to ignore my husband. He's overly excited. Can you please give us a minute?"

She whispered in James' ear. He whispered back. The whispers grew louder and they repeated the process like a lawyer advising a defendant in court. The rouge on her cheeks brightened as her already thin lips stiffened.

"If you could just get the transfer underway we would really appreciate it," said James. "We want to get home to our friends and family in Florida."

"Of course you do," said the agent, glaring at him. "Of course you do." He left the room, trudging off to prepare the arrangements for another lucky winner.

"Dee, I'm sorry. I didn't mean—"

"Shh," she said, raising a hand towards his face. "I get it James. You bought the ticket. It was your doing. And it's *your* show. Now we're rich because of it. Let's not ruin it."

When the lottery agent returned to inform them the transfer had been completed he still had the warmth of a cadaver but appeared more upbeat when he said, "With the penalty levied by the state of New York for taking the lump sum payment, along with applicable taxes withheld, the ten million dollars gross amount of your winnings has netted you a payoff amount of three million, one hundred and seventeen thousand dollars. Here is a receipt for your records. You have use of the room for the next hour to make any arrangements." He closed the door behind him and left as quickly as he entered.

Nobody moved. The only sound came from the cold air piping through the vents.

"Did that just happen?" said James, smiling. He held out his arms. "Did that just really happen?"

The kids lunged into him followed by Dee. The group hug was quiet the second time around, devoid of tears. They bowed their heads and James led them in a prayer of thanks, rambling, repeating himself. He flipped open his cell phone and dialed the number to his hometown bank he'd been a loyal customer at for over a decade. He entered the account number complete with security codes.

When the automated voice confirmed their new balance he grasped Dee by the arm and sank in a chair. His blue eyes bulged. Money, the missing link in his life, was no longer something to be feared. His money, Dee's money, and the Hortons' future had been secured in a Fort Knox vault. Nobody could take it away.

They drove to the nearest ATM and James withdrew the daily maximum allowed by his checking account of $400. For the first time in his adult life he had a semblance of play money in his wallet. He gave Dee half and the kids twenty bucks apiece. He pulled his wife close and palmed her fanny. In a rare display of public affection the married couple kissed like Hollywood stars on the set of a new hot movie.

He steered the Land Rover out of the city and passed through a Starbucks. They merged onto the interstate heading south. He sipped a scalding hot six-dollar mocha chai latte grande and burned the hell out of his tongue.

"Every day hun," he said. "Every single damn day. We can sleep in or work around the house. We can play golf and go out for lunch. Hit the beach if we want. Any beach. We can pretty much do whatever we want. How great is that? Whoever said money can't buy you happiness is either a two-faced liar or the biggest jackass in the history of the world!" James beeped the horn several times and barked an off pitched wolf howl as they sped down the New York State thruway. He was finally an alpha dog.

CHAPTER

5

J ames marveled at the beauty of the Hudson Valley as the miles of pavement eased along beneath the SUV. The sun shined brightly amidst a scarcity of clouds and the mountains were covered in walls of green. He cruised in the slow lane with a new pair of Oakley's shading his eyes. His coffee never tasted better, the radio never sounded clearer, and he couldn't recall a nicer view from atop the Tappan Zee Bridge. Dee nodded off in the front seat with a crossword puzzle strewn across her lap, half finished. Sports talk chatter filled the cabin while the kids were enthralled with their newest electronic gadgets.

He spotted their innocent faces in the rearview mirror wondering if they had a clue how many doors the lottery money would open. There'd be business opportunities, upward social networking, and unlimited travel adventures. They could afford to choose any college in the country. He hoped his offspring had the foresight and common sense to capitalize on it all.

The time displayed on the dashboard read 1:30 p.m. James smirked. That time of the day had been particularly difficult for him over the years. It signaled the beginning of his after lunch battle, a battle he usually wound up losing. He lost count how many times he sat in his windowless cubicle pretending to review an employee's call log record or feigning interest in an email while fighting his heavy eyes from closing.

At least twice a year he'd get busted dozing off, but never on a Wednesday. Every Wednesday at exactly the same time his boss' boss' boss, the big boss, would summon him to her office for a lengthy discussion regarding the latest team building concepts and offer suggestions of how to be a better employee. James replayed the resignation email again and again in his mind as his smirk blew up to a smile.

Their car rumbled across a gravel driveway and came to rest in front of a two-story white brick house on an acre of land with tall oak trees and stylish landscaping. The neighbors on each side were far enough away to afford privacy yet close enough for a sense of community. It dwarfed the quarter acre lot the Horton's home resided on and the ant colony feel of their development. James had always been a little jealous.

Mary darted from the house when she saw them pull up, darting at least for someone approaching the milestone of eighty. Her hair was dyed reddish, streaked with natural gray highlights, and she wore a silver necklace with a large cross dangling around her neck. She assaulted the kids first with lingering hugs and kisses.

"Isn't this a rare treat," she said. "I can't believe you came all the way up here spur of the moment like this."

"Mom, you look great," said Dee, embracing her, rocking side to side. "I know it was last minute, but James had to come to New York for work. He needed to use his frequent flyer miles. I couldn't wait to see you."

"James, you shouldn't have," said Mary. "When you do things like this, that's why you're my favorite son-in-law."

He laughed, obliging their long standing joke. "It would mean a lot more if I wasn't your only son-in-law."

"Don't you worry about that. Now come on inside. Let's get you a cold beer."

He helped Mary climb the porch steps and whispered to Dee, "God I love your mother."

For the next several hours the trio drank frosted mugs of light beer in the kitchen, retelling old stories they've heard numerous times as Mary peeled potatoes, seasoned the roast, and baked her lauded French apple pie. James played it stupid, Dee played it low key, and the kids played outside. They were saving their big announcement until right before dinner.

The dining room table was set with linen napkins and the good stemware reserved for company. Everybody held hands as Mary led them in saying grace. "God, thank you for this food we are about…."

Dee bowed her head but kept one eye open, hawking her mother, putting the final mental touches on her speech. She'd rehearsed it non-stop since leaving Florida but when she raised her glass and opened her mouth there was nothing. She swallowed and tried again. More silence. Her eyes welled up as she handed her mother an envelope.

"What's this?" asked Mary. "And why are you crying Dee? Is it something bad? Is that why you came here? For heaven's sake, I knew something was going on."

"Open the envelope," said James.

A check fell onto her plate. Mary picked it up, pulling on her glasses. Dee smiled while sniffling and took a picture on her phone. She was the only child to an aging widowed parent. She scooted her chair close to her mother and waited.

Mary stared at the check for $50,000 scanning the zeros and location of the decimal point. She glanced at her daughter, back to the check, and over to James. She looked at the kids.

"That check is a gift for you," said James. "It's some spending money to get you started. There will be plenty more to come. That's why we're here. That's what Dee wanted to surprise you with. I didn't come here for work. In fact, I quit my job. So did Dee. We came here because we won the lottery. We came to collect the money. Remember last month when Dee said we were going to Buffalo...."

The color seeped fast from Mary's face. She turned whiter than her normal white hue and her eyes glazed over with a shiny mucous. James didn't know if she was having a stroke or a senior moment.

"Mary?" he said. "Mary?"

She reached for her glass but it slipped through her fingers, spilling. She slumped to the left and fell to the floor, conking her head on the table. Dee screamed, jumping from the chair to see if their surprise had killed her. Mary had a pulse, wasn't bleeding, and her breathing was normal. James scooped up his light framed mother-in-law and carried her to the couch. Dee grabbed a cool wet towel and dabbed her cheeks, calling her mother's name. Mary didn't respond. They shouted about how to proceed and Cole dialed 911 when she opened her eyes and blinked several times, trying to sit up.

"Mom. Are you alright?" asked Dee, gently restraining her.

Mary lay motionless, gathering her surroundings from her favorite vase and a Norman Rockwell print centered on the wall. "I think I'm okay," she finally said. "What happened?"

"You fainted and scared the hell out of us," said James, handing her a glass of water.

She took a baby sip. "That hasn't happened in the longest time. Not since your father's funeral." Mary planted her feet on the floor and drank some more water. She looked at Dee. "Are you trying to kill me my daughter? You can't hand me a check of that size without any warning."

"Surprise," said Dee. Her arms were open and she grinned while crying.

"I'm getting too damn old for surprises," said Mary. She felt the lump on her head and flinched. "The lottery Dee?"

Ten minutes later they were back around the table enjoying the home cooked meal. They laughed at Mary's incident and had a good time at her expense. Cole performed a spot-on impression of his grandmother falling over in her chair. Each time it became more dramatic. Mary endured the ribbing whole heartedly with an ice bag pressed to her head. James respected her ability to not take life too seriously.

As one bottle of wine morphed into two it grew late. The kids wandered off to their bedrooms to text away and the ladies cleared the table. With dish duty underway James escaped to the living room, extending the footrest of a leather recliner. His fingers fell over the remote control. *Shark Week* was playing on the Discovery Channel and a big-time college football game aired on a major network. He flipped between the two like an old west gunslinger and when they both had commercials he searched the 200 channels faster than he could view the screen. That's when he saw the clock on the VCR. That's when it was time for his beloved Janie Chavez.

James hadn't watched the news in months. It caused him to get angry or depressed or both and with the economy in shambles it freaked him out even further. He told Dee it only made a bad situation worse. But up at Mary's house, on the outskirts of New York City, he always turned it on. And there was only one reason why. A woman named Janie Chavez.

She'd been the meteorologist at Channel 8 for five years and was born in the same small town as James, only ten years later. He met her once at the mall when she worked for an affiliate in Albany before she made the big leap to the city. She'd hosted a pet adoption drive for the ASPCA and he got her autograph and picture but decided against a dog.

Janie Chavez was a legend where he came from. She'd made it, broken through the barrier of ordinary, and was the most successful person to ever graduate from his high school. And while doing the weather on TV wasn't the big screen of Tinsletown and nobody handed out Oscars, Ms. Janie Chavez achieved rock star status in his mind.

He watched her point to the Doppler radar and explain the low pressure system drifting in from the west. Whatever she said, he believed. And as Janie broke down the partly sunny three day forecast, a broadcast statement continuously scrolled across the bottom of the screen. Insurance behemoth BGI, one of the largest companies in the world and a stalwart of the nation's financial sector, was on the verge of bankruptcy. It had officially asked the federal government for a bailout. They were begging for money in a sophisticated manner, like an upscale homeless person.

Bailout? thought James. That was a term he was unfamiliar with when it came to business. It evoked images of a small rowboat, maybe a dingy, sinking in the middle of a choppy sea with frantic men using wooden buckets to scoop out water as it sank. He thought of *Gilligan's Island* and heard the theme song pinging around his head.

James Horton never had enough money to participate in the high stakes game of Wall Street. He didn't read *The Journal,* thought the term *junk bonds* sounded stupid, and had zero clue what the Dow Jones Industrial Average represented or how it was calculated. Standard & Poor's might as well have been a housing project in the Bronx and derivatives, he chalked that up to a foreign language.

The only concept he understood is what he could touch and feel, what was tangible. And earlier that year, while dropping off a group of kids from Samantha's birthday party, he observed an unusual amount of FOR SALE signs littered throughout Florida's neighborhoods. One by one they dotted the landscape. Residential developments once bustling with scores of illegal construction workers throwing up stick framed houses at record speed grounded to an immediate halt. They had roads, advertising signs, and even street lights; but no houses. Commercial strips malls and business parks ceased being built halfway through construction leaving unfinished empty concrete buildings and vacant parking lots. The abandoned landscapes were covered in tall weeds and dirt, mimicking a modern day ghost town.

Phrases like *upside down* and *under water* became commonplace in the average American's vocabulary. The word *foreclosure* was mentioned in the news on a daily basis. "A house is a man's castle." That's what his father used to like to say. The old man failed to mention that throughout the course of history, many a castle gets sacked.

The Hortons bought their single family 1,800 square foot home for $275,000 and sank in another $25,000 to make it more modern. (The idea of living without granite countertops, a fridge with no ice maker in the door, and only one sink in the master bath was an abomination. Wall to wall carpeting was insufferable.) They wanted to put down roots for their kids' sake and establish the most important concept people obsessed over, the most important concept in the known world: equity. The school district was good, earning a solid B-plus in the annual rankings along with a low incident rate of shootings, and wasting money on rent no longer seemed the prudent option. It was time to grow up and become true adults, to leap towards respectability by joining the ranks of indebted homeowners.

The latest assessment from the tax collector placed the value of their home at $185,000 and dwindling. Losing that staggering amount of equity in thirty months with no guarantee of it ever returning caused James to re-examine his life. He'd done everything right, everything expected, and followed the middle class rule book with a blind devotion. And he still couldn't get ahead, only further behind. Yet for the sake of his family he soldiered on. He ignored his burgeoning resentment and maintained a positive delicate approach, regurgitating on command like a trained parrot the catch phrases he heard at the office. "The market is cyclical." "It'll automatically correct itself." "You've got to ride the wave."

But with a radical shift in perspective courtesy of six magical numbers he no longer cared about any of it. A three million dollar nest egg lay tucked away in his Trustworth Bank checking account.

Mary and Dee joined him in the living room, sitting on the couch, resting their feet on a coffee table. It didn't matter if the weather forecast was good or bad, nobody dare say a bad word about Janie Chavez.

"So Mary, are you ready to travel the world?" said James, lowering the volume. "You got your passport all set?"

"I sure do. I need to make sure it hasn't expired. It's been a long time. I was beginning to think I'd never use it again."

"We'll make a jet setter out of you yet."

"I can't thank you and Dee enough for the check you know. I love you both so much," she said, drinking some wine. She nudged Dee in the leg and laughed. "But of course, now I love you so much more."

"Okay, no more wine for the lady with a bump on her head," said Dee, moving Mary's wine glass to the far end of the table. "We're thrilled to finally be able to help you out. You'll never have to worry about money again. We'll take care of anything you want, right hun?"

"Absolutely," said James. "Anything at all. Except of course breast implants. We can't be a party to that type of irresponsible behavior."

"Watch yourself young man. I'm not too old to put you over my knee." He gave her a wink.

"So what's the plan now? What are you going to do?" asked Mary.

"Other than taking a long overdue vacation, we're not sure," said Dee.

"What about the kids and school?"

"Oh, they'll be fine. Two weeks off from school won't hurt. It's not like their studying corporate law. They'll get to see some of the country. We're stopping in Philadelphia, D.C., Myrtle Beach, and Atlanta. It'll be an education they can't get in a classroom."

Mary nodded and reached for her glass, drinking the remnants of her chardonnay. "How about the money? What about all that wonderful money?"

"James made an appointment with a stockbroker who's a friend of a friend when we get back in town. Until then, it'll sit safely in the bank."

"Be careful," said Mary. "I've heard people are losing a lot in the market lately. My friend Irma, remember her Dee, the lady who does the photography, she said she lost—"

"You don't have to worry about that," said James, snapping shut the leg rest of the recliner. "Our investments will be small and conservative. This money is generational. There's no way we're going back to being broke because we got too greedy or stupid. We'll splurge for the next few weeks then it's on to a sensible budget."

Dee confirmed his sentiment with an, "Uh-huh," and pulled a blanket off the top of the couch, covering her mother's legs. James began talking faster, motioning with his hands.

"We've all heard about those people who win the lottery or become famous only to blow it on things they don't need. Boats, cars, houses, restaurants, jewelry. It doesn't make any sense. It's beyond stupid. This money is more than enough to last us forever."

"Paying off the house alone will be a godsend," said Dee. "I remember when we bought it. We thought we got lucky. It was in a nice neighborhood at the end of a cul-de-sac. There were three other bids on it. It was hard to even find a house back then. They'd get listed and sold right away. And while we didn't think we could afford it, the adjustable rate mortgage made it possible." She yawned. "We never should have bought it in the first place."

"I think the builders were printing money back then," said James. "It seemed like that anyway. They must've had their own ATMs. We'd go check out a house and then a month later it would be five or even ten thousand dollars higher for no good reason. It was like a feeding frenzy. We thought the house would just keep going up in value over the next few years. We planned on selling when the kids graduated from high school." He leaned forward. "I thought real estate was supposed to go up in value, not bottom out from under you."

"Everybody thought that," said Mary. "It's usually a good investment."

"I know," said James. "It wasn't only the builders either. I knew a guy who got evicted from his apartment because the landlord was doing a condo conversion. They told him he either had to buy the apartment he'd been renting because it was now a condo or get out. I still don't see how that's freaking legal and when you hear about that stuff it makes me want to—"

"James," said Dee, raising her voice. "We get it. Relax. It's ancient history now. Why don't you see what's playing on the movie channels?"

He handed them the remote and grinned. "You're right hun. It's not a problem anymore. Nothing to worry about."

The worst financial investment of the Hortons' lives was no longer an issue. The shackle of debt had been released. He walked to the kitchen and asked, "Does anybody want more pie?"

CHAPTER

6

A knock at the door signaled his delivery. James sat up from a deck chair on the balcony and rose leisurely to his feet, stretching towards the sky. His back, once riddled with knots, felt loose and the color of his skin had transformed from a pasty pale to a golden bronze. He scuffed his feet against the tile floor in plush white slippers and wore a matching silk bathrobe with his initials embroidered on the front.

A young man from Ecuador sporting a goatee pushed a service cart into the center of the room, placing a bouquet of red roses on the counter. James tipped him generously on top of the already included gratuity and signed his autograph for suite 2084. He asked if the freshly squeezed orange juice had pulp in it. It didn't. The rest of the family was sleeping. He'd been up for hours.

He chomped on a piece of crispy bacon and dove on the couch, springing upright when his left shoulder touched the pillow. The constant throbbing had ceased but the sensitive area was still red and swollen. He felt the bandage to gauge if the blood soaked cotton had dried and removed it to allow his wound some air. The pain had been intense, much greater than expected, and James couldn't believe he'd gone through with it.

"It's forever you know," said Dee the previous day, protesting against his decision when he forced her to come along. She brushed her hair with firm strokes as he circled the block in search of a parking spot. "You can't change your mind in a week or a month or a year. Don't you think you're a little too old for this now?"

32

"I've never felt younger," said James. "Why would I change my mind? It's perfect."

"It's not going to look so hot when you're seventy."

He flicked on the directional and stopped, parallel parking next to a Prius. "Hun, we're not going to look anything close to hot when we're seventy."

She waited on the sidewalk near a pizza shack and drank lemonade, conversing with her mother to relay her objection. The kids watched with enthusiasm, documenting the event on their camera phones as a man in his mid-thirties with giant sized holes carved through his earlobes permanently inked their dad. James sat in the chair stone faced while the sharp needle hissed, burrowing trenches in the bottom of his sandals with his toes. He clenched his teeth and clasped the armrest, trying not to yell or scream, trying not to act like an overgrown wuss.

A tattoo was something he'd always desired but never knew what to get. A team's sports logo on his calf? A barbed wire ring wrapped around his bicep? The names of his wife and kids scrawled into his chest in cursive? They'd all been done and he wanted something different. Besides, he wasn't really a barbed wire kind of guy. But now the six winning lottery numbers would forever be stained on his skin, covering his left shoulder, serving as a new lucky charm. He contemplated having the numbers printed on T-shirts and hats for the rest of the family and buying a plaque to decorate his office.

James gazed out the opening leading to the balcony enjoying the crisp cool breeze coming in off the ocean. The sunrise broke over the Atlantic coloring the morning with shades of purple, orange, and blue as the white caps of waves rolled upon the shore. Fishing boats drifted out to sea, securing their nets for an abundant harvest, and the whole scene smacked of a postcard moment. He inhaled the gritty salt air and had to be reminded it was *him* and not somebody else living such an amazing life.

The deluxe suite the Hortons occupied was on the twentieth floor and had more square footage than their house in Florida. Each bedroom had its own private bath constructed from marble and granite and included a bidet nobody tried using. There were TVs in the shower and automatic blinds covered every window. The entire suite was wired for high definition surround sound. He fastened a pair of headphones to his ears and clicked the master remote, attempting to turn on the stereo, but accidentally ignited the fireplace while dimming the lights.

The morning newspaper was next to him. He picked it up, sipping a cup of tea. The front page headline read, "MORE BIG COMPANIES IN TROUBLE. GOV'T BAILOUTS CONTINUE." The article discussed the problems of risky investments, questionable mortgage practices, and the horrible financial mismanagement taking place at some of the top companies in the country. The words *greed* and *ineptitude* were used more than once. The word *irresponsible* was sprinkled throughout. Unsatisfied with the billion dollar profits they annually reaped, corporations experimented with ill-advised strategies to produce even more cash. But when the music stopped playing in the financial world, a severe shortage of adequate chairs existed.

The ominous headline escaped his attention. He didn't notice the large print words or care what the story had to say. It wasn't his mess. He adjusted his robe, pulled the belt tighter, and flung off his slippers. His toenails were jagged and cracked and he thought about getting a pedicure.

The sports section was wedged between Entertainment and Business and why it wasn't on top he'd never know. He flipped it open, seeing the New York Giants lost again. His cousin Harry would be due another fifty bucks. He tossed the paper onto an end table and closed his eyes, wondering what time the pool opened. He considered scheduling a late afternoon round of golf or maybe a hot stone massage.

"Good morning daddy," said Samantha, tapping him on the head, giggling.

He twitched. "Jeeze, you scared me sweetie. Is mom up yet?"

"I'm up," said Dee, entering from the bedroom in a flowing nightgown. She walked taller and straighter and the bags under her eyes had lightened. She kissed him, resting her head on his chest, and he enjoyed the smell of her spearmint mouthwash.

At his daughter's request he switched on the Cartoon Network and fixed them both a plate full of eggs. The morning breeze intensified and ruffled the curtains, folding back the front page of the paper, obscuring the headline. Their two and a half week vacation was coming to an end.

"What time does the pool open?" said Dee. "I want to work on my tan some more."

James dialed the number to the lobby.

"Yes Mr. Horton, how may I serve you today?" the concierge asked.

He smiled at his wife. It was good to be the king in the land of Hortonville.

CHAPTER

7

"Easy buddy. Take it easy," James said to Cole as the waitress left. She had long blond locks and a perfectly round derrière. Her large fake beasts stood at attention, commanding attention, and her cleavage was hypnotic to the eye. He tried not to stare himself, unsuccessfully.

The four of them sat in a booth at Hooters talking amongst the loud noise. It was bright and chaotic with a corner reserved to sell tacky memorabilia and neon Budweiser signs glowed everywhere. The Hortons had grown tired of fancy dinners and wanted something simple for the last big meal of their trip, waiting twenty-five minutes to be seated.

"They know you're going to look and they expect it," said James. "Why do you think they dress that way? But don't gawk. They don't like to be gawked at. Nobody likes to be gawked at."

"Leave the kid alone James. He's never been here before," said Dee.

"Trying to be a role model hun. That's all."

James observed scores of half-naked co-eds whirl through the dining room hoisting up pitchers of beer. They carried plates full of deep fried tastiness and the occasional salad, always with a smile. The caveman business model was so primitive, so simple, and yet so successful. He admired its concept and prayed to God his little girl never worked there.

Located in the opposite corner from their table was a trio of TVs bolted high up on the wall. To the left was a baseball game in the midst of a rain delay. He had no rooting or betting interest in either team. The middle screen played a re-run of the world's strongest man competition, the one where an American

36

became champion for the first time since 1982; and to the right, a cable news program aired a roundtable discussion of talking heads with breaking news flashing along the bottom of the screen. James had grown numb to the overabundance of constant breaking news. He found it distracting and determining crucial matters deemed necessary for the general public to be aware of versus nonsense for ratings became ambiguous for him. *Breaking news my ass.* He excused himself to the restroom.

Dee ordered refills on everyone's drinks and focused on her crossword puzzle.

"What's a four letter word for a Hindu princess?" she asked the kids.

Samantha mocked her brother's fixation with the waitstaff and they bickered endlessly. The siblings were due for a break from one another. The family was due for break. But not the kind they imagined.

James stopped on the way to the bathroom and peered inside the open style kitchen. He saw the cooks work the line of incoming tickets in a hectic rush, sweating, pumping out orders at an incredible pace. He moved on towards the patio where a small group of smokers huddled, lacquering their lungs with tar, and he contemplated joining his peeps to bum a clandestine cigarette. But he knew better. No matter how much he cleaned up it wouldn't matter. Cigarette smoke is like napalm.

The restaurant seemed louder when he exited the bathroom and while wiping his still damp hands on the back of his jeans he thought, *How long was I in there?* The music from the speakers had a heavy bass, vibrating through the floor, and a group of young men gathered around the bar to slam shots of tequila and argue over who was the sexiest waitress. By the time he wandered back to the table all three TVs showed the same program. They'd interrupted their regularly scheduled broadcasting for live studio coverage. A history making moment was being announced.

Reilhman Brothers, one of the oldest and most prestigious banking institutions in the country and in the world, a legend in the finance industry, had proclaimed their insolvency. They were straight up busted, going out of business like a failed pizza joint. James shifted his butt in the booth. He remembered their commercials growing up as a kid and could still sing the jingle. He had a savings account with them in his early twenties. A small one.

The back and forth dialogue from the panel of economic experts painted an unsettling view of the event. "Unprecedented Fallout", "*Titanic* Sinking", "Domino Effect", and "Cataclysmic Failure" were phrases being thrown around. Their words were powerful. They were successful. His stomach tightened. With the exception of a black and white couple in their fifties pointing towards the screen nobody seemed to notice. Or maybe they didn't care. He filtered out the noise and poked Dee in the side.

"Hun, take a look at the TVs. They're all saying the same thing. Can you read the closed captioning from here?"

"I think so. I lost one of my contacts this afternoon. Hold on." She strained her neck forward as he asked, "What do you think is going on?"

Dee read the screen and tried to make sense of the small and sometimes misspelled words. "It looks like someone at Reilhman Brothers screwed up royally. Aren't they the ones with that beautiful bank in lower Manhattan, the one with the sculptures and artwork? Mom and I, when I was a teenager, used to go there after—"

"Yeah, that's great hun. But what do you think it means for us?"

"What are you talking about?"

"Could it be an issue?"

"I don't know. Do you have an account with them you're not telling me?"

He shook his head no.

"Then what's the problem?"

"It just seems bad," he said. "They were so huge. It's not like a car company or insurance company or some kind of retailer. It's freakin Reilhman Brothers."

James scratched his chin and leaned back. He watched the TVs, consuming every single word until the panel was finished. When the baseball game finally resumed it was the bottom of the eighth inning. The strongman competition was long over.

Dee rubbed her eyes, slouching in the booth, as he fished out his cell phone from a pocket and dialed the number to the bank. He entered the account number while biting his lip and clanking his wedding band against a beer bottle. On the other end of the line was the smooth sounding voice of a new automated message James had never encountered before.

"I'm sorry. That information is not available at this time. Please try your call again later. Thank you. Good-bye." *Click.*

He held the phone at arm's length and stared at it with a scrunched up face as if the recording had been given in Latin. His legs started bouncing and he dialed the number again. The message was repeated. He pressed the phone harder against his ear, assuming there was a bad connection or maybe he'd misheard.

"I'm sorry. That information is not available at this time. Please try your call again later. Thank you. Good-bye." *Click.*

He called the bank five consecutive times and received five identical results.

"Dee, I can't get through to my account."

"So wait and try back later," she said, taking a bite of Samantha's dessert. "Are you ready to leave soon? It's almost nine thirty. The kids and I are tired."

"I did try them later. And then I tried them again."

"James, if our little bank was having a problem they would call us. We both know Tracy, the branch manager, and her daughter is in the same grade as Cole. I think you're overreacting."

"Did you know that Trustworth's customer service department won an award last year for excellence?" he said. "It doesn't seem so freaking excellent to me right now."

His jaw muscles bulged while he continued dialing and he released a few audible, "What the fucks?" at the table. After one more failed attempt he turned to Dee, percolating, ignoring any degree of decorum.

"I called the damn number nine times now. What in the fuck is going on?"

"First off, watch the swearing in front of the kids," she said. "You're starting to act like an asshole. Second, maybe the phones are down or the system crashed. You know how bad the thunderstorms get in Florida. It's our last night here and it's been a long vacation. So please don't spoil it, okay?"

He nodded yes like a chastised boy and rapped his knuckles on the table. His blood pressure spiked as negative thoughts crashed around his skull. James stared at a piece of lettuce on the floor, watching people trample it, and nibbled his fingernails. He waited for the kids to finish their dessert. Nobody was talking. *Fuck this shit.*

He flagged down the waitress and settled the bill.

"Alright, let's go. We're leaving."

"Good. I can't wait to hop into bed," said Dee. "Can we stop at a drugstore first? I need some aspirin."

"No. I mean we're leaving leaving." James slid from the booth.

"Back to Florida?"

"Yes."

"It's a ten hour ride back to Orlando. We'll be driving all night. I don't want to sleep in the car James and neither do the kids. Let's leave in the morning as planned."

"We need to get home to see what the hell is going on with our money," he said.

"The bank won't even be open by the time we get there."

"I know that. But when they do open, I want to freaking be there. Alright?"

Dee sighed. "Give me your phone." She hit redial and handed it back. "Now punch in the numbers."

The crease mark deepened between her eyebrows as she listened to the recording. "Has that ever happened before?"

"No. Never."

"When was the last time you checked the account?"

"I checked it four or five times at your mother's and then once about a week and a half ago. I've been using our credit cards to pay for everything."

"What?" she said, standing, her expression incredulous. "Why would you do that? You must have maxed out every single card."

"I wanted to get all the bonus points and it's easier than always running to the ATM. I'll pay everything off when we get home."

She shook her head and said, "Never mind," as he stomped off to the car. Her voice grew stern. "Cole, Samantha. Go use the bathroom. We're leaving."

The Horton family vacation had officially come to an unexpected end.

CHAPTER

8

The long ride home was hellatious for everyone. James weaved reck-
lessly through traffic, bee lining towards the freeway, and his behavior deteriorated as they drove deeper into the night. He called the bank every
fifteen minutes and listened to the disturbing response, each time erupting
with a combination of F-bombs, S-bombs, and C-bombs; among other letters.
Dee begged him to stop and he tried. But he couldn't.

At times he swore louder than others and twice he punched the top of
the dashboard. For long stretches of lonely interstate he whispered to himself.
But the worst part was his constant fiddling with the radio in a desperate
search for financial updates. He tuned into one station after another on the
AM dial, alternating between commercials, static, and Bible Belt preaching.

They arrived home at six in the morning and he roused his family from their
slumber. Dee and Cole stumbled into the house drugged with sleep, collapsing
into their beds. Samantha wanted to remain sleeping in the car but James carried
her upstairs and tucked her in. He was twitchy, wired on gas station coffee and
nerves, and didn't feel tired, or at least didn't know it. He took a hot shower, threw
on clean clothes, and a can of Pepsi served as his breakfast. Twenty minutes after
driving all night he found himself back behind the wheel of the car.

Palm Tree Shoppes was the name of the strip mall housing local branch
number thirty-five of Trustworth Bank. The bank resided on the far end of the
plaza next to a Chinese restaurant and included a nail salon, liquor store,
florist, and a Christian book store. A drive-up teller was available on the side
of the building and they had an ATM out front.

He pulled into the empty parking lot and situated the car with a bird's eye view of the lobby. The street lights were still on as he shined his high beams through the front window. Nothing appeared out of the ordinary. The carpet was vacuumed and the desks were neatly organized. The customer service kiosk was fully stocked with deposit and withdrawal slips and a green cardboard banner hung from the ceiling advertising their unbeatable home mortgage interest rates. Everything seemed ready for business as usual. Relief swept over him. Dee was right. It was probably just a bad storm or computer glitch. His stomach growled and he felt hungry.

He cracked the car windows and turned on the radio, reclining all the way back in the seat. His eyes, once alert with concern, grew heavy. The Stones sang "Sympathy for the Devil" on the oldies station as James imagined the plans for their next big family vacation, a month long visit to Europe. And after that, a three week cruise up the Alaskan coastline followed by a tour of the Pacific islands. He drifted off to sleep thinking about swimming in the warm blue waters of Tahiti.

Two car horns honking in a battle for air supremacy woke him. An accident nearly occurred in front of the florist shop. A young man in a sports car and a soccer mom rocking a station wagon waged battle over a prized parking spot. They flipped each other off, exchanging obscenities. The soccer mom won.

James opened his eyes and felt wet. He'd sweat through his shirt like he'd been running on a treadmill and his fingers were swollen from the heat. He glanced at his watch. Sleep had seduced his body for close to five hours.

The sun blinded him, demanding he throw on his shades, and leaned forward cracking his neck. The bank appeared no different than when he arrived. Employees were absent and the drive-thru teller lane was empty. Not one single customer scurried about. He licked his dry lips and adjusted the rearview mirror. Was it a holiday? Had all of the traveling screwed up his memory? He slid open his cell phone. The date was Tuesday, September 30th. Nothing special.

He marched to the front door with long firm strides as if the bank expected him and tugged on the thick metal handle. It didn't budge. He pressed his face against the glass, leaving an oily residue, shielding the reflection with his hands. It was dark inside and the only light came from the emergency exit signs.

Everything was in place for a busy day of transactions with the exception of human activity. He kicked the bottom of the door and slapped the glass before calling customer service. He kicked the door again, harder.

James patrolled the sidewalk searching for clues to the broken puzzle and talked to himself unabashed. The drive-thru teller counter showed a full jar of lollipops and a half jar of dog treats. He tried the ATM three times in a row, his account still unavailable, and he pounded on the large front windows of the entrance.

"Hello? Is anybody in there?" he said. "Hello?"

An elderly woman approached him from the Chinese restaurant slurping a near empty cup of soda.

"Excuse me young man. Is everything alright?"

"What? Yeah, I'm fine. Please go away."

"Are you sure? You seem rather upset."

He wanted to say something snarky and rude but upon seeing her he couldn't. She reminded him of his third grade teacher. "Well, let's see," he said. "I got back in town this morning and the bank is closed on a Tuesday for no particular reason. The customer service number won't connect me to anyone and as many times as I've tried, my account balance is nowhere to be found. I'm not sure what's going on. So maybe you're right ma'am. Maybe I'm not fine."

"Yeah, I thought you might be one of those," she said, gumming her straw. "That's why I came over."

"One of what?"

"You're the fifth one I've seen."

"The fifth of what?" said James.

"I guess you haven't checked your mail then, have you?"

He removed his sunglasses and dug at his eyes. "I don't mean to be rude ma'am, but it's been a long day already."

"Then you haven't heard the news. The bank sent every customer a letter telling them what happened."

He stepped closer. "A letter? What kind of a letter? What did it say?"

She pulled out a handkerchief and wiped her mouth. "It stated quite clear that they're done."

"Done? Done what? You mean done with some kind of marketing promotion?"

"They're finished you see. To be no more. They went out of business. It was made official last Wednesday. There was even a press conference. I saw it on channel eleven. I just love that Mike—"

"Out of business? What the fuck do you mean out of business?"

"That's a terrible word you know. You're a very rude young man," she said, turning to walk away.

He jumped in front of her and grabbed her by the shoulders. "Tell me what you mean by out of business. A bank can't go out of business. Tell me what you mean!"

"They went bankrupt you see. I may be old but I'm no liar. But not to worry, they were a proud member of the FDIC. I myself had over seven thousand dollars in my account and will get every red cent back. It's guaranteed by the federal government. That is the—"

"Oh my God! Oh my fucking God!" said James, clutching his head, spinning in a circle. "No, no, no, no, no!"

She continued talking, her words nothing but noise, as he hurtled to the car and laid a long strip of rubber on the pavement. His hands trembled on the wheel and he struggled to stay in his lane. "Please God no," he said, submerging himself into full prayer mode.

The Land Rover skidded to a halt in the driveway. He sprang from the car with the engine idling and sprinted to the mailbox. He threw letter after letter on the grass until coming across a simple white envelope addressed from the bank. It appeared as innocuous as his monthly statement. He tore it open, devouring the words.

September 24, 2008

Dear Mr. Horton,

It is with deep regret to inform you as a loyal customer at Trustworth Bank & Savings we've experienced extreme financial hardship in this devastating economic downturn. Thus, with no other options available, we're being forced to close our doors and file for bankruptcy after fifty-five years in business. As a long standing member of the FDIC program all accounts will be paid in full to the maximum allowed of one hundred thousand dollars *per* the date of our closing. Beginning Monday, October 2, you may call our new customer service number at 800-555-9876 to file your claim. We appreciate your business with us over the years. Thank you for your patience and understanding in this sensitive matter. God bless you, and God bless America.

Sincerely,

William H. Breg, CEO

He blinked and read it again. The words were hollow, surreal. His legs buckled and he reached for the mailbox to support himself. His brief promotion to the upper class had been nullified. He was catapulted into the past.

"Dee! Dee!" he yelled, barging through the front door.

She came out from the bathroom with her hair in curlers. "What's going on James? What's all the shouting about?"

"The money is gone! It's all gone!"

"What do you mean it's all gone? You're sweating. Why are you sweating? Slow down and talk to me."

He held up the letter and fell against the wall, melting into the ground.

"We're fucked," he said. "We're totally fucking fucked. They fucking fucked us." The tears were unavoidable.

She gasped reading the letter. "But. How can. I mean. Oh my God. Is this real? How can this be true?"

James was speechless, descending into economic shock.

"I've never heard of such a thing. It has to be a mistake," she said. "This all has to be some kind of big mistake. Because according to this, we've lost almost all the money. And if...." Her voice trailed off, fading, like there'd been a death in the family.

He nodded, eyes full of mist, unable to bring himself to say it. She joined him on the floor and cradled him. They held each other in one long wet and snotty soul crushing embrace.

"I think I'm going to be sick," she said, running back to the bathroom. James wiped his eyes and forced himself up, staggering into the kitchen. He uncapped a full bottle of vodka tucked in the freezer and chugged until he gagged. He then chugged some more.

Karen, the branch manager of the bank, was the first person he called but couldn't get through. He searched desperately for her home address with no success. Every number he found for Trustworth Bank was either busy, disconnected, or went straight to voicemail. Twice he heard the chirp of a fax. A pulsating vein surfaced in the center of his forehead and his bloodshot eyes were swollen.

He paced from the kitchen through the living room and into his office, repeating the loop like a caged animal plotting an escape from the zoo. His fists were wound into balls. Upon reading the letter yet again he lashed out and punched a hole in the wall, grazing a stud and ripping the skin from his knuckles.

James screamed and bolted to the garage where he rummaged through cluttered shelves before backing from the driveway. Dee chased after him.

"Get out of the car please. James? Listen to me. Where are you going?"

He rolled down the window. "I'm going to get our money back."

CHAPTER

9

He roared into the plaza with the tires squealing and nearly missed clipping a delivery van while rounding a row of parked cars. He ignored the speed bumps, crushing his muffler, and yelled at customers strolling through the plaza to, "Get the hell out of the way!" The brake pads ground into the rotors as the Corolla screeched to a whiplash stop on the sidewalk in front of the bank.

The door flew open and ricocheted back, hitting him in the knees as he climbed to the curb. James yanked on a pair of old work gloves and gripped a bat from Cole's days playing Little League, twirling the hard maple wood in his hands. Secured to his face were pink tinted goggles used the last time he went skiing.

The wall of glass was harder than expected and his wrists felt the reverb, tingling. The first swing felt like hitting concrete as did the second and third. The fourth swing produced a small chip. A man shouted, "Hey!" on his fifth swing and James lowered the bat, sensing the eyeballs probing him as a handful of bystanders pointed and recorded his rant on their phones. He gave them their Kodak moment and flipped them the bird while hollering profanities. His mind didn't go blank or black out. It turned red. A bullfight red.

He swung fervently, violently, and grunted with effort. The small chip turned into a crack, spreading, and three more colossal thrusts caused the twelve foot pane of glass to spider. It took a prodigious home run swing to bust it wide open. A refrigerator sized shard crashed to the sidewalk and sprayed the air with razor sharp pieces of shrapnel. He swung until the window frame was empty as a shower of glass rained upon him. The sound was loud and piercing. He breached the entrance, panting, hungry for more.

The alarm system triggered, hurting his ears, and an array of flashing lights clouded his vision. Jagged glass pebbles filled his shoes cutting his feet as he walked. His face and head were already bloody.

He rumbled through the lobby like a mean drunk and leapt across the teller counter, anxious to see what remained. With vigorous strikes, James bludgeoned the cash drawers but they wouldn't open. His baseball bat was no match for industrial strength metal boxes. He screamed, the arteries pumping hard from his neck, and smashed everything in his path. Phones, lights, pictures, pencil holders, coffee cups, computers, and keyboards were pounded into oblivion. Stacks of paper exploded on the floor. He tipped over desks, launched chairs clear across the room, and kicked large holes in the sheetrock. For five full minutes he emptied his rage into the bank.

His desire to continue wreaking havoc was strong but his out of shape body wouldn't comply. He bent over, holding his knees, gasping for air. It was the best cardio workout he had in years. He came to rest on a thin gray carpet with the vault door serving as a backstop. He flung off his goggles and gloves. A Camel Light hung from his lips and he fired it up, trying to catch his breath.

The police sirens echoed faintly in the distance, competing against the alarm, and grew closer. He shut his eyes and considered fleeing into the nearby woods to take the back way home in an effort to run for his freedom. But with the car right in front of the bank and his face captured by every video camera in the vicinity, the soon to be felon wasn't going anywhere. People already emailed snippets of his rampage to their friends and would tell everyone and anyone the exciting news of their day, embellishing the event with each new version. *Better to happen here than in front of the kids,* he thought.

He exhaled through his nose and stubbed out the smoke as fatigue settled in. His adrenaline pump had run dry. The flashing security lights induced a ferocious headache and his feet throbbed with every heartbeat. His back hurt, his face hurt, and his wrists were killing him. His *mind* hurt. He lifted his arm and grabbed his shoulder thinking he may have torn a rotator cuff, maybe a tendon.

Three squad cars sped into Palm Tree Shoppes plaza with their blue lights flashing and sirens booming. They formed a barrier around James' car, surrounding the financial establishment with an army of five. He understood what happened next when the police barged in, pumped up and edgy, not knowing what to expect from a hostile situation. Complete cooperation was atop his agenda. The last thing he wanted were two slugs in the chest for resisting arrest.

The officers infiltrated with military precision wearing bullet proof vests and hard rimmed helmets. A trio of cops knelt at the entrance, their 9mm Glocks aimed at his head. They barked orders and he couldn't hear a word they said but had no trouble reading their lips. The bank resembled a war zone.

He put one hand in the air along with the other and it turned eerily quiet as somebody disabled the alarm. Dee sped into the parking lot and pushed her way to the front of the crowd. James sighed. It was a frightening juxtaposition.

"Do whatever they say," she said. "You hear me? Do whatever they say."

The policemen threw him on the ground and dropped a powerful knee between his shoulder blades. They leaned their body weight on him, checking for weapons, and frisked him like a drug mule crossing the border. He groaned, unable to move, as the cold silver cuffs dug into his flesh. They dragged him to his feet and with an officer squeezing each arm, James was escorted toward the front door limping badly.

Dee waited on the sidewalk, sniffling, watching the nightmare unfold. She clenched a torn wad of tissues and wore a baseball hat, no makeup.

He was scared to make eye contact with his wife yet felt no shame for the act he committed. He never meant to upset her and convinced himself that given the situation, most people would have done the same thing. He was sure of it.

She followed him to the squad car as the crowd parted way.

"Meet me at the station. I'll be fine. Everything's going to be okay," he said.

He gave her a wink that fell flat and she held his gaze without speaking. An officer placed a hand on his head and forced him to bend down, slumping into the back seat.

The twelve minute ride to the station seemed like an hour and he observed every driver perfectly conform to the rules of the road. That was to be his only entertainment. With each passing tree, convenient store, stop light, and pedestrian the giant clusterfuck of his creation sank in. His problems mounted by the second.

The cops questioned him about the incident as he stared through the grate without saying a word, blood dripping in his eyes and trickling into his mouth. James had tremendous respect for the men in blue but knew to keep his mouth shut until speaking with an attorney. He had the right to remain silent. A lifetime of watching detective shows assured it.

CHAPTER

10

A tall slender man strutted into the interrogation room, his face taut, scowling. The lawyer for James wore an expensive double breasted suit, a Brooks Brothers tie, and a thick layer of arrogance. A platinum watch dangled from his hairless wrist and his black leather shoes were spit shined like mirrors. His reputation in central Florida was stellar.

"You know, I was on the golf course," he said, tossing a briefcase on the table. "And I wanted to play nine more holes."

James nodded, slightly.

"I don't normally even take these types of cases. Frankly, I hate them. You're lucky I work with your wife. Or used to anyway. I spoke with her out front. She's a basket case thanks to you."

Another small nod.

"What in the hell were you thinking? I mean really. It's amazing. People amaze me. They always amaze me. It never ends."

"Thanks for doing this Harris. I appreciate it," said James, his voice calm but hoarse.

"Don't thank me too quickly. I want you to know I'm doing this for Dee, not you. And I don't come cheap."

"So what am I looking at?" asked James, leaning forward. "How do I get out of here?"

Harris sat down, unbuttoning his jacket, throwing one leg over the other. "This may be one of the stupidest cases I've ever heard of. It's right up there anyway. It's almost as bad as somebody leaving their wallet at the scene

51

of the crime. You see, this is why I don't take these cases anymore. This isn't why I went to law school. Princeton, you know. Magna Cum Laude." He switched legs and re-buttoned his jacket. "Did you'd think you'd actually get any money? And if you did, that you'd get away with it?"

"It's been a rough day. I guess I wasn't thinking too clearly. Maybe I could plead temporary insanity?"

Harris laughed, a high pitched laugh, and snorted. "If I thought that would work, believe me, I'd try."

"Then what do we do?"

"You'll make bail. It'll probably be about five grand. Then we'll get a court date and I'll cut a deal." He paused. "James, I know you don't think so, but what you did, it's not like some unpaid traffic tickets. I'm good but I'm not a magician. I see a little time in your future."

"Time? How much?"

"Hard to say yet. Ten, maybe fifteen years."

"You're screwing with me right?"

"Yeah, a little, but I need to get something from this besides the money. Remember, I wanted to play nine more holes." Harris unbuttoned his jacket again, taking it off, and opened a bottle of water. "Listen, I'm not going to rip into you any further. I'll leave that for your wife." He smirked at James and unclicked his briefcase. "Now we need to get ready for the bail hearing."

It was late afternoon and a shift change in the police station was under-way. Judge Holloway stayed longer than expected, three hours longer, and let everyone know how she felt. Her arthritic knee was inflamed from an early morning tennis match and she'd recently changed medications. The case of James Horton was the third bank related issue she'd heard in the past two weeks.

"Mr. Horton," the judge said. "I've reviewed your case and can't say how disappointed I am with your lack of judgment. Economic times are tough for many people right now but it doesn't give you the right to display deviant self-righteous behavior. I understand your situation is unique compared to most people, but nevertheless, it is still unacceptable."

Harris' voice boomed, the elocution perfect. "Excuse me your honor, if I may, we're prepared to let—"

The judge flashed her palm and continued. "I can't have you being an instigator or stirring up trouble because you think you were wronged Mr. Horton. Not in my city. Where would it end? Trustworth Bank is the fifth financial institution to go bankrupt in Florida within the past month. Several other intuitions are teetering. These are perilous times and it's not the time to be playing cowboy. We must stick together. The general populous needs a deterrent no matter how small it may be. I'm setting bail for your egregious act at twenty thousand dollars."

"Your honor," said Harris, "with all due respect, that is far too high for my client who has no—"

"My decision is final."

The gavel banged with a thud louder than normal and she walked towards her chambers, tearing off her robe, favoring her left knee.

James looked at his suave attorney. "What the fuck was that?"

His look was not returned.

Imposition of the excessive bail presented a major obstacle for the Hortons. They didn't have any money. During their extended family vacation James spared no expense in racking up over $32,000 on their credit cards. The lottery money had vanished and the timetable for receiving the federal insurance claim was unknown. The married couple had barely $600 between them, no income, and no available credit.

Dee was permitted a ten minute session with her husband before he was led to a cell. Her face looked pale and weak as if she hadn't eaten all day.

"Hey there," said James, faking enthusiasm. "You come here often?"

"Only when my psychotic husband goes off his meds."

"The guy sounds like an asshole."

She didn't bite.

"Seriously hun, how you holding up?"

"I'm pretty freaked out James. The kids are freaked out too. It's scary seeing you in here. What were you trying to do?"

"I know, I messed up. I messed up bad and I'm sorry. Sorry to put you through this. It's inexcusable. Can you please forgive me?"

"Of course I can, you're my husband." She stopped to blow her nose. "What the heck happened? You ran out of the house yelling something about getting our money back."

He shrugged.

"By the time I got dressed you were gone. I knew you went to the bank and when I got there it was...."

"I really don't know what happened," he said, massaging his sore shoulder. "It's kind of a blur now. Like it wasn't even me. I drove to the bank thinking maybe there was somehow, some way, I could get our money back since it was stolen. It sounded right at the time."

"What do you mean stolen?" she asked. "What are you talking about?"

"Think about it Dee. One minute the money is there, safely in the account. And the next minute it's not. We didn't do anything different. What would you call it?"

"You're not serious, are you?"

"Look, it was incredibly dumb in hindsight," he said, grasping her hand and stroking her fingers. "I know it was stupid. I admit that. A simple knee jerk reaction to losing our dream money in the blink of an eye. When I read that letter, I thought my head was literally going to explode. Whoever heard of such a thing? I didn't even know banks could go out of business. Everybody gives them their freaking money. And the timing? Good God the timing."

"It makes no sense to me either. I'm upset about it too, believe me. There were so many things I wanted to do, places to see. But you only made it worse James, don't you see?"

He let go of her hand, raising his raspy voice. "Dee, what the hell am I supposed to do? Sit around while someone robs us for over three million dollars? Am I supposed to take a time-out in the corner? Write a complaint letter? Should I just act like a spineless wimp? That's what they want. That's what they expect."

"Yes to all of that and then some."

"Dee, listen—"

"You deal with it the best you can. Your macho solution achieved what? Take a look at where you are right now. Is this what you want? This isn't a movie you know. There are consequences, and not just for you."

"It was over three million dollars," he said. "Do you know how much money that is? People get killed every day for way less than that."

She looked at him as though he were stranger. "What people? I don't know those kinds of people. You don't know those kinds of people. Where would you come across those kinds of people?" She curled her lips and softened her tone as if speaking to a child. "It's gone James, alright? It's gone. That's the reality of it. For some reason God didn't want us to have that money. Otherwise—"

He pushed away from the table, standing.

"Are you serious right now? You're going to give me the 'everything happens for a reason' speech? Why in the world would God give us an amazing life changing gift and then tear it away in such a merciless fashion? Why would he do that? To teach us what? What could we possibly learn from that? What could anybody learn from that? It's all bullshit you know. Do you think God really is watching our every move and reading our every thought? And if he is, then this is a seriously twisted fucking joke and I don't appreciate it. You've got to get real Dee. The money was stolen, bottom line period. And there's no mystical or religious meaning why."

His face was flushed, covered in Band-Aids, and blood stains clung to his shirt. They stared across one another in opposite directions, their time eroding. She noticed the clock on the wall. "We can discuss this later. Right now we need to talk about getting you released. How are we going to get the twenty thousand?"

James took a deep breath. "Let's just ask your mother to borrow it out of the fifty we gave her? I hate to get Mary involved in this but she's going to find out anyway."

Dee paused, avoiding his gaze. "I already tried that. It's not going to happen."

"Come again," he said.

"It's gone."

"All of it?"

"Yes."

"What do you mean it's all gone? Your little old mother spent fifty thousand dollars in two and a half weeks? Does she have a major cocaine habit we're not aware of?"

"She did what we told her to do. She paid off her home equity loan and put a new furnace in the house. That only left about fifteen thousand."

"So get that then," he said. "We can try and scrape up the other five."

"Mom kind of loaned it to her friend Sally who was having some medical issues."

James slapped the table. "Isn't that just great? What planet am I freaking living on?"

"The cops suggested we use the service of a bail bondsman." She removed a business card. "They gave me a number."

"A bail bondsman? We just had over three million dollars stolen and I have to resort to a bail bondsman. And pay them a fee. No way. I'll serve my time first."

"Have you lost your mind? Time in county jail? You?"

"Screw it. On principle alone I'll do it. I'll stay here as long as it takes if I have to." He sat down and crossed his arms.

"You really have lost it. Today wasn't a temporary lack of judgment. Are you listening to yourself? To see you like this, I wish we never even won the stupid money. We were getting along fine without it."

He laughed. "You're joking right? What household were you living in? Because I want to move there. We were barely surviving Dee. We were hanging on by a thread and going down further each day."

"What point exactly are you trying to make by staying in jail? What does that prove? That you're a complete idiot. We have two kids in case you forgot."

They argued for the remainder of the time. She was rational, he was not. The more she talked the more stubborn he became.

They heard a pounding on the window of the door and a husky voice called out, "Time's up."

She rose and was about to speak but walked to the doorway instead. Dee had one foot in the hall and hesitated before stepping further. Her back remained to him. "You know, if we'd taken the payments like I wanted to, we wouldn't be in this situation in the first place." She slammed the door shut without glancing back.

He banged his head on the table, leaving it there, hiding his face with his hands. The knife cut deep. The truth cut deeper.

A guard brought inmate #10785 back to the holding cell until a vacant bunk could be located. His attorney was long gone and his wife was back home with the kids. It was dark outside. Within a span of thirty-six hours the former millionaire went from sleeping in the safety of a five star luxury penthouse to residing in a concrete cage.

CHAPTER

11

James walked, shimmying like a Geisha, with his hands cuffed and his legs shackled. He clanked down a bright hallway in an orange jumpsuit overtop a white T-shirt, a guard following one pace behind. His eyes were painted on the concrete floor as he was clueless what to expect inside the stronghold filled with society's derelicts. None of his friends or relatives had ever gone to jail. None of his known associates either. The only thing the middle-aged white man knew about jail was that he didn't want to be there, and never thought he would.

It was quieter than imagined inside the facility and his mind raced, buzzing, breeding thoughts of the worst of the worst. He thought of Clint Eastwood in the movie *Escape from Alcatraz*. He thought of the Bloods and the Crips, the Latin Kings, the Aryan Nation, and every other gang he'd seen on TV. He thought of the exercise yard, large men pumping heavy weights, and how to make a shiv from a bar of soap. But worst of all, he thought of tossed salad.

He'd heard about the grotesque act of salad tossing inside prison from a documentary. He and his friends used to joke about it on the golf course. The thought of licking another man's corn hole filled with syrup or jam made his balls shrivel up and his heart skip a beat. The last thing he wanted was to be raped by a gargantuan man named Bubba in the shower for refusing to commit the unthinkable horror. Losing over three million dollars because of greedy incompetent bank management was enough of an anal pillage for one day.

But his fears were soon laid to rest.

"Top or bottom?" a man asked, holding a pillow when inmate #10785 stepped foot inside the cell. The man was short, five six on a good day, well built, with a dark brown widow's peak. He had two different colored eyes and crooked teeth.

James pressed against the wall and clenched his butt cheeks. He sucked in his gut, transferring body mass to his flabby pecks, trying to look tough despite his white collar softness.

"What?" he said, almost stuttering.

"Easy newbie. I'm talking about the bunks." The man extended his hand. "The name's Victorio. Everybody calls me Tory."

James exhaled, his gut returning, his shoulders rounding. "Oh. Yeah. Right. Top I guess."

"Bottom it is then," said Tory. "You can peel off that wall now before you two become an official couple. Relax. I just got here myself. This ain't Rikers Island."

"I know. It's just that—"

"Dude, this is county. I'm in for back child support. I got four weeks. Third time. I drink too much. Know what I'm sayin?"

"Really? That's a relief," said James, making his way to the bottom bunk. "I mean that you only drink too much."

"Most of the guys in here aren't hard core criminals. It's a bunch of petty thieves and drug addicts. A ton of drunk drivers."

"Man, thank you so much for saying that. I was going all *Shawshank Redemption* in my head, replaying that laundry scene over and over."

"You don't have to worry about getting stabbed in the cafeteria or trying to prove you're a tough guy. Keep your gang signs low and you won't have a problem." Tory thumped his chest twice and flashed three fingers as they shared an uncomfortable laugh. "You'll be fine newbie. You'll be fine."

James crashed on the bunk like a dead man experiencing soreness in muscles he didn't know could get sore. Tory talked, yapping incessantly about the good old days, recalling a party in high school when he funneled twelve beers without puking and won twenty bucks. The next story involved a campfire, a tent, a girl named Erica, and the details of a lost condom. The one after that was worse. James was immune to his words, snoozing well before lights out.

It wasn't hard time he served; it was boring time, mind-numbing time. He would have preferred quarrying rocks with a sledgehammer or clearing the side of the road with a sickle. Cool Hand James would have preferred anything but lying in his bed smoking cigarettes faster than he could light them with only his tortuous mind as company.

He tried forcing himself to sleep even when not tired and with each ticking hour hopeless depression settled over him. Losing the money gnawed at his guts, overwhelming him. It physically hurt. He felt like a creature had sliced open his stomach and snatched his soul, making him watch as they ate it.

Every word of the harrowing letter replayed in his mind and he could still feel the paper, still smell the ink. The whole situation was incomprehensible. How could a bank of fifty-five years go belly-up weeks after he deposited millions? Why now? Why him? Why didn't he take the damn payments? The last question he asked was cruel and punishing. It would plague him for longer than he knew.

"Tory," he said after a four foot walk to the seatless toilet at two in the morning. It was night number three in the slammer and may as well have been three-hundred. "Tory, come on. Roll over man."

His cellmate was chopping some serious wood in the snoring department and James lay on his side with a pillow tucked over his head. He missed his queen size bed with the soft cotton sheets. He missed the way Dee twitched when drifting off to sleep and how gentle she was in the morning. He missed the kids venturing off to the school bus, the way they said good-bye, and he missed how once everybody left the house he could stroll around in only his socks and underwear. But most of all he missed the money. James mourned it, like a child on the side of a milk carton never to be seen again, knowing deep inside how much life was going to suck without it. He prayed to God for another miracle and gave the sign of the cross. He didn't pray for youth or glory or good looks. That part of his journey was over. It was only the money.

Dawn was approaching when he fell back asleep.

"Let's go newbie. Chow time," said Tory after getting dressed, hammering out push-ups on the floor.

James didn't move.

"If we get there late it'll only be oatmeal."

"Leave me alone."

"I heard you crying last night. And this morning, you were talking in your sleep, swearing up a storm."

"Sorry about that," said James in a weak voice. He leaned up on one arm, embarrassed, and popped a cig in his mouth. "I tried to be quiet. It's been—"

"Shit man. No need to fucking apologize. Everybody cries in here one way or another. We ain't as badass as we think."

Tory rolled over and began doing crunches.

"I don't know what you did to get in here or why you did it," he said. "And I have no idea how fucked up your life is right now. But you have to let that shit go man, or it's gonna take you someplace bad. I can relate, I been there."

"You been there, huh?" said James, feeling around for the lighter. "Then why do you keep coming back to this place? Isn't this your third time? This is someplace bad isn't it Tory? Seems kind of dumb not taking care of your kids. Seems kind of stupid."

"Easy newbie. Watch yourself." Tory jumped up and leaned over the bunk. He grabbed James' blanket and threw it in the toilet. "You don't want none of me. Not you doughboy. Believe it."

"Sorry man. Sorry. Just making conversation. Didn't mean to—"

"I told you already. I drink. I got a drinking disease. It's hereditary or some shit like that. It ain't my fault."

James turned towards the wall in a mound of self-pity and sucked on the cigarette like a pacifier, the tobacco crackling in the stale air. He was cold and still not hungry, skipping breakfast again.

You have use of the room for the next hour. That's all he could hear for the rest of the morning as the last thing stated by the lottery bureaucrat rattled around his head. James could still see the man's angry face and bald shiny head, his caterpillar unibrow. It was a miserable face. A face James once wore. A face he would wear again. If the man could ultimately see what happened to James Horton's winnings it would make his entire crummy job seem worth it.

Four days after being incarcerated Dee arrived with bail money in hand. They hadn't talked since their fight and upon seeing her he gave her a sheepish smile. He was covered in graying stubble and scabs and his body was frail along with his mind. He buried his head on her shoulder as she pushed her fingernails through his greasy hair. The longer they embraced the tighter he squeezed. He never wanted to let go.

"It took a little while to straighten everything out," she said, wiping the lipstick from his cheek. "Are we good?"

He rubbed his eyes and sniffled. "Yeah hun, we're good."

Chapter

12

"SUBURBANITE DAD GOES NUTS". It was printed in boldface on the left side of the newspaper following his arrest, smack dab in the middle of the Local section. Below it, a female jogger's near death experience with a twelve foot rogue alligator was chronicled and above it was the terrible tragedy of yet another high school teacher allegedly having sex with a student.

James' article was short, three quick paragraphs, and his mug shot was adjacent to a photo of the vandalized bank. The day was slow in the press world and his story was catchy. It caught on. Radio shows discussed the bad luck lottery winner and a grainy clip of his outburst was posted online. It went viral.

A news team showed up at the Horton residence unannounced. Dee was off grocery shopping and the kids, enamored with the camera, explained in detail their trip to New York, their incredible vacation, and the short lived saga of the lottery money. Their innocent comments to the media only fueled the fire. How much fuel nobody had any idea. James had become a phenomenon, a poor man's celebrity.

The Hortons exited the lobby of the police station arm in arm. The sky was an overcast sheet of slate gray but still bright enough to hurt his sensitive eyes. The flags out front, one for the country, one for the state, sat limp against a silver pole. He breathed in the stagnant air, chewing the mugginess like beef stew, and coughed. It was his first time outdoors since being incarcerated.

His middle finger, along with the index finger of his right hand, were a tobacco stained yellow from the non-stop puffing away and he wondered not if Dee would notice but when. He tucked the evidence in the back pocket of his pants as they walked towards the car.

"What's going on over there?" he asked, pointing to a crowd on the far side of the visitor parking area about fifty feet from their minivan.

"I haven't the foggiest," she said. "They were here when I showed up."

A small group of people gathered on the asphalt and formed a crude circle. They were mostly baby boomers in their first decade of membership into AARP with the exception of a good looking young couple in their early twenties who had a large dog. They sat on lawn chairs and the tops of coolers drinking bottled water and fanning themselves, too hot to stand. One person had an umbrella. They held up signs and talked loudly amongst themselves, at times chanting, at times singing.

James cupped his eyes and watched them as he moved closer to the car. He suddenly stopped and spun Dee around, draping his arms across her. He estimated the distance back to the police station. The car was closer.

"Don't look," he said into her ear. "Get the keys from your purse, get them ready. Be discreet."

"What's going on?"

"Those signs they're holding over there. I think I can read them."

"What do they say?" she asked.

"Keep your head down and pretend we're talking."

"But we are talking."

"Just make pretend."

The signs the crowd held up said WAY TO SHOW THEM JAMES!, GET UP—STAND UP!, and JAMES HORTON, MAN OF THE PEOPLE! They were made from white poster board and the words were printed in red marker with blue stars filling the gaps.

"Let's move," he said, gripping Dee's hand, quickening the pace.

"There he is," shouted a woman in worn out sandals and a beach hat. She fought the glare with one hand and had binoculars in the other. The crowd erupted in applause. They stood, cheering convict #10785 and somebody yelled, "You da man James!" People whistled. People approached him.

The Hortons fast walk turned into a jog and for the last twenty feet they ran. He locked the doors and slid down in the seat, shielding his face as the zombies descended.

"Go go go," he said.

Dee sped out the best she could, trying to avoid going over the fifteen miles per hour speed limit.

"What in the hell was that?" he asked, watching his supporters shrink in the side view mirror. "Is there an insane asylum around the corner I don't know about?"

She laughed. "Well look at my husband. The criminal turned hero. You're a regular modern day Robin Hood."

"Seriously Dee, those people, they're crazy." He adjusted his seatbelt and sat back up. "They do realize the money's gone, don't they? They know we have nothing to give them."

"I think so. They didn't seem to be looking for handouts."

"If they don't want money, why else would they be here?"

She turned left from the parking lot and passed along the side of the police station heading back towards the main road. James could still see the signs.

"What in the heck are they talking about? Man of the people my ass. What people? The stupid people or the poor people? We lost over three million dollars. Bunch of damn freaks."

Dee said, "While you were serving your time, on principle was it, your story took on a life of its own. You had a blurb on the internet and the local news ran a small segment. We've been getting phone calls, emails. We even had some media stop by the house."

"You're kidding."

"Nope."

"Can I ask why?" said James. "I committed a serious felony in broad daylight. I am now officially a criminal."

"Those people in the parking lot, they've had some losses too. I'm sure not like ours but for some reason they've identified with what you did. You've got to read some of the emails when we get home. I don't even know how people got my address. People from everywhere are writing to tell me about losing their jobs and how their four-oh-one-kay's have evaporated. The ones lucky enough to get pensions say they've taken a serious hit too. So many people are on the verge of losing their homes it's not even funny. One guy wrote and asked if we were going to be homeless. Said we could come stay with him and his family. He lives in Tennessee."

"Tennessee? They heard about this up there?"

"Yep. Don't ask me why or how, but in a weird way, you've touched them."

"Great. Wonderful. Yippee. Halle-fucking-lujah. I touched them." He hung his head. "I can't help them Dee. I can't even help us."

She reached out and caressed his arm. Her tone was reassuring. "I think you did something they all wished they could do but lacked the courage. Something everybody wants to do at one time or another."

"What's that?"

"Take action. Do something."

He flexed his hand, making a fist. His knuckles still hurt from punching the office wall and his shoulder was stiff. "Easy for them to say. We both know it was stupid. Everybody knows it. I'm never going to live this down. And besides, they didn't have to spend four days in jail listening to some guy jerk off at least once a night, sometimes twice. They don't have to pay for an expensive attorney or the huge fines. Not to mention the humiliation. Shouldn't they be looking for a job or something?"

"James?"

"Yeah?"

"It's Saturday."

They drove in silence past a fondue restaurant they hadn't frequented in years and an oil change place advertising UNDER NEW MANAGEMENT for the third time. They drove past the Post Office, Samantha's middle school, and a credit union he once considered joining. He leaned over and kissed her on the cheek.

"Thank you hun. You were right. I'm totally good with the jail thing. It's completely out of my system forever. I think I can check that one safely off my list."

"I thought you might say that but it's still nice to hear. Enjoy your brief moment in the spotlight. Within a week, nobody will remember your name or what you did. And if they actually do, they won't care. You won't have time to dwell on it either. You'll be too busy looking for a job. Your fifteen minutes are waning." She patted his knee and smiled. "You're welcome honey. You're welcome."

He stared out the window until they got home, his head smushed against the glass. The vibrations of the pavement jiggled his fleshy cheeks. The white line of the road flashed by in an unbroken stream and he noticed random pockets of trash littered on the side of the road. He saw a dead turtle mangled to pieces.

James had been dealing with everything as it came along but the thought of looking for a new job made his temples throb. Dee's statement was paralyzing. The word *job* and all that it entailed conjured up images of rush hour traffic, carpooling, conference calls, bosses, meetings, and hours upon hours on the phone. It was back to a peasant existence. He'd be forced to dust off the monkey suit and dance once again. His pride, if he didn't choke to death on it, would have to be swallowed first.

CHAPTER

13

He entered the house and was greeted to a warm welcome by two of his most favorite things in the world: a forty-two inch flat screen hi-def television and the most comfortable faux leather couch any reasonable man could expect to have. James hadn't seen a box score, update, or a highlight of sports for the longest stretch of his life. He hoped that never happened again.

The house was empty and quiet and the only sound came from the freezer where ice cubes dropped into a tray. Samantha and Cole were two neighborhoods over at the Smith's annual end of the season pool party, complete with a volleyball tournament and prizes. He could only imagine the trials they faced, the ridicule thrust upon them.

Dee made him a roast beef sandwich and joined her husband in the living room, sitting across the coffee table in a blue cloth love seat with a matching ottoman. She fussed with her rings, twisting them.

"I called Karen yesterday morning. She agreed to give me my old job back, same pay. They hadn't found a replacement yet so it worked out kind of nice. I start on Monday."

"That's good hun." He pressed the guide button on the remote, zipping through channels, and stretched out his legs.

"I figured we may as well get back into the swing of things as quickly as possible," she said. "Back on the horse so to speak."

"Right."

"We sure could use the money."

"No doubt."

"So what do you think you're going to do now? Any ideas? Because I heard the phone company is hiring customer service reps at the main office over on Lincoln Avenue. Maybe you could stop by and fill out an application next week."

He took another bite of his sandwich, pressing the buttons faster on the remote. "Sure," he said, stopping at channel 1035, ESPN.

"Don't feel much like chatting, do you?"

He brushed some crumbs off his lip. "I don't mean to be rude hun. Really I don't. But not right now, okay? How about tomorrow? We can figure everything out tomorrow. " He patted the couch, motioning towards it with a nod of his head, and was surprisingly horny. "Why don't you come lay down with me and watch a movie or something? Any one you want. You pick."

"James, there's something I need to tell you. Please don't get mad."

"Okay."

"I had to use the services of the bail bondsman to get you out. I'm sorry. The kids and I wanted you home so badly. I didn't see any other way. I know you were adamant against it but…."

He laughed to himself. *Companies are getting bailed out, now so am I.*

"Dee, it's okay," he said. "It's actually more than okay. I'm glad you did it. I don't know what I was thinking in the first place. And I kind of figured that anyway. We don't have that many friends, especially with money. You did what you had to and I really appreciate it. Jail pretty much sucked. I couldn't imagine being in there any longer."

James winked at her, raising the volume on the TV.

"Can you please turn that thing off for a second?" she asked.

He sighed, wishing the conversation was coming to an end. A new edition of *SportsCenter* was about to begin.

"I'm worried about you," she said, sitting on the edge of the chair. "Are you alright? You're not going to do anything crazy again, are you?"

"I'm fine Dee. Trust me when I say I have zero desire to go back to jail and hopefully your buddy Harris can see to that. It was an awful experience. Principle schminciple. That's a load of horseshit. I just want to eat my sandwich and watch a little television."

They didn't speak for the next five minutes and he heard himself chewing, wondering why it seemed so loud. He peeked at the remote, contemplating whether to hit the power button. His wife's eyes were upon him and he felt uncomfortable, thinking of the other TV in the bedroom. But he wasn't that dumb and knew he needed to stay.

Dee finally got up and walked across the room, placing a pillow on the floor near his waist. She knelt down and whispered in his ear. He grinned and set his plate aside, closing his eyes.

She rubbed his belly in small circles, sticking the tips of her fingers under his pants. The circles became larger as she undid the zipper, first kissing the denim, then kissing his skin. She watched him grow and teased him before taking him in her mouth, gliding up and down softly. He groaned louder and louder until his leg twitched like a dog before his body went limp.

"Welcome home," she said, throwing the pillow on the chair. "Don't worry, we're going to be fine. We've been down before. We'll figure something out. We always do."

He nodded and smiled and would have agreed to just about anything.

James dozed on the couch for the remainder of the afternoon. He slept hard despite sleeping all the time in jail and his skin was cool and clammy. His temperature seemed warm. He pressed the back of his hand to his forehead thinking maybe he'd contracted the flu and reminded himself to take a multivitamin and hit the sack early.

"What time is dinner?" he asked, tying his shoes, his hair wet from a long hot shower. After spotting his tattoo in the bathroom mirror he felt antsy, resisting the urge to scrape it off with a knife. The bright green ink was smooth against his skin. It was forever and condemning. He wanted to tattoo those numbers onto somebody's face. There was something he needed to do.

"It should be ready in an hour or so. I made one of your favorites," said Dee. "The kids will be home from the party soon. Maybe we could play a game later."

"Sure." He jingled the car keys in his hand. "I won't be long."

"James," she said. Her brown eyes met his blue ones.

"Yeah."

She opened a cabinet and grabbed the pepper. "It's nothing. Forget it." She untied her apron and set it on the counter.

Dee stood in the kitchen and watched him back from the driveway, watching the Corolla fade from the cul-de-sac, heading to the unknown. She leaned her hip against the granite countertop, near the undermount sink, and stared down the street long after he was gone before setting the table.

The businesses of Palm Tree Shoppes glowed bright against the encroaching dusk as the primetime hours of shopping and dining were in full swing. The only exception of course was the bank. Even by weekend standards, the 3,000 square foot commercial space leased by Trustworth Bank and Savings was darker than usual. The large plastic letters fastened on the bank's gray shingle roof, normally lit in a muted white, were turned off as were the row of flood lights illuminating the ATM. Inside, there were no red emergency exit lights, no light radiating from a computer screen left on by an employee, and with the windows gone, there was no reflection of any kind. The former financial establishment was a vortex of eerie darkness.

Large sheets of plywood occupied the gaping holes where windows once stood and were already splattered with graffiti while small fragments of loose glass overlooked by the cleanup crew were wedged in between crevasses and cracks along the sidewalk. Yellow caution tape surrounded the premise, wrapping it like a giant present. DO NOT ENTER signs were posted everywhere.

James crept past the front entrance, his foot riding the brake, and he pulled down a ball cap tightly over his head. He was shocked at the level of destruction. *Did I really do this?* he thought. It was a part of him he didn't know existed. He hadn't even been in a fight since middle school.

With each passing sweep of the bank he wanted to stop and analyze every detail of the crime scene with the precision of a forensic investigator. He wanted to cross out the peace sign spray painted on the plywood and replace it with something more appropriate. The word *thieves* came to mind. He wanted to burn the place to the ground and finish what he started but James was frightened. Not only of jail, but everything. He wasn't sure if even being there was a bail violation.

He lingered around the plaza until a cop car parked in front of the Chinese restaurant. Two officers exited the car, glanced in his direction, and took a call on their radios. James vacated the area immediately. He drove down the road with no destination in mind but didn't want to go home. The house and all of its chains were back. He wanted to sweep up his family and move to Hawaii or Iceland or Brooklyn. He wanted to go anywhere but *that* house.

A huge blinking sign that read HOT caught his attention as he cruised through a section of town with a never-ending row of fast food joints. The donut shop, a place he visited often in his younger days when the word angioplasty had no meaning, was filled with a steady line in the drive-thru and the smell of molten sugar flavored the air.

He sat at a two person mini table in the corner with his hat still low picking at a fried dough treat, observing the employees in action. One of them was a boy not much older than eighteen and reminded James of his son. The young man moved with a carefree grace and was full of life, full of hope. He was full of the future.

A small HELP WANTED sign hung in the window next to a poster for the new coffee-donut supreme value combo, available only for a limited time. James guessed they were paying minimum wage and last time he knew it hovered around seven dollars an hour. He looked at the sign several more times and added some basic math, shaking his head.

He faked reading a newspaper as the *what if* factor of financial freedom had been replaced by the *why me* factor of what could have been, what might have been, what should have been. The pain from losing the money was reminiscent of losing his best friend in high school from a car crash. It was dumbfounding, all encompassing. He didn't know what to do, how to feel, or how to act. His emotions oscillated between depression and rage. For his family's sake, he knew the appearance of a brave face was paramount. He needed to be a chameleon in order to survive the ordeal. That was his only chance.

A Hispanic couple with three little kids entered the shop scooping up two dozen glazed to go. They wore matching black shirts from a local church and each one had a different saying. The wife's shirt stated, "This Too Shall Pass." It was written in red cursive letters underneath a picture of Jesus on the cross. James stared at her, unable to look away. The saying became etched in his brain. *This Too Shall Pass.* He scribbled the words on a napkin, circling them repeatedly, recalling how his mother used to preach the same thing. He crumpled the napkin and tossed it in the trash. He wasn't so sure.

James took the long way home and stopped to buy Dee flowers and the kids chocolate ice cream. He also purchased a lottery ticket. A Pick 6.

Dee prepared an all-star dinner and the Hortons ate together as a close knit family. They didn't say grace that night and in an effort to appear wise and fatherly, he explained to the kids what really happened at the bank. It was a first rate sales presentation. He assured their young minds the entire event had been a giant misunderstanding and accepted the fact that Samantha and Cole didn't believe a single word he said. But he had to say it, had to try. He hugged them, kissed them each on the forehead, and told them how much he loved them. He suggested they go catch a movie in the morning.

The Horton clan circled around the Monopoly board, moving their irons and thimbles across Boardwalk and Reading Railroad and St. James Place until it was bedtime. Everybody knew their family roles and played it to perfection. It was an Emmy worthy performance on par with the Cleavers. James imbibed a few more beers than usual and almost died when Samantha said, counting her fake money, "You know daddy, at least we got a nice vacation out of the deal."

Smiling outside while crying inside he nodded yes, faking agreement.

CHAPTER

14

Amonth crawled by and the status quo of life returned seamlessly for the rest of the family. Dee resumed working full time at the law firm performing her paralegal duties with professional efficiency. She never complained about what might have been, falling back into a normal routine. The tormenting endured by Samantha and Cole at school had subsided with their classmates focusing their criticism towards the newest victim stung by the imperfection of being human. They'd made up all homework from the family vacation and hung out with friends as usual.

James' story had largely faded into obscurity. The media milked it for a short time using him as the poster boy for what's right or wrong with America depending on their agenda. Without condoning his actions liberals hailed the passion he showed, painting him as the victim of an out of control and unregulated capitalism. Conservatives denounced his behavior as the act of a common street thug who deserved to be punished to the maximum. The blog nation agreed, disagreed, and called him everything in between.

Day after day James found himself alone in the house, lost at sea, with the motivational level of a sloth. He'd sit in his office chair and stare at the grimy computer screen, reminiscing about the night of winning the lottery. Without purpose or aim he perused the dead-end job leads available online in between games of chess and went through the motion of job seeking for only one reason: material. He needed something to report to his wife.

With the exception of roaming centerfield for the New York Yankees or playing point guard for the Knicks, James had little interest in going back to work of any kind. What he wanted and wished for was the lure of returning to a life without worry. Choosing what golf course to play or what beach to visit next were the only decisions he desired to make. The former millionaire had turned into a scorned lover, unwilling to accept the terms of the financial breakup.

At half past noon on a Wednesday he twisted off a beer cap and checked to see how many people continued to write him. After weeks of being flooded with emails he still averaged over ten per day. The positive correspondence, the ones making him feel righteous for annihilating the bank, had all but disappeared. Supporters of his cause moved on. The only thing left was venomous hate mail.

The negative compositions tended to be lengthier and more colorful, pulling no punches in their unwavering ridicule. Strictly out of self-loathing curiosity he read every word they sent. Some of the emails were from former colleagues, particularly those he'd attacked in his flamboyant farewell. They threw his disparaging remarks back in his face tenfold. It was harsh but he couldn't blame them. He would have done the same thing. Going out in a blaze of glory had returned to burn him.

The phone rang. The caller ID indicated it was Dee. He flipped open a notebook and glanced at a list of companies to speak of, hoping not to repeat himself from the previous day. It was time for his daily checkup.

"Hey hun. How's work going?" he asked.

"I'm pretty busy. I have a meeting in five minutes. How's the job search? Any good leads?"

"Oh yeah. Quite a few I think. I sent out a bunch of resumes. Have to wait and see though. You know how it goes."

"Good, we can talk about them later. Right now I don't have much time. I spoke with Harris today and he has some great news. I mean really great news."

"How is that beady eyed son of a bitch?" said James, swiveling in the chair.

"You should be a little more thankful he even took your case. The man does high profile work." She paused. "How many beers have you had already?"

He didn't answer.

"I don't have time to get into the details, but you're going to flip. I'll tell you all about it over dinner. See you tonight. Love you."

"Love you too," he said, making kissing noises into the phone.

James yawned and cracked his knuckles, satisfied his efforts qualified for a full day's work. Less than two hours removed from sleeping he debated between napping versus drinking more beer. But Dee's teaser had triggered him. He speculated what the good news may have been. Less jail time? Reduced attorney fees? Perhaps even some kind of refund?

For three nights in a row he had a recurring dream. It centered on a gruesome boating accident off the coast of Miami involving every single high ranking member of Trustworth Bank and took place on Christmas Eve. The company threw themselves an extravagant party for another great fiscal year, patting themselves on the back. A twelve piece orchestra played and there were cases of rare vintage champagne. Caviar from the Black Sea was served by the bucket. Everyone danced on the deck of a private yacht until an oil tanker came out of nowhere and tore the vessel in half. Most of the executives died instantly but a few were maimed, experiencing a slow painful death. They were all covered in crude. The only survivor was the captain who had an uncanny resemblance to George Washington and didn't have a speck of oil on him. He somehow managed to steal all of their wallets and swim safely to a deserted island inhabited by the Harlem Globetrotters and the entire cast of *Baywatch*. James closed his eyes. He wanted to have that bizarre dream again. Maybe that was the good news Dee spoke of.

When the kids arrived home from school he snored on the couch with a puddle of drool on his shirt. The TV volume was on high. There were beer cans on the coffee table and an empty bag of chips on the floor. He reeked of cigarettes, having already graduated to a full pack a day. The married couple didn't argue over his disgusting habit anymore as their sex life no longer existed.

"James. Dinner's ready," said Dee, nudging him from his slumber. "Why don't you go clean up?"

He wiped his eyes, slightly disoriented, and put his feet on the ground. Something smelled fantastic. After washing his face and changing a shirt he joined his family at the table.

"When I talked with your earlier I mentioned Harris and the case," said Dee, passing around a plate of steamed veggies. "You aren't going to believe it."

"Good ol' Mr. Harris, my brother. Love that guy hun. The man with the funky suit jacket. Let me ask you this. Does he unbutton and then re-button that thing like a hundred times a day at the office? Can he get carpel tunnel from that?"

"Harris is fine, thank you. He received a call out of the blue this morning. You know who from?"

"Your mother," said James, laughing.

"No you drunken moron. Not my mother. A receiver acting on behalf of Trustworth Bank."

"The bank? I thought they were done."

"They are. But a small staff was temporarily assigned for the bankruptcy proceedings. Asset liquidation and that kind of stuff."

He sat up straight, his eyes narrowed.

"The money? They have the money? They were just fucking with us?" he asked.

"First off, watch your language please. Second, no, they don't have the money. It's still gone. But they have proposed a deal that would keep you out of jail."

"Well that sucks!" He slammed a beer bottle on the table.

"Didn't you listen to me dummy? They're willing to drop all charges."

He took a small bite of chicken and then one more. "Fine. What is the supposed incredible deal? Let me guess. If I give them a kidney or an eye they won't throw me in the clinker. Or how about they take all my blood?"

Dee set down her fork, folding her hands. "They've proposed to drop all charges if we pay for the damages to the bank and restore the building to where it was before you trashed the place, including the replacement value of the items destroyed."

He leaned back on two legs of the chair, holding the wall for balance.

"James, its prison we're talking about. Harris thinks they're being difficult about the case because they want to make an example out of you. They want to throw the book at you."

"And?"

"And you were only in there for four days last time. When I came and got you, you looked like a nomad wandering the desert. How about six months of that? Or a year? Or maybe longer?" She took a sip of wine and tilted her head. "You're not going to last in there. You're not cut out for that kind of environment. You won't make it. You know that, right?"

"Really Dee? I wouldn't be the bell of the ball?"

She disregarded his comment and focused her attention on the kids, asking the universal parental question, "How was school today?"

"I'm sorry hun," he said, setting the chair on the floor, saving the kids from answering. "You're right. I'm being stupid. So what is it? How much to take care of everything?"

"Thirty thousand dollars. But they said if we could do it cheaper that's fine, as long as the landlord approves it."

"Thirty thousand dollars? Whoa. That's a lot of cash. Can't they take it out of the three million dollars they stole?"

"Please not again with the stealing thing," she said. "Not tonight."

"Before I even consider giving those lowlife bastards one stinking dime, did Harris mention why in their good hearted nature they are willing to do such a thing?"

"No, not really. Maybe they felt bad or something. Who knows and who cares. Maybe it's their way of making a bad situation right."

James threw his napkin on the table. "Are you sure you want to have this conversation in front of the kids?"

"We're all part of this family. They're old enough to know the truth. And why are you getting so upset anyway? I thought you'd be excited. You know, because of the whole not going to jail thing."

"Fine then. Let's talk. I'm going to ask you a question and I want the truth. The honest truth. If somebody told you all you had to do was spend six months in jail, or maybe even a year, and you'd get three million dollars afterwards, would you take it?"

She shook her head no.

"That's three million cash. No taxes, no catch."

She shook her head again. "Why in the world would anybody do that?"

"Come on. You most certainly would. Who wouldn't? So I'm willing to consider the offer of course but please don't insult my mediocre intelligence by saying the bank wanted to make things right. Why? Does that mean they did something wrong? They aren't doing this because they feel bad or want to help. They have some kind of an agenda. They stole our money and they know it and there's nothing short of giving it back that can make things right!"

His face reddened to a frightening hue. The look in his eye was similar to the day he broke in the bank.

"Okay. Okay. Calm down. It doesn't matter why. Maybe you're right, but—"

"You're damn right I'm right!"

"I got it James. Relax. You're scaring the kids."

He ran a hand through his hair and took a deep breath. The kids buried their faces in the plates, pushing around their food. The air conditioning unit kicked on providing some much needed noise.

"You guys want some more mashed potatoes?" asked Dee, lifting a ceramic bowl. "There's plenty left. How about another glass of soda?"

James walked to the fridge and slammed the door, causing the magnets to fall everywhere. Once again he'd embarrassed himself in front of the kids. They'd grown used to his fondness for swearing but the screaming and yelling were never part of his repertoire.

He stopped next to Dee and kissed her on the head. The color of his face was normal.

"I'm sorry hun for losing my temper. Cole, Samantha, I apologize. I'm sorry. I didn't mean it. Your father is going through a rough patch right now, an adjustment period. That's all. I'll be fine."

He took his wife's hand. She pulled it away.

"You guys can be excused if you want," said Dee. "I brought home cupcakes for dessert."

The kids ignored the offer, moping all the way to their bedrooms. Dee picked at her plate, cutting her meal into pieces so small they needn't be chewed. The married couple finished dinner in awkward silence like two strangers enduring a bad first date. She cleared the table and when he got up to help with the dishes she said, "I got it. Just leave."

He put up no fight and slipped into the garage for a smoke. His blowups were becoming more frequent, adding tension to an already tense house. The bank, money, a job, jail, their future; nothing could be said to him. His pledge to morph into chameleonic mode around the family was failing. His plan for survival was failing.

The pillow on the couch was greasy and flat from the weight of his large head and his legs dangled over the edge. He slept little that night, tossing, with the bright light from the TV illuminating the room.

CHAPTER

15

James arose the next day sleep deprived with a stuffy nose and a headache. He stubbed his big toe on the way to the kitchen, splitting the nail on a corner of baseboard molding, and hobbled to the coffee maker grumbling. He was in a foul mood, fouler than normal, and began his hollow routine in preparation for nothing. A $30,000 burden had been added to his list of woes and money, as usual, wasn't far removed from his mind. He couldn't get the conversation from dinner out of his mind. Why would the bank make such an offer? Why then?

He watched *SportsCenter* five times in a row with the mute button on, memorizing the highlights without trying, thinking about the deal. He pictured his dad, not the used up old skeleton version limping to the finish line, but the vibrant youthful one with the freakishly strong hands who could handshake a person to the ground. James saw him clearly, sitting at a card table in the breezeway of the house he grew up in, clutching a non-filtered cigarette as he searched for the next piece of a jigsaw puzzle spewing platitudes. "If it's too good to be true, then it probably is." "There's no such thing as a free lunch." "There's always a catch." James heard those mantras dozens of times growing up and his father was a walking cliché, repeating information received from his own daddy who'd gone through the Great Depression. The two generations of Horton men with a pessimistic view on life spoke his language. James dialed the number to Dee's law firm.

Philip, a cousin of somebody high up in the firm who mattered, answered the phone. He was a newly hired secretary with a penchant for gabbing. He told

James how sorry he was to hear about the lottery money, how he once had an aunt who won five grand playing bingo, how she bought an expensive parakeet with the winnings, and how the bird died from lead poisoning after eating the paint on the cage. Philip rambled with a slight lisp, discussing his new used car and what a pleasure it was working with Dee. James considered pouring a jigger of bourbon in his coffee and jabbing a steak knife through his ear, wondering if the twenty-five year old man babbled incessantly to everyone. He'd never been so happy to be placed on hold.

A white plastic chair on the side deck of the house was covered in dirt and dark green spots of mold. James cleaned it with a damp paper towel and tucked the phone under his neck, sitting in the shade near a rusting barbeque. His toe was purple with a nasty blood blister as he elevated his foot on the railing. A mild wind knocked down the last stubborn leaves clinging to tree branches and from his vantage point he saw a huge pile of bear shit dead center in the lawn. The momma black bear had returned. One of the kids would have to be assigned cleanup duty.

James opened a scrapbook from the first week of their vacation. Samantha and Cole made it an effort to cheer him up. There were pictures of Six Flags Theme Park, the Liberty Bell, Independence Hall, Appomattox Court House, and Virginia Beach. One picture from the hundreds he'd taken was his favorite. It was of Dee, in a rare solo shot without their children, posing with a frisky smile next to the sculpture garden at the Biltmore in North Carolina. For some reason he couldn't identify it was the best picture she'd taken in a long time. Maybe it was the lighting on her hair, the sun bronzing her skin, or the new expensive water bra underneath a sleek yellow top.

She looked incredible even at the age of forty-two, even after popping out two kids, both times all natural and no epidural. Compared to the rest of the people at the law firm Mrs. Dee Eloise Horton was practically a supermodel. She was office hot, by office standards, and James married up in the physical appearance department. He surmised the only reason Harris even took his case was in hopes of one day bedding her. *How much of me is she going to tolerate?*

"Harris Winchester speaking," his lawyer said, interrupting the sound of smooth jazz elevator music.

James dropped the phone, startled to hear a voice.

"Um, hi Harris. James Horton here. How are you today?"

"James. What can I do for you?" Harris peeked at his watch hidden under a French cuff and opened a bag of trail mix. He was working through lunch again.

"Dee told me at dinner last night about the phone call you received from the bank."

"Yes, that is correct. They did call me."

"I was wondering why they would do that. Why would they make such an offer?"

"I'm rather surprised myself James. Very surprised."

"So what do you think about it?"

"As we discussed in jail, you do remember your glorious time in jail," said Harris, crunching a mouthful of nuts, "the crime you committed encompassed trespassing, breaking and entering, vandalism, and destruction of property. It's a third degree felony offense and punishable by up to five years in prison according to Florida state law. I've argued, on your behalf, that with no prior record to speak of and considering it was a first time offense, that sentence seems exceedingly harsh. The first offer I received was for sixteen months in jail with three years probation. I've been working hard to get that reduced and they've already come down to ten. Then, out of nowhere, I get a call on behalf of the bank with an unprecedented offer. Why do you think that is James?"

"I have no clue. That's kind of the reason for the phone call."

"No thoughts at all?"

James mouthed a few silent swear words. "I don't know. It seems a bit odd. They're going out of business so who cares if they get a little bad PR. They no longer exist."

"I agree with you."

"So?"

"So what?" Harris said.

James held the phone in the air. He pointed at it like he was holding a gun and fired a couple of shots. His toe throbbed and he put too much damn cream in his coffee. *I'm getting billed five hundred dollars an hour for this?*

"Look Harris, I know my case isn't a top priority of yours, but could you elaborate?"

Harris smiled. "James, you're right. You should have been a detective. You'd make an excellent Inspector Clouseau." He laughed at his own lame joke and continued. "The bank isn't doing this because they want to be nice or care about you or are worried about PR. In fact, I'm sure nothing could be further from the truth. They aren't going out of business either. They are out of business. It's a very big difference. Like everything else in the world, their decision is based on money."

"How so? I thought they had no money. Which is mindboggling considering they stole all of mine."

"Ahh. Your self-righteous conspiracy theory has surfaced. I was wondering how long before you brought that up. You're just like my other clients James, aren't you? The world revolves around you and you alone. You're the center of your own universe. For the hundredth time, nobody stole your money. You weren't the only person with money in the bank mind you. They did have other customers. Lots of them. The system in place has its faults and doesn't always work flawlessly. In your situation it was simply bad timing. Bad luck."

"Bad luck huh. That's what we're going to call it. Seems kind of funny that one minute my money is there and the next it's gone."

Harris kicked up his feet on the desk and leaned back in his plush brown chair. He spoke deliberately. "You know James, if you'd taken the payments like your wife suggested, this predicament would have been alleviated."

The pain in James' big toe ceased and he no longer had a headache. He bit his lower lip, sticking the whole thing in his mouth, and his hand trembled. He wanted to reach through the phone like Freddy Krueger and slash the attorney's face with metal claws. The insolent bastard had crossed the line and the insult to James Horton's honor demanded immediate retribution. But he knew upon seeing his lawyer next there wouldn't be a duel with pistols or swords. There'd be no punches, head-butts, slaps, or shoves; no MMA takedowns. Nothing but a dirty look and a disparaging remark, and probably not even that.

"James? You still there?"

He loosened his mouth and stood, his hand moving along with the words, slicing the air, when he said in an angry tone, "Stop fucking around. Why did the bank make the offer?"

Harris relented, sporting a grin. "You were informed the bank was going under on a Tuesday but they had declared their bankruptcy status the previous week while you were on vacation. As soon as they filed for bankruptcy it immediately nullified their insurance policy on the retail space for all of their branches. So the building you vandalized was uninsured. In the process of liquidation, every conceivable asset must be utilized to pay off debt to creditors. Having you pay for the damages to the bank, including the computers and furniture, and restoring it to its original value is of greater financial importance than your sitting in jail for months on end. It's that simple. If you have any further questions I suggest you contact the receiver for the bank or perform some other form of inquiry. Consider the bank's leniency a stroke of good fortune and don't overthink it. It's a good deal James, a blessing. You got lucky. Take it."

"But what about me?" he said, bubbles of spit exiting his mouth. "Don't they have a debt to pay to me? The landlord gets his but I don't get mine. What about my money? Aren't I in line to get something?"

"Good day James."

"But my money Harris? They stole my money. You know it's true. Everybody does. What about me? How about my debt? Harris? Harris?"

All he heard was a dial tone.

A neighbor's Pomeranian barked like a rabid psychopath as a landscaping crew showed up to fix a cracked sprinkler pipe. The dog's owner emerged from the garage wearing no shirt and scolded the beast. Upon seeing James he gave a perfunctory wave. James responded with an obligatory wave of his own and dumped his coffee on the ground, leaving the cup on the deck.

He limped to the bathroom in search of some Tylenol and felt a combination of lightheadedness and nausea. Paying for the damages he inflicted on the bank was equivalent to working as free labor. Worse yet, it was tantamount to actually paying the bank for the right to work there. It added a tragic insult to a critical injury, removing the last shred of dignity from a broken man. At least for then. He spent the afternoon in bed with the door shut and the curtains drawn, spooning a pillow. *Bad luck. Bad timing.* He didn't want to hear it anymore. It didn't make any sense. He wished his phone call to Harris had never gotten through.

CHAPTER

16

"**I**s there anybody else you want to invite?" Dee asked for the third time, verifying the guest list for a final head count. She tapped a pencil on the binder of her spiral notepad.

James shrugged and yawned. He pushed back the ottoman and slouched to the right of the chair, raising the volume. A game was playing on TV. A game was always playing on TV.

It had been three weeks since they received their check from the FDIC for $100,000 and it took less than an hour to spend. $32,000 went for their credit cards, an astounding $18,000 in attorney fees, $4,000 in back taxes, settling up with the bail bondsman, a new transmission for the minivan, Samantha's braces, fixing the air conditioning unit, Christmas presents, and the always looming mortgage payment. Then there was the little check they owed to the bank for $30,000 to keep James' pasty rear-end out of jail. With the remaining scraps left, Dee planned a New Year's Eve party.

"There has to be somebody besides Teddy," she said. "What about the guys from your dart league? Or how about that one guy from work you used to do stuff with?"

"Hun, I haven't played darts in about two years in case you didn't notice and the guy from work, that was Jason, the heavyset dude with the hearing aid who'd drink at least a six pack of diet soda every day. We'd make fun of him because he ate salad for lunch all the time and smother the thing with ranch or blue cheese dressing, sometimes both. He really thought he was eating healthy."

"Well call him. Wait, he wasn't one of the people you made fun of in your email, was he?"

James shook his head. "Nah. He's a good dude. But he married some chick from Nicaragua so she could get her green card. She won't let him leave the house. Kind of a control freak. They have twins and the last I knew she was pregnant again."

"What did he marry her for if she's so controlling?"

"She's not bad looking, he is, and he wanted to get laid."

"How romantic," said Dee, counting the names in the left hand margin of the notepad, getting a total of twenty-six. She plopped down on the arm of the chair. "You need to get back out there James. You used to have a lot of friends. Maybe you should try a little harder, join a club or something."

He waved a hand back and forth as if shooing a fly. "Dee, could you, I mean you're blocking the screen."

She pulled her hair into a ponytail and fastened it with a scrunchy. "Well I think this party is going to be a great way to ring in the New Year whether you have any friends here or not. We can put the past where it belongs and focus on two thousand and nine. It's going to be fun. Remember the word fun?"

"If you say so," he said without taking his eyes off the TV.

Dee straightened an ornament on the Christmas tree made from Popsicle sticks with a picture of Samantha in it. She adjusted a row of white and red lights that didn't need adjusting and bent down to check the water level in the stand, using her middle finger as a measuring stick.

"Oh, one last thing before I go to bed," she said, wiping the pine scented moisture on a towel. "Can you call my mother please?"

He threw his hands over his face and mumbled through his fingers, "You're killing me with the mother thing."

"I've invited her three different times and she keeps saying no. She denies it, but it has to be because of the money. I think if you called her it might make a difference."

James leaned forward and stretched his sore lower back. It ached where the spine meets the buttocks. His new sedentary lifestyle consisted of a strict routine: sitting, lying down, sitting some more, getting up to lie down somewhere else, sleeping, eating and drinking. His weight ballooned faster than the national debt.

"How many times do I have to tell you, or her, that I'm not mad. I'm not upset, sad, angry, pissed off or furious. I'm nothing. I'm glad Mary got a little money from our shitty deal." He whispered under his breath, "At least somebody did."

"I know, I know. I've told her that numerous times, but she won't listen. I told her you're not like that. But you know how mom is. She feels weird. Like she did something wrong."

"How about I send her an email? That's the best I can do right now."

"Fine," she said, rotating the one stocking hanging over the fire place that had drifted in the wrong direction, ensuring they all angled to the right.

Dee made her way to the kitchen for a cup of chamomile tea before heading down the hallway towards the bedroom. She asked in a loud voice, "Can you lower the volume out there tonight? I could hear the TV blaring until all hours of the morning. I slept terrible."

"Yeah hun."

"And James," she said, holding her notebook, displaying the guest list.

"Yeah hun."

"I guess I'll only put you down for one invite then."

Entranced by the bright talking box with the moving objects he said, "Yeah hun," unaware that his wife of sixteen years had left the room.

The house was decorated a la Martha Stewart and a tad overdone, pushing hard for the illusion of happiness. Colored streamers hung from the ceiling and sparkling confetti glimmered on the staircase and floors. A table near the door contained Happy New Year paraphernalia and a Christmas tree stood tall in the center of the living room. The smell of vanilla was strong as half a dozen candles lit up the fireplace and on every available surface were trays of homemade cookies and candy. The manger scene was to the left of the tree and had real hay in it, baby Jesus looking cute as a button, and a three foot stuffed Little Drummer Boy guarded James' office where he specified nobody was to enter. Dee hung mistletoe in the kitchen and in the living room and one near the bathroom. Shuffling in the eight disc CD player was a sassy ensemble of seventies holiday tunes and dance hits from the eighties, ensuring music long enough to escort the final buzzed person out the door.

James began drinking early, earlier than normal, and skipped his late afternoon lunch-nap ritual. He wandered about the house plotting his strategy and decided the corner of the living room located near the sliding glass doors was his. He'd scouted it out and staked claim to it and would fight to the death anyone who challenged its sovereignty.

His blue striped dress shirt was already wrinkled along with his slacks and the beard he insisted on growing looked dirty and unkempt. It was cool inside the house but as the guests poured in he was sweating, pulling on his collar. Dee confronted him wearing a classic black cocktail dress with pearl earrings and a necklace.

"I need you to be good tonight," she said, fixing his tie. "You promised. Now, why don't you go eat something and put some water in that cup?"

"I'm good hun. A O motherfucking K. No worries mate. I'll eat later, trust me," he said, tapping the basketball protruding under his shirt. "Does it look like I'm in the habit of missing meals?"

"Later is what I'm afraid of." She took his hand. It was wet and disgusting. "Come on. I want to introduce you to some people who moved in down the street. Their names are Peter and Michelle and they brought a bottle of Chambord to put in the champagne later."

He resisted her pull, broke away the grip, and shoved his hand in a pocket. "Nah. I kind of like the view over here at Fort James. You put me in charge of the ice remember and I take that very seriously. In fact, I'd better go check to make sure we have enough. I'll mingle later hun. Let me get warmed up." He leaned in for a kiss on the lips, would have settled for the cheek, and wound up smooching the air.

At parties, James used to refill people's glasses without being asked and always had a lighter ready to spark up a smoke. He'd share stories, embellishing small kernels of truth, and was known for cracking one-liners. But it was gone. He was gone, replaced by somebody else. Holding the most basic conversation had turned into a challenge.

To the guests in attendance James was an enigma. Everyone knew him or of him and not a soul inside the place hadn't heard his sad story in dramatic detail via the news, the internet, or secondhand gossip. Most people had grown frightened of him, preferring to keep their distance. He stopped showing up at soccer games or volunteer breakfasts. He was curt in public, rude when he wanted to be, and disinterested in anything. And his outrageous behavior at the bank wasn't the only thing. His physical appearance had undergone a significant transformation.

His face morphed into a permanent shade of red and always seemed sunburned. He was puffy and bloated and gave the general appearance of a rather unhealthy guy. His blue eyes, no doubt his best feature, became cloudy, and a look of angry desperation was always present. Over the course of three months James had aged in dog years. Avoiding him at the party was on most people's agendas.

The conversation with the Smiths went disastrous when he laughed inappropriately and he fared no better with the Quills. The Maloneys pretended they had a phone call when Dee dragged him over and the Portnovays, well, they were the Portnovays. By the time he was introduced to the Christies he surrendered. He tried to engage Dee's friends in small talk but the words weren't there. He ended up staring at the bottom of a glass that needed to be refreshed without speaking. He felt like a stranger in his own home, an insider amongst outsiders. James grazed on his fingernails, spitting little bits in the air, and every forty seconds dabbed his forehead with a hanky. The safety of the corner was his only solace.

An aggressive smack hit him on the side of the arm, catching him off guard. Somebody was squeezing harder than normal in manly affection.

"Happy New Year," said Bill, his neighbor from the other side of the development with the nicer houses, the side of the development James never visited. "Thanks for the invite. Great party."

"Thank Dee. She did it all."

"I haven't seen you at the driving range in a while. We have to play some golf hombre. I bought a sweet new driver. Destroying it off the tee. Shot an eighty-four last week."

"Good for you Bill. Fan-fucking-tastic," said James, emptying his vodka tonic in a swig.

"Next week I'm playing with a few guys from church. You want in?"

"Church guys? Let me think about that for a sec. Ahh, nope."

James searched for Dee through the crowd. He searched for the kids, forgetting they were staying at friends.

"Your loss. Maybe some other time?"

"Probably not."

Bill cleared his throat. "You know James, that stuff at the bank, that was something. Top shelf batshit if you ask me." He took a step closer and held a beer bottle with both hands, tearing at the label. "Some people I work with have talked about it. I told them I know you. Said we were friends. They think it was pretty cool, except for this one lady who says you should be locked up in a mental hospital. But I have to ask. That must have been some rush, right?"

James disengaged from the conversation and turned without speaking, going to get more ice. Bill followed, chirping.

"What was it like James smashing the place to hell and being on the news? How did it feel that everybody knew your name? Come on, you can tell me. I won't say anything. What was it like being in jail? Did you have to kick the shit out of anyone?" He grinned. "Did you have to pay for protection with a carton of cigarettes?"

James was a heavy six four, Bill a scrawny five foot nine. He looked down at his guest, noticing the bad hair plugs, and observed the brown penny loafers with no socks. There were actual pennies in the slots and they were shiny. He still didn't utter a word and once again turned to walk away. Once again, Bill followed.

"So you were in there for what, about a week, right? Did you see anybody get stabbed or shanked? Did you—"

With surprisingly fast reflexes for a big guy he cupped Bill's mouth with one hand and grabbed him by the back of the head with the other, pressing the two together. "I'm going to need you to shut the fuck up now. Okay little Billy?" He smiled and shoved him against the wall. "Now why don't you return to the rest of the party and talk about your new speedboat or the price of soybeans or the fake tits you bought your wife so you'd stop sleeping around, and leave me the fuck alone." He slapped Bill across the face, a half-slap, but hard enough to leave fingermarks. He stepped back and saluted him, spun on his heel, and had one leg out the sliding glass door when somebody called his name.

"James Hot Sauce Horton. I'd know that ugly son of a bitch anywhere."

James stopped and turned around. He approached the man and tried to snarl but his face lit up. "Those are big words for such a little guy." They shook hands and pulled each other close, embracing in a tight hug as both of them said, "I missed you man."

"This jackass won't return my phone calls," said Teddy London to nobody in particular.

James smiled for the first time all night. "Hey Teddy, you want to do a shot with an asshole like me?"

CHAPTER

17

The two men spent the next few hours matching each other drink for drink. They grew loud at first, then even louder, receiving the occasional uncomfortable glance from a guest. Dee asked them to lower their voices three times and shot James the death stare. She finally gave up, ordering them outside. With the exception of a couple lone smokers, they had the backyard to themselves.

The moon hung over the tree line in a crescent shape and there weren't many clouds. They could see the stars ancient light flickering from the Orion constellation, the only one James could identify, and as they talked, they unknowingly migrated around the yard. Every time a squirrel or raccoon or some other small creature made the tiniest noise in the woods, James envisioned the big black momma bear charging at them to protect her cubs. He warned Teddy about the piles of shit he'd been finding on the lawn.

"Sorry man to hear what happened," said Teddy. "It don't seem fair."

James took a hit off the joint Teddy provided. "What can you do? I'm jinxed," he said in a constricted voice. He unleashed a long burst of smoke and coughed hard, scraping the back of his throat. "You're supposed to be cheering me up man, not turning into a buzzkill."

"I know dude. But I just found out about that FDIC thing the other day. A little salt on the wound if you ask me."

"It almost seems appropriate at this point. It's just the fecal icing on my turd cake," said James, bogarting the joint.

The weed was good. It was strong. James couldn't remember the last time he partook.

"If that fucking bank of yours could've at least gone out of business just a few weeks later," said Teddy, "you would have gotten so much more money."

"A hundred and fifty thousand dollars more money."

"Ain't that a motherfucker."

"It's the motherfucker of all motherfuckers my friend. Besides the place going bankrupt in the first place." James put his glass to his lips but it was empty. "Kind of hard to believe too. My shit-hole bank goes bankrupt and I get a hundred grand. That's the deal. Now, because of people like me, and everybody freaking out about the economy, the government raised the minimum amount to two hundred and fifty thousand."

"They've got to keep the faith brother."

"That's right. Keep the goddamn faith. Wave that magic wand and change the rules. Abracadabra. And it's good and all, makes perfect sense. But it don't help me one bit." He inhaled another vacuum cleaner sized hit off the joint and Teddy reached up to grab it.

"Take it easy big boy. This shit is pretty strong."

"You pussy."

"You're a real policy changer Mr. Horton. An inspiration for change. Maybe you should run for senate."

James laughed. "Senate? Hell, I'll run for president. No, screw that, I want to run for the FDIC. How do I get elected to the FDIC? Those sonsabitches. It's like they're watching me man." He leaned against the house, his buzz multiplying by the second.

"Nobody is watching your fat ass. Except maybe the cops."

James threw his glass in the woods, hearing it break on a rock.

Teddy extinguished the joint and placed it in his cigarette pack. "You know, Heather said that when people experience bad luck it means they did something bad in a past life."

There was an enormous gap in the fence providing a freeway access for the bears and James made a mental note to take care of it. He didn't hear what his drinking buddy said and then forgot why he was staring at the fence in the first place.

Teddy nudged him and repeated himself.

"That's what you get for dating a hippy," said James, swaying a bit. "They say weird shit like that. Where is your hairy armpitted sweetheart anyway?"

"She's home. Says she's sick. Coming to get me later."

"Ah hell Teddy, maybe she's right. Maybe I was the guy who worked the guillotine in the French Revolution or the dude that shot Abraham Lincoln. Maybe I fucked a billy goat or something in the fifteenth century when I was working on a farm and now I'm paying for it. Bestiality is a sin my friend," he said, pointing a finger, laughing. "Speaking of Bill, where is that little twit? Get him over here so I can smack his ass again. I want to spank him with his stupid penny loafers."

"You did hit him pretty hard," said Teddy. "I saw that slap a mile away." He lunged at James with a big open hand, moving in slow motion, striking him in the face.

James stepped back, nearly falling, and held his jaw. He pretended to cry and stuck a thumb in his mouth.

That was it. That's all it took. The two clowns got on one of those rolls where they couldn't stop laughing no matter what they did and everything seemed funny. Their stomachs hurt and in order to calm down they retired to separate corners. When Teddy stepped in bear shit, it sent them over the edge.

Everyone gathered around the television as the countdown for 2009 closed in. James opened the sliding glass door and the light struck his eyes like he'd been stuck in a coal mine for decades. The house was warm and cozy and the heat penetrated his body, transforming him into Gumby. His eyes were slits of glossy redness and the drunkenese dialect emanating from his mouth was a new hybrid version containing a great deal of mumbles. He gave himself the internal pep talk. *Move slowly. Don't say too much. Be cool. You can do this.*

One careful step was followed by another and his strides were calculated, as if on a balance beam. The wall served as a guide.

People hummed kazoos and blew party favors while throwing confetti in the air. They had their toasts prepared and resolutions ready in anticipation of improving their lives once again. Drunken hugs and sloppy kisses were about to infect the room as everyone chanted in unison, "Thirty, twenty-nine, twenty-eight, twenty-seven...." The ball in Times Square was ready to drop, a mob of partygoers screaming.

Standing near the coffee table was Dee. She gave her hubby a cute little wave and he panicked, seeing three of her, but took a deep breath and waved to the one in the middle. His mouth was drier than dry and he would have paid a thousand dollars for a breath mint.

"Twenty-six, twenty-five, twenty-four, twenty-three...."

He let go of the wall, took a sharp left, and advanced towards his beautiful wife. She was only ten feet away.

The widow Myers hadn't moved from the couch since arriving and as he tried scooting around her James caught his foot on the cane tucked under her feet. He got top heavy and began to tumble while gravity did its thing. His three steps to the right were countered by four to the left and when he overcorrected, his momentum couldn't be stopped. With his gut leading the way he fell forward like a spring breaker in a belly-flop contest. James only managed to get one hand partially in front of his face before slamming on top of the coffee table.

"Twenty-two, twenty-one, twenty...."

The floor shook when he pounded it and the cheap wooden structure exploded into splintering pieces. The shockwave reverberated off the windows, rattling the single pane glass, and everyone ceased chanting. The only voice to be heard was the TV host anchoring the festivities.

James lay on his stomach covered in cookies and potato chips with onion dip matted in his hair. He moaned, holding his lips and chin, blood coloring his graying beard.

Teddy and Dee rushed over, rolling him on his back. James looked around with one eye half shut and already swelling. The faces, the walls, the fireplace. Everything rotated in a dense fog.

"I told you to go easy on that stuff," said Teddy, trying to help him up.

A ringing noise filled James' ears and he wanted to speak but couldn't. His tongue felt numb. He managed to get to one knee before projectile vomiting all over the place, spraying the bottom of people's legs. The crowd gasped and separated as he crawled to the staircase.

"James," said Dee, gripping his shoulder. "Lay down on the floor. I'll get you some ice."

He grunted and pulled himself up by the railing. Teddy ducked under his arm for support but James thwarted him off. He stumbled to the front door, bumping the walls, nearly falling again. Once outside he entered the garage and locked himself in. His party was over. The Horton's New Year's Eve party was over.

The guests filed out in fire drill fashion, skipping the faux gestures of helping to cleanup. They devoured the juicy gossip of James' spectacle like a pack of hungry vultures and the news would spread fast. Dee did her best damage control and created excuses for her husband, intimating he hadn't slept in days, suggesting he'd been taking medication for an ear infection. She apologized more times than could be counted.

Once barricaded in the safety of the garage James puked some more until dry heaving himself to sleep on the concrete floor using a tiling sponge for a pillow. Dee knocked on the door.

"James? Are you alright? Can you hear me?"

She pressed her ear to the door and heard snoring.

"James? Come on now. Wake up and come inside." She shook the handle several times and couldn't remember where they'd put the key. The garage door opener was in the minivan but instead of retrieving it she blew a strand of hair from her forehead and went back inside, turning off the lights.

At seven in the morning he unglued his puffy eyes, wondering where he was with no recollection of getting there. He shivered, drenched head to toe in urine, and his bottom lip was gashed as well as his chin. *What the hell happened?* he asked himself, rubbing his head, trying to configure the fragments of his blackout episode.

He stripped off his clothes and chucked them in the washer, reeking of an incontinent wildebeest as he walked in the house buck naked hoping nobody saw him. The first thing he noticed was the trainwreck sprawled on the living room floor. *That can't be good.* He jumped in the shower.

Dee lay awake and heard him come in. She'd been up all night.

After brushing his teeth and rinsing with Listerine twice he strategically maneuvered into the bed, lying as close to the edge as possible. He vowed to never ever ever ever drink again.

A lamp clicked on. Dee sat up.

"James. Hey James. We need to talk." She pushed him hard in the leg and slid back to distance herself from the emanating stench.

"Hun, I know what you're going to say. I know. I'm so sorry," he said, going on apologetic cruise control. Although unsure how the night unfolded, he without a doubt knew it was bad.

"I don't even know where to begin," she said, her hands clutching her shoulders, the corners of her mouth turned down.

James spoke in a wounded voice. "I know I embarrassed myself, but more importantly I embarrassed you, the kids, and the family. It will never happen again. I mean it."

"You see, that's the thing. You've been embarrassing us lately about a lot of things. I can't cover for you anymore. Ever since getting home from jail your attitude has been terrible. Tonight was the last straw. This isn't working. Something has to change."

"I'm not going to drink anymore," he said. "I quit."

"Yeah right. You've been saying that for months."

"I promise."

"You've promised before."

"I promise promise. I'm done."

"It's more than the drinking. That's just the tip of it. It's the constant negativity. We're all stuck walking on eggshells because of you. It's like we can't breathe. We're suffocating. Can't you see it?"

"I'm trying hun. I really am. It's been difficult for me."

"That excuse is getting so old James, it really is," she said, shaking her head. She pulled her knees up to her chest, wrapping her arms around them. "This whole thing has been difficult for everyone in the family but we've seemed to move on. We're managing to be alright. But you, with your endless self-pity and explosive anger. Tell me, how is that really trying?"

He rolled over to face her, holding his stomach. "I don't know, but in my mind I'm trying."

"As far as I can see, you aren't trying hard enough. Things need to change for real and quickly or—"

"Or what?" He sat up and turned on his own lamp. "What are you trying to say? We've had problems before and they always seem to work out fine."

"This is different. We've gotten through tough times in our marriage as a team. I got through them with a sweet caring man. I can't do this all by myself. It's too much. You aren't present James. You're a totally different person than you were a few months ago. It's like I don't even know you."

She looked away as he clicked off the light and fell under the covers. "Tell me what I need to do hun. You name it and I'll do it."

"I think you should see some kind of therapist."

"Really? A shrink?"

"Yes, a shrink. Last night was beyond humiliating. I can't even imagine what people are saying today. That can never happen again. That will not happen ever again. You understand? I deserve better than that and so do the kids. I don't want to live with this kind of drama."

"You're right Dee. I can't argue with you. Maybe talking to someone can help. I'll do whatever you say. Set it up and I'll go."

"You need to do this for the sake of the family."

"Okay hun," he said, his eyes getting heavy.

"And maybe get some anger management as well or attend some kind of recovery program."

"You got it."

"And I was thinking we could start taking walks after work to get back in shape. Maybe join a gym or something?"

"Okay hun."

"And get you some new clothes. Nothing fits you anymore."

He started to doze off, to dream, but managed to fire off one more, "Okay hun," before going out.

"And James," she added. "The smoking thing has got to go. You know how much that turns me off and I want you to…."

She noticed his heavy breathing and saw he was asleep. Her husband was dead to the world once more. She watched him for a minute, brushing his hair to the side. His big gut had grown bigger in the past few months and the shirt he wore stretched hard to cover it. A single tear leaked from her eye, ran over her cheek, and cascaded down her face; leaping onto her robe. None followed.

CHAPTER

18

The economy in central Florida as well as the nation continued to crumble. Unemployment rates skyrocketed and a current of fear swept from sea to shining sea. People with jobs felt lucky to have them, no matter how insignificant, and jobs once considered lowly or easy to attain became competitive. Employees logged whatever hours their companies demanded and despite growing workloads with stagnant wages, they kept their mouths shut. They complained to their families and friends but nobody else. The media tagged it as the worst time in American history since the Great Depression. For most people who never came close to missing a meal or going to bed with their bellies grumbling they couldn't grasp what that meant. James Horton was no exception.

Finding a job of some sort, any sort, had always been easy, ever since high school when he worked fixing sandwiches in a sub shop. A dedicated person with a determined mindset could always land work doing manual labor, bussing tables, or serving as a cashier. Jobs were there to be had, or they used to be. But jobs paying well, above the poverty line, were increasingly a thing of rarity.

After revamping his resume for the third time with the assistance of an expensive online service, little action was happening. The opportunities for interviews of any kind were non-existent. He flooded the internet and its thousands of suspect job boards with application upon application upon application, never knowing where they went or if somebody actually received them. He tried, after getting badgered from Dee, to re-enter his former industry but it was more than far too late. James was considered a pariah, a loose cannon, and a borderline psycho. He'd been reckless. Anybody that checked into his obnoxious farewell as junior corporate trainer at Snake Hill Hot Sauce Company would see that.

He knocked on a blue metal door and peered in both directions of a hallway, praying not to recognize anybody and be forced into conversation. He was twenty minutes late.

"James, good to see you," the therapist said, reaching out his hand, still wearing a college class ring from a small school in the Midwest. Dr. Novak was a young man, thirty-two years old, and specialized in obsessive compulsive disorders. He wasn't James' first, second, or third choice. James didn't have a choice. But Dr. Novak was one of the few doctors who accepted the health insurance Dee's place of employment offered.

"I didn't think you were going to make it," he said. "Come in. Have a seat."

"Me neither, but I had to. I got fired again yesterday. I need you to talk to Dee for me. Last time. I promise."

"What? Fired again? It's only been three weeks since I last saw you."

"I can make my co-pay on a credit card, right?"

"Of course," said Dr. Novak, swiping the card through a portable machine prior to the session starting, ensuring it would go through. He sat down and scanned his patient's notes, crossing his legs at the knee. "So let me get this straight. That was your fifth job since January?"

"That seems about right." James removed a black leather flask. "It could be six. It could be seven."

"It's three o'clock in the afternoon James. The flask? Really?"

"I haven't had a drink in almost two weeks. And I'm here aren't I? And I'm paying."

Dr. Novak paused and ran an index finger over his top lip, letting it navigate the scar from his cleft pallet. "So what happened with the job this time?"

"I'll tell you what happened, I'm too old and out of shape to be loading cargo trucks. My back hurt so bad every morning I was taking eight ibuprofen just to go to work. It had herniated disk written all over it. And besides, I couldn't keep up with the younger guys. They were calling me gramps."

The doctor nodded and scribbled on a pad. "Go on."

"I didn't complain or nothing. At least not out loud. I tried my best. But it was obvious how much slower I was than everybody else. They told me to leave after lunch. I get my final paycheck next week."

"I'm sorry James. I'm really very sorry to hear that."

James took a nip of the flask, washing it down with a Diet Coke. "You're sorry. Wait until I see my wife. I texted her."

Dr. Novak went to the water cooler and retrieved a paper cup, handing it to his patient. "Can you at least pour your libations in here and drink like a gentleman?" He made some more notes in the file and removed his glasses, tucking them in his shirt.

"It seems to be a pattern with you. Losing your job."

"A pattern?" said James. "What pattern? Are you serious? These jobs, the ones I've been able to get, they're freaking garbage. They're all minimum wage. If I could ever find a real job I would stick."

"You think?"

"Listen, I used to be a junior corporate trainer for a large hot sauce company. Four years there. It wasn't a glamorous job but I made almost forty-eight thousand a year."

"So what does that mean?"

"It means I had a pretty good job, even though I didn't know it. It means I know how to keep a job. I showed loyalty, a team player mentality. But then, out of the blue, I became a millionaire for a few weeks. I wrote a stupid email I shouldn't have. I made some mistakes. What do you want from me? The job market is brutal. I tried working some commission only sales jobs and was terrible at it. I tried working in a lumber yard, being a store greeter, and delivering pizzas. Did you know somebody actually stole three large pepperoni pies from my car when I delivered at an apartment complex? Unbelievable. Heck, I even stooped to being a goddamn sign flipper for a jewelry store. We Buy Gold. That's what it said on the sign. Guess how many people yelled obscenities at me on a given day? I can tell you it's north of ten."

He ran a hand over his face, around his neck, and over his face again. "I'm pushing fifty doc. Fifty damn years old. I've tried everything but can't seem to find a real job. I'm blackballed from the only industry I know to make any real money. I'm starting to feel hopeless, like somebody hexed me, like one of those voodoo dolls you see in the movies. And I don't know who's pushing the pins."

"I understand James. It's tough out there. But don't give up just yet. Hang in there," said Dr. Novak, offering his deep professional insight. "We're running a little behind so let's change gears for a minute. How are you doing with losing the money? Do you still believe it was stolen?"

James tightened his lips. "Nope."

"No?"

"You heard me, I said no." He mimicked the voice of a robot. "I realize now that my money was not stolen and that there are no guarantees in life. The bank did nothing wrong."

"You don't seem very convinced."

"That's because I'm not. But I don't want to sound like a crazy person anymore either. I'm sick of everybody telling me I'm freaking nuts. I'm working real hard to let that go doc. I really am. When it comes up now I say it was bad luck. That's what Dee told me to say. We even practiced it with role playing. That's what people need to hear, right?"

Dr. Novak nibbled on the end of a pen. "Well let me ask you this then. Do you still feel guilty about the money? Like the whole thing was your fault for not taking the payments?"

"God I hate coming here," said James.

"You're here now, so why not talk about it? Tell me about the money. Tell me how you think you let your whole family down because you took the lump sum. Tell me how much that pains you."

For the remainder of the session James retreated into the region of his mind where there were fields of flowers and chocolate bunnies, rollercoasters and cotton candy. His lips flapped and words came out, vibrating through air particles on invisible waves, reaching the therapist's eager ears. But they were contrived and rehearsed, delivered with an automatic ease.

He looked at the oversized framed diplomas hanging on the wall behind Dr. Novak. There was a B.A., an M.A., and a PhD. James did a quick word scramble: bad, mad, dam, bam. He even came up with phad, knowing it's not a real word. He wondered how much those seven letters cost to attain and bet his therapist was still paying off his student loans. He shook his cup. It was empty.

It had been five months since he'd made a fool of himself at the Christmas party and stained the family name. Going to therapy was a big part of the healing process in returning things to normal, keeping it all intact. But like a new drug, working so well initially, the effectiveness began to dissipate. Missed appointments were routine, tardiness common, and his record for active participation was spotty at best. The family life was mud sliding with household morale at an all-time low. A cavernous rut deepened amongst the Horton clan.

On the way home from Dr. Novak's a yellow gas light demanded his attention, blinking on the dashboard. The fuel needle waffled on empty. With only a five-dollar bill he resorted to the change cup, digging hard for the quarters. Gas was at an all-time high and creeping higher each month with no logical explanation why, inflating the price of everything. He pumped in half of a quarter tank and bought a ninety-nine cent carnation in the beginning stage of wilting. He added a forty ounce beer and a Slim Jim. And a lottery ticket.

James sat in the parking lot of the 7-Eleven listening to music that was hip and popular during his glory days that he never knew were supposed to be glorious. He prepared for his side of the argument. Dr. Novak was no help, refusing to call Dee, but he felt confident in his litany of excuses. He believed to have a pretty tight case for his day drinking and losing his job, a case that grew stronger when he turned left at the stop sign in the development and saw the empty driveway of his house. It provided valuable time to clean up.

His stomach churned while watching a show on the Lifetime Network, his new secret obsession, and he thought about having a smoke. But he'd just showered and wanted to smell clean. James checked his watch every ten minutes, listening eagerly for the sounds he'd grown accustomed to: the kids slamming the car doors, Dee scolding them not to do so, and the clunk of his wife's high heels up the sidewalk.

When 6:00 p.m. rolled around he imagined they were simply running late. Traffic was horrible near their house and road construction made it worse. By 7:00 p.m. he was convinced they'd stopped for a slice of pizza or maybe some tacos, maybe even Chinese. By 7:15 he worried, calling Dee's cell, texting the kids. By 7:30 he considered calling the cops, by 7:45 the hospitals, and at 8:00 p.m. he tied his shoes.

James navigated the house searching for clues to their whereabouts and flicked on all the lights. Both kids' beds had their sheets removed and the blinds were drawn shut. Cole's room wasn't the usual wall to wall carpet of dirty/clean clothes. It smelled different, and the Spiderman poster hanging over the headboard was missing as was the titty magazine hidden under the mattress James knew about. Samantha's stuffed animals were gone and her favorite books she read over and over were nowhere to be found. When he looked down the wall and noticed her pink Barbie night light was absent too he needn't investigate further.

He descended the staircase slowly, holding the rail hunched over, one lonely step at a time. James didn't yell or scream or holler. But inside, where the voices can be the harshest, he shredded himself with dismay. Why did he push it so far? How could he not recognize how off kilter everything had become? Was he that imperceptive, that blind? When he entered the kitchen it was there all along, directly in front of him. A small purple envelope containing his initials was propped up against a crystal fruit bowl with no fruit in it and the envelope was tucked in, not sealed.

The letter was long and messy and written in a shaky hand. Dee specified her feelings with every detail, catching him off guard. Her words were so honest and blunt, so mean and cruel. He read it only once. Her words were so true.

James watched a group of ants march under the sliding glass door, going back and forth at will, over and around the traps he set, not missing a beat in their mission. Worker ants working, doing what came natural. Doing what had to be done for survival.

He stepped out into the humidity as the sun sat behind the horizon. The sky was streaked with shades of orange, violet, and dark blue. He lit the corner of the letter from a burning cigarette and watched the glowing embers drift away in the breeze, disappearing like they never existed. *I can change Dee. I know I can change.*

CHAPTER

19

On the desk lay a single piece of paper worn thin from being crumpled and then un-crumpled, the process repeated twice. The note, or rather his script, was typed out doubled spaced with words crossed out, words added, and reminders to stay calm in the margins.

James took several deep breaths and read it slowly, leaving three well-rehearsed messages on the voice mail of Dee, Cole, and Samantha. It'd taken him two days of agitated self-destructive phone calls to reach that point, ignoring his wife's request for a time-space buffer in order to figure things out and self-analyze.

After the initial shock dissipated and his abandonment became reality, the numbness turned into sadness, spilling into anger. He considered jumping in the car and racing up to White Plains, demanding his wife and kids return to their rightful home in Florida, demanding they be together. But he knew better. Dee would never respond to a demand.

The house seemed bigger with nobody in it and he felt like a bachelor minus the fun. Spread along the coffee table were pictures of the kids. Samantha was dressed as a ballerina for Halloween, Cole that year was Wolverine. There were class photos, pictures from the beach, and sports shots from the soccer fields to the basketball courts. Year by year their bodies grew, their facial structures changed, and James took particular interest in the family photos involving him. He was dumbfounded how thin and in shape he once was and whether he knew it or not, he actually looked happy. He wondered if he had the capacity to be his definition of happy again. He wondered if he knew what happiness meant.

His cell phone rang and he sprinted across the living room, swiping it off an end table. *Dammit.* He wished it was somebody else and let it ring one time shy of going to voicemail.

"Hey Mary," he said in an unwelcoming tone.

"Hello James," she said, speaking softly. "Dee doesn't know I'm calling. Her and the kids are playing a game."

He regretted answering it and thought about hanging up, saying his phone dropped the call. But he couldn't be that rude. Not to her. And now he was stuck.

"How are you?" she asked.

"Fine. Fine."

He sat on the staircase, head between his knees, scratching his arm.

"It's been a while since you and I talked," she said. "I know things have gotten a little out of sorts, and I don't want to interfere."

"You're fine Mary. You're fine."

"I'm calling because there is something you should know. In spite of everything that's happened James, we all love you very much. We need to hear that sometimes. I love you, the kids love you, and Dee loves you."

An air bubble formed in his throat.

"I know it feels like you're being deserted right now, like the world and everyone in it is against you. But they aren't. And you're not alone. Time apart can be good sometimes. You simply have to see that. And use it."

Her words were kind and he was surprised how easily they stirred him. It felt as though Mary was next to him, combing his hair like a small child, reassuring him that everything would be alright. All he needed was a glass of warm milk and his Superman pajamas.

He breathed heavy into the phone, his face tight, fighting it.

"You're a good man James. And a very good father. Don't be too hard on yourself. We tend to do that too often. We're always so hard on ourselves. Why do we do that? And you're still so young. So very very young. At least compared to me."

His jaw quivered. "I'm sorry."

"I know you are. But there's nothing to be sorry for. It's not your fault."

"I'm sorry," he repeated, sniveling. "I am so freaking sorry."

"It's okay James. One day you're going to be even stronger from this."

The tears ran over his cheeks, dripping off his chin. "It's like there's this hole inside of me Mary, and I don't know how to fill it. I know it sounds stupid and people say that kind of crap all the time, using it as an excuse to act weak. But I don't know what to do. I feel miserable and have no clue if I can ever get back to the way I used to be."

She grinned. "Do you honestly remember the way you used to be James? Do you remember how you felt? Feeling less miserable than you do now but still kind of miserable anyway? Always feeling stressed out but putting on a brave persona because you knew it was the right thing to do for your family? You hid it well but I saw you. I know how you were."

He released a slight laugh and a slight cry, wiping his nose on a sleeve. "That was me."

"The good old days weren't always as good as we remember. Things tend to get rosier in hindsight," she said.

James held his thumb and index finger an inch apart. "I was so freaking close Mary. I was so freaking close to having it all, so close to winning the game."

"But that's just it. It's a game you can't win. It can never be won. There are no rules and no scorecards among us. That part is up to God. That is one of the rare privileges in getting older. You get some real perspective."

Samantha called her grandmother in the background, stating it was her turn, and Mary said she would be right there. "Take this time and put yourself back together. We want you back. You know what you have to do, right?"

"I'll try."

"I didn't call to give you a lecture. That's not how you and I are. We go back a ways. Forget about the money. You had everything you ever needed before that. It's what's inside that counts. Now give the situation a chance. Give Dee and the kids some time. You can't force it right now."

"I'll really try," he said, sniffling some more.

"I know you have it in you James. You're stronger than you think. You lost your way. It happens sometimes."

"Mary. Thank you. I needed...." His voice broke off.

"It's going to be okay. We'll all be together before you know it. We're going to laugh at this someday. Now take care of yourself and do what needs to be done."

He couldn't speak.

"I'm going to hang up now James. Have a good night. You'll be in my prayers. And remember, we all love you very much."

He fell onto the couch, plunging his head into a pillow. For the first time since jail he set his manhood aside and the crying that started on the phone elevated to a full-on blubber. He purged his emotions until he was physically and mentally spent. That night's sleep was the deepest most nourishing sleep he'd experienced in a long long time.

Beams of light woke him the next afternoon as the sun pushed its way through a slit in the curtains and gathered on his face, warming him. He embraced it rather than getting annoyed and instead of hiding under the blankets, he sat up, stretched, and moved about. Two heaping scoops of dark roast grinds were dumped into the coffee filter while he thought about Mary's phone call. He felt like somebody gave him a B12 shot. There was work to be done.

First on his agenda was to create an agenda. James needed a list. And number one on that list was finding a well-paid respectable job. It was also number two and number three. There would be no more dogging it on the computer, getting sidetracked with sports blogs and Hollywood gossip, getting sucked into the world of free porn. The pity party was over.

He scheduled an appointment for the next day with an employment counselor at the state run career center to take a skill and work aptitude test. Maybe he'd go back to school and become a chef or a teacher or a nurse. Maybe he could get certified to coach sports. He was definitely headed back to the church.

James broke out the boom box and cranked up the tunes. Guns N' Roses was in the disc player and he hit the repeat button, singing along to the lyrics of "Welcome to the Jungle" as he slipped into his work gear of frayed jean shorts and a wife beater with paint stains. The house had been ignored and it showed.

Multiple notices were taped to the front door from the homeowners association. The Hortons were in violation of serious punishable offenses. The lawn was too high and there was a medium-sized brown spot that needed reseeding immediately. The leaf debris in the driveway had piled up, they were over the allotted weed quota in front of the shrubs, and the color of the mulch faded from a deep red to a dull brown.

One by one, sweating through his clothes in a 101 degree heat index, he completed the assigned chores. It was well after eight o'clock before he finished. He cracked open a beastly cold beer and chugged the whole thing, enjoying the burn of chilled hops as a tasty reward.

A frozen dinner baked in the oven with the aroma of Salisbury steak dominating the kitchen. He peeled off his sweaty socks and rubbed his sore feet, popping a blister. He clicked on the TV and surfed up and down before remembering item number five on his list. It had been stated quite clearly to, "Chill the fuck out watching so much TV." James powered on his laptop instead, gearing up for an all-night marathon of solitaire.

He glanced at the remote control and then the TV, wondering why they had so many channels to begin with. Logging onto the cable company's website, he brought up their account. Dee had always been in charge of the household finances and when he saw a $250 payment past due he was shocked. The cable bill cost far more than water or electricity. A closer examination revealed the normal bill to be $200 with an extra $50 for a pay per view boxing match he ordered when alcohol had impaired his judgment. He didn't even remember who won. James was disappointed, knowing damn well that pay per view anything was a luxury he couldn't afford.

The doorbell rang, followed by a knock, and in walked Teddy.

"What up Hot Sauce?" he said, drinking a bottle of Gatorade and carrying a half-eaten bag of chips. A red bandana covered his head and his work outfit smelled of lawnmower exhaust and two stroke engine oil.

The oven timer beeped and James removed his dinner, pulling back the plastic cellophane covering the peach cobbler. He took a bite of the Salisbury steak and it was salty as hell. "You want some?" he asked.

Teddy crinkled his nose and crammed his mouth with a handful of chips. "That stuff is dog food man. It'll kill you."

"Pretty much," said James, carrying it back to the coffee table. "But it does the trick." He looked at his watch. "So what brings you by?"

"Wanted to see how you're doing with Dee moving out and all."

"How did you know about that?"

"Seriously? You know her and Sheila still talk sometimes."

"Oh, right. Sheila, wife number two."

Teddy smiled and made an hourglass symbol with his hands. "Best body I've ever seen on a woman even til this day, including the young chicks. Scouts honor."

"Dee moving out is only temporary my friend."

"If you say so. But that's what I thought when wife number two moved out?"

A pile of self-help books were spread on the floor and Teddy picked up one, leafing through it. He read the title out loud. "Raging Against the Rage. Why Anger Hurts." He skimmed the introduction and snapped it shut. "Give me a break. That shit really helping you?"

"No. I don't know," said James, snatching it from his hands. "Maybe. Haven't made it past page ten of that one yet. Hey, can I ask you a question?"

"Shoot."

"How much you paying for cable?"

"Practically nothing. I got one of those black boxes that does the descrambling. I can get you one. You want me to hook it up?"

"Nah," said James, chewing a mouthful of potatoes. "I need to start paying down some bills so I can keep the damn house. The mortgage adjustment kicked in and the payments are getting serious now. I'm cancelling everything this week. No more cable or renting movies or magazine subscriptions. And no more internet either. I can use the computers at the library for free. I'm streamlining Teddy."

"Good for you buddy. But no cable? What are you going to watch?" He took a slug from his Gatorade. "Anyway, it doesn't matter. You can come by my house when football season starts."

"Will do."

"Hey, there's something I want to talk with you about," said Teddy. "Something you should know." He lit a cigarette. "You haven't by any chance heard the news today or read the paper?"

"Not today or yesterday and it's a pretty good bet I won't be hearing about it tomorrow either. But I did read the back of a Fruity Pebbles box if that makes you feel any better."

"I figured as much. You know, you may have been onto something Hot Sauce. You just may have been onto something."

Teddy began typing on the laptop, blazing around the keyboard like a pro. "For a while there I was starting to think that maybe you were going off the deep end a little. You white guys have a reputation for being some crazy bastards. Not that it would matter because I think everybody is kind of crazy in their own way and we'd still hang out and all. But you know what I'm saying."

James wolfed down another big bite of the mystery meat and spoke with his mouth full. "I really don't know why I hang out with you. My therapist says you're a bad influence. Says it's not very good for my self-esteem. Are you aware of that?"

"Yeah, well, your therapist is a giant dipshit. I'm the only person who can tolerate your miserable ass." Teddy clicked on a local website and stepped back, removing his bandana. "Brace yourself Hot Sauce. Your body may spontaneously combust."

The headline on top of the screen jolted him.

"FORMER BANK EXECUTIVES QUESTIONED."

"In the past two days questions have surfaced about a local defunct bank amid the continuing economic crisis. Trustworth Bank and Savings, a company headquartered in central Florida and serving the entire state since 1953, abruptly went out of business last September. With so many banks failing across the country controversy now surrounds the procedures and timetable for Trustworth's collapse. It's been uncovered that four high ranking executives may have received potentially huge bonuses on the eve of its own demise. A source has gone on record stating that senior VP Pam Gindefeld received a four million dollar bonus as did VP Bobby Stafford and CFO Frank Cally, while CEO William Breg is reported to have received almost double that. No official charges have been filed. When reached for his reaction to the story Mr. Breg's attorney had no comment. An investigation is pending."

James clasped the computer, pulling it close. He scanned the story, processing, choking on the bombshell thrown down his gullet. He started rocking and wheezing like a cat about to cough up a fur ball.

"You alright?" Teddy asked, brandishing a hand in front of his face. "You need some water or something?"

He rocked harder and the wheezing intensified until an aluminum tray flew against the wall, carrots and peas tumbling on the floor. The laptop soon followed as James screeched the cry of a man who'd rather be rich than right.

"You've got to be fucking kidding me!" He pounded the couch cushions. "After all this time. And now? You've got to be fucking kidding me!"

Teddy picked up the computer, assessing it for damage.

"I can't…." said James. "It's amazing that…. nobody wanted to…." He shook his head.

"I know dude. Its heavy stuff."

He pointed at Teddy. "Why the hell did you show me that? Why the hell did you come over here and show me that today?"

"Easy big man. I'm not the enemy. I figured you'd feel better knowing you may have been right the whole time about the bank stealing your money."

"May have?" said James. "There's nothing may have about it."

The wheezing stopped and his rocking subsided. One hand covered his eyes and the other plowed through his hair as the room went quiet.

Teddy crushed two more cigarettes, offered one to James, and eventually said, "So what do you think?"

"I think I got robbed with a fucking computer, that's what I think. Not a knife or a gun or a gang of hoodlums with lead pipes. A goddamn computer."

"Looks like a sophisticated mugging if you ask me."

"In broad daylight. In front of everybody."

"Maybe you could sue them," said Teddy. "Organize a class action or something."

"They'd bury me in court fees. It could take years to resolve, maybe decades. By the time anything happened all my money would go to pay an attorney. They know that. They rely on that. It's their strategy. And on top of it all, you know their attorney is going to be a hell of a lot better than the one I could afford."

"I guess so. You'd probably have to get some D-list attorney who graduated one-hundredth in their class from an online university."

James slithered down the couch and tilted back his head.

"The article says an investigation is pending," said Teddy. "That's a good thing. Something could come of it."

"What kind of investigation will they really do? Think about it dude. This is a small city. These people know people. Important people. Influential people. For fuck's sake nothing is going to happen. I'd be better off doing an investigation myself."

"Hey, look at the bright side. At least you know you're not nuts. That's got to count for something."

"They got me," said James. His temples throbbed, pushing out the skin, reverberating pain back to the core of his mind. "They sure as hell got me good."

"Smooth as assassins."

"Smoother."

"You know, my Uncle Slocum always used to tell us as kids, 'That's the way the cookie crumbles', whenever something bad happened. It's not very original and pretty cheesy, but what can you do sometimes? It's out of your control. Just the way it is."

"Just the way it is, huh? Well go tell your stupid Uncle Slocum that my cookie hasn't been crumbled. You can lick crumbs off a table. Sweep them off the floor. My cookie has been obliterated into thin air."

Teddy finished his Gatorade, dropped a cigarette butt in the bottom, and capped it. "I'd better get home soon. Five in the morning comes pretty early for us folks keeping the lawns of America pretty." He walked over to James. "I know you're upset man. I get it. But I thought you should know. You were right all along. The rest of us are idiots." He fixed his gaze on the floor and held out his hand. "I'm a dick for ever doubting you. And I'm sorry."

James spoke just above a whisper, as if talking to himself. "Now that it's true, it's so much worse." He gave Teddy a feeble grip and focused on the ceiling, on the popcorn texture he hated so much. His stomach hurt and he rubbed it, a tsunami of nausea crashing in.

He didn't hear the front door close and didn't care if it was left wide open. He remained stuck on the couch, rehashing the previous night's phone call with Mary.

"There are no scorecards among us," she'd said. "It's a game you can't win." *Bullshit,* he thought. *I did win. I didn't do anything wrong. And I'm tired of having to pay for it.*

He cursed Teddy's intrusion for ruining his one day of hopeful peace, his one day of optimism, never knowing if another would fall upon him. How dare his ignorant friend?

The pep talk from Mary never stood a chance.

CHAPTER

20

J ames was a no-show for his career counselor appointment the next day and never bothered rescheduling. Instead, he hopped in his car and drove. He drove all the way to Miami, four and a half hours with traffic, only to purchase a Cuban sandwich, refuel, and drive all the way back. He repeated the pattern for a week straight, road raging any blue-hair retiree that risked driving in the fast lane too slow. Wherever his location, he wanted to be someplace else. But no matter what time he arrived back in town, the former millionaire always wound up at exactly the same spot.

The corner tenant in Palm Tree Shoppes replacing Trustworth Bank was a greeting card store named Brenda's Nook. It sold party supplies, chocolates, and items for scrapbooking. They were gearing up for the next big holiday, their next big cash cow, and the store was plastered with red, white, and blue everything for the Fourth of July weekend.

He'd park his car directly in front of the place and look through the front windows, reminiscing about a flipped over desk or a kicked in wall. Only nine short months had elapsed since smashing the bank to pieces yet it seemed so much longer. No evidence remained in the plaza of Trustworth Bank whatsoever. Like James winning the lottery, it apparently never existed. Both of them had been erased.

The sun beat through his windows as he cruised on the Florida Turnpike dialing a memorized number he'd been calling every day.

"Orlando Daily News," said a female voice he guessed to be around the age of thirty.

"Sarah Martin please. Yes, I can hold," said James. He'd grown tired of Cuban sandwiches, tired of the long trek to Miami, and began taking smaller trips. Sometimes it was Jacksonville, sometimes Tampa. Today he returned from Cocoa Beach.

He wasn't officially placed on hold and it sounded more like somebody covering the receiver with their hand and doing a pretty bad job of it. He heard two women speaking, thought one of them said, "Tell him I'm not here." But he couldn't be sure.

James waited and changed ears with the phone, reminding himself to get a headset. His investigation of the bank was in full swing. His results were not.

"Mr. Horton, what can I do for you?" Sarah said after making him wait for another five minutes, increasing the odds of a hang up. She spoke in a Caribbean accent, perhaps from the island of Trinidad, and recently celebrated her twenty-fifth birthday.

"Good afternoon Ms. Martin. I'm calling to see if there was any update on the case."

"Not since the last ten times you called Mr. Horton," she said, rolling her eyes.

"Nothing? I find that quite hard to believe."

"As I've told you repeatedly sir, I'm just the person who wrote the story. I write a lot of stories for the paper. All kinds of stories. If we hear any updates about the Trustworth Bank situation we'll print it. Then you'll know. So instead of calling every day you can go to our website and check for yourself." She put an index finger near the side of her head and twirled it, motioning towards her co-worker.

"That's it?" said James, pressing the gas pedal harder, maneuvering around a chartered tour bus. "That's the same thing you said yesterday. There has to be something. Why aren't you out in the field looking for leads?"

"We're not the police sir, just a newspaper. Why don't you call them instead?"

James paused, thinking of a comeback. He didn't want to let on that he'd called the police several times and was told the accusations against the Trustworth Bank executives were just that; accusations. Nothing could be done without further evidence. When he'd pushed the officer about the protocol for making a citizen's arrest they advised him to stand down.

"Where's the hard hitting investigative reporting our media used to be known for?" he said to her. "Where is the breaking news for news that really needs to be broke? Haven't you ever heard of Geraldo Rivera? Or Dan Rather?" He raised his voice without knowing it. "Didn't you take some kind of journalistic pledge in college, to dig for the truth, to sniff out a story and follow it through until justice is served for the average man? What the hell did you go to college for in the first place if not that? It has to be more than writing articles."

Sarah held out the phone, imitating him. She whispered to her co-worker to pick up the line, saying, "He's at it again."

She coughed and said, "I'm sorry Mr. Horton. The phone cut out for a second. Could you repeat what you said about a journalist pledge? It's soooo interesting, I have to write it down. Is that similar to the Hippocratic Oath med students have to take?"

The two women laughed and did little in the way to conceal it. James Horton, or the Trustworth Bank guy as they called him, was entertaining for the tenth day in a row. They yanked the cord and he performed on cue, happy to do so.

He rambled full steam ahead and after rifling off journalists names from Diane Sawyer to Connie Chung, he somehow managed to go off on a tangent about his favorite weather girl from New York. He droned on about her integrity, her professionalism, her beauty, and said, "If Janie Chavez worked at your paper she'd solve this case."

"I didn't know meteorologists reported on crime stories," said Sarah. "I can just see the headline now. Weather girl solves mysterious sunburn case and charges are forthcoming. In a stunning turn of events, the sun did it."

Her co-worker added, "Abominable Snowman solves riddle of the elusive frost bite killer."

The car began shaking and a loud popping sound erupted from the back left tire as a piece of rubber launched across the highway. James dropped the phone and needed both hands firmly on the wheel to guide his Corolla safely onto the shoulder. When he picked back up the phone Sarah Martin was gone. He knew they were making fun of him. *Fuck em',* he thought. *I'll call back tomorrow.*

James shredded the skin off one of his knuckles unscrewing a lug nut and blood dripped on his shorts and sandals. Traffic raced past him dangerously fast only feet away and he wondered how many motorists die each year changing a tire on the side of the road. He decided to get AAA.

The rest area he stopped at had nice clean bathrooms and an impressive selection from the vending machines. He parked in one of the few shaded areas and watched two little dogs do their business in the pet friendly area, both taking dumps, and was amused as the owners pretended not to notice. With three bars left on his battery he sipped a diet Sprite and continued his new full-time occupation as telephonic investigator extraordinaire.

The Attorney General's office instructed him to go online with any issues he wanted to comment on and the Better Business Bureau had a hard time taking him seriously when his official complaint against the newspaper was, "They were making fun of me." He contacted a different police precinct about the protocol for making a citizen's arrest and when asked for his name he said, "Vern Hertzburger," a minor league baseball player from Albany he met when he was a kid. He called Dee and got voice mail, the same with Teddy, and by the time he dialed Harris Winchester's office James only had one bar left.

"What is wrong with you James?" said Harris in an angry tone. "Stop telling my secretary it's an emergency and that one of my family members has been injured in a serious accident."

"It works doesn't it? And besides, you won't take my call."

"There's a reason for that."

"Don't hang up or I'll just call back. And if you refuse to take my calls Harris I'll have to come down there in person. I can wait by your car. You still driving the green Jag these days?"

Harris rolled up his sleeves and looked at the clock. He had court in an hour.

"You've got two minutes," he said. "That's it. And why aren't you following up with the list of lawyers I sent you that are better suited to help?"

"You mean better suited to my finances," said James.

"Now you've got less than two minutes."

"I did call them. They won't call back. And besides, I don't have any money for a retainer."

"Then why are you calling me?"

"Because I already paid you like a million dollars. Remember? You owe me."

Harris sighed. "So says the man I kept out of jail. I can see gratitude is not one of your strengths. What do you want?"

"You know what I want," said James, opening a notebook and clicking a pen.

"If I give you a nugget of information will you promise to leave me alone?"

"Maybe."

"I'm serious James. This has to stop or I'm going to have to get legal on you. What would Dee say about all this?"

James started the car to run the air conditioning. "I would appreciate you not telling Dee about any of this, about my investigation. Okay? This is strictly man to man. Now what do you have?"

"If you ever repeat what I say I'll deny it. Do you understand?"

"Yes."

Harris lowered his voice. "There isn't going to be any case against Trust-worth Bank. Your so called investigation is futile. From what I've heard the source of the story to the newspaper was a former disgruntled employee who seems to have changed his mind."

"What the hell do you mean changed his mind?"

"Let's just say he used to drive a Kia and he seems much happier in his new Audi."

"An Audi. A fucking Audi. How did—"

"I have to go James. I have real work to do with real people who need it." He paused and a smile lit up his face. "You can go ahead and close the case now Inspector Clouseau."

"A goddamn Audi," said James, hitting the steering wheel. "What model is it? Is it an A8? It better not be an A8."

"What difference does it make? It doesn't matter. Do you even know who William Breg is? Who he really is?"

"A dirty lowlife thief."

"If you honestly believe that, then you are much dumber than I ever gave you credit for. Give my regards to Dee."

He drove home with the donut tire on going exactly the posted speed limit, driving like the people he reviled. He parked his car at Brenda's Nook in a spot he considered his own. Harris was right. James didn't know who William Breg was. He didn't know a thing about any of the Trustworth Bank executives who stole his money. Maybe that needed to change.

For his last call of the day he tried Teddy again. His phone was about to die. This time, he got through.

"Dude, I need a big favor."

C H A P T E R

21

The car was a top of the line two-door roadster with a retractable roof and carbon fiber chassis. The doors went up when they opened, not out, and the futuristic design wasn't quite the Batmobile, but not far behind either. Its supercharged engine boasted a top speed of 200 miles per hour that would never be reached and it accelerated from zero to sixty in under four seconds. It was that quick, that ridiculously fast, with a price tag higher than the combined income of several middle class families. It seemed almost too nice to drive.

The posh automobile stood out, even amongst Florida's elite, and for all the cool gadgets and technological features, one innocuous item on the piece of modern artwork caught James' attention. The vanity plate read BNUSGRL. He became transfixed and the hubris was too much, smothering him in disbelief. *Why don't they just rub a load of shit in my face?* he thought. The license plate had to be taken.

He stalked his target for the second straight day and enjoyed it, contemplating a new vocation never imagined. Maybe Harris was right. Maybe James should be a detective. But rather than Inspector Clouseau, he was thinking more Magnum P.I. minus the seventies porn stash.

The hunt began at her home followed by a trip to the mall, over to a friend's house, and finally a trendy restaurant/bar named Chico's in the renovated artsy district of the city. Teddy had been many things in his past life, one of them an IT geek. It was a good gig paying well until he got fired for falsifying travel expenses. But he was still able to hack around with the best of them and locate her home address, driving record, employment history, and GPA in undergraduate school.

Pam Gindefeld bordered the age of fifty-three and had been a superstar within Trustworth Bank for over a decade. Intelligent and committed, ambition was her greatest strength. The job requirements at the senior VP level were demanding and extracted a significant toll on her personal life. She was twice divorced and saw her kids sporadically as they got older. After yet another failed relationship she returned to the dating arena once more. Her trek out to Chico's that evening was a girl's night out for margaritas, dancing, and cougar surveillance.

James sat in his car with binoculars draped around his neck, admiring her beautiful ride from across the street. He held a recent picture of Ms. Gindefeld. She had above average looks for her age group and a supreme confidence assisted by the cosmetic scalpel. Gone were the crow's feet that should have been and her skin was pulled back tight with bee sting lips. She looked good, a bit odd, but still good.

He parked near a burned out streetlight after a twenty minute canvass of the neighborhood and resisted the common sense urge to flee. Empty beer cans, crushed flat in the center, piled up on the passenger seat floor and the ashtray overflowed with half-smoked butts. His stomach gurgled as he crunched a handful of Rolaids.

The headlights of a car shined his way and grew brighter and brighter before turning into the parking lot. He sank in the seat and then sat up slowly, peering just above the window, trying to look without being seen. James scanned the area like the Terminator, searching the restaurant for muscle-bound bouncers and security cams.

His legs bounced hard and hit the steering wheel as he clutched the door handle for the third time. *Big breaths,* he told himself, finally ready to pull it. *Big calming breaths.* James counted to three, then ten, then twenty, and then started over at three again. He slammed his head back against the headrest, disparaging his cowardice with a slew of effeminate offensives.

One face infiltrated his mind as he considered his probationary status and the probability of returning to jail: his former cellmate. Would Tory be there waiting for not paying child support again? If not, would the next guy he bunked with be so nice? Would he make James his lap dog? His fuck rag?

He shuddered at the idea of being locked up once more, imagining Dee remarrying and moving to a farm in Pennsylvania, the kids moving with her and taking their step-dad's name as he rotted away in the slammer. James liked fresh air though rarely going outside and food with real flavor was a good thing. A private bathroom was invaluable, something he'd donate a pinky for. "Top bunk or bottom?" he recalled his cellmate saying.

The car felt smaller and hotter and the windows started to fog. If he left he could still catch the end of the game. He picked up the article written by Sarah Martin. "FORMER BANK EXECUTIVES QUESTIONED." No need to read the rest. The 149 word document had been committed to memory and four names were circled in red. Pam Gindefeld was the first one mentioned.

He wiped a hole in the fogged up window and looked over at her car. He looked at the article. To the car. To the article. To the car. Back and forth he went like a tennis match at Wimbledon as he argued with himself in silence, each side presenting a persuasive case. When a split second occurred where the voices of reason were ballgagged, he pulled the door handle for real and stepped out onto the street.

The poorly lit parking lot needed a pave job and was packed full for the evening's festivities. A cover band jammed inside Chico's and could be heard for two blocks in either direction. Patrons drank away the work week and danced to a mixed blend of eighties pop and top forty hits. The conditions were perfect.

He approached her car from the side and ducked behind the trunk feeling suffocated in his long black shirt and sweatpants. The ski mask itched against his beard and his breath was heavy. It stunk. He flipped open a Swiss Army Knife, a Christmas present from Cole, and used a flathead screwdriver to remove the license plate. James then scampered across the ground slashing each tire along the way, watching the car shrink a few inches until the tires went flat. No alarms sounded. No lights flashed. He reached in his backpack for phase two of the master plan when a voice stunned him from behind.

"Yo bro, you alright?" said a young man escorting his drunken lover to a car they had no business driving. "Whatcha doin' down there anyway?"

James made a puking sound and spit.

"Oh, that's nasty man. You okay? Here, let me help you up"

"I'm good," he said. "One too many kamikaze shots is all. Thanks."

"C'mon, let me get you on—"

"Fuck off," said James, his right hand clenched.

"Alright bro. Happy puking."

They continued stumbling on their way, laughing.

He ripped the ski mask above his nose and leaned against the car, panting, his heartbeat echoing in his head. For the second time he delved into the backpack extracting a can of spray paint. He shook it, composing himself as the ball bearing rattled inside, and spelled out the word THIEF in large green letters on the passenger side. Come daylight, he knew it would contrast brilliantly against the metallic silver car.

James shuffled around the front bumper to the drivers side, repeating his accusation for all to see as the hissing sound of the spray paint added to the noise emanating from Chico's. The cover band wailed away and ramped up a furious roar to the end of their first set.

His tongue poked from his mouth while he sprayed the letters and he was careful not make a misspelling. Three exclamation points finished phase two and it was time for the grand finale. He held a brick in his hand. It too had the word THIEF painted on it. *Throw it at the windshield. Run.*

He gripped the brick tightly, like a quarterback ready to launch a spiral, and used his muscular legs for leverage. James cocked his arm and was about to unload when a glowing light distracted him. He dropped to the ground and saw Pam Gindefeld walking to her car texting, immersed in a silent conversation.

He moved quickly, crawling on all fours, and grabbed his bag while scolding himself for not leaving sooner. One frightened step towards the safety of the street was followed by another and that's when it happened. That's when his size fourteen clown foot betrayed him. His sneaker clipped the side of the paint can and it made a high pitched *tink* sound when it hit the ground before rolling towards the car's owner. The can rolled fast, with the accuracy of a GPS lock, and when Pam Gindefeld looked up to see where the object came from she spotted a large hulking figure in a ski mask only yards away.

She screamed and pivoted at the same time, dropping the phone, but her high heel pumps made it difficult to run.

James froze, his body and mind in a tug of war, and unsure what to do he lunged at her feet and smacked her ankle. He felt like a bystander watching it unfold when her legs crossed up and she fell to the ground, piercing the skin of both knees.

Pam screamed again as they wrestled and flailed, slapping at each other like two preppy girls in a cat fight. He covered her mouth but she bit his hand. She kicked him, clawing at his mask, and the words *bonus girl* flashed through his head as they struggled. He thought of his family, the family he'd lost. He thought of the money, the money he'd lost. He screamed too and his jilted brain gave the green light command.

James landed a quick jab in her doughy stomach and silenced her immediately. He heard the air exit her lungs and smelled what she'd been drinking, what she'd been eating.

He stumbled backwards and looked at his fist as if it were somebody else's. The music stopped, replaced by a cacophony of bugs, and Pam Ginde-feld moaned, rolling over on her side. He picked up the spray paint to toss in his bag but stopped. Nobody was coming his way and the parking lot was clear. He shook the can lightly at first, then harder. He leaned down next to her and unleashed a green torrent, aiming only inches away from the senior vice-president's face. Her mouth was slightly agape and the four million-dollar bonus girl received a late night snack of Krylon chemicals.

"Why did you steal my money from the bank?" he said, close to her ear, barely touching her skin. "Why did you steal my life?"

He wiped a glob of paint from her mouth and added, "Shame on you for making me do this. This isn't what I wanted. Shame on you and the bank. You're an embarrassment to the rest of us."

James took her purse and cell phone and ran to the car with his head down, his outfit splattered with paint. He called Chico's to inform the manager a person had passed out drunk in the parking lot and may need medical attention before wiping the phone for prints and tossing it in the bushes.

He left the downtown area cautiously doing the speed limit and merged onto the interstate, driving in the slow lane as both hands shook on the wheel. Every pore of his body, every cell and synapse, tingled with energy. He felt like he could climb a mountain or bench press a car. He was alert, more than alert, and whatever drugs flowed through his system he wanted more of. But for an inexplicable reason and one he wasn't prepared for he began to cry. For the next five minutes he cried hard, violently, with heavy sobs and whole thrust body shakes.

When the getaway car entered the driveway his body had melted. The elusive *off* switch he so desperately sought had been clicked in his mind. No worries over money, the lottery, the bank, his family, or the future. No worries over life. Everything was going to be fine. Just like Mary said. Maybe she was right after all.

He walked into the house leaving the rest of the beer in the car and crashed on the bed. No more alcohol was needed that night to achieve his drug induced fix. He'd found something. Something he never knew he had.

CHAPTER

22

Eleven hours later James woke to the sound of a neighbor's leaf blower pushing pine straw across a short driveway where a tree root buckled the concrete. When he opened his eyes and regained his bearings he found himself in a setting that'd become unfamiliar. He slept in the master bedroom as though drugged by a roofie, drooling in a dreamless stupor, and it was the first time since Dee left for New York he ventured into the queen size bed. He was still in his clothes, shoes and all, and green paint was smattered on the covers, the sheets, and the pillow cases. He even had a few splotches on his face.

He squeezed his index finger and it was sore from being bitten with a purple ring forming on the skin. But that was the only casualty. He felt like he'd lost thirty pounds or received a positive prognosis from a medical scare. James was flying high when he stripped down naked for a shower, his saggy butt and belly flab jiggling as he laughed aloud, mocking the time spent agonizing in therapy sessions with Dr. Novak. "Tell me how that makes you feel," he said in a condescending voice.

The self-help books sprinkled throughout the house, the ones he was strongly encouraged to purchase by the doc, cost a small fortune and he'd plodded through them for months on end looking for an answer, looking up words he didn't understand. They all said the same thing. Violence inflicted on those who have crossed a person only leads to further erosion of the situation and ultimately makes a person feel worse. They may have been wrong about James Horton.

His clothes from the crime scene were tossed on the floor along with the sheets. The incriminating evidence of his felonious activity was rolled in a ball and stuffed into the bottom of a large black garbage bag. Trash pick-up was still two days out but an abandoned construction site nearby offered the use of industrial size dumpsters. He'd wait until the cover of nightfall.

James closed the blinds and sat in the kitchen sipping hot coffee with the contents of Pam Gindefeld's purse spread on the table. Nothing was out of the ordinary and many of the items were similar to what Dee used to carry around. There were tissues, tissues, and more tissues, a variety of make-up and lipstick, breath mints, diet pills, a small box of candy, and a panty liner. He opened her wallet and grinned. James hadn't stolen anything since swiping a pack of bubblegum from the neighborhood convenience store in the fifth grade. He got caught by the owner, grounded by his mother, and whipped by his father.

Four credit cards were inside the wallet, two gold, two platinum, and dozens of receipts from the mall to the coffee shops. She had pictures of her kids, a driver's license, and a wad of cash totaling $800. He leaned back fanning out the money. It was more cash than he'd seen in quite some time. The money was tax free and tangible. It was his. And it was money he was owed.

He shredded the remaining paper trail of his loot, hid the license plate in the garage, and joined Teddy at a sushi restaurant he hadn't been to in years.

"Order whatever you want," he said, perusing the extensive menu. "It's on me."

The restaurant was small, seating only ten tables, and for three years in a row received an award from the Zagat survey. They sat up front near the windows and had a less than desirable view of a busy two lane road running past a cemetery.

The two men devoured an artistic basket of colorful sashimi in the shape of a sailboat and washed it down with the finest hot sake available. They talked about sports, mentioned the possibility of an upcoming hurricane, and debated whether the new golf course opening near the airport would offer discount greens fees for their first month of business.

"So did you win one of those scratch-off tickets you been playing or something?" asked Teddy after consuming the majority of the Pacific Ocean. He belched a horrifyingly stinky fish burp and made no attempt to conceal it.

"What?" said James, covering his nose.

"I mean yesterday you were broke as hell, and today this," said Teddy, motioning at the table.

"I uh, I found some money in the couch."

Teddy met his eyes and took out the newspaper. It was already folded to the local crime scene. "I thought you were just going to mess up her car."

James put down his chopsticks, wiping his mouth. Business was picking up with a mixture of white folks and Asians. He leaned forward, his voice light.

"I did mess up her car. Like I said I would. Don't worry about it."

"Talk to me," said Teddy, adding more wasabi to his soy sauce. "I need to know."

After summoning the waitress James ordered another bottle of sake. He pulled his chair around the table so the two were right next to each other, lovers style. He picked a strand of rice from his teeth and flicked the mushy substance on the floor. "So you see, what had happened was...."

For the next twenty minutes James talked, pausing only to gulp his sake, and Teddy listened, interrupting him twice. The first time he asked, "The drunk kid really said happy puking? Who says that corny shit?" and the second time he asked, "Why do you think she left the bar so early?"

When James was done Teddy had both elbows on the table. His left ear was warm from the sake and he tugged on it making it worse. "Could I be in trouble for any of this?"

"No Teddy, you're good," said James, shaking his head. "You provided a little data. You didn't do anything wrong. The FBI won't barge into your house and seize your computer. Your life isn't going to unravel for an internet search." He squeezed his finger and pointed at the newspaper. The little bruise was really starting to hurt. "Did you even read the whole article you gave me? I mean the whole thing. Because if you had you'd notice she never mentioned to the cops what I said to her about being a thief and stealing my money and getting what she deserved."

"You painted the word thief on her car dude. I think that says it all."

"I know that, but she never mentioned what I said about the bank. Don't you get it? She never mentioned the bank."

Teddy pushed his chair back from the table and folded his arms, watching the cars crawl by in the congested traffic.

The restaurant chatter grew louder with the dinner rush cranking into high gear. James observed the sushi chef working his magic behind the counter, eyes down, focused and serious. He noticed his white headband with the gray trim sprawling out from the center in all directions.

"A woman?" Teddy finally said. "You hit a freaking woman? I have to say this. That's about as low as it gets."

"It's not something I'm proud of, believe me. I didn't plan on doing it. But things got out of hand. It happened so fast. I thought I was going back to jail." He took a sip of water and cleared his throat. "She was screaming her freaking head off. I was scared. I panicked, okay? What was I supposed to do man?"

"Run."

James' face reddened. "Let me tell you something about this woman you think is so divine, that you're so concerned for. Who is fine by the way. She got the wind knocked out of her, that's all, and a little paint on the face. It's a small price to pay for stealing millions of dollars and getting away with it if you ask me. As far as I can see she's nothing more than a goddamn lowlife fucking thief. Her and her cronies. Man, woman, penis, vagina. I don't care if she was a fucking alien. She had it coming. And then some." He took a deep breath, exhaling loudly. "What would you do if somebody stole your entire life's savings?"

"I wouldn't hit a woman."

"You make it seem like I battered her around for not having my dinner ready on time, as if I'm some kind of monster. I told you, I panicked."

"I'm just saying I wouldn't have done it."

"You weren't in my shoes Saint Teddy, so how do you really know? And you're full of shit anyway. Remember a few years ago when you won some money playing poker and that one guy owed you what, like a hundred bucks. You talked about kicking his ass for a month."

"It was only talk. That was different. I was never serious."

James made eye contact with the waitress and signaled for the check.

"Come on man, you know my story. You know me Teddy. I mean look at the article. She told the police it was a mugging and nothing else. I spoke right into her ear about stealing the money. About the bank. But there was no mention of it at all."

"You ever think maybe she didn't hear you."

"She heard me. There's no doubt she heard me." He poured the last of the now cold sake. "I'll tell you this Teddy. If I'd gotten her at her house instead of a parking lot she'd probably never even call the police. Only a guilty person does stuff like that. Think of O.J. running from the cops, driving the white Bronco."

Teddy sported a faint smile. "If the glove don't fit you must acquit."

"Exactly."

James moved back around to the opposite side of the table and set his plate to one side. He raised his miniature cup, killing the contents.

"How long do you think before she gets all the paint off her face?" asked Teddy.

"I think Ms. Gindefeld is going to be E.T. for a while."

"You gave her the scarlet letter huh?"

"I was improvising."

"So that's that then," said Teddy. "You got it out of your system. You squared the deal. It's over."

"Not quite. There's a few other people I'd like to introduce myself to. I seem to be the only person working this investigation."

"Is that what you're going to call it?"

"It's the truth," said James. "Now, do you think you could help me with that? Get me some intel?"

"What is this, the set of a movie? What are you a fucking Charles Bronson character?"

"A highly underrated actor if you ask me. Did you ever see *Death Hunt*?"

Teddy shook his head side to side. "Are you being serious right now? I can't tell."

"What? It's a good movie."

"You really are a crazy fucker. It's gone too far already. Whatever you're thinking Hot Sauce, it's a bad idea. Abort."

James picked up the black wallet left by the waitress and opened it.

"You said business has been slow lately, right?"

"Scary slow," said Teddy. "There's so much competition for landscaping it's not even funny. Any asshole with a lawnmower and a weed whacker thinks he knows what he's doing. And these guys are charging next to nothing just to get the business."

"Maybe this can help," said James, peeling off $200 from his billfold, handing it over. "The VP's name is Bobby Stafford. That's what the story by Sarah Martin said. Come by tomorrow and give me the lowdown."

"James?"

"Wow. That's the first time you called me by my name in a while. No Hot Sauce?"

Teddy hesitated, looking at the money. There were two crisp fifties and a c-note. "You're just going to do something simple, right? Maybe egg his house or smash his mailbox?"

"Is that what you need to hear my friend?"

Teddy nodded, avoiding his eyes.

James handed him another $100 and patted his forearm.

"Sure Teddy, it'll be something simple. Maybe I'll toilet paper a tree in his front yard or steal the stereo from his car."

The sun was fading as darkness set in. James had to go. He needed to get home and take out the trash.

CHAPTER

23

Bent Oaks development consisted of thirty-one high-end houses in a suburb of Orlando that'd been farmland pasture only five years earlier. Bobby Stafford's house was the first one built all the way at the end. Had there been any hills in the area, bona fide hills, the house would have assuredly been perched atop one. It was a 5,000 square foot red brick home with a three car garage and backed up to a small parcel of woods bordering a wetland. A yellow sign stating BEWARE OF ALLIGATORS was posted near a fence, half as a joke, half not.

James sat in a rented BMW from Euro Imports with the engine idling. He'd been waiting ten minutes in the blue colored sedan for a neighbor, visitor, or pizza delivery guy to arrive on the scene so the long metal gate would swing open. There were no security guards and no need to sign in. At least not yet. A construction project was underway on a small tract of bulldozed dirt, bisecting the tall wrought iron entrance and exit gates. When completed, the guard shack would be the size of a two man tollbooth.

He let his foot off the brake and followed a Lexus around a bend doing twenty miles per hour. The sidewalks were double in width of his own neighborhood and the driveways were legitimate driveways, not parking spots, most up to fifty feet long. A perfectly trimmed combination of tall green hedges and thick Bermuda grass dotted the landscape. James tapped his fingers on the stick shift, chewing a whole pack of gum, and when the Lexus turned left at a fork he went right, heading to the first house built in the development.

His hair was slicked back and appeared unrealistically dark along with his beard; both casualties of a botched dye job. A pair of wire rimmed glasses

134

completed the simplistic disguise. His suit was neatly pressed and James knew a white guy driving an expensive car would never be looked at twice.

He pulled into a brick paved driveway cutting the headlights and parked as close to the garage as possible. A motion light kicked on when he opened the door. He smelled smoke, a good smoke, a BBQ smoke. He hadn't been able to eat all day.

Bobby Stafford was the only offspring of Rudolph and Valerie Stafford, a long time Orlando power couple who descended from a long line of powerful power couples. A Yale University drop out, he was forty pounds overweight and got busted for a DUI and possession of cocaine in his late twenties, nine years earlier. His father had been instrumental in the growth of Trustworth Bank and upon retiring his son was appointed vice-president of the real estate division despite several more qualified candidates. Bobby worked hard to earn it though, a whole eighteen months. It was textbook nepotism at its finest.

James ran up the sidewalk, trying to walk, with a brown leather briefcase purchased from a pawn shop and touched his hair, then his suit jacket. He straightened his tie and rang the doorbell, checking behind him, anticipating a Rotty or Shepard or Doberman Pinscher charging with gnarled teeth.

Inside he heard a commotion, like furniture getting shoved around, and there was a loud repetition of yelling. He swallowed as the footsteps grew closer.

"This better be good," a man's voice said.

James twisted his head, unsure where the voice came from.

"To the left. Turn your head to the left. Now, look up."

Attached to the wall above the doorway was a twelve inch black and white monitor with Bobby's bloated face staring at him. James gave a pathetic shy wave, like a frightened child acknowledging an intimidating parent.

"Who the hell are you?" said Bobby. "And what do you want?" He took a sip of what appeared to be a wine cooler.

James clutched the keys in his pocket. "I'm sorry for the inconvenience Mr. Stafford. I'm with the bank oversight committee. We need you to sign one additional document that was previously overlooked. It's important sir. The bonus package you received wasn't the correct amount."

"What are you talking about, not the correct amount? Wait here. I'm calling my attorney. And why are you at my home on a Sunday night at nine. What's your name anyway?"

"My name is Tom Smith," said James, reaching on his tippy toes, stretching his torso to inch closer to the monitor. "Before you do anything sir you should know the banking error is in your favor by a substantial dollar figure."

"How much in my favor?"

"About three hundred thousand dollars sir."

The two men stared at one another, their images distorted by the lens. The pause was long, longer than expected.

"Why?" said Bobby, swirling his drink. "Why was there an error? Who told you there was an error?"

"I don't know why the error occurred sir, just that it did. That's why I'm here at such an unconventional hour. This is supposed to be under the radar. Very hush hush given the latest media attention. This needs to be done quickly and discreetly sir."

"So what do you need from me?"

"I need you to sign some paperwork so we can release the additional funds to an offshore account by midnight tonight. Call your attorney if you like. This is imperative. I have a few more stops to make so if you don't mind sir," said James, pushing in all his chips of the high stakes poker game.

Another long pause ensued. His neck hurt from staring up at the camera and he swung it sideways to release the tension, hearing it crack. The street glowed orange from the hovering lights, casting long shadows, and a neighbor's garage door retracted open. The sound of an engine starting filled the void.

Nothing was happening as Bobby disappeared from the screen. Was he calling the cops? His father? The FBI? James stepped back, shying from the camera, and whipped out the car keys. He was about to unleash plan B, a full scale retreat, when the lock on the door went *click* and the rest of Bobby Stafford appeared before him wearing flip flops and a poorly fit bathing suit, nothing else.

James followed his host down a hallway with salt water fish tanks on opposite sides. To the right was a full length pool table near a juke box designed to appear retro. A movie poster hung from the wall of Al Pacino in

Scarface blazing a gun, the caption reading, "Say hello to my little friend!" To the left was an antiquities room exhibiting a life-size Knight in chainmail and Japanese swords encased in glass. The house stunk of cherry incense and Polo cologne infused with the funk of stale weed. He assumed Bobby Stafford was single or in between maids.

The lighting in the kitchen was bright, department store bright, and he saw the back wooden deck where Bobby was grilling. A TV played near the fridge and a large marble island anchored the room. James opened the briefcase and removed an official looking document printed on high quality stock. He placed it upside down on the black and white stone, sliding it over. Bobby emptied his drink with a tilt of the head, pulling the paper towards him. His eyebrows and nose, along with the skin on his forehead, raised in confusion.

"Is this some kind of joke Tom?" he asked. "Is this for real?"

"Is there a problem?"

"The problem is that these are the fucking lyrics to the "Star Spangled Banner"." Bobby crumpled the paper into a ball and threw it, missing his target by at least three feet. "You think you're funny don't you? Did Pam put you up to this? Did Cally? My father isn't going to think this is so damn funny. Do you know who the fuck he is?"

James shrugged. He wanted to say something cool, something witty. He wanted the perfect one-liner. But when his lips parted ways he was speechless. He took a step forward.

Bobby moved to the right, maintaining eye contact, searching the countertop with his fingertips. He reached for the butcher block and unsheathed a bread knife.

"Stay right the fuck there," he said, pointing the serrated blade like he was going to slice a loaf of pumpernickel. He opened his cell phone and was about to dial when a stream of pepper spray hit him in the eyes, the mouth, the nose, and the eyes again. He grabbed his face and let go of the knife as the phone ricocheted in the corner. The knife fell straight, shaving a chunk from his ankle, and Bobby screamed but faded in volume quickly as the fiery capsaicin constricted his airways.

James bent over and rested on his knees, catching his breath, his forehead bubbling with sweat. He thanked God the canister of pepper spray had retained its potency. Three years earlier he gave it to Dee when his out of town work training seminars increased in frequency. The thin red canister still had the price tag on it.

He snapped on a pair of latex gloves reminding him of a long overdue prostate exam and waited for his target to crumble to the floor before bounding him with duct tape. About fifteen minutes were needed until his host would be able to speak clearly again.

It was the biggest house he'd ever been in and James wandered around the abundance of rooms placing items of small value in a garbage bag along the way. He searched in vain upstairs for a coveted safe with the mother lode and the majority of artwork was far too large to carry. But he did manage to snag three Rolex's and a nice little cache of jewelry.

Bobby moaned when he re-entered the kitchen and the shallow wound on his foot had begun to coagulate.

"You're a cheap fuck, you know that?" said James. "You only had fifty bucks in your wallet."

"I can get money," Bobby pleaded in a hoarse tone. "I can pay you. Tomorrow morning I can pay you."

"Tomorrow doesn't do me any good today."

"I'm sorry, I'm sorry. I don't keep a lot of cash in the house."

"Yeah, I kind of noticed," said James, grabbing the knife from the floor. It still had a blood spat on it and he wiped it on Bobby's arm. "You're not going to try and scream or do anything stupid, are you Bob?"

With his body shaking, he shook his head no.

James lit a cigarette, exhaling a cumulonimbus cloud. "Good. Because I don't like knives and I'm not a big fan of guns either. I saw your shotgun collection in the study. Now, I know you and your bank buddies stole my money along with thousands of other innocent people who trusted you. As an independent investigator working this case I want to know. Whose idea was it?"

"Wha.... Wha.... what money? Wha.... what are you talking about? I've never stolen anything in my life," said Bobby, his eyes red and drippy.

"Given the fact that you were born with a silver spoon implanted in your sphincter I almost want to believe you. Seriously. It makes sense, right? Why would you steal? You don't want for anything. It's not like you're stressing over the mortgage payment or your credit card bills like the rest of us slobs. You're not considering getting a second or third job to help pay for your kids' college tuition, are you Bob? No? I didn't think so." He squeezed Bobby's cheeks and brought them together. "You do realize, when you were born, you hit the gene pool lottery, right?"

Bobby nodded and continued to cry.

James got down on the floor and sat Indian style, flicking his ash onto Bobby's curly hair. He slapped him lightly across the face.

"Stop crying you big pussy. I haven't even done anything yet."

"Are you doing this because I'm gay?" asked Bobby.

"What?" said James, confused. "What the hell are you talking about? I could give two shits if you're gay. Move to Vermont with your boyfriend and adopt African babies if that makes you happy. I'm doing this Bobby because you're a lowlife thief. It's that simple. Now stop trying to change the subject. Who came up with the bonus idea?"

"I…. I don't know what you're talking about."

James took another long drag of the cigarette, stoking the coal, and leaned on Bobby's neck. He brought the glowing ember close to his face.

"Don't make me Bobby. I swear I'll put this fucking thing out in your eye if I have to," he said, bluffing, knowing he never could.

Bobby yelled and James covered his mouth.

"I'm going to count to ten," he said. "And then I want an answer."

He only made it to seven Mississippi when he felt something strange through the glove. He stopped and pulled it away.

"Did you seriously just lick my hand?"

Bobby coughed up a phlegm ball and lips were beginning to swell.

"I'm allergic to latex" he said, sucking in air hard. "It was all Breg's idea. Please, whatever you're going to do. Stop."

"William Breg, the CEO?"

"Yes."

"Why didn't you tell me that in the first place? Why would you protect him?"

"He's good friends with my father. He's a powerful man, a scary man. He can make things difficult."

"So can I," said James, trying to stand. His right leg went numb and his low back was on the verge of spasming. "Where's your liquor cabinet?" He threw the gloves in the trash.

"In the game room. Near the pool table."

James returned with two bottles of scotch and put one in his briefcase, unsealing the cap of the other. He took a long methodical belt and smacked his lips, making an unpleasant face. He poured a couple shots down Bobby's throat and chased it with a couple more.

For the next half-hour James was engrossed as the vice-president of Trustworth Bank's real estate division blabbed about the inner workings of the company. Bobby discussed in detail how they organized the scam, pulled it off, and when he knew it was going down. The entire plan was so simple, so easy. It was too easy.

"So who was the guy that leaked the story to the press? Was he in on it?"

"In the beginning, by mistake," said Bobby. "Until Breg realized he didn't need him anymore. He was low level anyway. Never should have known about in the first place. He was fired a week before we closed up shop."

James looked around, noticing the oversized French door refrigerator and the six burner stainless steel Viking stove that no doubt cost more than his car. The deck in the back was two stories high with an eight person hot tub recessed into it.

"Are you right handed or left handed?" he said.

"I write left handed but eat right handed. Why?"

"Let me make this easier for you. When you're jacking off to some dude, which hand does the jacking?"

"I can use either."

"I'm sure you can sweetheart, now pick one."

"Left."

Most people are right handed. James assumed he was lying.

Moving Bobby's dense body into the required position took more effort than expected, requiring a few smacks of persuasive encouragement. He placed him faced down with his arms spread over his head in the shape of a V. Three strips of duct tape covered his mouth and his legs were wrapped together tightly. Bobby's wrists and hands were secured to the ground, palms flat on the floor.

James turned up the volume on the TV and searched the kitchen drawers for an instrument of choice. The bottle of scotch was diminishing. He was close to ready.

"Have you ever heard what they do to thieves in the Middle East?" he said. "They supposedly cut off one of their hands, the one they thought did the stealing. It seems kind of harsh, don't you think? You could never do that shit in the States. But then again, I bet it's one hell of a deterrent. Walking around with a stub. People pointing and staring at you. Knowing what you did. At least that's what I've heard anyway. I have no idea if it's true. Could be some kind of Middle East urban legend."

The meat tenderizer had a shiny square handle and was probably purchased from William Sonoma or Bloomingdale's. He held it in his hand, pounding the flat side against his palm. The weight was good. It felt solid. The jagged metal spikes, triangular in shape, reflected in the overhead track lighting. He ran his fingers across them. They were no doubt sharp.

Bobby whimpered through the tape and tried squirming. He wasn't going anywhere. The whites of his eyes were the size of silver dollars.

"I won't lie to you Bobby. This is going to hurt you a whole lot more than it's going to hurt me. Try to breathe through it. You ever notice that's what everybody says. You have to breathe." He flexed his hand, tightening the grip, and cut a practice swing in the air. "I still can't fathom why you did it. It boggles my mind. But you did. And because of it, you pretty much ruined my life. My wife and kids are gone. I'm unemployed. You made me live alone in a house I might wind up losing anyway. And the real question I guess is why? Why, why, why? Why did all this happen? Because you stole money that you didn't need. Money that's not yours. And for what? This house is freaking amazing. So freaking amazing. A house most people can't imagine living in. What, it's not big enough for you? Not enough rooms to hold all your stupid shit, all your stupid antiques? You have three sweet ass cars in your garage. Do you know that? Three. I'd kill just to have one of them." He threw down his cigarette, crushed it under a shoe, and shook his head. "It just boggles my fucking mind."

James leaned on Bobby's forearm with his left hand, steadying himself. "Now it's time to take your meds like a big boy. Daddy Warbucks isn't here to bail your ass out."

He raised the meat tenderizer, teeth side down, staring at the sausage fingers of his culprit. They were the fingers of a cyberspace thug, a modern day John Dillinger, creeping through miles of fiber optic cable undetected. He imagined those fingers emptying his bank account with a few simple key-strokes, transferring money to some kind of slush fund until the band of merry thieves could divvy it up.

"Ahhhhhhhh!" James yelled, striking down hard, his head cocked to the side and his eyes barely open. The tile cracked when he hit it, not Bobby's hand, and a bolt of pain penetrated from his wrist to his elbow.

"Son of a fuck piss shit!" he screamed, running around the kitchen holding his arm. He laughed because he wanted to cry and wrapped his wrist in duct tape. After a lengthy timeout, he returned to Bobby's side.

James thrust down again and grunted, watching this time as the sharp metal edges gashed off chunks of skin and flattened knuckles. A fingernail exploded and dislodged with the force of a bullet, blasting through the air into the unknown.

Blood flowed on the travertine.

He'd never seen what lied beneath a human fingernail, never wanted to. It resembled the filling from a chewy Fig Newton, maroonish in color and sticky. There were specks of white that could have been cartilage, could have been bone.

He dry heaved and burped all the way to the sink, puking so hard a blood vessel popped in his eye. Bobby screamed into the tape until his energy gave way and his body conceded. James rolled him over and helped him onto a chair, securing him again, covering his crippled hand with a cool damp towel. He wrote the word THIEF on his forehead in permanent ink.

In a corner near the wall laid Bobby's cell phone. Two people were selected at random from the contact list and received the same message.

"thru out back stuk on floor pls come ovr"

James packed his briefcase and looked at his creation, at what he'd been forced to. His shirt was untucked and he ripped off his tie, messing up his hair while tucking his glasses in a pocket. He turned off the TV, then the lights, leaving the kitchen in darkness, and walked down the hallway between the fish tanks. But he stopped. There it was again. He stared at the poster of Al Pacino in the movie he hadn't seen in years. Tony Montana. The llello. He read the caption out loud. "Say hello to my little friend." James cracked a smile and thought, *I just did.*

He headed to the car controlling the rush of adrenaline and no tears were shed for perpetrator number two. Not even close. He backed from the driveway and left the development with the sunroof open, a full moon lighting the sky. Twice in two weeks he felt incredible, he had hope, as if the Universe was realigning.

CHAPTER

24

A hurricane originating from the warm air rising above the Sahara swept across the Atlantic. It slowly traversed the ocean sucking up moisture like an elephant trunk and reached as high as a category three before fizzling. By the time it reached the Bahamas it was downgraded to a category one and by the time it made landfall in Florida the once mighty behemoth was reduced to a tropical storm.

For three days straight the meteorologists had an orgy amongst themselves, pointing at their green screens with contained excitement, rehashing the latest computer models every 5.2 milliseconds, predicting scenarios of doom. Every man, woman, and child needed to immediately bug out to the safety of a nuclear bunker with an abundance of K rations in order to survive the end of the world ordeal. It really just rained a lot. A lot.

The storm stalled off the coast of Cape Canaveral scrubbing a long scheduled rocket launch and swirled in a clockwise pattern collecting massive volumes of water, then uncollecting it. It rained hard for sixty consecutive hours. The Horton's house held strong for the first two days but eventually sprang leaks. First the light fixtures in the kitchen ceiling, then the seal of the sliding glass doors. Moisture found every opportunistic crevice from the roof to the foundation and dark spots formed on the walls resembling images of a Rorschach test. James put down buckets and pots, covered the floor in towels, and watched as the front lawn turned into a pond. He left the house only once to pick up a pizza and wings. He was also running low on smokes.

"Faithfully" by Journey played on his cell phone while James emptied a bucket of water in the sink. He'd been calling his wife at the pace of a stalker, anxious to boast of the progress he'd made, and it was imperative for Dee to hear all about it. Over a month had passed since she'd left and their last meaningful conversation was long before that.

"Hey there," he said, his voice higher than normal, the empty bucket back on the floor already pinging with drips. "You're one tough person to get a hold of."

"Hi James. I've been meaning to get back to you. Sorry it took so long. How are you?"

"Hun, couldn't be better. Well I could be better if you guys were here."

"Are you taking care of yourself?" she said, spinning a ring on her finger.

"Would you believe I actually started working out again? You know that stupid ab-roller turbo thing we put in the attic?"

"The one you bought off the infomercial and never used once? I forgot we even had that."

"Me too. But I've been using it every day. I'll have a six-pack before you know it," he said with a sarcastic grin. "Or maybe a twelve-pack. Hell, maybe even a case." He slapped his stomach, wishing he didn't.

"Speaking of which. How're you doing with the drinking? Are you cutting down?"

James glanced at the beer on the counter. At least it was a light beer. "Absolutely hun. No more hard stuff for the most part."

"And the smoking?"

"I've got to be honest with you Dee," he said, a warm butt smoldering in the ashtray. "That one is going to be a work in progress. I'm thinking of trying those hypnosis tapes you hear about on TV. You can rent them at the library for free."

"That's good James. That's really good. That's really really good."

Neither of them spoke. The phone was quiet. Dead air, the conversation killer. His smile vanished.

"Dee. You alright? Something on your mind?"

"I'm fine. A little tired."

"You don't seem fine. We haven't spoken in a while and when we actually do, I feel like I'm being interrogated by the Gestapo." He took a deep breath and changed his tone, softening it. "I miss you hun. I miss the kids."

More silence. Silence upon silence. He waited for a sniffle or a sob or an, "I miss you too James." He waited for a sigh, a snort, a laugh, or a hiccup. He would have settled for a belch. He would have settled for anything.

"I know this time apart has been tough on everybody," she eventually said, nodding at her mother, her mother nodding back. "But I think it's been good for us to grow and evolve as people. Don't you?"

He threw another towel on the floor and went into the living room. A tree branch fell in the back yard and was leaning on a section of the fence. He paid it no mind. The phone was pressed tight to his ear, glued to his jaw. "I guess. For a little while. A month is long enough for me though. More than enough. I'm ready for you guys to come back. I'm ready for a Horton family reunion."

"I know, but I was thinking maybe a little bit longer may be the best thing because—"

"Hey hun, can you hold on a second?" James covered the phone and held it above his head. His heart raced quicker than the falling rain. He was going down fast. He was going down hard. He needed to change the subject.

"Dee, I have some amazing news. You know how you said we were going to lose the house. Well, I figured out a way to keep it intact. I came up with a plan."

"Did you get a new job or something?"

"Kind of. I'm still ironing out the details. But it doesn't matter. We have the house. And we're going to keep it. The house is ready and awaits your return my lady. I even painted the chipped up side of the garage and fixed the squeaky hinge on the medicine cabinet that used to drive you nuts."

The mascara of her face was blotchy and she held a wrinkled tissue in her hand. "James, there's something I want to tell you. I'm glad you still have the house and it sounds like you're pulling yourself together. It really does, but—"

"But what?"

"But please don't get mad," she said.

"This doesn't sound good."

"I've enrolled the kids up here for the fall semester."

"This fall?" he asked. "You mean this fall that comes after this summer?"

"Yes."

James stopped circling the couch and sat down, listening to the rain pound the windows and assault the roof. The dark gray light gave the illusion of dusk but it was early afternoon. He ran a hand through his thick short hair, fresh from a visit to the barber, and moved it towards his chin. The clean shaved skin felt strange and tacky.

The recent mortgage payment, along with the previous two that were never made, had all been taken care of courtesy of the Bobby Stafford heist. James figured with a few more trips to the pawn shop he'd scrape up enough money to make a couple more. He'd convinced himself that's one of the reasons for visiting Bobby in the first place. At least part of it.

"Hello? James? Are you there?"

"No, yeah, I mean I'm here," he said, his shoulders slumped. "I don't know what to say. I wasn't expecting to hear that. What about their friends? What about your friends? What about the law? Is that even legal?"

"Who do you think a judge would side with right now? So let's not go there, okay? And besides, it'll only be for a few more months if you think about it. Christmas is right around the corner and will be here before you know it."

"Christmas, huh? That's what we're aiming for now? It's like five months away."

"I need more time," she said, her mother's arm draped around her.

"Can't you see how good I'm doing Deidra? How hard I'm trying." He smacked his chest. "I even broke out the stupid ab-roller."

He emptied another bucket in the sink and watched his weird neighbor walk her three small dogs down the street. They all wore matching pink slickers. Dee continued talking and explaining and he finally said what he'd thought all along.

"This is about the payments, isn't it? This is some kind of payback because I took the lump sum. I mean who in the world could've imagine that happening with the bank Dee? You resent me, don't you? I want to hear you say it."

"That's just it James. It's not about that. It's not about any of that. It never was. You can't seem to get that through your head. This is what I'm talking about. This is why we need more time. This is why you need to be in therapy."

"Dr. Novak didn't seem to be doing a whole lot for me other than giving me a bill."

"You should go back to him James. Harris called. He told me about your investigation."

"Harris called? That backstabbing prick. I didn't realize you and him were so chummy."

"Please," she said. "Don't be ridiculous. He was concerned. What is he talking about? What is this about an investigation you're doing into the bank? What are you up to?"

James fired up a smoke, exhaling into the phone extra loud for effect. "I have to go. You know where I am when you find what the hell it is you're looking for."

"Please don't be—"

"Can you put the kids on the phone so their father can say hello before they forget all about me?"

He spent the rest of the day on the couch watching re-runs of *Sanford and Son*, the only station the TV picked up for free. Official size puddles were now in the kitchen and near the glass door as the buckets spilled over the edge. He replayed the conversation with Dee over and over in his mind, second guessing himself, wishing he'd said something different. But what was there to say?

The rain eventually diminished to a steady drizzle, a light sprinkle, and then stopped. But he never knew. Accompanying him for the majority of the evening was the undefeated, undisputed, and reigning king of heavyweight knockouts; a Mr. Jack Daniels. It was well after midnight before he passed out spread eagle on the floor with a half-eaten slice of pepperoni pizza resting on his chest.

25

The house was empty except for the couch, refrigerator, toaster oven, dishwasher, and about a third of his wardrobe. He carried the last box of stuff downstairs and stopped to stretch, his low back sore, both hips stiffening. It was quiet as he tapped his foot on the fake hardwood floor and heard the hollow sound of cheapness. The guy who installed the floor said that may happen; after he'd finished. *What was the point?* James asked himself.

The living room walls had rows of small bumps pushing to the surface where the sheetrock screws bulged and a contractor stated the house was settling and the problem was common. It could be covered up with two coats of knock-down paint and be good as new, all for the low low price of only $2,999. James turned his attention to the fireplace. The realtor tagged it as a selling point when they were on the fence about buying. Visions of romantic dinners with Dee and cooking s'mores with the family filled his head. They used it exactly twice. The second time he burned his hand stoking the flame. He hadn't a clue why anybody would want a fireplace in one of the muggiest places he'd ever known.

It had been a week of agony for James after Dee's shocking call, a week stuck in mental purgatory. He couldn't wrap his head around it. Her words continued to penetrate his mind, bombarding his brain with arrows of confusion. Was she ever coming home? Was Teddy right about wife number two? He picked up a box off the stairway, grimacing, and walked outside. He mumbled to himself and continued to disparage the house: the non-stop battle with the bugs, the mold surrounding the sky light, the constant maintenance of the air conditioning unit. He would have gone on but was interrupted.

"Yo, how much for the TV?" asked a skinny man of compatible age, tracking James down across the driveway. He wore a Tampa Bay Bucs jersey under a large cross, had a shaved head, and his white socks were pulled up to the bottom of his knees. He was the first customer of the day.

"Which one," said James, pointing, "The large or the small?"

"No doubt the large. What up wit the DVD player and stereo speakers?"

James flipped on his sunglasses as beads of sweat already sprinkled his face. He strolled over to the forty-two inch high-def television he purchased two years earlier, rubbing the top. It'd cost $2,600 and in a genius financial move was funded by their tax refund. He released a nostalgic sigh. For a long time he considered the material object a dear friend. They spent countless hours together watching all the big games and there was no other place he'd rather be nestled in front of for an old school action flick marathon. But he knew that friends come and go.

"Seven hundred bucks," said James.

"I'll give you three."

"How about six?"

"How bout three twenty-five?"

"How about five?"

"Three-fitty is the highest I'll go," the skinny man said.

Brand new models were retailing for less than a grand. James looked at him, wiping his brow.

"Fine. Take the damn thing. But I'm not helping you load it."

That's how he spent the remainder of his Saturday; fielding a ridiculous amount of questions and haggling with strangers like a Tijuana shopkeeper. The small ad he placed in the local *Penny Saver* stated that everything inside, outside, and surrounding his property was negotiable. It produced a much bigger turnout than expected.

He wandered about the lawn with a fanny pack on like a tourist at Disney, baffled by the odd collection of souls scouring his yard for secondhand junk in the ninety-three degree heat. Some people drove up in a Mercedes, others a jalopy. There were black people, white people, Latinos and Asians. There were college kids, rednecks, old people, lesbians, and do it yourself dads. He believed them all to be the same. They too were hoping to win the lottery by discovering a rare painting nobody knew was rare or unearthing a historically significant document tucked away in a dresser drawer. Cashing in on his naiveté was their clandestine agenda.

Teddy arrived three hours late in a beat up green truck used for his business. Painted on the side was TL & SONS LANDSCAPING despite neither of his sons ever working with him. It overflowed with a love seat and chairs, a basketball backboard, and two garbage bags full of not so valuable sports memorabilia. Everything was secured with bright orange bungees and he resembled the Beverly Hillbillies driving out to California, if the Hillbillies had been people of Middle Eastern descent. James smiled and waved, relieved to have someone to hang with.

The crowd dispersed long before sundown and the temperature cooled to a balmy eighty-seven degrees. Mosquitos were in full flight, hunting, buzzing through the air in search of human blood and bit the two men everywhere as the scratching began.

James dragged the remaining unsold items to the curb, the ones he didn't want, and placed a sign in front that read FREE. The vultures would be out first light of the morning to pick everything clean.

They sat on lawn chairs in the garage listening to music, the smell of a citronella candle burning, counting the tax free money from their depreciated merchandise. James netted a hair over three thousand and Teddy pocketed a respectable two-hundred. A raccoon stared at them from the edge of the lawn, acting like he was owed a share of the cut, waiting for his nightly assault on the garbage cans. James was glad it wasn't a black bear.

"So what's the next move with the house?" said Teddy. "When you told me you were having a yard sale I didn't think it was everything you ever owned. It's empty as shit in there. What're you going to do Hot Sauce, get a lantern and camp out?"

"Don't know yet. Maybe," said James, shrugging. "I could eat hot dogs and beans from a can like a hobo."

"You've got to do something."

James changed the channel on the radio and wacked it, adjusting the antenna. He threw an empty beer can at the raccoon and yelled. The raccoon didn't flinch.

"With my family gone, maybe I'll burn this fucker to the ground," he said, staring at the floor. "You know, for the insurance."

Teddy laughed, an uneasy laugh, and counted his money again.

James picked up a putter, the only golf club he didn't sell, and his ten foot putt bounced along the concrete floor before lipping the side of an overturned coffee cup. Teddy ripped off a twenty spot from his wad of cash. "What do you say? First one to make five putts wins."

James matched his twenty. "I'm in." He took another swing and once again his putt hit the side of the cup. He adjusted his stance. "Dude, I need a big favor."

"Another one?"

"Yep."

"Everybody needs a big favor."

"Well this everybody needs a report on the former CEO of a certain company."

"You're talking about William Breg, aren't you?" said Teddy. "The big guy."

"I would say there's a prominent local thief who goes by that name."

"You talk about that guy a lot you know. It's like you got some kind of man crush on him."

"Man crush? No way. Money crush? Maybe," said James, handing Teddy the club. "I think it's time for an intro." He excused himself to the bathroom.

A white van approached the house, turning around in the cul-de-sac. It was the classic white cargo van, the creepy one with no windows, and it stopped in front of the FREE sign to investigate. Two figures jumped out and threw everything inside, including the sign itself. When James returned with a bottle of vodka from the freezer he saw a flashlight piercing the dusk and closed the garage door.

"This will be it then?" said Teddy, swatting his neck with a ball cap. "Tell me this will be it."

"Seeing as Frank Cally has moved out of state, I'm pretty sure I can say right now that yes, this will be it."

"I might have some time on Monday, but don't get your hopes up. This isn't very high on my priority list." Teddy leaned against the wall, scratching his left ankle with his right foot. "I'm not defending what she said but I have to agree with Dee on one thing. Maybe you should get back to seeing your therapist. I think you need to talk with somebody."

"I'm talking with you right now."

"She's right you know."

"What, you're taking her side now? Don't make me hurt you little man."

"I'm serious dude. You keep messing with these high profile people man and you're going to end up back in jail or something. Maybe worse. These kind of guys don't fuck around. You got kids man. You should keep pushing forward with the lawyer idea."

"I know what I'm doing, okay grandma? It's under control." James reached in his pocket and removed something shiny. He polished it with the bottom of his tank top.

"Here," he said to Teddy, dropping a cold metal object in his palm.

Teddy inspected it. "Damn dude, is this a Rolex? Is this real?"

"Sure as hell is. It's water proof up to a hundred meters. The Navy Seals wear these things in combat. True story. Saw it on TV."

"Where'd you get it?"

"It's compliments of a friend," said James, holding a finger to his lips.

Teddy strapped it on and extended his arm in admiration, bending it at the elbow. The gold watch fit nice and snug on his wrist.

"Thanks Hot Sauce. I don't really know what to say." He held out his hand and they exchanged a long firm shake.

"You deserve it my friend. I just wanted to say thanks for everything." James straddled the golf ball and scratched behind his ear. "You know Teddy, you really need to come up with a new nickname for me. I haven't worked at that hot sauce company in a long time now. It's getting pretty old."

They traded belts from the bottle before Teddy said, "But James, you're a perfect Hot Sauce. It's a perfect nickname. I can only take a little bit of you and you're a real pain in the ass."

James laughed. "You sound like my wife now."

"She is the smart one in the family."

They played putt-putt until the vodka was gone and they lost track whose turn it was. Last he remembered, James was in the hole for eighty bucks.

CHAPTER

26

A security guard leaned out the window with a blue shirt and a matching hat, the letters Y.E. emblazoned on both in red. A walkie talkie hung next to a cell phone from his hip. He was tall, at least six five, and his athletic physique suggested he was no stranger to the gym. He smiled on command and finished every conversation with an obligatory, "Have a nice day," regardless of what transpired. Two other beefcakes joined him in the mini one-story house masquerading as a booth.

James was third in line, sandwiched between a white Porsche and a dry cleaning delivery van, with the air conditioning blasting a cool breeze off his gel-coiffed hair. Replacing his wire rimmed glasses were a pair of Oakley's and a dark brown mustache was glued beneath his nose. His suit, brand new from J.C. Penny, had a matching tie and pocket square and an American flag button was pinned to his lapel.

The brake lights of the Porsche vanished momentarily and he rolled ten feet further up. James spoke aloud as if somebody was in the car, glancing at himself in the rearview mirror, practicing his spiel.

Huge queen palm trees flanked the roadside leading to the entrance while lavender and gardenias sweetened the air. A long stretch of grass butted up next to the woods and displayed in the center was a modern art sculpture of inverted triangles constructed from old railroad ties. In front of the guard booth was a bowl shaped fountain with a mermaid perched atop, holding a comb, her breasts exposed to the world.

"Please sign here sir," the security guard said in a deep tone, handing over a clipboard, smiling. "And could I please see some ID?"

James scribbled a signature and reached in his pocket. He frowned, reaching in the other. He gave a wry grin and patted both sides of his jacket and pants like he was frisking himself before snapping open the glove box. He unbuckled his seatbelt and lunged towards the back seat, running his hand along the floor mats.

"Excuse me sir. I'm going to need to see some ID," the security guard repeated.

James slid his shades toward the end of his nose, resting them on the tip, and unwrapped a piece of gum. "You won't believe this," he said, shaking his head. "I must have left my wallet in the wife's car. She took the Maserati today. Women, you know?"

He released a short obnoxious laugh and saw a butterfly float across the windshield as a Bentley approached the exit gate. "You guys have any bottles of water in there?" he said. "I'm heading over to the club later for tennis. Big match. Need to hydrate." The guard didn't answer and took a step back.

James sat in the car listening to the splash of the fountain and tapped his fingers on the shifter. He looked out the passenger window and faked a dramatic yawn. When his head spun back six eyeballs awaited, staring, and the three large men folded their arms. He chomped down on the gum, biting his tongue, tasting a little blood.

"You can turn around right over there sir," one of the guards said, not smiling, pointing to an open space. "Have a nice day."

"Yeah, that's great fellas," said James, exhaling loudly and nodding. "And I appreciate you doing your job. Well done. But I'm actually here to meet somebody. A Mr. Ronald Stephens, the real estate agent. He does a lot of business in here, a lot of business, and I'm thinking of buying one of these shacks for a flip." He blew a bubble, snapping it. "We're supposed to meet at half past four and I know I'm early, but I was hoping to check out the neighborhood beforehand." James turned up his wrist to show them the time, the large face of a Rolex shimmering in the light. He handed them a piece of paper. "Anyway, here's his number."

The three guards made a combined income of thirty-three dollars an hour and glanced at one another, tugging on their utility belts, the line of waiting cars growing. One person honked and another revved their engine. "You can wait over there sir," one of them said, motioning to the right. "Sorry for any inconvenience." James heard the words, "Have a nice day," fading as he closed the window.

He pulled to the side and threw off his shades. The dry cleaning van drove past him followed by a Lamborghini. He watched two squirrels chase one another up and around a tree, fighting over food, and as more cars passed he leaned towards the passenger seat tilting his head, shielding his face.

Ronald Stephens, a reputable real estate agent who hadn't seen a commission for the longest stretch of his career, was contacted a week earlier to inquire about a six-bedroom seven bathroom house for sale in the upscale community of Yorkshire Estates. James was surprised when after only a fifteen minute phone call the realtor waived the credit check. He was even more surprised when he was able to successfully evade Mr. Stephen's questions of financial solvency, some of which he didn't fully understand. He kept repeating the words *portfolio* and *diversification* and threw in a *Martha's Vineyard* for good measure.

The house he called about was heading into foreclosure and courtesy of Teddy's research James knew it. The 12,000 square foot home decreased in value every day and had become a blight for the neighbors, an embarrassment to the community. The gossip concerning the former millionaires turned poor white trash was at a high school level and all parties involved, particularly the homeowners association, were willing to do anything before further monetary erosion occurred. Reputation was at stake.

Mr. Stephens drove a black Mercedes E-Class and James followed him through the majestic gates as the pair quickly vanished into the maze of riches. He kept a safe distance back, about fifty feet, and there were MapQuest directions on top of a briefcase with an address highlighted in blue. More palm trees lined the streets and there was a median the size of a freeway. There were more flowers, more bushes, more fountains, and more sculptures. There was more everything.

Thick trees taller than the Great Wall of China provided a natural fence and obscured any view to the majority of homes. The only evidence structures existed behind the green barriers were the ceramic shingles of orange, red, and brown stretching high in the air. The houses were fortresses, hidden inside the land of forbidden suburbia, and nobody jogged on the sidewalks or rode bikes or took walks. There were no mothers pushing strollers or kids playing.

He held the directions above the steering wheel while noting the various landmarks along the way. It would be easy to get lost with so much beauty blending everything together. They took a left near a lake and a right at the fountain of manatees. Another left, another small lake, two rights, and a hundred yards of picturesque pine trees.

Mr. Stephens lead him through two miles of the 190 acre community traveling thirty miles per hour as James pulled at his itchy collar, searching, waiting to make his move. An opening in the median finally presented itself and he stomped on the brakes, watching the Mercedes continue over a small hill. He cranked the wheel to the left and slammed the gas pedal, smoking the tires, hoping he'd never see Mr. Stephens again.

James sped down the road and after u-turning twice and clipping the side of the curb he turned onto a street called Gingerbread Lane. It had a long row of gates, some with the owner's initials, others with the family crest, and he crept along until coming across a brick pillar with the number twenty-two on it. He double-checked his highlighted address. Twenty-two was a match.

A bevy of landscapers and gardeners buzzed about the hive, accessing the estate for their weekly duties. The sound of lawnmowers and hedge trimmers vibrated in the air and the men using weed whackers had towels slung over their heads. James parked behind a large pickup truck hitched to an empty trailer and killed the ignition.

His phone rang again for the fourth time. Mr. Stephens was frantic in his messages and James put the realtor at ease, texting that his wife had gone into labor and he needed to leave immediately. He turned off the disposable track phone and stuffed it into a pocket. With a final peek in the rearview mirror he grabbed the briefcase, gave the sign of the cross, and opened the door to the smell of freshly cut grass.

CHAPTER

27

William Breg occupied a palatial estate that made Bobby Stafford's spread look like a shanty. It was 20,000 square feet of extravagance on a ten acre plot and the guest house alone would qualify as a dream home for most ordinary people. His garage contained ten vintage cars and he was rumored to have one of the finest wine collections in the city. His neighbors were professional athletes, politicians, TV personalities, and high ranking business associates. They were powerful and elite, writing the rules by which they played in a cocoon of their own little world.

James rang the doorbell in the massive front entrance, squeezing the briefcase, his fingernails jutting into his palm. He hummed a song he'd heard on the radio to calm himself and waited before a heavyset Hispanic woman greeted him wearing jeans and a sleeveless shirt.

"Hola," she said, smiling.

"Good afternoon," said James, surprised, expecting a bald white man in a tuxedo by the name of Jeeves who spoke in a snobby British accent. "My name is Dick Royce. I'm a business associate of Mr. Breg. Is he in today?"

"Señor Breg es no home," she said.

"Do you know what time he'll be back?"

"Señor Breg es no home."

James hovered in the doorway and mashed his lips together, peering into the opulent foyer. *Dammit Teddy, Breg was supposed to be here.* He saw a huge vaulted ceiling with a glass chandelier and the staircase curved up both sides of the wall. There were life-size paintings of people he assumed to be family members and as he continued taking inventory the maid interrupted him.

"Cómo le puedo ayudar?"

He grinned, clueless what she said, and ran a hand along his face. They stared at one another until a gardener traipsed around a corner with a hose wrapped over his shoulder. He looked at James and then at her. She looked at him and back to James.

"There must have been a scheduling error with Mr. Breg," said James. "Sorry to have bothered you."

He looked at the gardener again and stepped towards the car. Some puffy gray clouds rolled in, blocking the sun, cooling the temperature a few degrees.

"Wait," he said, turning to approach the maid as she closed the door. He motioned towards his throat. "Agua por favor." His one class of community college Spanish came to the rescue.

"Sí," she said. "En la cocina."

She brought him to the kitchen and poured a tall glass of ice water, adding a lemon wedge.

"Gracias. Una momento por favor," he said, holding up an index finger. He dug the cell phone from his pocket and faked dialing a call. James spoke loud for effect as his voice bounced off the exotic stone counters and slate floor. He meandered to the right of the kitchen, towards the archway, and felt like one of those cheeseballs he'd seen countless times at the airport, pretending to close a million dollar deal while standing in line for coach. "I'll have my secretary fax over the paperwork to you and your partners and I'll cc you on the email I send to your BlackBerry." He didn't even know what cc meant.

She opened a bin of silverware and began polishing it for the dinner service as he continued talking, first resting an arm on a hip, then throwing it above his head in exasperation. He shook his head yes, shook his head no, and inched further towards the edge of the room. James winked and smiled at her before crossing the threshold, babbling his non-nonsense into the silent phone.

The formal dining room was bigger than the first floor of his house and had a table the length of a school bus. The chairs were crafted from walnut with unusually high straight backs and when he sat in one it was no more comfortable than the pews in church. A green checkered rug covered the floor, squares of copper were arranged on the ceiling, and floral print wallpaper was plastered everywhere. There were oriental vases and silver candelabras and the whole room bragged of old school money: stodgy, ugly, and very, very expensive.

He passed through a library filled with leather-bound books and came to a door where the aroma of tobacco was strong. He entered a cigar room, blown away by the view it afforded. The sprawling backyard was not much smaller than a par five fairway and had the greenest grass he'd ever seen. There were rows of citrus trees alongside a reflecting pool and an intricate hedge maze in the shape of a circle. He saw a large white gazebo near the lake and the room faced west to capture a sunset most people vacation for, the kind advertised on brochures. James imagined Breg and his cohorts standing in front of the windows, sipping brandy, puffing away, congratulating themselves for being the smartest self-made men and women in the world. "Hear hear," they would say, clanking their glasses, playing the role of conquistadors in the twenty-first century of capitalism.

He snatched a handful of stogies from the walk-in humidor along with a cigar cutter when he noticed a box inscribed with the words *Especial-Cubano.* Underneath it, sticking out, was a letter written by the CFO of Trustworth Bank, Frank Cally. He grabbed it, about to read the contents, but heard the maid call out, "Señor Dick. Señor Dick." She raised her voice. "Tiempo para ir!"

James enjoyed one last view of the lake and met her in the hallway. Her smile was replaced by a scowl and one hand was filled with forks, the other a damp rag. She pointed with her fist in the direction of the kitchen. "Vámonos." He followed her back through the library and across the dining room where he ducked into one of the many bathrooms. "Una momento," he said, closing the door.

Even if he had to relieve his bladder or empty his bowels, the bathroom wasn't a real a bathroom at all. It was a bathroom museum. The toilet had a gold-plated handle and there were two pieces of artwork, both still lifes of fruit, both framed and signed by the artist. He ran the water and stole everything available including the handcrafted soaps, the silk flowers, and the softest toilet paper his ass would ever have the pleasure of feeling.

The knocking on the door ceased and he no longer heard, "Señor Dick," or "Tiempo para ir." He fiddled with his mustache and glanced at his watch. Fifteen minutes had elapsed since entering the compound. His glimpse behind the curtain was complete. James would have to find some other time, probably some other way, to introduce himself to the former CEO of Trustworth Bank.

The maid was absent when he opened the door but his joy was short lived. A burly man with a goatee in a gray suit had taken her place. He had dark hair, not much of a neck, and his head was in the shape of a bucket.

"Excuse me sir. Can I help you with something?"

"I uh...." said James. "I was looking for—"

"Esmeralda said you won't leave and that you didn't have an appointment. Is that true?"

"She did?"

"What the hell do you think she was saying?"

"I wasn't sure. I don't really speak Spanish. I needed to use the bathroom."

A crushing blow on his shoulder forced him to bend to the left and he was escorted to the kitchen before getting shoved into a chair.

"Don't move," the man said, picking up a phone, his muscles popping through his jacket.

James' voice grew high, cracking like a pubescent teen, and he cleared his throat. "I just need Mr. Breg to sign some paperwork. I'm an associate of his from the bank."

The man let go of James and stepped back. "Hi Wendy. It's Marty from the house. Is Mr. Breg available please? Yeah, I can wait."

"So you know Mr. Breg personally?" he asked.

James nodded.

"That's strange. Because people don't normally show up at this house unannounced to talk business. Ever. And judging by that piece of shit off the rack suit, I'd be hard pressed to believe he's doing any kind of business with you."

"I have a very important document for him to sign," said James, unhinging the latches of the briefcase.

"Settle down, I'm warning you." Marty turned his attention back to the phone. "Yes, hello sir, I have somebody here who wants to speak with you. I don't know sir. I'm not sure sir. It's unclear sir. He says he knows you sir."

James reached inside the briefcase with his right hand, searching under the toilet paper and silk flowers until clutching a thin red canister, maneuvering it in his palm. With his left hand he accepted the phone.

"Hello William. I'm with the bank oversight committee. I'm here because—" James sprang from the chair and tossed the phone in the air. He whipped his right hand from the briefcase and lined up the pepper spray towards Marty's lunging face, pulling the trigger. Marty moved, trying to dodge, a second too late, but not before wrestling James to the floor and obliterating his nose with a ferocious elbow. He wrapped his forearm around James' throat and leaned back, squeezing, trying to choke him out. But the burn was too deep and he had trouble breathing. He was forced to let go.

James saw a bright light with tweety birds dancing and a whooshing sound rumbled through his head. Blood gushed down his face, splattering his shirt like a Jackson Pollock painting. He crawled to one knee, sprayed Marty again, and punched him square in the ballsack. Esmeralda clung to the wall, motionless, as he staggered from the kitchen holding his nose.

He ripped open the front door to encounter three gardeners with rakes in their hands and upon seeing his mangled face they ran. James hopped in the car and tore from the driveway using his pocket square for a bandage. His eyes pumped tears, mixing with the blood.

The tall black exit gates were closing behind a motorcycle and upon approaching the guard booth James accelerated, darting through the opening, scraping the side of the car as sparks lit up the afternoon air. He weaved through traffic and passed two cars on a double yellow line before running a red light and almost t-boning a taxi. When he rounded a ramp leading to the highway his heart slowed a beat and his jaw unclenched. The path to freedom was secure. Or so he thought.

The normal rush hour traffic was compounded by a four-car pileup of tourists on their way to a theme park. Everything was backed up as far as he could see and the traffic moved at the pace of cold honey, taking ten minutes to go half a mile. James smacked the dashboard and yelled at the people gawking, pointing to his damaged BMW.

He chucked the mustache out the window and took the next exit, parking in a three-story garage with a scarcity of tenants. He reclined in his seat until nightfall, cowering, calling Teddy numerous times only to get voice mail.

His nose was broken, no doubt about it, and an hour elapsed before the bleeding stopped. The bags under his eyes turned purple and he started resembling the raccoon that frequented his yard.

When James got home he sat on the couch in his underwear listening to Bob Marley wail about freedom, competing with the ringing in his ears. He snuggled with a bottle of Smirnoff and iced his face. His crooked nose had duct tape across it with nuggets of dried blood stuck to the nostrils. He felt proud and pitiful at the same time.

The effects of the alcohol and a grade two concussion skewed his thoughts as he considered the possibility of revisiting Breg's compound. The lakefront seemed the logical entry point. He'd need an inflatable raft, a paddle, a wet suit, and night vision goggles. The theme from *Mission Impossible* filled his empty head. Once inside the estate he would scale the wall to the second floor with grappling hooks, cut out a section of the bedroom window with a laser guided suction cup tool, and subdue his victim with a tranquilizer gun. Only then could he interrogate Breg to find the safe and recoup his money.

It sounded so good. It sounded so real, so do-able. There would be alligators and miniature cameras and unexpected run-ins with beautiful women. When his eyes creaked open the next afternoon the sunlight from the curtainless windows battered him. He rolled over on the floor, groaning. Underneath him were long lists of schematic drawings approximating distances and heights with crossed out and re-written figures. They were as sophisticated as a fifth grade book report.

His head hurt, his body ached, and he'd felt like he kissed a frying pan. But James laughed, a weak laugh. He pulled himself onto the couch and lightly touched the bridge of his nose, wincing, wondering who shit in his mouth. "The name ish Bond, Jamesh Bond," he said in a terrible Sean Connery impression, licking his lips before walking to the bathroom. The only thing he had in common with 007 was the same first name.

It was time for a new direction.

CHAPTER

28

A young lady stood on the sidewalk in blue leather pumps, holding a Louis Vuitton, puffing a clove cigarette. She was gorgeous and knew it, or at least should have. The name given over the phone was Misty, a genuine stripper classic. She was no older than twenty-five and had full glossed lips, short smooth legs, and an aura of raw sexuality. Her skin tight mini skirt complimented an even tighter white top and James was shocked when he opened the door inviting the temptress in. She far exceeded his expectations.

The agency Misty worked for charged a flat rate of $500 an hour plus a non-negotiable tip of fifty bucks. Cash was their only acceptable means of payment. As the two parties exchanged money for the business transaction James' garage sale profits came in handy. Less than an hour had passed since he'd placed a phone call to the escort service advertised in the yellow pages and the process was as efficient as ordering a pizza for delivery.

Misty strolled towards the only piece of furniture left in the house and sat down. He soaked in her body, her face, and noticed a small piercing on the left side of her nose. James hated piercings. But it looked good on her.

He turned *up* the lights and glanced at the windows covered with sheets, double-checking for an opening, fearing any second the cops would kick down the front door with bomb sniffing dogs. Helicopters would swirl above and a SWAT team with video cameras instead of guns would storm the house. He'd be featured on a cable program titled "Pervert of the Month" and be forced to register as a sex offender. He took a chug of tequila and grabbed two Budweisers from the fridge.

"Thanks for the beer," said Misty, placing it on the floor instead of the overturned bucket serving as a coffee table. She brushed away a patch of brown hair from her bare shoulder. "Before we begin we need to set the ground rules, okay? I don't do anal whatsoever but will stick my finger up your ass if you want. You can't cum on my hair or face no matter how much extra you pay me and you have to wear a condom even if I blow you. No exceptions. The price quoted over the phone is only for you to pop once. If that only takes ten seconds or ten minutes then the rest of the time we can talk but if you want to pop again it'll be another five hundred. I don't do rough shit, choking, or golden showers. Are we clear?"

He nodded yes with a blank gaze.

"I hope so, because there is a very large black man sitting in the car outside named Darryl. He will come in here and royally fuck you up should there be any violation of these terms."

James was no prude but was stunned to hear the sexual debauchery emanating from the young woman's mouth. While working up the courage to utilize the escort service and debating whether he wanted to go through with it, he assumed the prostitute they sent would be of average attractiveness. But upon seeing her in person, Misty commanded at least a nine on the universal female rating system.

He recalled memories of his late teens and early twenties when the women doing porn were average looking at best. His girlfriends during that time period had wild savage bushes the size of Texas with stray pubic hairs creeping out the sides of their granny panties and thought shaving their legs in the middle of winter was optional. James couldn't compare them to the women he viewed on the internet and the incredibly beautiful girl sitting on his sofa. They could easily pass for models.

He tipped back his beer, crossing his legs.

She stood up, removed her top, and hiked down her skirt like they were old friends hanging at the beach. Within fifteen seconds she wore only a yellow thong and matching bra. Her stomach was perfectly flat and as Misty sat close to James he never knew cheap perfume could smell so good. She rubbed his leg with her fingernails, whispering in his ear. She leaned into him, pushing her perky breasts onto his chest, and moved up and down slowly, moaning. He was almost finished.

His face turned three shades of red and he untucked his shirt to hide the monster lurking in his pants. Misty was by far the hottest woman he ever had a realistic possibility of having sex with. He knew the average middle-aged guy like himself had a zero chance of acquiring the attention of such physically blessed girls unless they paid for it. Those particular kind of upper tier women are reserved for rich men, famous men, or men posing on the cover of a magazine with eight-pack abs. He'd rarely even seen a girl of Misty's caliber in his everyday travels, let alone interact with one, theorizing they didn't have regular jobs, didn't mingle with average looking people, and ran in wild packs of a secret society.

His caveman urge was strong and primal as fantasies from doggy style to the reverse cowboy were on the verge of becoming a reality. She straddled him, nibbled his ear, and unhooked her bra; running a nipple along his lips. Misty grinded her sweet spot on him, cotton on wood, dry rocking hard. She breathed heavy and he lightly caressed her ass, feeling the curves of a firm ripe apple. She rubbed his chest, his stomach, and went for the zipper when he stopped her. He looked into her sparkling green eyes with regret.

"Is something the matter?" she asked.

"Yeah," he said, pushing himself away. "Something is definitely the matter." He picked up her clothes off the floor and handed them over. "Here, put these back on."

"What? You want me to put my clothes back on? Now that's a first." She grabbed her top. "What are you like a queer or something?"

James sighed. "No. I'm not a queer. Although I'm feeling kind of gay right now. The thing is, I'm sort of married. Even though we don't live together and I'm not sure she loves me anymore and I have no idea if she's ever coming home to—"

"Don't worry about it," said Misty, reaching over, rubbing his leg again. "It's okay baby. Most of my clients are married. At least half anyway. Nobody's going to find out. Not unless you kiss and tell." She touched the tip of his penis overtop his jeans and a bolt of electricity shot through him. "I'll only use my hand if you want. That's not really cheating you know."

Misty had small hands, the kind to make a man look big, and James wanted the young vixen to do anything and everything to him. He counted *one Mississippi, two Mississippi*, and utilized all the will power left in his moral inventory to scurry to the stairs.

She said, "Well I can't have you calling back the agency telling them I didn't get you off and backed out of the deal. That's not good for my business."

"Relax, I'm not calling anybody. Looking at you sitting there practically naked, I must be insane. I've never cheated on my wife and I'm not about to start now. I'm a lot of things, but not that. I just want to have her back in the house with the kids."

"Alright," she said. "It's your money mister."

She took a sip of beer and put on her bra.

"If you love her so much, then why don't you make it happen?"

"I'm working on it, believe me," he said. "It's a long story. But that's not the reason I paid you to come over here tonight. I have a business proposition for you."

She continued dressing, pulling up her skirt, climbing into her top. James committed every sensual detail of her body to an ironclad memory and the second she disappeared from sight he would have no choice but to finish what had been started in the privacy of the shower.

For the remaining hour the duo drank more beers and discussed the specific parameters of his plan. He outlined the job, informing her it was to be a solo act not affiliated with the agency, and stressed that it needed to be very low-key. They went over the location, the time, what to wear, and how to act. Her fee was hefty, triple the normal charge, but considering his lack of involvement, he thought worth it.

James handed her two photographs, half the money, and printed instructions of what they discussed. He walked her to the door like a gentleman and extended his hand. She bypassed his formal gesture, planting a sweet kiss on his cheek.

"Are you sure you're not gay?" she asked again, grinning.

"Yeah, I'm sure."

"This has been an interesting session. I wish they were all this easy. By the way, you never told me your name."

James went blank as the answer to the simple question flustered him. He felt stupid and not knowing why said, "Bond. You can call me Bond."

"Alright Mr. Bond. You little weirdo. I'll play along and see your gay ass when the job is done to get the rest of my money. In the meantime, feel free to call me anytime you want to spend five hundred dollars and not have sex."

She laughed as he watched her drift down the sidewalk into a car. He looked but didn't spot Darryl, the large man she spoke of.

James leaned against the side of the house and sparked a smoke in the warm night air. The taillights faded, disappearing, and once again he was alone. His shirt was ripe with Misty's perfume and he inhaled deeply. *What the hell am I doing?* he thought. *What in the hell am I doing?*

CHAPTER

29

Ten long days went by after the sexless encounter with Misty and James had a headache and stomachache for all of them. He set up his laptop in the kitchen and waited every afternoon playing game after game of solitaire. The faintest sound of a vehicle approaching the cul-de-sac caused him to attack the window and pace back and forth like an animal waiting to be fed. He'd cup his eyes and squint until realizing it wasn't the right person. When the postal truck did stop at the end of the driveway he fled to the mailbox, only to be greeted with a dirty look from the mail carrier and a fresh stack of bills. The day his long awaited package finally arrived, it only made matters worse.

His beard grew back, gray hairs everywhere, and his appetite had been severely diminished. Lack of sleep reached an all-time high and although James wasn't counting, he swore his nightly trips to the bathroom increased in frequency. Once again the ab-roller turbo machine was covered in dust.

After multiple phone calls and a persistent amount of badgering, Teddy was finally able to get James out of the house, to drag him from isolation. He used a free round of golf as bait.

Cries of, "Fore!" were heard as waves of golfers missed the green on the eighteenth hole near the clubhouse, spraying white dimpled balls into a small pond promoted as a lake. The municipal course was crowded as always, even with a slight whiff of stank emanating from the nearby sewage treatment plant when the wind blew from the east.

James and Teddy sat in their cart, both wearing shades, pressing buttons randomly on the broken GPS unit. They waited thirty minutes as cars

169

continued to pour into the parking lot faster than the hot temperature climbed. People in short sleeved collared shirts and mismatched shorts practiced on the driving range while groups of old men already finished playing for the day and were knee deep in the scotch around a card table. James smothered his arms and the back of his neck with sunblock.

"Have you been showering?" said Teddy, fanning himself with a baseball hat. "Your hair is looking kind of greasy dude."

"Sometimes."

"Well take one tonight. It looks like shit. Plus, you have some serious B.O. kicking."

"I know. I'm grossing myself out man. I've been wearing the same underwear for three days in a row."

"That's just plain old fucking nasty."

James shrugged.

"So did you bring them?" said Teddy, scooting to far edge of the seat.

James removed a manila envelope from his golf bag, took out a stack of photos, and handed them over. "They came the other day. You can keep them if you want. I have copies at the house."

Teddy smiled, sifting through the graphic pictures of Misty seducing William Breg. There were shots of her fully naked performing fellatio, shots of her riding on top, and shots of Breg taking her from behind. It was obvious who the man in the X-rated photos was.

"Holy shit," said Teddy. "These are awesome." He lowered his voice to a whisper. "This chick you hired is unbelievable."

"Yup."

"Did you write the word thief on them before sending them out?"

"Yup."

Teddy set the pictures on his lap. "What's wrong man? You're acting more mopey than usual." He smacked his friend on the back. "I thought you'd be ecstatic with the results. They came out great."

James rubbed his temples, then his forehead. "Between Misty and the guy I paid to take the pictures, I'm in for around three grand. I need that money right now to pay some bills."

"It cost that much?"

"Apparently this type of thing doesn't come cheap."

"Sell something then."

"There's nothing left. Except this," said James, holding up his wrist to display a Rolex. "I wanted to keep this one as a souvenir."

Teddy looked down at his own wrist, at the watch James gave him. He tucked his hand in his pocket and jumped from the cart to stretch.

The first tee box had turned into a log jam. A foursome of young men gave the starter a hard time about the wait and one gentleman in particular complained louder than his friends while texting and smoking a cigar. He explained in great detail the nature of his super busy, super important day. The starter, a Korean War veteran with a U.S.S. *Missouri* cap on, held a clipboard in one hand and sipped coffee from a Styrofoam cup in the other. He called out the next name of the party to tee off without looking in the young man's direction.

"You know what the major flaw in my plan was?" said James, watching Teddy struggle to touch his feet with his hands, the blood rushing to his face.

"I would assume not banging that goddess of a woman?"

"Let's put aside my priest-like performance when she was sitting on my couch rubbing my thigh, whispering in my ear how much she wanted me. And please don't bring it up again. But I have no idea what the outcome was. No clue about his reaction. Who the hell knows what happened when Breg, or his wife, or his former colleagues at the bank received the photos. It could have been horrible and embarrassing or could have been no big deal."

"Did you see the pictures? Her titties are flopping all over him. How is that no big deal to a married man?" said Teddy, bending his leg back to loosen his quad, softly counting to ten.

"Maybe Breg and his wife have an open relationship. As disturbing as it is, maybe they're swingers. Maybe she knows about his cheating ways but stays because she likes the money and power, like a politician's wife. Maybe she doesn't want to be by herself. He could always say he was set up or the pictures were photoshopped. Guys at that level in life have many enemies." He shook his head. "I guess I'll never know. It was a stupid idea. Definitely one of the stupidest I've ever had. And a costly one."

They moved a cart length closer and Teddy stuffed a pinch of chewing tobacco under his lip. James wanted to go back home, back to bed. He popped open a beer instead.

"But the worst part of the whole thing," said James, brushing the foam from the lid, "is that I didn't get to feel anything. Nothing at all. Even if the pictures caused Breg some kind of pain I would never get to feel it. Never get to see the look on his smug face when I cracked him. There's complete emptiness inside me. Not to mention I didn't get any money." He paused. "You see, with the first two thieves I took care of, they got what they deserved. With them, the pain I caused made me feel better, like I was doing the right thing, and not just for me, but everybody. It made me feel whole and—"

"There's a lot of ears around here," said Teddy, raising his hand, looking around. "We can talk more about this later."

They played the first three holes, waiting forever in between shots, and were on pace for a grueling five and a half hour round. James took extra care to park in the shade and after losing a new sleeve of golf balls in the first seven holes he removed his shoes and rested his feet near the windshield. He'd watch Teddy play and search for the cart girl to replenish their beverages.

"So are you finished?" said Teddy as they headed for the back nine.

"I'm not feeling the golf thing today. Sorry man. I'll pay you back for the club rentals."

"I'm not talking about golf. I mean your unofficial crackpot investigation of the bank."

"I guess so," said James. "I don't know what else to do. I don't think I'll be able to finagle my way back into Breg's house again. Not sure if I want to anyway. And he's either there or at the very private, very secure country club. That only leaves Frank Cally, the CFO. And we know that piece of shit lives up in Virginia now."

"Good," said Teddy, mocking him with applause. "It's about damn time. You've had your fun. You can exit gracefully. Now listen, there's something I want to ask you." He spit a wad of brown saliva on the grass. "I had one of my guys quit last week. Felipe. He's been with me for the last two years. Best guy I have. But he's moving back to California for family reasons."

"So?"

"So, I have an opening. Come work with me for a while. It'll be good for you."

"I don't know man. I'm not really cut out for manual—"

"Stop being such a candy-ass. I just picked up a decent size contract for a youth soccer complex. You can work on your tan while you get back in shape. You need a little structure in your life right now and I can finally help."

James flicked a cigarette in the air. He saw three hawks floating on air currents without flapping their wings. "I guess I could try it. Maybe you're right. Do you think it would help with Dee coming back? If she saw me working hard again?"

"It couldn't hurt dude. It couldn't hurt."

Teddy landed a chip shot ten feet to the right of the hole and posed in his follow through to admire it. James hopped off the cart, dropped a ball, and hit it high in the air, aiming even closer to the pin. The ball sailed on a gust of wind and water splashed up near a flock of geese swimming in a pond.

"Yeah," he said, jamming the pitching wedge back in the bag. "I think I'll just wait for the cart girl."

30

J ames spent the evening piddling in the garage, searching through the stuff that didn't sell in the garage sale, the small amount of stuff he actually considered keeping. He looked for his work boots and the pair of ratty gloves with the holes in the thumbs, knowing they'd have to make do until getting to a store. Teddy was picking him up at six in the morning, sharp, and James couldn't remember the last time he'd done a solid day's work for a solid day's pay. He rubbed his palms together and they were dish pan soft. In a few days, he knew they'd be covered in blisters.

It was trash night and he heard his neighbor scraping the pavement with the bottom of plastic garbage cans while dragging them to the curb. His own garbage cans overflowed on the side of the house, festering with maggots. He placed them next to the recycling bin and stood in the driveway wearing dirty socks, listening to some rumblings in the woods. The raccoon, or maybe a hungry black bear, were salivating in anticipation. He finished in the garage and locked everything up, turning off the lights.

A bottle of coconut water replaced his beer and he gushed down the electrolytes in a last ditch effort to hydrate. He scratched his head, second guessing his decision to work as a landscaper for Teddy. Was it too late to call and back out? Six in the morning was early, a time James hadn't seen in a while. Not unless he pulled an all-nighter.

He took off his shirt and recoiled from the smell. Teddy was right. He was riper than an outhouse. The rejuvenating power of a hot shower awaited.

James walked past the corner office and down the short hallway but stopped. Above him, to the right of the doorway, was a shadow, a shadow he'd never seen. It resembled a small square on top of a large square. He heard a creak, saw the shadow move. Adrenaline injected into his bloodstream yet his legs felt heavy. The shadow grew bigger and when he gathered the courage to spin around a beast of a man was atop him. He covered his face and screamed while getting body slammed to the ground. A blow to the side of his skull thrust him into darkness.

His vision was blurry when he opened his eyes. His mouth was taped and hands and feet were fastened with zip ties. He sat shirtless against the bedroom wall with the door shut and heard men talking but he couldn't make out what they said. James dozed in and out of consciousness for the next half-hour, the bump on his head sticky with blood. When he opened his eyes again and became lucid, the men noticed.

"Hey, there he is," a voice said. "Welcome back." A man snapped his fingers and another man removed something from his jacket, broke it in half, and held it under James' nose. The ammonia from the smelling salt burned, frying his sinus cavities, and he whipped his head back, clanking the wall.

He slowly blinked as his vision returned to normal and James felt nauseous. His mouth began to water. He knew it was coming, tried choking it down, but was unable to stop it. The vomit bounced off the tape, up through his nose, and leaked from his nostrils. He exhaled hard, pushing it along to breathe, as regurgitated chunks of hot dogs and chips slithered over his lips, down his chin, and plopped onto his belly.

Standing in front of him dressed in a light gray suit was Marty, the no-neck buckethead from William Breg's house. He wore a big smile and pointed at James, saying to his partner, "This is the guy George. This is the fucking guy that punched me in the nuts."

"That's a cheap shot," said George, wagging an index finger side to side. "A real man code violation if you ask me."

Marty knelt next to James and patted his hair, wiping his hand on a hanky. "The tape is staying on. Nod if you understand."

James complied.

"You know James Horton, you are one stupid motherfucker," said Marty. "Ballsy, I'll give you that, but very very stupid. And not just because you trespassed onto Mr. Breg's estate. George, tell him how stupid he is."

"You used your personal credit card to pay for the rented BMW. There are cameras everywhere at Mr. Breg's house. You can't see them because they are hidden. Did you know there was a very small sticker in the bottom right hand corner of the windshield that said Euro Imports LTD and gave a toll free number? It was very small, easy to miss. We got the license number plate too. And it's not your fault because you're so damn stupid."

"It only took a few days to track you down," said Marty. "We've been watching you James. To see what you're going to do next. You are one boring son of a bitch, you know that? Not too much of a people person are you?"

"He's boring and stupid," said George. "The guy's a loser. And he completely sucks at golf."

It was hot in the house and all three men were sweating. James was on the cusp of crying, trying to contain the tears. He was helpless and searched his mind's databank but no *MacGyver* ideas were springing to his head. It wasn't a TV show. The tension around his wrists cut off the circulation as his hands went numb.

"Mr. Breg wanted to be here in person, but that's what he pays us for," said Marty, taking off his jacket. "But he did give me a letter for your dumbass. First though, I need to ask you some questions."

He rolled up his sleeves and his forearms were massive, covered in tattoos of pin-up girls and overgrown hair.

"From the records of the car rental it shows you previously rented that same car the day Bobby Stafford was assaulted in his home. That was you, wasn't it?"

James looked around for a miracle. An earthquake would have been nice. Maybe a giant sink hole. He didn't answer.

"George," said Marty, snapping his fingers. "Show him your toy."

George pulled back his jacket, displaying a silver handgun tucked under his belt.

"James, I need you to listen very carefully. George here is not in a great mood. He's been having some issues with his stomach. It's a whole dairy lactose thing I don't want to get into. But he loves to eat cheese. And right now he can't. He gets grumpy when he can't eat cheese. So go ahead, answer the question."

James stared into his black eyes. They were big and scary, just like the man. He moved his head slightly.

"And before that, you attacked Pam Gindefeld in a downtown parking lot, correct?"

He nodded again, trembling.

"We know James. We know it had to be you. It's all connected. Leaving the word thief on everything is a pretty stupid calling card."

"It's hard to believe how stupid this guy is," said George.

"I have to agree. Especially writing it on those pictures of Mr. Breg fucking that whore."

The room began to rotate upside down and side to side as his body shrank and his head expanded. James thought of Dee and the kids and what the newspaper would say in his obituary. If he was lucky, he'd have an obituary. They could mourn him. If unlucky, he'd disappear without a trace, adding his name to the long list of people who go missing every day. Speculation would plague the rest of his family's lives about the man they once knew. What happened? Where did he go? Theories of an alien abduction or being sold for black market body parts would be tossed around. He'd simply rot in an unmarked grave.

"Let's do this already and get out of this dump," said George, turning up his watch. "I'm starving."

Marty stepped back.

George cocked the handgun. "Where does Mr. Breg want it?"

"Same as usual. Two in the head. Two in the chest."

James couldn't breathe, his lungs seizing up, with the barrel of the gun pressed to his forehead. He closed his eyes and George backhanded him across the face. "Keep them open. Or we'll cut them out."

He looked away at the empty wall as images of his beautiful children crushed him. There were images of Dee, his estranged mother, his hard working father. Within a second that lasted an hour he thought of the afterlife, contemplated God, and prayed to Jesus. And when the trigger was pulled the gun went *click*. George pulled the trigger again. Another *click*.

"Did you really think we were going to kill a parasite like you?" said Marty, smiling. "You ain't worth it James. Not to me or Mr. Breg."

His body tingled, like frostbite thawing, and his pants were warm from wetting himself. James fulfilled the definition of shitting one's pants. Marty removed a letter. "Mr. Breg asked me to read you this. He hates any unwanted attention and goes out of his way to avoid it." He ripped the letter into pieces and scattered them on the floor. "Let me summarize Mr. Breg's demands for your dumbass. Get the fuck out of Florida and never come back. Ever. You have one week and we'll be watching."

Marty cut James free, standing him against the wall.

"You know, before getting the pictures, Mr. Breg was just going to give you a harsh warning, to let you know about his disapproval of stopping by his house without an invite. You hadn't done anything to him personally but steal a few toiletries. Although Esmeralda was pretty shaken up. Poor girl. But considering now, we're going to—"

With an uppercut to the nether region he pinned James' balls to the bottom of his ass. James bent over, grabbing his crotch, and a vicious knee pounded his face, re-breaking his nose. Another knee split open his eye. "You never hit a man in the nuts," said Marty. "It's not right." He punched him again below the belt as George landed a hard right to the mouth, knocking out a tooth, followed by several body blows. When they let him go James crashed to the floor, tearing off the tape, gasping for air.

"George, hand it over," said Marty, wiping his forehead.

The cylinder was small, all black, adorned with a red stenciled spider. "I have a buddy in the police department. This stuff can only be issued to them. It's not street legal. You got me good last time dumbass. My eyes burned for days. Yours are going to burn for a week." He pointed the nozzle at James' face. "Put your fucking hands down."

"Please," said James through a bloody swollen lip, slurring his words, barely audible.

Marty squeezed the trigger of the industrial strength mace. "How do you like it fuckhead?"

James rolled around the floor like he was exorcising a demon until getting mule kicked in the sternum.

"One week," said Marty, putting his jacket back on, brushing off some lint on the sleeve. "Consider yourself lucky Mr. Breg is not a violent man. You should thank him. Maybe send him a nice card or a fruit basket. I know you have his address."

"Have a nice life loser," said George as the two men left the room, exited the house, and made their way through a small patch of woods into a nearby neighborhood.

George finished texting Mr. Breg and started the car. "That dumbass didn't even know the gun was a fake. Did you see the look on his face?"

Marty nodded. "I told you he was stupid."

James lay on the fake hardwood floor in the fetal position until he passed out. The next noise he heard was the doorbell. It was six o'clock. Teddy was there. It was time for work.

CHAPTER

31

The bag of ice had a microscopic hole in it somewhere and James didn't know how it got there, didn't care. He was too lazy to change it. Droplets of cold water leaked down his thigh as he continued battling the swelling of his testes. They no longer resembled overripe grapefruits and while it still hurt to walk he started to turn the corner on day four of his post ass-kicking beat down. He popped two pain pills, his stash getting low, and trudged towards the bathroom.

His nose, destined to be crooked for the rest of his life, was heavily taped, and the impacted blood-snot mucus began breaking up. He could wheeze a little, producing an inadvertent train whistle as a bonus. It didn't hurt to cough or laugh or breathe so much and his lips deflated from full and pouty to white boy thin. His eyes still crackled with a vibrant red and the gash on his head had scabbed enough to become itchy and annoying.

James stared in the mirror running his tongue over the gum line where a tooth once resided. It was smooth and slimy and he vowed to floss more often to ensure keeping the rest of his chicklets. He pulled back his upper lip, knowing he resembled a redneck hillbilly, but decided to be positive. It made him look tough, or so he thought, and at least it wasn't a front one. But when asked about the missing tooth he needed a good story. Maybe he used to play semi-pro hockey or lost it ski jumping in the Alps. Maybe he lost it working as a secret agent.

The front door rang twice and then swung open.

"Hello," a female called out.

"In the bathroom," said James. "Be there in a sec."

Melinda walked in with a brown paper grocery bag and set it on the floor. Her hair was pulled back in a bun and she wore white sneakers, no socks, and a yellow top.

"How you feeling today Mr. Horton?" she asked as James limped into the living room dabbing his eyes with a tissue.

He grinned. "Much much better. Check it out. I can breathe through my nose again."

"It's a start," she said, opening the bag and removing a gallon of orange juice. "I'll make you a sandwich." She threw him a film case with a few stinky buds of weed in it. "Teddy wanted me to give you this."

James reached for it slowly and it bounced off the heel of his hand, careening into a corner where a dust bunny lived. She retrieved it, handing it to him. He opened it and smelled the skunk trapped inside, handing it back. "I'm good. But I'll take some more OxyContin if you have it. And would you please tell my friend Teddy he doesn't need to send you over here anymore. I'm fine. I'm really fine."

Melinda was the girlfriend of Teddy's oldest son and studied dental hygiene at the local college. She was a big girl, not fat or heavy big, just big boned big, standing over six feet tall. Teddy's son was five foot six, short like his dad. They were an odd looking pair.

"Why don't you tell him yourself?" she said. "I can see your phone on the end of the couch."

"He won't take my calls right now."

"How come?"

"He uh, fears the phones might be bugged."

Melinda shook her head. "I'll tell him Mr. Horton." She disappeared into the kitchen.

Since finding James semi-unconscious Teddy had become persona non grata around the Horton residence. He asked repeatedly if the goon squad had mentioned his name or had any idea of his involvement in collecting information. More importantly, he was concerned about the ill-advised photos of Misty and Breg briefly in his possession. James reassured his friend nobody had mentioned him but Teddy didn't seem very reassured.

Melinda helped with the dishes and folded the laundry in the dryer. He watched her work, admiring her without her knowledge, and for a reason he couldn't identify, she reminded him of Dee. Maybe it was the way she wound his clean socks into a ball or the way she rinsed off the plates before putting them in the dishwasher. Maybe it was the color of her hair or the way she ignored him when he asked stupid questions. Maybe, because aside from paying a hooker mucho dinero to spend an hour with him and just talk, Melinda was the only female companionship he'd known longer than his lonely soul cared to remember.

She didn't know the full story of why she went to a stranger's house to help out but she did it. As would have Dee. And in that moment James knew it was time. It was more than time. It was over time. If the wifey wasn't coming to him, then he would go to the wifey. He'd be the knight in shining armor every girl dreams of, every woman wants. He popped another pain pill, feeling good, and fantasized about the fairytale about to be created. Melinda caught him staring.

"Why are you looking at me like that?" she said, blowing away a rogue strand of hair that escaped from the bun.

"You remind me of somebody is all," he said, smiling big, smiling creepy.

"Alrighty then. I think I'm done here today."

"Melinda wait." James took two twenty-dollar bills from his wallet. "I want you to have this. And you don't need to come back again. Thank you so much for everything. You're very kind. So very kind."

"I hope you feel better Mr. Horton," she said, pocketing the cash. "Really, I do. Take care of that face."

"Can I ask you one last thing?"

She searched her purse for the car keys. "I guess."

"How much do you think it would cost to rent a horse for the day? Like a white stallion."

"What?"

"You know, the knight in shining armor on a white horse thing. From the books and the movies. When I go win back Dee."

She walked towards the door. "I'll tell Teddy maybe he should send somebody else tomorrow. I'll mention the pain pills but you need to be careful Mr. Horton. You really should go see a doctor." She left the house and he yelled after her, "I told you before, I don't have any health insurance." He waved his hand in the air as if she couldn't possibly understand.

James ate his tuna sandwich chewing gingerly on the left side of his mouth. Sports talk played on the radio and he debated calling the show to express his concern with the latest Yankees trade. He set his plate in the sink and saw a black Dodge Charger sitting outside his house again, on the far side of the cul-de-sac near a pine tree with a dead limb that needed a trimming. He had no idea how long they'd been there or how long they'd stay.

He snapped a picture of the car on his phone hoping they didn't notice, or if they did, thought he was trying to be funny. Breg's goon squad lived up to their word in giving him a week. They were real men of honor, a true asset to the nobility of thumb breakers around the world. Only a few days were left before it was time to leave. And James intended to use every one of them.

32

T he closet in the master bedroom had heavy mirror doors, the kind that slid. The one on the right always slipped off the track and James pulled back the other, gripping a shelf for support, reaching for something buried under a heap of clothes not worn since embarking on a health kick four years earlier. He cursed his *skinny* clothes, knowing those days were over, and sifted through them. His knees cracked twice and his back cracked once as he stood and carried a small wooden box in the living room clutching his ribs.

The keepsake had been a gift from his parents on his thirteenth birthday. His mother told him it was hand carved by Native Americans and was over a century old. But upon inspecting the box with a magnifying glass he discovered a faded stamp on the bottom that read MADE IN CHINA. The whole charade added to its storytelling appeal.

He opened it, running his hand through a pile of quarters, nickels, and dimes encased in clear plastic shells. He searched for one item in particular, his favorite. It was an 1877 Morgan Silver Dollar listed in good condition. James delved into the hobby of coin collecting during high school and accumulated a respectable amateur collection. But once they bought the house any money he managed to save for a rare proof or uncirculated coin set always went towards something that needed to be fixed, or in the middle class status of the Hortons, needed to be upgraded.

James stared at the coin, inspecting the intricate design of the relief and attention to detail. He admired the serious face of Lady Liberty, her stoic beauty, and her uplifting message of freedom and equality. The idea inspired him as a patriot and made him want to eat apple pie, vote, say hi to the neighbors, milk a cow, go to church, and play baseball. Yet when he thought of William Breg and his band of piggish thieves it made him angry; angry enough to blow a whiff of oxygen into his beaten body and keep a nearly dying flame flickering with life.

He twisted the coin in his hands and wondered about the latest value before dropping it back in the box, adding his treasured Rolex. He rubbed the top to say good-bye and placed it in the trunk of his car near some family photos. Come first thing in the morning, he'd take his collection to a pawn shop.

A map of the east coast was spread over the couch and to the left were his bills and financial statements. To the right was a book of matches and an eight ounce aluminum tin of lighter fluid. James lifted a fifth of bourbon to his lips and swallowed his last three pain pills, the best drugs he'd ever known.

Two places were circled on the map with a black magic marker. The first was a small town in northern Virginia, the second was White Plains, New York. He removed a plaid collared shirt he'd worn at the office for years and threw it on the floor, sprinkling it with lighter fluid. Next were his socks and pants. It approached four in the morning as James struck a match and sparked the last smoke of his pack.

He sat on the couch, droopy but awake, daydreaming. It was the same dream he'd experienced countless times before, the one where he's eighteen again, a high school senior, a youthful blank slate ahead of him. Dr. Novak concluded it was indicative of a classic midlife crisis, representing his fear of impending death and the realization that time is speeding up in addition to running out. James disagreed. He only wanted to fix everything, to wash away the coulda, woulda, shoulda that plagued him; to wash away the lost opportunities of *if only*. He took another drink and flicked the cigarette on his clothes, glancing at the map one last time.

The corner near the sliding glass door burned first. He contemplated the fire extinguisher under the sink and the timeframe to grab it but his skin was already warm, the process underway. The room glowed, then radiated, then overpowered as the flames ate the wall like a tiger assaulting its prey, flashing across the ceiling in a chain reaction of combustion. He walked to the door and waited until he needn't wait any longer. His body was loose, his mind even looser.

James sauntered over to the neighbor's house as if picking up a date for the dance. He tried playing the part of a frantic homeowner, a part he had no business playing, and knocked on the door with the force of an unmotivated salesman. He lingered on the steps and rang the doorbell once before a light flipped on and the widow Myers appeared in her granny gown, frowning and pissy. She sniffed, smelling the smoke the instant she opened the door, and screamed, "My house! My house!" while the fire growled in the quiet night air. She limped with her cane towards the garden hose and doused her cedar plank siding, yelling at James to dial 911.

The fire engines marched down the street in full regalia with sirens blaring and red lights flashing as neighbors flocked to witness the awesome display of Mother Nature flexing her muscles. People snapped pictures and recorded videos, documenting the spectacle with excitement. James stood alone in his tighty whities straining to appear upset to the outside world but completely at peace inside. He looked around for the black Dodge Charger but was unable to find it.

"Is anybody else in the house?" asked the fire chief after barking orders to his men.

"No. Just me," said James in a soft voice. "The house is empty."

The fire ripped through the home like a pile of dry kindling, the beams whining and hissing. The power of the flame was humbling and with a fifteen minute head start the structure was doomed.

"There isn't too much we can do," the fire chief said. "No sense in risking the safety of my men. We'll water the area down for the safety of your neighbors, try to keep it contained." He unbuckled the strap on his helmet. "I'm sorry. She's a goner."

James hung his head and focused on manufacturing a single solitary tear. But the ducts were bone dry. The fire chief threw a blanket around his shoulders.

"You should go sit somewhere safe. The best thing you can do is try and stay out of our way."

The cul-de-sac turned into a brightly lit parking lot with the arrival of three local news teams. Hoses pumped full of high pressurized water littered the ground while the firemen valiantly battled the blaze. The heat was intense, even from far away, and James was in awe of the reality TV show unfolding.

An orange glimmer reflected off his eyes as the 2,000 square foot abode representing everything he'd grown to resent vanished one crumbling section at a time.

The fire reduced the Horton's quarter acre lot to a smoldering pile of burnt rubble. The sun changed the sky from black to purple to blue and the bystanders dispersed back to their dens in preparation for the work day. The show was over, the energy evaporated. All three news teams departed after getting their sound bites and photo ops and James wandered around with the blanket speaking to a myriad of investigators.

A small white car pulled onto the scene while the firefighters packed up their gear. It had a logo of a red circle inside a yellow circle inside a green one, surrounded by violet stars. Out stepped a very attractive young black woman wearing a gray pant suit sculpted to her body. She had thick black glasses shielding her brown eyes with the word Prada decorating the side and she carried a clipboard.

"Are you a Mr. James Horton?" she said, offering a friendly professional smile. Her teeth were super white, super straight, and her eyebrows shrank together when she looked closer at his face. "Oh my God. What happened to you? Did you have an accident or something?"

"Pretty much," he said, combing his hair with a hand. "Something like that anyway."

For the first time all morning he became self-aware, embarrassed by standing around mostly naked. He sucked in his gut and rearranged the blanket to cover his burgeoning man breasts, praying no skid marks or pee stains were present on his undies.

"My name is Debra Sands. I'm an adjuster with Four Star Insurance Company."

"Nice to meet you Ms. Sands."

"We're a subsidiary of a subsidiary of a branch of our parent company. I know you've heard of us. You've had us for quite some time. I'm sure you have seen our commercial."

James recognized the logo and said, "Oh, Four Star. Right. The one with the dog doing a trick for the mother whose cooking dinner, where he rolls over and gets a treat. And the father, yeah, the father is building a swing set for the kids, they're handing him tools, drinking lemonade, and then wham; the hot water tank explodes. Blows out the side of their house. Great special effects."

"That's the one."

"Whatever happened to the grandmother? She was knitting a scarf and sitting in the rocking chair near the window."

Debra Sands handed him her business card. "We sell life insurance too."

The gray wool blanket was itchy but he pulled it around him tighter. "How did you get here so fast? How did you know about the fire so quickly?"

"That's what we do Mr. Horton. We're the experts." She clicked her ball-point pen several times in succession. "Can you tell me what happened?"

James walked her to where the garage used to be, stepping in an ashy paste that coated the driveway. He sold his story one more time with conviction.

"I think I feel asleep with a cigarette in my hand," he said. "Last thing I remember was watching TV."

"A cigarette huh?"

"Yeah, nasty habit. Gross, I know. I'm trying to quit. Been using those hypnosis tapes you can get at the library for free?"

"Were you drinking at all?"

"Not really. Only apple juice. Maybe one beer. Perhaps a glass of wine. Mostly water. But as you mentioned, about my appearance. I was in a bike accident earlier this week. I crashed into an illegally parked car driven by an illegal. Guy didn't even have a license. I'm on pain meds. They make me groggy."

"So the car was parked or somebody was driving it?" she said.

"Everything happened so fast. I'm lucky I didn't choke to death on the smoke. All I can say Ms. Sands is thank God for the person who invented smoke detectors."

As the bullshit flowed from his lips, the top one still healing, he inhaled her body through her clothes. James noticed her womanly curves, her sensual skin, and could smell her lotion. Was it green apple? Maybe honeydew melon? Dee used to wear something like that. Was it peach? His mind wandered, an erotic memory of his wife creeping in, and he forgot what he was saying. He felt something move in his underwear and looked down, staring at a mid-sized chubby.

"Mr. Horton? Hello? Mr. Horton?" she said, touching his shoulder before catching a glimpse of his mini-bulge.

He spun around and she lunged back. They retired to separate corners like two boxers in between rounds of a prize fight. When they met again he tried to apologize.

"I'm so sorry about that. I've been taking these pills, well, not those kind of pills, at least not recently, but—"

"Can you tell me about the assets inside?" she said, directing her attention far over the top of his head. "Did you keep a list of valuables along with their serial numbers, purchase dates, warranties, and prices? Maybe some pictures. Do you have any receipts?"

He laughed, tasted his breath, and didn't laugh again.

"Did I say something funny?"

"No. I mean yes. I mean people really do that? They write down serial numbers and save them?"

"Of course," she said.

"But wouldn't they just get burned up in the fire?"

She removed her glasses, cleaned one lens with a tissue, and put them back on. "Some people have safes. Fire proof ones for important documents. They're pretty cheap, and quite common."

"Oh, yeah, right. Safes. Makes sense." He leaned against her car. "I don't have any of that stuff Ms. Sands. It was kind of empty inside. I'm in the process of a complete home makeover for when my wife comes back."

"Where is Mrs. Horton? I see her listed on the policy."

"On vacation. It's like a work vacation actually. But with the kids. We're going to give the house a face-lift, spruce it up a bit. New windows, new stove. Paint the walls. I'm having all the popcorn removed from the ceilings and thinking about putting a low flow toilet in the upstairs bathroom. This is our dream house. We love it here." He shook his head and sighed. "I don't know how I'll tell her. She's going to be devastated. Will you guys cover therapy sessions to help her cope with the loss?"

"We're not that kind of insurance company Mr. Horton. I think you have us confused with somebody else."

James continued rambling, talking too much as most men do in the presence of attractive women, when the black Dodge Charger entered the neighborhood. It parked on the street near a neighbor's mailbox and flashed its lights. He knew Marty and George were watching, noting the time, the hour-glass draining. They revved the engine and flashed the lights again.

"You know Ms. Sands. There is one thing I forgot to mention. For the past week I've noticed a strange car hanging around the area. It was never here before. I'm not saying they had anything to do with it, because they probably didn't. But the timing and their presence in this small quiet neighborhood does seem a bit odd. I was thinking about calling the police. It may be worth looking into."

She wrote down something on the clipboard and nodded. "Maybe."

He smiled at the goons and waved. They flashed the lights one final time before driving away.

"I have a picture of the car on my cell phone," he said. "I think you can make out the plate."

The sound of rush hour traffic on the main road intensified. The widow Myers, still in her granny gown, shut off the sprinklers and wound up the hose. James looked at the large open space surrounding his driveway and thought of Four Star's stupid commercial. He felt hungry and exhausted and was jonesing for coffee as a hangover settled in. He contemplated napping in his car but it was time to flee the peninsula. He had a long drive ahead of him.

CHAPTER

33

A hard breeze jostled his car as he drove on the highway. The clouds shifted fast and the few times they separated the sun was at the precise angle to be blinding. James squirted the windshield washer fluid to remove the dotted cream cheese shmear of bug guts but spread them out even further. He'd been behind the wheel for six hours and felt sluggish from a belly full of junk food and the omnipresent heat, crashing from a mid-afternoon caffeine buzz. To conserve on fuel he resisted the pleasure of air conditioning and the car radio had already grown stale. The miles ticked by slowly on his sojourn to the north.

He passed mile marker 181 coming off an on-ramp and spotted what seemed to be his umpteenth hitchhiker of the day. James could hear it. Like she was sitting right next to him, he could hear his mother's words, her stern lecture about the danger of picking up strangers. But with three more hours until bunkering down for the night he couldn't resist.

"Where you headed?" he asked a man about ten years his junior. The man sank into the passenger seat catching his breath from the jog up to the car. He wore baggy camouflage shorts and threw a large brown duffle bag in the back seat.

"Canada."

"Canada, eh?" said James, a nervous little laugh. "What brings you there?"

"Got anything to eat?"

James handed him the bag of beef jerky he'd been working on and repeated the question, pressing the gas as a tractor trailer raced by.

"Don't know. Cept that I've never been there."

"Wow," said James. "Flying by the seat of your pants. Exploring the world. I like that." He put on the cruise control and lit a smoke with the car lighter.

"No. I have my reasons."

"Well, we've got time on our hands if you care to elaborate. Just the road ahead of us."

The hitchhiker didn't speak, diving into the beef jerky. He had dirty blonde sideburns and a black tattoo in place of a wedding ring. He smelled of campfire smoke and bug spray.

James turned on the radio and asked more questions but didn't get a response. Then, without a warning, the hitchhiker unbuckled his seatbelt, sliding back towards the door. He coughed up a lugey and hocked it out the window. "Mister, you ever put a cat in the microwave and watch it explode?"

"What?" said James, swallowing, pretending not to hear. He tapped the brake and merged into the slow lane, debating how fast he could grab the pepper spray. The hitchhiker stared at him and made a low guttural sound of, "Meow, meow." James thought of driving off the road to hit a tree or a pole and launch the unbuckled freakoid through the windshield.

Laughter erupted from his co-pilot. It was coarse and loud. "I got you man," he said, smacking his leg. "I got you big time. Ah shit, you should have seen your face. I thought you might cry. Damn that was funny."

"What the fuck?" said James, tapping the brake some more. "What the fuck dude?"

"I'll admit, it's a little twisted, but most people that pick us up think we're deranged or something. That's the rap on us hitchhikers, ain't it? Like we're all fucking serial killers." He laughed again. "Not sure why you people pick us up in the first place. But it got your heart pumping, didn't it? Now you got a story to tell your friends."

James loosened his death grip on the wheel. "I picked you up because I was bored. On the verge of falling asleep. Not for a goddamn story."

"And I do appreciate it brother. Praise the Lord. Amen. The name is Alex. I'm going to Canada to visit my daughter." He stuck out his hand. James hesitated, observing the residual grease from the beef jerky, then relented.

"What's your name anyway?" said Alex.

"You can just call me Bond"

"Like the guy from the movies?"

"It's a nickname. I'd rather not talk about it."

"Okay, Bond. Whatever floats your boat." He bummed one of James' cigarettes. "I haven't seen my daughter in a couple years. She lives in Montreal last time I knew."

James hit the windshield washer fluid again. More bug guts. He needed new wipers.

"See, I lost my wife a few years back," said Alex. "She got sick. Medical bills broke me. Tore me a new one. Some shit about a pre-existing condition. I dunno. Never could get a straight answer. I was driving rigs on the west coast at the time. Started gambling, trying to get it back, trying the only thing I knew to make big money fast. Won some in the beginning but then, you know, it didn't last. Now I can't stop. Cannot stop. No matter what. Begged and lied to keep it going. Even stole some shit. Ain't proud about that. Believe me. Lost it all brother. I'll do anything for money. Then I gamble it all away. Can't keep it. It's never enough."

"I'm sorry to hear about your wife Alex. When did it happen?"

"Goin' on eleven years now."

"Eleven years?" said James, looking at him sideways. "And you still can't stop gambling?"

"Nope. I know it's insane, that's what you're thinking. Right? This guy's off his fucking rocker. But unless you're in my shoes, you wouldn't understand. It's not an obsession or addiction. That's what people think. That's what they like to tell you. But what the hell do they know? It's kinda hard to explain. It's like it's all I got. You see, there ain't nothing else for me. Ain't nothing left. Win or lose, gambling is what I do. It's who I am."

A blue sign on the highway stated gas and food were fifteen miles ahead. James glanced at the odometer and did the math. He stopped asking questions and squished up against the door, his arm hanging on the frame as the wind rushed by. Alex polished off the remaining beef jerky, crumpled up the bag, and let it fall on the floor. He licked his fingers and wiped them on his shorts.

"Got anything to drink?" he asked.

"No."

"It's alright, it's okay. I'll manage." His voice changed. It became softer with a tinge of self-pity. He seemed younger for some reason. "Now listen Mr. Bond. Speaking of money, I'm kinda short right now. And seeing as you and I are kinda like good friends, I was hoping to borrow some."

"Are you kidding? I met you ten minutes ago. You told me you gamble everything away."

"That's true. But I didn't get to finish. You see, sometimes I win. I win big. And I got a sneaky feeling I'm gonna win big at that casino in Montreal. I had a vision about black eight coming up on the roulette table. It's gonna hit for sure. I promise to pay you back every penny. With interest. Cross my heart Mr. Bond."

James didn't respond, humming along to the radio.

"Alright," said Alex. "I get it. You're skeptical. But how about this? And think it over first before you decide. I'll take fifty bucks for a handy."

"A what?" said James, passing a minivan.

"You know, a handy."

"What the hell is a handy?"

"A little tug tug on your partner. A medicinal release to help you relax down there. It'll help take your mind off things."

James rubbed his eyes and debated jumping from the car into on-coming traffic. "I think I'll pass Alex. I'm not really into the whole man meat homo thing."

"A handy don't make you gay Mr. Bond. It's therapeutic. Like a massage."

The next exit couldn't come fast enough. James sped for the first time on the trip and had a policeman pulled him over, he'd welcome a ticket.

They arrived at the gas station and he handed Alex a twenty-dollar bill. Painted on a cinder block wall of the mom and pop enterprise was a mural of a shark wearing sunglasses, eating a taco under a blinking Tecate beer sign. The shark said, "Muy delicioso!" and the day's special was only five bucks.

"Can you grab me a pack of smokes while I fill the tank?" said James.

"I'm your man."

"And get yourself a taco while you're in there."

"Thanks Mr. Bond."

The second Alex entered the store he jammed the car in gear, leaving the brown duffle bag next to a gas pump. It was the best twenty dollars he ever spent.

He drove until the murky light of dusk settled in as the temperature cooled with the humidity taking a rare hiatus. He thought about what Alex said regarding money. "Can't keep it. It's never enough." James deemed the man a fool, an ignoramus, but felt something stir inside him, felt something ring true. How foolish was *he*? How close was *he* to becoming like Alex one day? If things didn't get better in the next eleven years or things got even worse, would he ever stoop to offer some dude a handy? Would he still drone on about Trustworth Bank and how they screwed him, stuck in a perilous state of mind, never moving forward? Would that become his identity?

Money. The switch had been flipped and his head hurt. He wanted to hit the off button and leap from the merry-go-round to make it stop. The burden had become so tiresome for James. He didn't want to think about it ever again but couldn't think of anything else. He hated money. Absolutely hated it. Yet he loved it. Absolutely loved it. And the only reason he hated it was because he didn't have it. It was a non-negotiable necessity, like oxygen. And he needed it. Worst of all, he once had it.

He flicked on the low beams and noticed the lines of the road for the first time in thirty minutes with no recollection of driving. James was happy to be heading north. The Horton clan had a good run in Florida but it was time to move on, like a hunter-gatherer, to plow new fields. He reflected on his childhood and concentrated on the aspects of New York he enjoyed growing up: apple picking in the fall, skiing in the winter, hiking in the Adirondack mountains, the smell of spring as flowers bloomed and life renewed itself. Change is necessary. Change is good. He convinced himself to believe that.

A light appeared on the dashboard somewhere in the Carolinas. The gas tank was critically low. Ten more miles, maybe twelve, and he'd be pushing. Gas was selling for over three dollars a gallon and climbing each month with no end in sight. It hurt to fill up and as he opened his wallet perhaps Alex was correct. There was never enough. That was the purpose in visiting Frank Cally. Money always seemed the purpose for everything.

Bars covered the windows of his motel room and guests had the option of renting by the hour. Room sixteen was funkified, combining a unique blend of wet carpet and mystery odor that lacked a proper name. He endured an icy shower and dressed in blue jeans and a long sleeved shirt, pulling his socks all the way up. He threw the always disgusting comforter on the floor and avoided thinking about the bed bugs and dust mites sharing the place. The blood stains, fecal stains, semen and urine stains were to be ignored. He fluffed the cardboard pillows and clicked on the console TV.

James opened the letter from Frank Cally, the one he'd confiscated from William Breg's house while snooping around the cigar room. He read it for the fiftieth time. The letter was four months old and written in proper cursive. Frank Cally thanked his long time BFF for their spontaneous three week jaunt around the Mediterranean and stated what a brilliant idea it was to take the wives this time and not the girlfriends. With his uber busy schedule of philanthropy and civic duty, "it was nice to get away from the chaos for a spell." James wanted to puke. He imagined what Frank Cally looked like. Would he be handsome, tanned, and debonair like Breg? Would he have aged beautifully as a product of living the good life, the stress free life? The answer undoubtedly had to be yes.

An energetic preacher occupied the television and bellowed away, demanding his flock dig deep in their pockets, deeper than deep, and give generously to the Lord. He commanded it. He demanded it. He expected it. And as he paced the stage sweating in a frenzy and pimping out the Lord he stopped his bullying words only once. He needed to wet his throat in order to continue.

James felt sleep overtaking him, seducing him, washing over his sore and aching body. The TV played until the screen went fuzzy, the preacher relentless in his message. There was no escape. Money. The true blood of man. The God of most people. Nobody in the world can breathe without it.

CHAPTER

34

A tow truck backfired in the parking lot mimicking a shotgun and woke James immediately. He got dressed fast and while brushing his teeth a cereal jingle played on TV. The catchy upbeat tune would be stuck in his head for the rest of the day. Honey Nut Cheerios, his fourth favorite cereal. He sang it out loud, over and over, and thought of his kids. It would be another week before he rolled into New York. He wanted his wounds to fully heal. He wanted to dry out. He wanted a bowl of cereal.

He traveled the back roads in the heart of the Deep South breaking around noon for the best soul food meal of his life. It rained off and on, mostly a light drizzle, and the sky was an infinite gray. But he didn't mind. A full night's sleep without the aid of pain pills nourished his body.

James drove along winding roads that cut through swaths of dense forest and there were fields of tobacco, peanuts, and corn. He saw farm houses with tall red barns and absent were the billboards so prevalent on the highway, the ones advertising country smoked hams or stating VIRGINIA IS FOR LOVERS! He drove over covered bridges and pristine lakes, fishing hole ponds and colorful mountains. The state was beautiful. He'd never really noticed, the two times passing through it.

Fresh air rushed through the car swirling cigarette ash as James became focused with his destination closing in. He breathed heavy, the seatbelt expanding across his chest, and positively visualized how the afternoon would unfold. It was James Horton's world doggonit and everyone else was just visiting. That's what one of his self-help books said anyway. Or maybe it was Dr.

Novak. He could have heard it on the radio or saw it on TV. It didn't matter. He needed to believe it.

He touched the brakes of the Corolla and rounded a bend, coming across a planation style estate with a white house and a grain silo fifty yards back to the left. There were horses grazing in a field alongside some companion goats and a pasture of cows. A wooden fence, weathered to a dusty brown, enclosed the entire perimeter except for the driveway which had an arching metal structure above the entrance but no name. James checked the directions and looked at his map. It was the first house he'd seen in twenty minutes. It was the house of somebody who didn't want to be found, the house of somebody who longed to disappear.

Two weeks after the bank bonuses had been issued Frank Cally skipped town, relocating from Orlando, his home of two decades. James drove by his mansion several times and the eight-bedroom Colonial sat vacant and untouched, still without a FOR SALE sign on it. The manor appeared well maintained and ready for a gallant return when its owner was done hiding out.

Frank Jefferson Cally, the youngest of three boys, was raised outside Boston to a family rumored to have bloodlines linked to the *Mayflower*. The articles James managed to find, and the ones Teddy discovered for him before they broke up, were that of a hardcore old school conservative who would karate chop his mother for an extra buck. His nickname in college was Callous Cally. It was even printed in the yearbook next to his hobbies of fly fishing, moose hunting, and traveling abroad. James had to admit, the former CFO's reputation intimidated him.

Frank was the fraternity brother of William Breg and the two men bonded instantly during their hell week together of pledging. They'd run the finances at Trustworth Bank for over fifteen years and were labeled The Wonder Twins, the extra-terrestrials from the *Justice League*. But rather than utilize their superpowers to mutate into a bucket of water or block of ice, they transformed into money making machines.

James parked the car in a tobacco field opposite the driveway and uncovered the latch of the visor mirror. His reflection was still unsightly and the dark purple bruising had lightened to a bluish green. He smiled. The missing tooth was a blessing. He counted, "One Mississippi, two Mississippi," and gripped his nose, twisting, biting down on a pen.

The spigot opened with a warm salty drip trickling into his mouth followed by a stream. The blood pooled in his palm and he dabbed it over his face, allowing the war paint to leak onto his clothes. It took ten minutes and a stack of napkins to turn the spigot off.

He banged on a door knocker in the shape of a rooster. The house was silent. He banged it again louder and reminded himself to act like he was in pain. A spider plant hung next to a window and he peeked inside, cupping his eyes, when a deadbolt slid and the door cracked open.

"Can I help you?" asked an elderly woman wearing a flour sprinkled apron overtop a beige dress.

James limped towards her, grunting.

"Excuse me ma'am," he said in a nasally voice, holding his nose. "My name is David Williams. I'm sorry to bother you but I've had a slight accident. My car blew a tire and I smashed into a ditch. Could I use your phone to call an ambulance?"

She scanned his face noticing the bruises and blood. "Goodness Lord," she said, swinging open the door and grabbing him around the waist while shouting, "Celia, can you come here please girl?"

A black woman dressed in blue hospital scrubs with matching sneakers greeted him. Celia helped James to the kitchen and removed an ice cube tray from the freezer. She popped the cubes in a towel and pressed it over his eye as the elderly woman blotted his face with a damp washcloth. The ladies were sweet and caring and it bothered him, making the job even harder.

"Did you say you hit your head? Where did you hit your head?" said Celia. "Show me where you hit your head."

James pointed to the front, the side, and the back; then rubbed his chest and said, "I hit it pretty hard on the steering wheel."

"I'll be right back," said Celia, running upstairs for bandages.

The elderly woman, who had to be Mrs. Cally, fussed with the washcloth and wiped his face some more. She began asking questions.

"Where did you crash your car? Was anybody else hurt? Where are you headed? Where did you come from?"

James observed her as she spoke and took note of her hazel eyes and narrow chin, her pronounced jaw line. She was thin, but a healthy thin, and he guessed her age thinking she must have been a real looker back in the day before the cruelty of time ravaged her. She helped him to the dining room table and propped his feet on a chair.

"I'll be right back," she said. "I'll fix you a nice warm plate." She ventured off to the kitchen.

This could be it, he thought. *This could be my only window.*

The refrigerator opened and closed along with the oven and he dashed into the adjoining great room. It was empty. He moved quickly through the sun room, the living room, the atrium, and the study. All empty, all quiet. It wasn't until he wandered towards the back of the house near the laundry room that he heard something. He followed the noise with his hand glued to the pepper spray and like a policeman entering an unpredictable environment he moved forward slowly. His nostrils flared and his eyes were wide when he slipped into an opening of a doorway leading to a converted bedroom.

"Frank Cally," he said. "Don't you fucking move."

The man obeyed. He didn't move or blink or flinch.

"Frank Cally," he repeated. He was about to tell him not to move again when he saw a chair. Not the cushy reclining chair the man sat in, but the one next to it, the wheelchair.

James tucked the pepper spray in his pocket and inched closer. The man still didn't move, didn't notice anyone there. He walked around to confront him directly and looked into a pair of hollow eyes. He waved a hand, brushing it against the hairs protruding from the tip of the man's nose, and snapped his fingers. James continued staring, the wrinkles of his forehead tight. Was this Callous Cally? It couldn't be. The man was catatonic.

Frank was slouched in the chair and had drool cascading from the corner of his mouth. The whole right side of his face was saggy. He was devoid of life and resembled a corpse except his eyes were open, fixated on the TV as if it were the only thing he'd ever known, yet he wasn't watching it either. James couldn't stop staring and waved his hand again. He flipped Frank the bird, turned it upside down, then sideways, and rested it on the bridge of his nose, pressing into the skin. He flicked him twice on the forehead and left a small red mark.

The drool festered in a pool of white foam and bubbled with each labored breath. James was disgusted but couldn't turn away. He pulled a tissue from the box and said, "Uh, that's so nasty," as he wiped Frank's mouth with an outstretched arm. He threw it in a trash bin already filled with crumpled tissues and wanted to immediately wash his hands. Or use hand sanitizer.

You son of a bitch Cally, he thought. *You fucked me again.*

"Hello? Hello sir?" Celia's voice rang out.

He didn't answer, imagining the man in front of him to be an imposter. It had to be. Cally and Breg were the same age, the invincible Wonder Twins. And the one time James managed to get a glimpse of William Breg in person, one afternoon when he left the country club, Breg appeared fit, like he could run a marathon or climb Mount Kilimanjaro. He looked freaking good. And it made James despise him all the more.

"There you are," said Celia, holding a box of different sized bandages and the ice pack from the dining room.

"Oh there you are," said Mrs. Cally holding an overflowing plate of hot food.

They both smiled.

"I'm sorry," said James, sitting on a folding metal chair. "I felt disoriented and needed to stand. I still feel a little dizzy."

"It's alright," said Mrs. Cally. "I phoned for an ambulance. They'll be here shortly."

James picked at the food and felt obliged to eat as the two women stood above the stranger with the bruised bloody face. He couldn't believe it. He was embarrassed to be there.

"Is he okay?" said James, motioning to Frank. "What happened?"

"Celia, could you please fetch our guest a glass of sweet tea?" The women exchanged glances as she left the room.

"Unfortunately David, my husband Frank suffered a major stroke about a month ago. It was so sudden. He was in perfect health, planning a scuba diving trip to the Bahamas. He's a good man." She kissed him on the cheek, her eyes watering. "Such a very good man. And a kind man too. Hasn't missed a Sunday in church since the day we met. Sings in the choir. Always works the holiday food drive. He has an honorary plaque in the new Bible study wing we helped build. My name is on there as well." She kissed him again, this time on the head, and wiped his mouth. "We're dealing with this tragedy the best we can."

James felt sorry for her, for her loss. He could feel her love, sense her pain, and from what he could tell, Mrs. Cally deserved better. As for Frank, that was a different story. He knew the man was an all-star hypocrite among the pantheon of hypocrites who deflected his guilt through a façade of altruism. But he still felt bad for her.

He nibbled a piece of corn bread as the TV aired an episode of *I Love Lucy*.

"He seems so at peace," said James, lying.

"We're doing the best we can," Mrs. Cally repeated a little softer.

"Ma'am, would it be alright if I stayed with him until the ambulance arrived? I used to watch this show with my father when I was a kid. It was his favorite."

"I think he'd like that," she said, touching James on the hand. "I think he'd like that very much. The company may do him some good." She left the room. Celia never returned with the tea.

He set the plate on a shelf, threw the ice pack in the trash. Frank Cally was frail and colorless. His arms were like pixie sticks and his sunken face looked skeletal. The once powerful man no longer existed. "How is money helping you now Frank? What are you going to buy now?" whispered James. "Was stealing my money worth it?" He spotted Frank's watch. It was a Breitling. Very expensive. The fancy chronometer would demand a high price at any reputable pawn shop. He viewed his own watch, a Timex from Wal-Mart. Not so fancy. It costs forty bucks.

The room stunk of piss and soiled adult diapers, moth balls and cleaning solutions. It reeked of that most heinous stench with the Grim Reaper hovering and waiting. He remembered the stench of death from when his father got sick. It's truly unforgettable.

He flipped Frank the bird again feeling ashamed, feeling pathetic, unsure what to do. James wanted to slap him, punch him, kick him, spit on him and push his stupid wheelchair down a flight of stairs. It would be so easy. He thought of ripping that expensive watch off Cally's bone withered hand and robbing the place blind. His desire was strong and his motivation justified. But he couldn't. As much as he tried, the predatory nature of a shark or a lion wasn't in his DNA. He lacked the killer instinct. James Horton wasn't a closer. *There's got to be more.*

The audience laugh track vibrated through the speakers. It was the episode where Lucy crushes grapes with her bare feet in a wooden tub alongside an Italian lady and they wind up fighting. He'd seen that one before, thought it was funny. He looked at Frank. Poor rich Frank. Alive but dead. Wealthy but wasted.

The money debacle was over for the day and fate had ensured that Frank Cally had gotten his comeuppance, if James believed any of that. He left a thank-you note on the chair and snuck out a side door leading to one of the fields, the one with the horses, and crawled under a barb wired fence. He was off to New York. He was off to see his family.

35

James procrastinated in the car a block from Mary's house behind a maroon SUV with New Jersey plates. He snapped on a wad of nicotine gum the size of a clementine chewing like a cow. His stomach churned and he rubbed it, feeling it gurgle, hearing the bubble-guts erupt in mini explosions. Droplets of perspiration leaked through his shirt and his eyes were moist from plucking a stubborn nose hair. Clutched in his hand were a dozen red roses and a box of Godiva chocolates.

He walked up the sidewalk with his head down wearing tan pleated Dockers and a navy blue blazer, hoping he hadn't gone overboard with the samples of cologne from the mall. He breathed into his palm for a breath check but was unsure if that really worked, blasting his throat with a stinging spray of Binaca. His fingers shook when he pressed the orange doorbell and his mouth had already gone dry.

Since leaving Florida James had an erotic vision of exactly how his triumphant return would unfold. Inspired by either a shampoo commercial or a letter he'd read in *Penthouse*, Dee would answer the door wearing a low cut sundress with no panties or bra, her lips colored red, her hair blown back by an imaginary wind. She'd leap into his arms and wrap her legs around him, pulling him tight, saying how much she loved him, declaring how she couldn't live without him. They'd embrace passionately as he carried her upstairs like a new bride to make tender yet powerful love for days at a time until crippled with exhaustion.

When the door finally opened she smiled. It was a big warm smile accompanied by a giant hug and kiss on the cheek. His triumphant return was off to a positive start and would have been a thousand times better had it actually been Dee and not her mother.

"James," she said. "It's so good to see you. You look great. Come in. Come in. I can't believe you're here. I was just thinking about you."

"Thanks Mary," he said, masking his disappointment. "Good to see you too. Is Dee here?"

"Darn it, you just missed her. Left about an hour ago. She'll be home later tonight. Probably about supper time. Her and the kids went shopping and to the movies."

"Oh, I saw her car in the driveway so I figured, you know."

Mary glanced at Dee's car in the gravel driveway. "She must have gone with a girlfriend."

He entered a hallway cluttered with sneakers and the kids' knapsacks. A fan oscillated on top of a china cabinet as a fake fern swayed in the breeze near a stack of newspapers. A new Norman Rockwell print hung on the wall, the one with the little girl getting her bathing suit pulled off by a dog. He fumbled with the pack of nicotine gum in his pocket and avoided Mary's eyes.

She gave him another big hug and led him to the couch. "Please, sit down. So how are you James? How's Florida? How's everything going?"

"I apologize for showing up on your door step unannounced. I probably should have called first. I don't mean to bother you. I just thought.... I wanted it to be a surprise." He started to stand. "Maybe I should come back another time."

"Nonsense," she said. "You're here now. That's what counts. And I haven't seen my son-in-law in far too long. Stay put and I'll grab us a beer."

He wiped his sweaty forehead with the back of his sweaty hand and removed his sweaty blazer. They talked, pseudo style, engaging in one of those generic conversations James excelled in. They discussed the Yankees, the weather, and the latest political scandal. She mentioned the idea of getting a pet and he chimed in about the gas mileage of the new hybrid cars. She fixed him a sandwich and the issue of the vanishing lottery money remained buried in awkward chit chat.

James finished his beer and looked at his wrist. Time to say goodbye. Return in a couple hours.

"As always Mary, thank you for the hospitality. Please don't tell her I came though. Okay? I'll be back tonight and still want to make it a surprise. Maybe I could pick up a pizza from Fratelli's. Bring over some cannolis for the kids."

"Are you sure you don't want to stay for one more beer?" she said. "I can make you another sandwich."

"No thanks. I've got to run."

The corners of her mouth turned down. "James, there's something…. You see…. I think that…." She yanked on her necklace. "You know I love you. But there's something…." Her voice broke off again.

He stood and folded his jacket over an arm. "Are you alright?"

"I lied to you earlier," she said in a solemn tone. "There's something you should know."

"You? Lie? I find that hard to believe Mary."

"But I did."

"About what?"

"Dee."

"Is everything okay?" he asked. "She isn't sick is she?"

"No, no. Nothing like that. My daughter's healthy as a horse." She scooped a beer cap off the coffee table, pressing it into her thumb. "It's been a tough time for everybody you know. These last few years. The world sure is changing. That's what my Rudy used to say. I remember when I was in my fifties and I got a job working in the mayor's office. It was over on Eighth Street. I really liked that job. Back then you could get a loaf of bread and a gallon of milk for—"

"Mary," said James, holding up a hand. "What's going on?"

"Right." She fiddled with the beer cap some more. "I'm sorry, but Dee's been seeing somebody for the last couple weeks. That's the friend she's at the mall with. I thought you had the right to know. I didn't want to see you get blindsided."

He grinned, a disbelieving grin. "What are you talking about? Seeing somebody? We're not even divorced. Just going through a trial separation until I get back on my feet. It happens to couples all the time."

"She has a new friend. A special friend. They've been spending time together."

"You mean like a boyfriend?" he said, his jaw muscles grinding.

"He's a teacher at Samantha's school. They met at an open house for new students. He teaches social studies and has two kids of his own. She didn't mean for it to happen. She wasn't sure what was going on with you."

"So this is my fault?" He stepped closer and stared down at her. "Are you sure you got your facts straight? Are you and your daughter on the same page here?"

"I'm sorry."

He spun away with his hands on his hips and saw their family portrait above the fireplace; the one they'd used two years in a row for their Christmas cards. His eyes darted back to Mary. "If you're messing with me, for whatever reason, I don't appreciate this kind of shit. I really hope you're not messing with me. Are you messing with me?"

"Of course not. Why would I?"

"No. No way. No fucking way. I don't believe you."

"I'm sorry."

He swung his leg to the right and launched a terracotta pot against the wall, dumping soil on the ground. *I was too late. I waited too long.*

"James. Listen to me. It's going to be alright. Trust me when I tell you—"

"Trust you? Isn't that what you told me before? That I needed to give it time. That everything was going to be alright. Well Mary, I can honestly say that everything isn't going to be alright. Everything sucks. So please spare me one of your bullshit grandiose speeches."

"Don't go James. Let's talk about this. Can I get you another beer? Do you want another sandwich?"

She reached for his arm and he jumped back like a threatened snake, glaring at the home wrecking meddler. He whipped the flowers over a chair, scattering petals everywhere, and threw his blazer on the floor before storming outside.

Mary followed, stumping on the porch, waffling between rationalizing her daughter's behavior and offering her son-in-law words of encouragement. James heard none of it as he disappeared from view. The knight in shining armor had been reduced to a lowly court jester.

He drove around White Plains for the rest of the day without a clue where to go. His throat was scratchy from screaming and he feared a broken hand from punching the hood of the car. The image of another man mounting his wife occupied his fragile mind. Some dude sticking it to the mother of his kids, the light of his life. Some dude sticking it to him. It played out like a horror movie on an endless reel.

Without knowing what to do, how to act, or how to deal with the latest update of his own personal breaking news, James Horton did what James Horton did best. A liquor store beckoned him offering the mind numbing emotional escape he relied upon. It's what he did. It's what he'd become. One day it's all he may have left.

36

The manager of the Gateway Motel ripped off the DO NOT DIS-TURB sign hanging on the door and handed it to his assistant. He swiped a magnetic card, entering the room. Both men covered their nose as the smell of vomit was strong. The curtains were taped together and empty bottles lined the dresser, table, and nightstand. Makeshift ashtrays were everywhere.

James leaned against the headboard of the bed with the glow of a cigarette illuminating his face. He wore checkered boxer shorts and different colored socks, watching the two figures navigate the room in search of the lamps, trying to screw the bulbs back in. He squinted when the lights flickered on as a man of Indian descent yelled, "Get out!" He pointed at James and flailed his arms. "You get out right now!" The manager pulled the curtains apart, tearing a long strand. "You will pay for this," he said. "Khalid, get rid of these bottles right away."

James had sweaters on his teeth from not brushing in days and his breath was vile. He blew a smoke ring in the funky air. "Khalid, you touch any of my shit and we're going to have a problem. You don't have to listen to this miserable tyrant." He jumped from the bed and stood, his oafish frame domineering the room.

Khalid dropped a bottle of tequila as the manager yelled at them both. James grabbed his wallet and opened it, holding his dwindling reserve of cash. "This should do it," he said. "And could I get some fresh towels please? Tell room service an order of pancakes would be nice."

The manager counted the money and displayed two fingers. "There's enough here to cover yesterday and today. Then you're out. I don't care. People have been complaining. You're a filthy animal. You stink."

"There's enough there for at least three days Assid. Count it again."

"Damages cost."

"Oh fuck you," said James, sitting back down on the bed. "I already paid your ass for the cracked mirror and the piss stains on the mattress."

"No no no Mr. Horton. That is not enough. My room is full of garbage now. So go fuck you instead."

"No, fuck your mother Assid."

"No, you go fuck your mother Mr. Horton. Fuck your mother's mother."

"No, fuck your mother's mother's mother Assid."

"Tomorrow asshole, then you're out."

"Don't forget the towels," said James as the door slammed shut.

The sunlight was blinding and forced him to search for his sunglasses. He felt like a prisoner in a movie who'd just been released from the darkness of solitary confinement and it took ten full minutes to re-tape the curtains together.

He lay on the hard mattress and knew Assid's description was correct. James was a filthy animal, a lowly beast plowing the fields of misery. He was ashamed but didn't care. Four days holed up in a cheap room and he resembled a savage. A rug burn ran the length of his leg and bruises covered his chest. His left eye twitched.

He found his cell phone under some fast food wrappers and powered it back on. The green button blinked and there were five text messages plus eight voice mails. They were all from Dee. He set it down and waited but he'd already waited too long.

"James," she said when he called back. "Thank God you're alright."

"I'm alive anyway. If that's what you mean."

"I was worried sick. Are you okay?"

"Fan-fucking-tastic Dee. Couldn't be better. How are you on this amazingly wonderful day?"

"I'm serious."

"So am I," said James.

"Can we talk?"

"I'm not stopping you Benedict Arnold. Go ahead and blabber away. I hear the dating scene in New York is spectacular this time of year."

"Let's not do this on the phone."

"Why not?"

"Because we need to meet in person," she said.

"Do we?"

"My mother told me what happened. We really need to talk."

"Good ol' Mary." He found a bottle with a spit-line hanging in the bottom and held it above his outstretched tongue, getting less than a mouthful. He tried to sound stout but his voice quivered. "When?"

"Tomorrow at noon. At the diner on Gibson Street. The one where we take the kids for pie."

"Fine," he said hanging up, chucking the cheap plastic bottle at the ceiling. He set the alarm while he still could and figured a wake-up call seemed pointless.

James arrived two hours early to marinate on some pre-battle cocktails and picked at an overcooked cheeseburger. When Dee parked the minivan his heart fluttered like a teenager attending the prom. He watched her feed the meter and analyzed the way she walked, the outfit she wore, and her new sassy hairstyle. Her body looked amazing. He couldn't move his eyes. Had she gotten better looking? Taken a magic pill? She appeared to have traveled fifteen years into the past.

He tore the edges off a napkin and his legs bounced shaking the table. Dee walked down the aisle of strangers in slow motion as if in a music video. Everything he'd rehearsed since their phone call evacuated his mind. He didn't know if he should stay seated or stand. Would kowtowing be a sign of weakness?

"Hi," said Dee, smiling. "Thanks for meeting me."

James nodded and noticed the indentation from years of wear on her bare ring finger.

"This is kind of weird, huh?" she said.

"You think?"

"I'm not sure where to even begin."

"Don't ask me. This was your big idea," he said.

"I want you to know that none of this.... Wait. What happened to your tooth?"

He touched his gum. "It's nothing. I'll tell you later. So what did you want to say?"

Dee was efficient. She was concise. She explained her side of the story for the next forty minutes, at times wiping away tears. The teacher she'd been seeing was a friend, maybe more than a friend, she wasn't sure. She was confused and needed somebody to talk with. They were leaning on each other during tough times and "He was someone I could confide in," she said. "Unlike my mother as of late."

James listened while folding and refolding packets of sugar, tearing one open, wiping the crystals on the floor. He wanted to kiss her lips as she talked, hold her hands as they moved. Her skin was so smooth and her face so pretty. Was she like this all along? Where had he been?

When Dee handed him the baton to reply he signaled the waitress for another drink and cleared his throat. His ego was wounded and tough guy James felt the need to put on a persona of a man he was not.

"Well," she said. "Don't you have anything to say?"

"I burned the damn house down."

She leaned back as if somebody pushed her. "Come again?"

"That's right. You heard me. I burned it to the ground. That blood sucking hell hole is no longer in existence."

"Keep your voice down," she said. "For God's sake."

"Do you know why I did it?"

Her upper lip disappeared as did the lower. "I don't want to have this conversation anymore." She gathered her coat. "This was a mistake. I came here to talk. To have a rational civilized conversation like adults. To tell you how I feel and express what's going on in my life, to see if we have anything left. You just sit there like a tree, drinking whatever it is you're drinking, and then when it's your turn to share the first thing you tell me is this. I can see not a whole lot has changed."

He grabbed her forearm as she rose. "Alright, I'll be quiet. But do you know why I did it?"

"Because you have become mentally unstable over the last year."

"No, I did it for us." He crunched a celery stalk and stirred his drink.

212

"Wait a minute," said Dee. "Are you saying you burned down the house for me? So we could get back together."

"That's exactly what I'm saying."

"I'm not sure I follow. How is that going to help? You burned down our house with all of our stuff."

James tipped back his glass and took a long pull, smacking his lips. He grinned.

"Technically Dee, we didn't lose our stuff. I sold it about two months ago in a garage sale with Teddy and used the money to pay the bills so we could keep the damn house. But I did also try to kind of blackmail the CEO of Trustworth Bank who stole our money because—"

"Still? The bank thing?" she said, shaking her head. "Are you freaking kidding me?"

"What do you mean still the bank thing? I got about three grand and it seemed like a good idea at the time. You see, I rented this hooker, well technically she was an escort. Misty was her name and I think you would have liked her. She was a sweet kid. We didn't have sex, she was somebody I could confide in, just like your friend, but I had to use this sleazy photographer—"

"Stop it, just stop it," she said, sliding from the booth. "I don't want to hear any more of this insanity. You've completely lost your mind."

"Wait, I haven't told you about the other lowlife bank thieves I was able to take care of. The ones that robbed us of our lives."

Dee folded a scarf around her neck. "You think this is funny, don't you? You're enjoying this. It's all some big kind of joke for the macho James Horton. I came here to talk. And I wish you would."

"I'm simply trying to explain what happened, to be honest, that's all. Like you did, about my replacement."

"First off, Baron is none of your damn business. Second, so the house is really gone? You really did it?"

"It's a pile of ashes hun. But more importantly, the guy's name is Baron? Seriously? Let me guess. He lives in a castle in England, drives a Volvo, and has feudal serfs working the land."

"Why would you do something so dumb? Why James?"

He rubbed his fingers together. "For what else Dee? Money."

"You burned down our house, where we had a lot of good times and a lot of good memories, and maybe a future, for money? I'll entertain your ignorance. Enlighten me. Please."

"Do I have to spell it out for you? With the insurance money we're going to get we could start over. Fresh. All of us. A family again. We could get a new place, up here if you want. Your mother could even live with us. Maybe we can move to Europe. Or Canada. They have free health insurance there."

"You really don't know anything about how insurance works, do you?" said Dee. "No wonder I used to handle everything."

"What are you talking about? I've heard about this kind of stuff, seen it on TV. People are doing it all over the country. You know, the people that are getting foreclosed on and losing their homes. It's simple economics. It's common sense." He polished off his drink and accidentally swallowed an ice cube.

"Common sense huh? I didn't realize you'd become such an economic guru."

James coughed, massaging his throat, and coughed some more. "We pay the insurance company and when something bad happens they give us money to fix it. Simple as that. Easy peasy japa-fucking-neasy. Remember a few years ago when we got in that fender bender coming out of the movies? Samantha got sick from eating too much popcorn so we left early. And Teddy had a friend who could fix it for like a third of the price of the estimate. We pocketed the rest of the money. Do you remember?"

"You'll be lucky if you don't go to jail for this," she said. "Are you aware of that? Is that what you want? For Samantha and Cole to visit their father in jail?"

"I'm just saying that—"

"Well don't say anything. Do you know how upside down on that house we were? Do you even know how much money we owed?"

"Of course I do. I've been making the payments haven't I?"

"They just don't hand you a big fat check for what we paid and the money they do give you is contingent upon rebuilding on that site, over a period of time for what the house would be currently worth not to mention the private mortgage insurance and everything else. You won't be getting any money you can put in your pocket to move around the country or vacation. That's not how the policy works."

James' face went blank. He scratched his head like a dazed baboon.

"It seemed like such a good idea at the time," he said. "I mean I was taking a lot of pain pills for the near death beating I took from Breg's goon squad."

"So that's what happened to your tooth. For God's sake James, everything seems like a good idea when you're drunk and angry all the time. You need to go back to Florida and straighten this whole mess out before it gets worse. I'm serious."

"But it seemed like such a good idea at the time," he said again. "And besides, as far as Florida is concerned, I really can't go back."

"Why's that?"

"I'm not allowed."

"What do you mean you aren't allowed to go...." She pulled on her coat, throwing a purse over her shoulder. "You know what? I don't want to know why you can't go back to Florida. I'll make arrangements for you to see the kids while you're here."

He stretched out his arm to stop her but she walked right through it.

"Stop," he said, raising his voice. Forks and knives ceased moving and the diner grew quiet. "Are you sure it's not like getting in a fender bender? A tiny scratch on the quarter panel you can live with?"

She never turned around, never broke stride. He watched until the minivan vanished from sight.

James held court in the booth for the remainder of the afternoon minding his own business, until he didn't. He was ushered from the diner by two cooks, a waitress, and a manager with a ponytail. When he stumbled outside his car was straight ahead one block up the street. He looked left, then right. Eeny, meeny, miny, moe. James went right. It may as well have been left.

CHAPTER

37

"You think he's dead?" asked a policeman, removing his cap. Flakes of dry skin fell on his shoulder adding to the speckled dandruff. A bald patch was carved on the crown of his head and he wasn't a fat man but a few extra miles on the treadmill wouldn't have hurt.

"Let's find out," said his partner Nate. He stuck a black leather shoe on the vagrant's hip and pushed, rolling him over. He fanned his face stepping back. "He's breathing, that's for sure. Smells like a fucking brewery."

It was early morning and the park brimmed with joggers and bikers, speed walkers doing their weird little shimmy. A small black dog humped another small dog as the owners tried to untangle them, getting tangled in the leashes themselves, all the while holding their Starbucks high in an effort not to spill.

"Is this the same guy we found behind Valenti's Pub a few days ago?" Officer Nate asked. "The one passed out on the loading dock near the dumpster hugging a loaf of sourdough bread?"

Officer Ray Leonard, a veteran of twenty years, bent down. "Yeah, I think so. He looks kind of familiar. He's got that one missing tooth."

Nate joined him, gripping the man by the cheeks, turning his head. "You're right. That's definitely the guy that puked on your shoes."

Ray jabbed a night stick into his stomach. "Rise and shine sweetheart. It's check out time."

"Ahh," James cried, gripping his belly. "What the fuck?" He opened his eyes. Everything was cloudy and blurry as an unseasonal warm front swept through New York, confusing him. Was he on his front lawn? A golf course? Maybe he was in the backyard of William Breg's estate.

"Five more minutes mom," he said. "I promise I won't miss the bus this time." His pants were soaked and blotches of barbeque sauce decorated his shirt, dirt and grass clippings sticking to it. He shielded his eyes. The two men appeared as Manhattan skyscrapers standing above him, swaying with the wind.

Officer Ray pressed his night stick deeper into the pudgy flesh, holding it there. "Let's go smart- ass."

James coughed and spit up, wiping his mouth. He leaned on an elbow. "I need water."

They hoisted him up, pushing him forward. He nearly tripped before gaining his balance and walked two wobbly paces in front of them. His shirt was untucked and his dress shoes were replaced by Velcro strapped sneakers. The three of them walked at a leisurely pace as he heard the officers talking.

"I'm telling you this Nate. That kid comes home with another bad report card and I'm throwing every fucking video game in the house out the window," said Ray.

"Isn't that what you said last time your little Einstein came home with straight C's?"

"This time I mean it."

"You see, that's the problem right there," said Nate. "False threats. I bet you're the type of dad who threatens to count to three every time you want him to pick something up or clean his room. Hell, you probably even go two and a half, two and three quarters, but never quite get to three. Do you? And because you never get to three, your little guy knows it. He calls your bluff and does what he wants. Basically says screw you dad. You have to treat him like a perp Ray. You have to follow through. Otherwise nothing changes."

"Easy for you to say."

"Why don't you just crack his ass anyway? Slap the boy upside the head. He'll get the message real quick. That's how I learned," said Nate.

"Wish I could but the wife won't let me. We're taking a different new age approach. I'm supposed to count to ten and verbalize my anger in a non-threating manner."

"You see, right there, that's why I'm never having kids. It's always something."

"Yeah, well, you can't keep having abortions forever Nate."

"Go fuck yourself Ray."

They walked through a section of fresh cut lawn covered with acorns and dried leaves, the birds singing their mating songs. Pedestrians stopped the officers twice asking for directions and the second time James collapsed to one knee. His neck muscles stiffened as he opened his mouth and gagged. Nothing came up, but something came out. His underwear was layered with fudge.

How did it come to this? he asked himself, feeling a humiliation never thought possible. *How did I fall so far?* James stared at the ground thinking of his life, running his hand along blades of grass. He listened as people strolled by and caught snippets of their conversations. *Why can't I be normal like them?* He wanted to dig a hole and hide, or maybe even die. He wasn't sure anymore.

A night stick in the craw of his back nudged him along. "Keep it moving Nancy." James grimaced, stumbling once again.

The squad car was parked in a handicap spot and they pushed him against it, reading him his Miranda Rights as they cuffed him.

"Is this really necessary?" mumbled James, his chin kissing the metal roof.

"Shut up," the partners said in unison, like they'd rehearsed it, like a cop buddy show, and clamped the cuffs tighter. They spun him around.

"You sure you want to do this?" asked Nate.

"What? Why?" said Ray opening the back seat door. "What the hell do you mean?"

"I mean this guy smells like straight up shit. The motherfucker stinks. I think he shit his pants."

James closed his eyes bracing for the inevitable.

"Did you just shit your pants?" said Officer Ray, sniffing.

No answer.

"I asked you a question."

"I'm sorry. It was an accident. It slipped out on that last dry heave. My stomach is—"

"You son of a...." Officer Ray cracked him on the head dropping James to the ground. "Help me get him in."

"Come on, he's going to stink up the fucking car. Do you want to smell like shit all day?" said Officer Nate, looking at the bridge leading to a highway. "I planned on stopping by Vanessa's shop after lunch."

"You're pathetic Nate, you know that? Put your dick back in your pants. Roll down the window if you have to. Now stop bitching and help me get him in."

"Can't we just give him a ticket or something? It's not like he did anything serious."

"You see this asshole here," said Ray, pointing to a heap in the back seat. "He's been hanging around for about three or four days now, on our beat. We don't need that. He makes us look bad. I don't want to see his fat sorry face again. And I don't want another complaint. We already gave him a warning, didn't we? And it seems a simple ticket isn't getting through this bozo's head. Look at him. He's still drunk. Probably wouldn't even remember getting a ticket. Probably forgot about the one we gave him before. If your new little hussy don't like the way you smell, then what can I tell you. Put on some extra perfume or wash up at the station. You'll figure it out."

He peered over his shoulder as he backed up the car. "You've got to follow through with these perps Nate. We wouldn't want to give him a false threat, now would we? You've got to follow through."

Nate gave him the finger. James snored in the back seat.

He didn't know why they called it the drunk tank. That it made it sound cool, almost enticing, and it was probably the name of a bar somewhere. There were no drinks besides water and you certainly couldn't get drunk. It wasn't even a tank, but a classroom sized room with no windows, and it contained the biggest screw-ups he'd ever seen. They should have called it the hangover tank or the detox tank. Maybe the loser's tank. Anything but the drunk tank. And James spent three rough days in there drying out.

The air was cool and moist when he exited the station as the warm front had passed through to the east. The temperature returned to normal. He blew on his hands and searched for his wife. It was chilly for somebody accustomed to living in Florida.

Dee waited on some concrete stairs near a poplar tree shedding its leaves. She read a magazine and a shopping bag of clothes was next to her. He spotted her, as she did him, and they nodded like two co-workers acknowledging each other in the hallway.

"Thank you," he said, accepting the bag.

"You're welcome."

The minivan was parked two blocks away and the walk was a slow one, a quiet one; James heading to the principal's office yet again. It'd recently rained and the sidewalks were wet. They passed a vendor selling hot dogs and another roasting nuts. Dee held an umbrella as James was a stride behind her, wondering when it was coming, waiting for the well-deserved lecture to begin.

She was calm when they reached the car and spoke like she was reading a letter. "You got lucky my father used to work with the judge's brother at The Port Authority. That he even remembered my mother. You realize you're still on probation, right?"

"Yes."

She handed him a piece of paper. "You have to go to these meetings for the next ninety days to stay out of jail. That was the deal. Make sure you get them signed and bring them to the court. And you can't drink anything. They may test you."

He nodded.

They leaned on opposite sides of the minivan staring at one another as it began to sprinkle. James looked tired. Dee looked sad. She opened the door, hopped in, and started the engine. He remained outside with his hands in his pockets when she waved him in through the window.

"Come on. Get in."

He forced a smile and shook his head, mouthing the word, "Thanks." He continued down the street, his clothes getting wet.

"James. Hey James," said Dee, swinging open the door. "Where are you going? Come on. Get in. We'll head back to mom's and figure something out."

"I need to get my car."

"I'll take you."

"I don't know where it is."

"Then how are you going to find it?"

He shrugged. "It has to be in White Plains somewhere."

Dee followed him. "What are you doing? Would you stop for a second?" She grabbed his shoulder. "Would you please stop for a second?"

"I need to find a job," he said, the rain mixing with his tears.

"Okay. That's a good thing. But why don't we concentrate on finding your car first."

"I'm serious Dee. I've been thinking. I'm going to move here, to New York, to be near the kids."

"All the way up here? I guess you weren't kidding about not being able to return to Florida."

"It's not about that."

She put the umbrella over their heads. "I know James. I know. Why don't we talk about it later? It's damp out. You're going to catch a cold. Come on, let's get in the car."

He held her gaze. "I'm sorry. And please don't worry. I won't interfere with your life. You do what you have to do. I get it now. I really do. But I got no place else to go Dee." His voice faded, crackling, and he dropped his head. "I got no place else to go."

"Come here," she said, wrapping her arms around him, gently rubbing his back. She too was teary. "What am I supposed to do with you?" Dee held him tight, he held her tighter. "Listen, a few days of mom's home cooking and you'll feel so much better. We need to get you some proper nutrition and a good night's rest."

He took her hand and pressed it against his face. "I appreciate what you've done for me. I can't thank you enough. And I appreciate the offer. But I've created this mess myself. This is all my doing and I've got to figure it out. I finally understand that now."

"Where are you going to stay?"

"For starters, I was thinking my car. The seats recline and I could make do for a little while. Until it gets really cold. Maybe then I'll try a shelter or a men's home. I don't know. It'll be a like a social experiment I guess."

"That's some kind of experiment, don't you think?"

"Maybe it'll do me some good to be a lab rat. Teach me some new tricks to earn my cheese. I know you don't understand and it doesn't make sense, but I have to do this. I have to do this for me. I'm going to call Wilson's first thing in the morning. Remember them? That grocery store I worked at when we first met."

Her eyes lit up briefly and she grinned. "James Horton. The customer service department assistant manager. You were so adorable in that dorky uniform when you screwed up my money order on purpose so we could talk longer."

"You see, I never was very good with money even back then. And I still get nervous around beautiful girls." He kicked a stone off the curb into the street. "But I was thinking something more behind the scenes. Maybe stocking shelves or unloading the trucks. My people skills aren't so good these days for any kind of customer service related position."

They both laughed.

"I'll call you when I get settled," he said.

"Is there anything I can say to make you change your mind? To come stay with us until you get a solid plan."

"Unfortunately hun, this is my solid plan."

"You're a crazy man James Horton. You know that?"

"I'm nothing more than an eccentric former millionaire." He winked at her. "And I don't care if you have a boyfriend, I'm still in love with you." He blew in his hands again and did an about face, heading in search of the Corolla.

"Wait," she yelled after him. She ran over and pushed something into his hand. "Before you say anything, I'm not giving this to you. It's a loan until you get turned around. I want you to take it. Please."

"Dee, you've done enough. Thank you but I don't—"

"It's not a suggestion, alright?"

They hugged again and he kissed her cheek, brushing the corner of her lips. He tasted her lipstick, savoring the waxy flavor. "Tell the kids I love them."

"I will. And call me if you need anything. Anything at all. Be safe. Please be safe." She straightened his hair, letting her hand rest on his cheek. "You can do this James. Don't give up on yourself."

He stared, taking a mental snapshot with the tears flowing fast, until he needn't stare any longer.

"By the way," he said, backpedaling. "What will the interest rate on this loan cost me?"

"You don't want to know."

Dee watched him disappear and spoke softly to herself. "And I'll always love you too James."

CHAPTER

38

His car windshield was a collection of parking tickets and bird poop and it cost $300 to remove the iron clad boot locked on the front tire. Somebody key-scratched the trunk and a Grateful Dead sticker had been fastened to the bumper. But the car was paid in full and insured until the end of the year. The only thing needed was gas and his portable hotel awaited. James was excited in a way. His new adventure would be the cross country road trip he always longed to take but never quite got around to: hiking in the Rockies, swimming in the Pacific. Nothing but the freedom of the road. At least the freedom of the road in the city of White Plains.

It only took three days of sleeping in the car before James woke up freezing his coconuts off and said, "Fuck this shit." It wasn't like taking a nap on the side of the road or sleeping off a hard buzz. He could never get comfortable no matter how many positions he contorted his large framed body into. His knees ached and his back hurt. He developed kinks in areas of his neck he never knew existed. Ninety minutes was the most he could sleep without waking up and dealing with his late night urination issue was a nightmare. He'd park the Corolla in shopping centers and corporate office parks during the day, questionable streets in sketchy neighborhoods at night. The whole time he was paranoid, constantly on the look-out for cops. He was trying not to drink and scared shitless.

It only took one night of sleeping in the homeless shelter before he said, "Fuck this shit." He waited in a Disneyesque line all afternoon amongst society's misfortunate simply to secure a bed, barely making the cutoff. Once inside the whole place reeked of a rotten nuclear fart bomb. One guy three bunks over with no front teeth kept staring at him, like he was going to murder him or penetrate him or cut out his body parts and cook them in a stew. James lay awake all night grasping the canister of pepper spray. He was trying not to drink and scared shitless.

On day five of his lab rat experiment a short lady donning a mustache most men would be jealous of asked, "Do you have the title? I'm going to need the title."

The title? James thought. *Dammit. It burned with the house.*

"I don't have it on me. But I can get you a copy."

"And then I can get you a check."

"How about cash?"

"How about it?"

"I prefer cash," he said.

"Don't we all?" She rubbed her nose near the nostrils and didn't officially give it a pick, but it was close. "We can do cash. If that's what you want. But it's going to be less."

"How much less?"

"Twenty percent."

"Seems kind of steep?"

"Do you want to sell your car or not?"

James looked around the lot. It was small, maybe an acre, and standing in the center was a gray mobile home doubling as an office. An American flag covered one of the windows. Hanging over the door was a banner that read FINANCING AVAILABLE! and a string of blue and white pennants ran from the corner of the building to a utility pole. Granski's Previously Owned Autos was the name of the place and Mrs. Granski asked him again, sniffling loudly.

"So do you want to sell the car or what? I got other things to do sweetie."

"Yes. Yes I do."

"Good. Get me the title and I should have your money around five."

James walked over crushed stone and passed in between two Hyundai Elantras the same color green. He climbed the steps to the trailer and opened the screen door, then the main door. There were three chairs with armrests, the newspaper spread open on one of them. Free coffee was available complete with powdered milk and a bowl of mixed hard candy was compliments of the house. The TV aired *The Jerry Springer Show*, two cousins fighting over the same man, and for fifty cents customers could buy day old donuts. James made a few calls and double-checked the fax number. It was a little after eleven. He sipped his black coffee and read the sports page, eating a borderline stale Boston cream. It was the best day he had in a while.

"Hello, my name is James," he said to a group six weeks later. He was one of thirty people sitting in a circle of a community hall basement.

"Hi James," everyone chanted in the same disinterested tone.

"I'm just going to listen today."

Pete, the guy running the group and the guy responsible for signing everyone's paperwork, the most important guy there, glanced up from the word jumble on his desk. He had thick white hair and wore a gold loop earring.

"Bullshit Horton. You say that all the time. Sharing is part of the deal. Now say something."

"I don't have anything to say. What do you want me to say Pete?"

"Did you complete the assignment I gave you? The mandatory assignment."

James ran a hand from his hairline to his chin. Six more weeks of this he told himself. He crossed his legs and leaned back as the lady next to him whispered, "Don't piss him off asshole."

"Yes I did as a matter of fact," said James.

"Then read it."

"Pete, come on. I don't think I should—"

"One call. That's it you know. One tiny phone call from me and your ass is sitting behind bars for God only knows how long. Ask Michael over there. He'll tell you all about it. I heard you didn't like being locked up so much when you were in Florida James. Didn't handle it so well. I heard you cried a lot." Pete stood and walked to the center of the circle, a pencil behind his ear. "You'll have to excuse James everybody. He's above the rest of you. You probably didn't know it but sitting among you miscreants is a man of wealth and nobility. Well, a man of former wealth. A regular Robin Leach. If Robin Leach were dead."

"Pete, that's enough man. You've made your point."

"No, it's okay. Tell them about the money. Tell them about the bank and the lump sum and—"

"Fine, I'll read the stupid assignment. Just stop talking please."

"Atta boy," said Pete. "I knew you had it in you."

The group muttered as James unfolded a piece of paper from his pocket and took a deep breath.

"This asinine assignment I was forced to do is titled 'Why I Drink'."

His face was hot like a cherry pepper and the paper shook as he held it.

"I drink because I'm happy. I drink because I'm sad. I drink because I'm rich. I drink because I'm poor. I drink because the sun rose. I drink because the sun set. I drink because it's windy. I drink because it's calm. I drink because I'm busy. I drink because I'm bored. I drink because I drink. Unfortunately, it's what I've learned to do."

There was a smattering of applause. One guy booed, another called him a dickhead. Pete said, "Not bad Horton. You bought yourself another day. Now who do you want to call on next?"

He stuck around after the meeting to help clean up and maybe earn some brownie points when he noticed the clock on the wall next to the state flag for New York. "See you guys tomorrow," he said to the three people he'd become acquaintances with. "My shift starts in an hour."

"Don't forget to cut the cheese," one of them said as he left. It was the same joke every time.

Working in the deli at Wilson's grocery store wasn't the ideal situation for James or his first choice. But that's all they had available and he was in no position to be picky. He hated wearing the hair net, it made him feel feminine, and he tried in earnest to be nice to every customer including the annoying ones. At times he got blue, dwelling on his anemic paycheck, daydreaming of the millions he once had. He'd exercise restraint when people complained the slices of meat weren't thin enough no matter how razor thin he sliced them and he never spit in anyone's salami or snuck a booger into a pound of roast turkey. But he couldn't say the thought never crossed his mind.

"James, when you're done with your shift I want you to take apart the machines and clean them thoroughly. You do know what the word thoroughly means I hope. And make sure this time you get all that coagulated meat out from under where the knob turns so nobody can see it," his manager said to him.

"Yes Mr. Styles," said James, sweeping the floor. He was twelve years older than Rick Styles, the deli manager, yet always had to address him as mister. James thought about smashing Rick's bulbous head through the glass of the deli cooler more than once. The middle-aged man was making progress but still had a long way to go.

He rented a room twenty minutes from work, twenty-five from Dee. The room wasn't much bigger than his jail cell in Orlando, but it wasn't a cell, and at least he wasn't in jail. It had everything a grown man needed to survive: a bed, mini fridge, and a working TV. There was even a small window. The only major drawback was having no control over the thermostat and sharing a bathroom with four other strange men where the accumulation of pubic hair was everywhere.

For over three months James did nothing but show up for work on time and sit in his room watching TV. Each day he checked off his mandatory meetings on a calendar until they were done. He bought a bike from his neighbor for thirty bucks and rode it a handful of times before the chain snapped. After that a bus pass worked fine. Once a week he'd meet the kids for burgers or a movie, although he would have preferred twice, and he even managed to have some encouraging conversations with Dee. James was surprised how simple it was to fall into a basic normal routine. Life could be easy when he let it.

He started a savings account and joked it would only take 400 more years to return to millionaire status at his present rate. Unless he got a raise, then maybe 375. He considered venturing back to college to earn a bachelor's degree or enrolling in a trade school. Plumbing or accounting, carpentry or teaching; it beat the hell out of slicing meat.

Acceptance of where he was in his unfulfilled life began to settle in. Personal growth was atop his new list. James Horton was right where he was supposed to be. That's what he told himself. It was a comforting lie, like a warm blanket on a cold day, and he pulled it over him frequently. Everything happens for a reason. That's what Dr. Novak said. That's what the self-help books said. That's what Dee said. But nobody ever told him the reason had to make sense.

CHAPTER

39

James fell asleep with the television on as usual, the background noise serving to be his only companion. He'd skimmed through less than three pages of a new golf magazine and couldn't stay awake long enough to watch his hometown hero Janie Chavez deliver the weather. After a co-worker called in sick that day he was voluntold to work a double shift and everything spiraled downhill from there.

A five year old kid threw up from eating too many free cookies the bakery provided and although it wasn't his department James was paged over the P.A. system to clean it up. They ran out of the advertised bologna on sale, one of the meat slicers broke, and the tuna salad had to be discarded because of an unusual odor. To top it off, he accidentally served Mrs. Kline a pound of regular ham when she ordered the low sodium.

"Nothing like this ever happens at the other store," she said, raising her voice for all the customers to hear. She demanded to see the manager.

Rick Styles listened to her complain for twenty minutes, nodding emphatically, and apologized over and over until he said, "You need to pay a little more attention back there James. Mrs. Kline is on a strict low salt diet. You could have killed her. Now give her a free pound of whatever she wants and make sure you get it right this time. And then apologize."

"Yes Mr. Styles," said James, avoiding eye contact with them both, his lips flapping quietly. It was one of the longest work days of his life.

He woke to his cell phone vibrating against the windowsill. A green light blinked indicating he'd missed a call and the TV was loud. Why was the TV always so loud in the morning? A late night infomercial was playing and operators were standing by for the next ten minutes only. Supplies were limited. Something about a non-stick frying pan that could transform into a waffle machine. He was sleepy.

He grabbed the phone, saw there was no message, and didn't recognize the number. James would never be mistaken for Mr. Popularity and without the weekly text messages from Samantha and Cole stating what time they would meet or the occasional call from Dee, nobody ever contacted him. At least nobody he wanted to speak with.

The mortgage company called to discuss various financial parameters of the house and it was imperative he called back to answer important lengthy questions. The fire department called asking for his new address. They wanted to send over a final copy of the arson investigation. While the circumstances of his situation were suspicious, not enough evidence was found to bring forth any formal charges. Two credit card companies called promoting their identity theft protection program and informing Mr. Horton he was eligible for a credit limit increase. His dentist called about a teeth cleaning, the proctologist's office about the appointment he no-showed for. There were the telemarketers, the political polls, the wrong numbers, and then there was Debra Sands from Four Star Insurance. She'd been hounding him for the past three weeks, sometimes leaving messages, sometimes not. Apparently he needed to sign some additional paperwork so she could transfer the case to the next department. Dee was right. They weren't going to cut him a big fat check. Not even close. He'd have to rebuild on site and the money would be doled out in small increments over time. There were details and particulars she needed to discuss. Official protocol. How could he tell her he was never returning to the Sunshine State, that he wasn't allowed, that he'd been banned like a gambler caught counting cards in a casino?

Morning traffic rustled at the intersection near his building and a garbage truck backed up below his room. He stretched out his arm and searched under the sheets, wondering when they'd invent the technology to have the most important gadget in the world surgically attached to his hand. But the remote control rested on the TV stand at least eight feet away. It may as well have been in Siberia.

James lay in bed, the light from the television filling the room, and stared at the mold spot on the ceiling growing bigger by the day. He fantasized about getting a car and vacationing in Tahiti. When the infomercial ended he wondered if golfing at Pebble Beach would ever become a reality.

"Business in America" was the opening segment as the news began and he scolded himself for not leaving the TV permanently on ESPN. The only news he cared about is whether the Knicks won and what the injury report was for the Giants game. He whipped off the sheets and lunged for the remote while the anchor was in mid story on the teleprompter.

"....Egg is the new chairman and CEO of the prestigious Sun Equity Royal Investments banking firm. Analysts expect his first order of business is to lay off fifteen thousand employees in an effort to offset losses stemming from the mortgage crisis and reach Wall Street's earnings expectations for the second quarter. Up next is Vince with your morning commute."

James lit a cigarette and cracked the window after changing the channel. The early morning calm had turned into his favorite part of the day. None of his roommates stirred about and the diner on the corner always packed by eight was empty.

The word *egg* sounded good as he zipped up his pants. Maybe he'd get them scrambled, maybe poached. His phone vibrated again and he still didn't recognize the number. The area code was Florida and it was probably Debra Sands wanting to set a meeting, wanting to do her job. He ignored the call and opened his Bible, flipping to a passage he clung to every day. "Ask and it will be given to you; seek and you will find; knock and the door will be opened to you. For everyone who asks receives; he who seeks finds, and to him who knocks, the door will be opened."

He lit another smoke and gulped down the carbon monoxide. The first few smokes of the day were always the tastiest. He held the cigarette at arm's length and stared at it in between puffs. *One thing at a time,* he told himself. But at nine bucks a pack the smokes were killing him.

The phone vibrated again.

"It's a kind of early for business calls, don't you think Debra? I planned on calling you but—"

"Who the hell is Debra?" a man's voice said.

James paused. "Teddy? Holy shit man. Is that you?"

"Sure as hell is my friend."

"Oh man. Great to hear your voice."

"You too Hot Sauce. I've been trying you all morning. Wanted to touch base before I started work. What, you got a girl up there or something?"

"Yeah," said James, flexing his hand. "I got two. Sally Palm and her sister. They've been keeping me up all night, rubbing my dick raw."

"Just don't fall in love," said Teddy, laughing.

James smiled. "Didn't know it was you or I would've picked up earlier. Should have left a message."

"I hate leaving voice mails. Never know what to say. And besides, I changed my number. Even changed carriers. Didn't want Breg stumbling onto my old one."

"I can't blame you there. But I'm glad you called. I've been thinking about you buddy. Hell, it's been too long."

"Four months."

"Damn, that long Teddy? You should come up and visit. We can catch a Knicks game. Maybe hit a Broadway show if we wanted to act like a couple of homos."

"You always did like show tunes."

"Can't get enough," said James, turning off the TV. "So what's up man? What's going on?"

"It's official dude. You and me, we're finally off the hook."

"Off the hook for what?"

"The coast is clear for your safe return to Florida"

"Good ol' Florida. Year round golf, no state income tax, and amazing beaches. The best freaking orange juice in the world. It sure is nice but I don't think I'll be seeing any of that soon. Lord Breg still rules with an iron hand."

"That's the reason for my call," said Teddy. "Lord Breg will no longer be an issue."

"What are you talking—"

"You have no idea how relieved I am. Ever say since they beat your ass silly I've been looking over both shoulders all the time. I know you said they have no clue about me but still, I mean look what they're capable of. I kept thinking I saw Breg's men at the grocery store or the gas station or driving home from work, like they were following me. It's stupid, right? But better than—"

"Take it down a notch Teddy. I haven't even had my coffee yet. What's with all the Florida talk?"

"You mean to tell me you still don't pay attention to the news after the bank bonus scandal? I thought you would have learned to be more aware."

"Why should I?" said James. "Are they giving away free cars or handing out money?"

"You're just like my sons, I swear. You guys watch nothing but sports."

"Don't forget about the weather."

"Please don't get started on your girlfriend Janie Chavez."

"For you, I won't. But that's all we need my friend besides a daily update of juicy Hollywood gossip."

"You really are a homo. No joke," said Teddy.

"I take pride in my rainbow T-shirt."

"I'm sure you do. So I guess you haven't heard then? They reported it down here a few days ago on a website."

"What happened?" said James. "Did the widow Myers die? Did the Dolphins actually win a football game?"

"No. It's William Breg. He got a new job."

The phone was wedged under James' neck as he tied his shoes. "Well good for him. We wouldn't want the man to starve. I hope it's as a clown in the rodeo. Maybe he'll get trampled by a bull."

"It's a pretty big job dude. Very high profile. And it's up in New York. That's why he's leaving Florida. That's why we're off the hook and you can—"

"Whoa whoa whoa," said James, snapping a shoelace. "What do mean up in New York? My New York?"

"What other New York is there? Breg is going to be the head a large investment banking firm on Wall Street called Sun Equity Royal Investments. He starts the first of the year."

James recalled the morning news, hearing only the "Egg" part of the journalist's newscast. He shook his head. "You're not serious are you?"

"It's a done deal. Who ever thought he'd leave his adopted home state? Is that great or what?"

Something within James shifted, pulling him, like a bird drawn to magnetic north. He tried to be cool and sipped some water. His mouth moved sharply as he spoke. "Nah, I get it. People get jobs. I got a job. You got a job.

Now he has a job. I mean, you know, whatever. These things. It's like, you know. It's fine."

"It's over Hot Sauce. You're a free man. Now me and Heather were thinking about throwing you a welcome back party. It was her idea actually. We can have it at that Mexican place you like and since a hotel will be pricy I was thinking you could stay with us until you rebuild the house. We have room now because—"

James' heart raced, beating way too fast for six in the morning on a Tuesday. "Until that crook looks me square in the eye and tells me he's calling off his hounds, I'm not making any plans of moving back to Florida. My life is up here now and...."

He grinded his teeth without knowing it and felt lightheaded. He sipped some more water.

"Hello? You there?" asked Teddy.

"It's amazing, actually mindboggling, how a former CEO who bankrupted a freaking bank for crying out loud lands on his feet and gets a super important high paying job with an even bigger bank. How in the world does that happen? I write one nasty email in quitting my job and can't even get a sniff of decent employment. It seems the man can do no wrong no matter how much he does wrong. He fails upwards, just like those schmucks at my last company. And what do I get? I get to go back to slicing liverwurst for some old hag visiting her daughter from Yonkers."

He stood, pacing, and his voice grew louder. "There's unfair Teddy and then there's plain old fucking ridiculous. This is even worse. How many more lives will he ruin now? How many other people will he steal from? How many more people is he going to bully? There's no telling what that piece of shit is capable of with that much power. And these are the scum that are leading us. Nothing but criminals. Leaders of the so called free market. Pillars of our mother fucking society. A bunch of cocksucking shit bag thieves with no sense of right or wrong if you ask me!"

"You're looking at the whole thing all wrong," said Teddy. "The guy that kicked you out of Florida will no longer be there. You're safe to come back. He'll be so busy with his new job he won't have time to think of you. You just got a free pass. You're off the radar. I thought you'd be psyched."

"I'll tell you something dude, I'm not sure if any of that karma shit is true. It can't be." James kicked the dresser, holding his foot as he fell onto the bed. The room seemed smaller, the walls dirtier. The conditions he'd grown to accept seemed unacceptable. He snapped the Bible shut and tossed it in the nightstand.

"Why does he have to come here?" said James. "Why he can't he go to L.A. or Miami or Chicago? Or China for that matter. Why can't he go there? Why can't he go to China?"

"New York is where the company's headquarters are. And who gives a shit where he goes? As long as he goes."

"I care. What am I supposed to do if he finds out I live here? Will Lord Breg ban me from New York too? What's next, Connecticut? Might as well make it the entire east coast. And after that? Arizona? Oregon?"

Teddy was quiet and then finally said, "I really thought you'd be psyched."

"I don't mean to be a bummer about this, but you don't understand. Just hearing his name, it makes my skin crawl. I haven't thought about that prick in a while and now he's going to be living near me."

"White Plains isn't the city man. I doubt you two will be sharing doormen."

"It's not as far as Plattsburgh, I'll give you that, but it's close enough." James paused. "It's like he's toying with me, rubbing my face in it even more."

"Anyway," said Teddy. "I'm sorry you don't share my enthusiasm for our safety. I should probably get going."

"Come on man, I'm glad you told me. I guess I'd find out sooner or later. I'm happy for you. But it doesn't do much good for me. It makes a complicated situation more confusing." James pinched the bridge of his nose and closed his eyes. "I want to thank you Teddy. And say I'm sorry. I never told you that. Getting you mixed up in my situation wasn't right. It wasn't fair. I put you in a bad spot. I put us both in a bad spot. It was a shitty thing to do."

"What are friends for?" said Teddy, polishing the Rolex James had given him. "But if you feel that bad, come down and work with me. For free of course. You always said how you hated the long winters and all that shoveling crap."

"The winters do suck the balls," said James. "I don't know about the whole work thing, and I'm definitely not moving, but maybe a quick visit isn't a terrible idea. Get out of town for a few days. Spend some time at the beach. Maybe hit the driving range." He paused. "I want us to be friends again. I miss you buddy." His voice was higher than normal and he realized it, adjusting back to full manliness. "But enough about me and my whining. How are things going with you? How's the business?"

"It's been tough lately," said Teddy. "The bank I normally do...."

James leaned on some pillows, his mind scattered like shotgun spray. William Breg was etched into his psyche once again. He listened like a burnt out therapist, not hearing a word his friend said, but knew when to interject the appropriate social cues of "uh huh", and "really", and "no kidding." He missed Teddy discuss how his business was in trouble, how the revolving line of credit had been cut by the bank, and how the banks tightened up lending even after receiving unprecedented loans from the government. He missed how ex-wife number two had a breast cancer scare but the tumor was benign and he didn't hear that Teddy's oldest son moved to Pensacola with Melinda. And when he needed to talk, to say something, anything, his pre-occupied brain spewed out one mindless cliché after another. "Hang in there buddy." "You'll turn it around." "When one door closes another one opens." "What doesn't kill us only makes us stronger." He added, "Tomorrow's a new day," before breaking out of the trance. His generic rambling was embarrassing.

"You know Hot Sauce," said Teddy. "I might take you up on that offer sometime. I've never been to the Big Apple."

"It's an open invitation. But you will have to get a hotel room because I'm living in a one bedroom shit box."

Teddy laughed and lowered his voice, sounding parental. "Be careful James."

"About what?"

"Just be careful."

James was thirty minutes late for work after missing the bus. His deli apron was wrinkled and he didn't shave. He yelled at a co-worker, argued with Rick Styles, and considered smacking a difficult customer who demanded a third free sample of cheddar. He took more cigarette breaks in the first two hours than he normally does all day. At lunch time he nicked his pinky with the slicer, cutting it from the tip to the second knuckle. The rest of the afternoon was spent in the hospital waiting to get stitched.

The next morning James called in sick, repeating the pattern for the three days straight. On the fourth day he didn't bother calling at all. He could have worked, the pinky was fine, but he didn't want to. He isolated himself in his room, mingling with the company of resentment and anger.

It was cloudy outside and snow was in the forecast. He packed his suitcase after paying his rent in advance, ready to visit someplace warm. Life was easy when he let it be, hard when he didn't.

CHAPTER

40

After twenty-eight hours in the confines of a bus James never wanted to see another Greyhound again. He couldn't sleep despite being tired and if not for a window seat things may have gotten ugly. A divorced mother of three accompanied him through the first leg of his journey ranting about her meth head ex-husband. She was followed by an older gentleman who'd lost his driver's license after side swiping three mail boxes and hitting a dog. The elderly man raved about the miracle of Viagra, detailing his love life at the senior center, and crossed the line of oversharing regarding his recent bout of chlamydia. The two people after him were nice and quiet keeping their noses in books. They took him all the way to the border of Georgia. And then he met Farrah.

"I got a half ounce of shrooms in my backpack," was the first thing she said after introducing herself. She had dreadlocks as thick as bananas and sucked on a grape flavored lollipop. A tattoo on the inside of her wrist read *Kyle*. Another on her neck spelled *Love*. She asked James if he wanted to trip, said it would make the ride more interesting. He politely declined. He had enough of a trip ahead of him.

James didn't call Teddy when he arrived in Florida and never made it anywhere near the beach. Playing golf was not an option. He didn't do much of anything after setting up base camp at a motel besides shadowing William Breg. At least he tried to, when his car cooperated. Twice it stalled, once at an intersection where it had to be pushed, the other in front of a Taco Bell. A new alternator seemed to be the fix.

He drove a 1997 silver Pontiac Grand Prix with 178,000 miles on it. James didn't rent the car, learning his lesson, and bought it outright with cash from his paltry savings. It cost him $1,200 and the owner added a vanilla air freshener because she said he was cute. The car had new windshield wipers and the sunroof opened three-quarters of the way using a hand crank. The tires were bald, not balding, and rust spots were pocked all over. But the junk box ran and he didn't expect more than that.

A high end grocery store cattycorner to the entrance of Featherby Country Club, or FCC as the members called it, was where James spent most of the first week. It had two levels, the top one consisting of a cafe and smoothie bar. The parking lot was elevated above a sloped hill and a short row of palm trees provided shade by early afternoon. He stared through binoculars while chain smoking and drinking cold coffee, trying not to fall asleep from boredom. The stakeout business was tedious and mind-numbing and unlike the two days he followed Pam Gindefeld, not a whole lot happened. He shuddered at the notion of a career as a P.I.

The car he followed shocked him. It wasn't a limousine, an Aston Martin, a Rolls Royce, or anything he expected. It was a black Lincoln Town Car circa 2007. There were no vanity plates and nothing screaming to the outside world, "Hey, I'm over here. Look at me." The car was boring and it blended in, resembling the plethora of upper class snow birds returning from their six month escape to the north.

Every day at 9:10 a.m. the Lincoln emerged from Yorkshire Estates and traveled twelve miles to the country club. William Breg played nine holes of golf, ate lunch, and played nine more. He'd ride ten miles on a stationary bike and get a one hour full body massage before hopping back in the car at 4:15 p.m. and returning to his fortress of solitude.

William "The Weasel" Breg rode in the back, always getting in on the driver's side, while Marty "The Gorilla" drove. George "The Squirrel" was designated shotgun. James "The Bear" made notes of everything, enjoying his code names. He wrote down the weather, what they wore, how they acted, and documented their one trip to the gas station as if researching a book. He snapped pictures and phoned the country club asking, "Are you currently hiring? Can I sign up on a trial basis? Is the manager available for a newspaper interview?" and, "Would you like to donate to charity?" The answers were, "No. Members only. No. Get lost."

James pondered every conceivable angle to devise a workable plan, to convince himself he was doing right by his fellow mankind. He'd made progress and would continue to do so, chipping away in an intelligent and rational manner. But back at the motel, when he'd lay in bed eating chips and watching re-runs of *Knight Rider* and *The A-Team*, the truth of his situation told him otherwise. His plan wasn't coming together. He didn't love it. And on the second day of week number two it hit him. A viable plan didn't exist. The perfect opportunity would never present itself. Once Breg arrived in New York they'd double his security, maybe triple it. His profile would skyrocket and he'd become an untouchable. James couldn't let that happen.

A real man makes his own luck. He'd heard that once in a movie. Easy for the actor to say, he's playing make believe in fantasyland. But James couldn't argue that through a conscious effort of bold decisions a real man makes his own *something*, whatever that may be. And the next day he awoke determined, fearless of the animal lined in his cross hairs. Wherever, whatever, his primitive mindset ensured *something* was going to happen.

The Lincoln bypassed the entrance of the country club, surprising him, and veered onto the highway towards downtown. Twenty minutes later it entered a parking garage in a high-rise building formerly owned by Trustworth Bank and Savings. Marty parked on the seventh floor near the elevator in a spot with a sign stating RESERVED FOR W. BREG still bolted to the wall. He escorted his boss inside while George stayed with the car.

James parked one level further up next to a Cadillac and changed into baggy ripped jeans, a brown flannel shirt with holes, and a pair of steel toed work boots purchased from the Goodwill store. He wore a beard that stretched to the top of his chest and a bandana was wrapped over his gray colored wig. After dousing his clothes with a bottle of rum he plodded through the parking lot using a cane, a cardboard sign tucked under his armpit.

George Naku, an employee of William Breg's for three years and a transplant from Hawaii, leaned against the warm hood of the Lincoln talking on his phone and smoking a cigarette. James meandered over displaying the sign that read HOMELESS VET. ANYTHING HELPS. GOD BLESS.

"Could you spare a few bills for a vet?" he asked in a gruff voice. "I haven't eaten in days."

"Don't touch the car," said George, shooing him away.

"Could you spare a few bills for a vet?"

"Keep moving before I call security."

James planted his feet. "But I haven't eaten in days."

"Hold on, let me call you back." George stepped towards the trunk, throwing his smoke on the ground. "Smells like you been drinking old timer."

"Could you spare a few bills for a vet? I haven't eaten in days."

"You served? In what branch?"

"Navy. Seaman first class aboard the *Constellation*."

"Navy huh? My dad was in the Army. Vietnam. Two tours."

James tapped the lid of the pepper spray, drawing it from his pocket when he stopped. The next move surprised him.

"Here," said George, removing a fifty-dollar bill from his money clip. "Get a good meal somewhere. Get a steak or some chicken. Try to eat some protein. And don't drink it all. You understand?"

James nodded.

"Now beat it before you get yourself in trouble. Take care yourself old timer." He opened his cell phone hitting redial.

The stiff new bill felt nice in his hands and James hadn't seen the face of Ulysses S. Grant in quite some time. He added panhandling to his list of employable skillsets and was speechless when he heard, "And thank you for serving."

An Acura SUV drove by as he stared at the skinny man from the big island. Was that the same guy who shoved a gun in his face and busted him in the mouth? He turned and looked at the ramp leading to level eight. It would be a thirty second walk to his car, a half-hour drive to the airport, and a two hour flight home. Maybe he could beg Rick Styles for his job back, register for those classes he spoke of. He touched his gum where a tooth used to be and turned back around. Maybe not.

"Can you spare a cigarette?" he said. "I haven't had a smoke in days."

George covered the phone and shook his head. "You got some shrapnel in that brain of yours old timer? I told you to beat it."

James rested the cane against the Lincoln and brushed his hand along the tail light. "Nice car."

"Sorry. I'm going to have to call you back again. I got a little situation." George kicked the cane into the aisle. "What the fuck is your problem?" He nudged James in the shoulder. "Are you deaf? I said to stop touching my—"

James squeezed the pepper spray and a light mist drizzled out followed by nothing. The canister was empty. George coughed, gripped him by the shirt, and pushed as the two men stumbled backwards twirling and grunting. They butted heads in a battle for leverage until George let go to swing. He swung wildly and punched James in the ear and the side of the head, forcing him to lose his balance and drop to one knee. As the blows reigned down James dove at George to go in for the tackle. He went in low and fell sideways onto the Hawaiian's knee, bending it in a direction knees aren't designed to bend. George screamed as James rolled over and scrambled to his feet, silencing the man with three quick shots to the face. He taped him up and stuffed George in the trunk of the car before slashing a front tire. He leapt in the driver's seat and crouched down with his ears ringing loud and bumps already forming on his head. Another SUV drove by.

The building's occupancy rate hovered at thirty percent and was the lowest in twenty years. A handful of people passed through the elevator and walked by the Lincoln but nobody reported a strange man in a nice car that appeared out of place. If you see something, say something. They never got the memo.

A security guard rode by on a Segway listening to an iPod while drinking a Slurpee from 7-Eleven. The guard made his rounds every fourteen minutes and wore a white helmet with a chin strap. James observed the time and had his head on a swivel, waiting for the rest of his party to join him. And wait he did, for almost two hours. He didn't feel shaky or nervous or scared. He felt calm. He was doing the right thing.

The seventh floor light lit up and the elevator button went *ding*. Marty exited with Breg on his hip and immediately noticed their car leaning down to the right. "George?" he said aloud. "George?" He inspected the flat, touching the slash with his fingers. "George?" he said again, turning to his boss. "Don't know where he could be sir. Wait here sir." Marty dialed his phone.

The theme from *The Good, The Bad, and the Ugly* whistled from under the driver seat of the car. James lay on his back with his knees coiled to his chin, cocked and ready.

"George, what the hell you doing in there?" said Marty, walking to the door. "You better not be sleeping."

He pulled the handle and a pair of size fourteen boots blasted him in the sternum. He staggered back and clutched his chest as James bum rushed him. They locked arms, their stomachs touching like sumo wrestlers, and Marty was the stronger of the two as they danced. He flung James into the Lincoln and dented the door before tossing him against another car. He raised his leg for a kick to the head but James avoided it, grabbing the tree trunk flying at him, hugging it with both arms. He bit into the fleshy part of the thigh and Marty howled, swiping him across the face and tearing loose the beard. Marty recognized his assailant's face and paused. The pause was slight and that's all it took. James punched him in the throat and sprang up, kneeing him in the stomach. He demolished Marty's nose with a hard straight right and heard something crack.

Breg, initially paralyzed, yelled for help and ran. But with the elevator on the twenty-eighth floor and no clue where the stairs were, the new CEO of Sun Equity Royal Investments ran the wrong way, running up the levels instead of down.

"Stop it William!" hollered James, huffing, leaning on one knee. Marty lay on the ground blinded with pain and for old times' sake James hammered him between the legs.

Breg ran faster than expected and wasn't getting caught by a pack a day smoker. Not until he rounded level eight and collided with the security guard. His ankle got crushed under a tire while a handlebar ripped across his face. James lumbered over wheezing and vowed to quit smoking the next day.

"Call an ambulance," said Breg, blood streaming from a deep cut on his cheek.

James struck him hard above the eye and there was no need for a standing eight count. His opponent was out.

The security guard's elbows were scraped to the bone and his hands looked like they'd been rubbed on a cheese grater. His shirt was spotted with raspberry Slurpee.

"You'll be fine," said James. "Relax." He removed the fifty-dollar bill George had given him and made sure the guard saw it, tucking it into his pocket. "Give me three minutes and then you can call it in. You never saw me.

You never saw any of this. Make pretend you're unconscious until I leave. Unless you want to be unconscious."

The security guard didn't move or utter a word. He closed his eyes feigning sleep.

The Pontiac idled with the air conditioner on as James threw Breg in the back seat after dressing the wound on his cheek. He covered him with a blanket. It would be five more hours until nightfall and after finally doing something, he needed to wait a little longer.

CHAPTER

41

James snapped his fingers and peeked through the curtains.

"William?" he said. "Can you hear me?"

The parking lot was full with pickup trucks and trailers in town for a National Motocross event. A NO VACANCY sign flashed in front of the motel and the soda machine was broken leaking water. People were hanging in lawn chairs and drinking cold beer on the sidewalk while firing up their portable grills.

He checked the window every five minutes searching for Marty or George or somebody worse, waiting for his victim to wake up. Breg did wake once at the rest area off the highway. But when the sixty-eight year old father of three and grandfather of seven became problematic, James had no choice but to crack him again.

Breg, dressed in a fine blue suit sans the tie, lay prone on a thin green carpet decorated with flowery prints of hibiscus. His right foot rested atop three stacked pillows with a bag of ice strapped to it and the blood on his shirt as well as his face dried to a dark reddish brown. The swelling on his face had stabilized.

"William?" James said again. "Come on now." At five six and 152 pounds he was easy to maneuver. James propped him up against the bed, being careful about the foot, and peeled off a gold watch, gold rope bracelet, and a gold pinky ring with a ruby in the center. He examined the pinky ring, never quite understanding the concept. Breg's platinum wedding band was welded on after forty-four years of marriage.

Breg moaned and moved his head to the right. "Martha?"

"Not quite William. I'd be one hell of an ugly Martha." James handed him a plastic cup. "Here, drink this."

"What is it?"

"Go ahead. You're probably dehydrated."

Breg smelled the fruit punch flavored Gatorade before gulping it down, asking for more.

On the far side of the room near a small TV and a dresser was a brown plastic table with matching chairs. Displayed on its surface were hedge trimmers, a hammer, and a drywall saw. Breg looked at the tools and didn't say anything then noticed his hands.

"My hands are green. You painted my hands green."

"Good to know you aren't colorblind at your age."

"What the....?" said Breg, feeling the bald shaved stripe down the center of his head.

"That's right William. The kids call it a reverse Mohawk. I have to say you look ridiculous."

"Why did you do that?"

"I was bored. And you're a thief."

"I could scream you know."

"And I could cut off your fingers with those hedge trimmers and smash in your face with the hammer."

Breg sighed, holding the cup in the air. "Can I have some more please?"

"Since you asked so nicely."

"So you must be the infamous James Horton," said Breg, cringing upon touching his bandaged cheek. "We finally meet face to face."

"What gave me away?"

"Who else could it be?"

"Oh, come on William. I'm sure a lot of people hate a scumbag like you. Don't sell yourself short."

Breg grinned at that one, briefly. It hurt to grin.

"Contrary to what you've come to believe James, I'm not the devil. Sure I have people who don't like me. Who doesn't? But you've taken it to a new level son."

"First off, I'm not your son. I'm not your pal, buddy, homie, or compadre. And how do you know you aren't the devil?"

"You don't look anything like a James," said Breg. "Do people ever tell you that?"

"What is a James supposed to look like?"

"I don't know. But not you. Marty never showed me your photo. I was expecting somebody different. You seem more like a Jamie to me."

"My father used to call me Jamie. So please don't call me that. My name is James. Do you think you can handle it?"

"Where is your father now?"

"He's dead. The man worked and worried himself to death. He was never able to get a decent...."

James' voice trailed off.

"He was never able to get a decent what?" said Breg.

An image of his sickly dad floated through his mind and James kicked his captive in the leg like a disobedient dog.

Breg winced. "I know what this is all about and I want to go on record stating we were investigated thoroughly by an independent auditing group and they found no major wrongdoings at the bank. You can check it for yourself if you'd like. I'll give you their name. Now I'm sorry you lost your money, but a lot of people lost their money. I lost some money in the market too. It was simply bad timing in a bad economy."

"Say that again."

"What?"

"Repeat the part about the bad timing."

"Why?"

James picked up the hammer, smacking it into his palm.

"Okay. It was simply bad timing in a bad economy."

He kicked the pillows from under Breg's foot and the injured ankle dropped to the ground, smacking with a thud. Breg screamed but was smothered by a large hand suffocating his face. "Embrace the pain William. Just like I have."

The music in the parking lot intensified as more people gathered around. "Sweet Home Alabama" pumped through a boom box and the smell of charcoal and lighter fluid floated in the air.

Breg clutched his jaw breathing heavy. He strained to pull his foot back on top of the pillows. "So this is what we're going to do? This is why I'm here? If you don't like my answers you're going to hurt me."

"Just so you know," said James. "I've barely touched you. We haven't even begun the hurt part yet."

Breg swallowed and stared at the door. "You're doing all this I presume because you want the truth. But the fact of the matter is you don't really want to hear it. You don't like the rules of the game because you don't know how to play it. How typical of your ilk?"

"Did you really just say the word ilk? Not sure I've heard that one before. Sounds like an S.A.T. word." James looked through the curtains after turning on the television. "I don't like having my money stolen William and I don't like being lied to. Bobby Stafford fessed up to everything."

"Bobby Stafford is an incompetent fool."

"Then why use him? Why even hire him in the first place?"

"I had no choice. If it wasn't for his father, for some connections of his, that dimwit of a man would be working a cash register somewhere at a convenience store."

"Do you deny what he told me?" said James, unzipping a bag and removing a roll of duct tape. "Do you deny that you and your team of Bobby, Frank, and Pam stole millions of dollars right before the bank went out of business and tried to pass it off as some kind of legitimate bonus program?"

Breg noticed the tape and shifted his bodyweight. "It's a complex situation Jamie." He held up his hand. "I'm sorry. I meant James. Listen, things are never as black and white as they may appear. Nothing ever is."

"And?"

"And what I'm saying is.... Look, were there certain liberties we may have taken at an opportune time? Were the lines blurred to a gray area of questionable standards? Perhaps, depending on how you view it."

"Perhaps?" said James. "I like that. So let me translate, help you cut through the bullshit. What you're really saying is that you did some very shady stuff but you don't want to come right out and admit it. Which makes no sense because either you did or you didn't. You can't lawyer up here William. The Fifth Amendment does not apply in the walls of this room."

"What do you want from all of this? Everybody wants something James. What is your ultimate goal here?"

"I'm trying very hard to understand a mindset I can't comprehend. You see, I used to mind my own business. Not ask a lot of questions. Just move along with the herd. Isn't that what my ilk does?" He walked away from the window and lit up a smoke. "I want to know why you did it. No, forget that, I need to know why. And the sad part William is that I don't know why I need to know. Just that I do. Maybe it's so one day I can go back to working in a deli or being a plumber and have some kind of closure to this nightmare you created. I can say, 'Oh, okay, I get it now. That makes sense. That's why my money is gone and I'll have to work until I die.' Now do me a favor and fill in the blanks. You want for nothing and live a life most men dream of. You seemed to have it all. Why fuck over regular people who are only trying to survive?"

"Could I have one of those?" said Breg, motioning towards James' cigarette.

James threw him the pack.

"First smoke in thirty-five years, not counting cigars." Breg took a long drag. "You aren't going to kick me again are you?"

"Not right now anyway. Go on."

"I helped that bank grow over the years and become very successful. Very successful. Made them a lot of money. There were some discrepancies between myself and the board along the way and they were getting worse. They began demanding decisions that led us to going down a questionable path, decisions I didn't particularly agree with. And when it became clear it wasn't going to work, that we were going to crash, I was the one who'd be taking the fall. That was my job. But it didn't seem right. I felt like I was owed that money. I felt like I deserved it." He flicked his ash and tilted back his head, gazing at the ceiling.

James waved both hands at the floor. "Nope. Sorry. No fucking way. You've got to do better than that William. Much better. Tell me you took it because you secretly have an orphanage in South America or you're helping eradicate a disease in Africa. Tell me you took it because you're running for public office and need campaign money and tell me you took it because your wife wants you to buy her a private island. But please don't talk about deserve. It's pathetic."

"You don't understand the dynamic of what I achieved for them. I was instrumental in the acquisition of—"

"You were instrumental in a well-coordinated conspiracy."

Breg pointed to his chest, poking himself. "Listen to me. I no doubt deserved, at the very least, the respect and compensation of bringing that small time institution to the level—"

"You're boring me William."

"I said listen to me goddammit!" Breg poked his chest harder. "I deserved—"

"The only thing you deserve is to be in prison for a very long time. The idea that you'd hide behind such a bullshit excuse and feel sorry for yourself is embarrassing. Did the bank owe you back pay or something? No? I didn't think so. It's not like you were making minimum wage as a drive-up teller. You weren't some underpaid mid-management lackey only trying to feed his kids so spare me the—"

A flash of anger overtook Breg and his eyes hardened. "I took it because I could you moronic imbecile! Are you that obtuse? I took it because it was there to be taken! It was money I was sure as hell owed and I don't need a lecture from some white trash loser who thinks he can—"

"Now there's the William Breg I know of," said James, clapping lightly. "Now the party's started. There's the guy who sent his goons to beat the shit out of me and banished me from the state of Florida. There's the guy who bribed the one witness who could bring him down and there's the guy who no doubt has people in high places on the payroll. I knew you'd come out to play eventually."

"Forgive me," said Breg, tugging on his neck where he usually had a tie. "Please forgive my outburst. My intentions were not to insult you and suggest—"

"Yes they were William. I expected nothing less."

Breg cleared his throat. "The point I'm trying to make is that people don't get to the top of anything in life by playing nice in the sandbox. I saw an opportunity and took it. If you didn't think you'd get caught you'd have done the same thing."

"Nah, I don't think so."

"That's easy to say that when opportunities never present themselves."

"I don't care what kind of opportunities came my way," said James. "I wouldn't do it. Not when I was already set. I mean how much is enough? I read somewhere you were worth like fifty million dollars?"

"There is never enough. Ever. And fifty million is a bit of an overstatement."

"How can there never be enough?"

"There just can't be," said Breg. "It's like the expanding universe, infinite in its appetite. You can always add another buck to your account. The wealthiest man in the world, no matter how wealthy he may be, is always going to stop if he sees a twenty-dollar bill lying on the ground. And he's going to pick it up. Who wouldn't? Now what if you could make that twenty appear whenever you wanted? It can be a tricky thing to handle." He threw up his arms. "Someone like you couldn't possibly comprehend that."

"You're right, I can't." James sat next to him. "And I probably never will. But here's the part that I really don't get. Don't you feel bad knowing you wiped out the retirement savings of thousands of people who were relying on it? Doesn't that have some kind of effect? I mean you crushed people's lives, destroyed their futures. How do you sleep knowing you robbed children of their college funds? Doesn't that make you feel the slightest bit of guilt?"

"Guilt is a curse for the weak I released a long time ago. Do you know if it weren't for people like me who grow businesses and provide jobs and secure solid returns for investors then none of it would matter anyway? Our economy would implode. You need people like me. People like me are the reason the system works, the reason there's a system in the first place. We're the cogs that run the machine. So once in a while I dip a little, to get what's mine. It's part of the checks and balances and a small price to pay for the value I bring to the table. And I've known plenty of people who've done a hell of a lot worse."

"You make it sound like I should thank you for stealing my money, maybe give you an award."

Breg pulled himself up, sitting straighter. "I hate to break it to you James in your Boy Scout quest for a righteous and all-encompassing answer. But there isn't any magic bullet or deep meaning to what happened at the bank. It happens every day all over the world, from big businesses to small ones to nonprofits to the government. For all our sophistication we're nothing more than barbarians at heart. We want something, we take something. Technology changes, people don't."

A commotion erupted in the parking lot and James dashed to the window expecting to find Breg's cavalry. What he saw instead were two young guys flexing their beer muscles in a wrestling match gone awry. A heavyset man in a cowboy hat separated them as Johnny Cash replaced Lynyrd Skynyrd on the radio.

"So what do you think will happen when you die then William?" he said. "You think none of this bad stuff you do is going to matter, that there's no repercussions? Do you plan on slipping St. Peter a few grand at the Pearly Gates and buying your way into heaven?"

"Now we're getting into religion. You're a deep thinker James. Not the mindless ape I assumed you'd be."

"Don't be so sure about that."

"I don't worry what happens when I die," said Breg. "Who knows? It'll probably be nothing more than decomposing into the ground. I'll never know I'm dead because I'll never remember being alive."

"That's a tad bleak isn't it? Don't you believe in God? Don't you have any faith?"

"If colleagues like my good friend Frank Cally go to church every Sunday it's simply a charade to uphold an image. I believe in the scientific method of empirical data and the power of observation. And lying here, looking at you, my senses are telling me you're in way over your head. Enough of this gibberish philosophy. Let's make a deal. Let's end this feud amicably."

A deal? James thought. He hadn't prepared for that. He leaned against the wall exhaling smoke from his nose.

"What kind of deal?"

"Stop what you're doing right now and let me go. I promise I won't go to the police."

James smirked. That angle was covered. "Mr. Breg doesn't like unwanted attention. That's what Marty said after beating me half to death. When I saw the kind of car you drove I knew it was true. Your deal blows William."

"Just because I prefer to be under the radar it doesn't mean I won't go to the police and—"

"Let's continue with me asking the questions so we can get to the fun part of evening. Shall we? So, if there is never enough money then how do you become happy? What's the point of it all?"

"You're wasting time," said Breg. "Somebody's going to come barging through that door any minute and you better pray it's the police."

"Answer me," said James, raising his voice.

"All I can say is most people make the mistake of trying to be happy when they should really be content just being satisfied."

"What?"

"Everybody puts so much emphasis on being happy yet people are more depressed than ever. Why is that? It's a broad subject James and we could go on lamenting about it forever. Given the cauldron of our predicament, is that really what you want to discuss? Forget about this nonsense."

"You'd like me to forget about every—"

"I can get you back some of your money." Breg said it fast, tapping his opponent with a quick jab.

James felt as if he'd jumped in a freezing cold lake, like the time he joined the Polar Bear club in high school. His body went numb and his mind became cloudy. Money. His long lost love was still alive.   "Give me a number," said Breg, "and I can get you back some of the money we took from the bank. We'll go our separate ways and never have to see each other again."

"After everything you put me through you think I'll cave for a few dollars? You think it's only about the money?"

"Of course. Why else would I be here?"

"It's more than that William."

"Don't be so naïve James. You sound like a juvenile. Now give me a number."

"You can't just get away with what you've done."

"Why not? I have before and will do so again. It's the way the human race is designed. It's the way your God set it up. The Golden Rule is the universal law among us and always will be. When I'm gone someone else will take my place. People will do anything for money. Absolutely, positively anything. Watch the news and study your history books. If the price is right, somebody will do it."

"Not always," said James, gnawing a thumbnail. "Everybody isn't like you William."

A look of amusement fell over Breg's face. "If you disagree, then take a hard look at yourself Jamie, at what you've done, at the crimes you've committed." He counted on his green painted fingers. "Let's see. There's assault, kidnapping, breaking and entering, theft. Very serious stuff. Should I continue? Did you ever think you could do it? Did you ever think when you were twenty or thirty or forty years old that one day you'd be a jaded felon? Probably not. Who would? But look how far you've gone. How much further are you going to take it? And say what you will to justify it, we both know it's all about the money."

James wanted to respond and defend himself but he had nothing. Breg continued.

"Now I'm not the devil son, as I've said, but you can bet your ass that if somebody could make a fortune doing business with him they not only would, but there'd be a line around the block and an all-out war to do so. So stop lying to yourself and face the truth. Give me a number so we can end this."

The hair on the back of James' neck stood up and goose bumps ran down both arms. He glared at the man he came to assault and clearly envisioned a number in his head, hating himself for doing so. Doubt creeped in, over, and through his mind. "Are you sure you aren't the devil?" he asked. "You seem pretty evil to me?"

Breg tried to suppress a grin, holding his bandaged face. "If you only knew the half of it Jamie, you'd consider me a swell guy, a regular angel."

James slipped a towel over his neck as he perched himself on the toilet after running the shower. He wore a scowl of torn confusion, listening to the contending voices argue in his head. He didn't like what he heard or what he thought. He didn't like what he felt. It was time to regroup.

"I can lecture you all night how things work in the real world," said Breg, watching James mumble to himself in the bathroom. "We can talk until the sun comes up if you want. But you're wasting time. It doesn't matter what I did, what you did, what we all did. Nobody's perfect. I accept that. I understand your frustrations. Stop this now and we can make it right. Why don't we discuss more practical matters at hand? Let's discuss matters more pertinent to the future of our lives."

The duct tape made a harsh tearing noise as James tore off a piece with his teeth. "We're done talking for now," he said, holding a strand end to end. He closed in on Breg's face, second guessing his priorities, and thought about his plan. He thought about the money. Always with the money.

CHAPTER

42

The bathroom was foggy with the door cracked open and the vent on high. James changed into a black collared shirt and tan pants, rubbing his freshly shaved chin. He buckled his belt and used a mirror near the bed to comb his hair. He wanted to look good for his upcoming trip and picked at the green paint stuck under his fingernails that no amount of scrubbing would remove.

Breg, with his eyebrows raised and forehead crinkled, pleaded for relief from the tape. James reached down, tearing it off.

"Ahh," said Breg, licking his lips. "Thank you. Could I have more to drink please?"

James ignored him, didn't glance his way.

"Have you given any thought to what I said Jamie, about a number?"

No answer once again.

Breg hesitated, fidgeting. "I see you're all dressed up. Are you going somewhere? Because I'm sure my wife has begun making inquiries by now. Marty and George will be searching for me everywhere. The clock is ticking. You really need to—"

"William, the time for chatting is over."

James fumbled with a button on his cuff and checked the window. The group outside had thinned as the charcoal withered to ash and the music softened.

"So as we were discussing earlier," said Breg, scanning the room, his voice unsettled, "about philosophy and the financial structure of our economy, I wanted to add that—"

"Shh," said James. "I've heard what I needed."

He taped Breg tighter than before and walked to the table, circling it, running his hands along the tools.

"People don't get to the top of anything by playing nice in the sandbox. Isn't that what you said William? Weren't those your exact words?"

Breg nodded yes, then no, then yes. He shrugged. His head swirled like a bobblehead.

"And you're probably right. Maybe that's why I've never been able to get ahead. Maybe I'm too nice. And I imagine everybody is nice to you William, aren't they? I'm sure throughout the day you're surrounded by professional ass kissers and dedicated brown nosers. People probably laugh at your horrible jokes and agree with whatever you say. No one dare risks offending you."

The hedge trimmers had red fiberglass handles and when clasped together they resembled the sound of scissors.

"Now, let's get to the reason you're here."

The blades were shiny and James chopped the air several times; first near Breg's nose, then his lips, then his ears. He finally set it in front of an eye, holding it under the lashes.

Breg tried to remain still but trembled.

"I could jam this into your eyeball. Scoop it out like a melon baller and make a pirate out of you." He brought the blade close, within millimeters of the pupil, his hand moving slightly with every heartbeat. Breg held his breath and stared at the blade as James let it linger. "But that would be gross William. Make a hell of a mess for the maid to clean up. They don't get paid enough for that."

He chucked the hedge trimmers on the bed and picked up the hammer.

The tears flowed and Breg's head collapsed towards his chest. He squealed into the tape when James grabbed his forehead and tilted him back, inserting the claw of the hammer into his nostrils.

"I bet you have some remorse now for what you did at the bank." He lifted up, stretching the skin until it turned white, and pulled slightly forward. "I bet you have so much remorse for getting caught by a nobody like me."

He yanked harder on the handle as the cold metal claw etched deeper and a trickle of blood emerged. James watched him twitch and wrangle in pain. "I'm sure you heard about Bobby's hand, about what he made me do, and about the exploding fingernail. Very very nasty I assure you. But with you William, I have to take it further. You were the mastermind of the bonus scam. It was your idea. And because of that, you need to be made an example of, like the judge did with me. I want it to make headlines across the country when they find your disfigured body." He removed the claw and slapped him across the face. "Maybe my ilk aren't a bunch cowards after all."

James set the hammer atop Breg's mouth and pushed on the tape, rotating it side to side. "I can feel your teeth in there William. They feel strong. My advice is to breathe through your nose because in less than a minute your mouth will be full of sharp fragments. But don't worry. With all your stolen money you can no doubt afford the best plastic surgeons. I think I see DaVinci veneers in your future."

He drew the hammer high in the air and let it descend slowly, stopping an inch above Breg's face. He tapped him gently. James raised it again and repeated the process over and over, picking up speed. He counted, "One, two, three...." and his arm crashed down, rushing by Breg's face, barreling into the foul smelling carpet. James reloaded and thrust down once more on the opposite side.

Breg convulsed like he had a seizure and sobbed uncontrollably, blood and mucus draining from his nose. James backhanded him and grabbed the drywall saw, inspecting it for sharpness. He started at the neck, near the Adam's apple, and ran it the length of the torso, tearing Breg's shirt and scratching the skin along the way. He stood over the thief and waited before cutting him free.

Spit dangled off Breg's lips when the tape was removed and he touched his teeth to make sure they were there. His chest heaved and he shrank into a ball, clutching his nose, whispering prayers of thanks.

"You seemed to have found religion in a hurry," said James. "I thought you didn't believe in all that God and heaven stuff."

"You're a sick psychotic beast of a man!"

James threw him a towel and offered a smoke as the grown man cried.

"Were you scared William?"

"Of course I was. Only a fool wouldn't be."

"And you're no fool, are you? It doesn't feel so good. And yet that's how the game is played. It's a crucial piece of the puzzle the rest of us don't understand. Maybe we don't want to understand it. You scare the shit out of people William. That's how you play."

Breg sniffled, drying his eyes and cleaning his face. He peered at the tools on the bed. "Why did you stop?"

"I'm sure you won't understand this, but I wanted you to know fear, real fear, if only for a moment. Sounds dumb doesn't it? But that's how it feels when your money is gone, when you realize life will never be the same. That's how it feels when you lose the security of your family's future, of your own future. You feel helpless and lost. You feel hopeless."

"So you're not going to hurt me like Bobby and Pam?"

"Do you actually think a man of my background ever wanted any of this?" said James. "My big plan was to play golf three times a week and travel the world with my family. I even considered giving ten percent of my winnings to the church. Beating and torturing bank executives wasn't very high on my priority list. But here I am in a crappy motel, trying to scare an incurably greedy man into experiencing a mindset he will never understand. It's not who I am. It never was."

"Then why risk so much just to scare me?"

"I had no choice. Something inside was driving me that I couldn't overcome. My therapist couldn't figure it out. Neither could my wife or best friend. Forget about those stupid self-help books. You needed to be dealt with in person for me to move on. That was my only remedy."

The two men were silent, the sound of the TV buffering the tension. They smoked cigarettes and drank the rest of the Gatorade.

"So what now?" said Breg after reassembling his pride.

James lowered his head. "Now…. Now I…." He ran a hand through his hair and closed his eyes, speaking with disgust. "Now I give you a number." It sounded worse than imagined.

"How much?"

"Three million," he said, turning away.

"In light of your disclosure in wishing me no harm, that number seems rather excessive. Do you plan on kidnapping me forever?"

"Forever? No. But the trunk of my car could be your new home for the next few weeks, maybe longer. Do you really want to stick around and find out? Three million is the amount you stole from me. It only seems fair."

"I'll give you five hundred grand to get out of my life forever," said Breg. "All you have to do is walk away and mention this to no one."

"You really don't like unwanted attention do you?"

"It's not good for business."

James hesitated, scratching his head.

"Say yes and we can fix this whole mess right now," said Breg.

"I don't know William, I think we've gone too far to fix anything. I'm pretty sure I hate you."

"If I could only do business with people who liked me then I wouldn't do much business at all. You said it yourself earlier, you've got to have faith." He wiped some blood still dripping from his nose. "A half a million dollars is a large sum of money for a person such as you. This is your second chance lottery Jamie, your only chance lottery. There will be no more opportunities for a man of your age. Are you smart enough to see that?"

"I'm smart enough to know that five hundred grand is nowhere near what you stole from me."

"Who's the one being greedy now? Ask yourself this. How long would it take you to earn that much money working at a job?" Breg's body language became demonstrative, his tone assertive. "You brought me here to find out the truth. As ugly as it may be, you said you had to know. Well here it is, staring you in the face. The decisions you've made are what put you here tonight. Not me. People make money every day and people lose money every day. You deal with it and move on. You can still live the life of your dreams."

"Two million," said James.

"Seven hundred. Give me my phone and leave right now and you will have put seven hundred thousand dollars in your pocket."

James didn't know whether to laugh or cry. Should he pat himself on the back or plunge his head in the toilet?

"Here is your chance to play golf and travel," said Breg. "Isn't that what you want? Here is your chance to change the perception of James Horton. You can enhance your bloodline, alter your lineage."

"A million and a half."

"Eight fifty. Final offer."

A beer commercial played on TV and James slumped in a corner as the *what if* factor of the good life encapsulated him. He envisioned buying Cole that cherry red Mustang for his birthday and one day giving Samantha the wedding of her dreams. He could pay for their college with a simple scratch of a check and ensure they never struggled financially. He could buy a new house and win back Dee and with his family reunited they could embark on that vacation to Tahiti. He'd give to the church, help out Teddy, take care of Mary, and donate to good causes. Maybe he'd get something named after him back home like a park or a library. Maybe a statue. He felt light headed and his stomach hurt. He opened his eyes and belched. Maybe James Horton could finally be a respectable gentleman.

"How would I get it?" he said.

"I'll have it wired into your account first thing tomorrow. You'll be able to draw on it by noon."

"How do I know you'll come through? You're the least trustworthy person ever William. How do I know you won't screw me again and start this mess all over?"

Breg motioned for James to come closer. "I want you to look at me. Look at my face and take a good look at my eyes. And I want you to listen. I've dedicated my entire life to the game of money. I was bred for it. It courses through my veins. There is nothing in the world I take more serious. When it comes to money, I never fuck around son. Ever. I guarantee you'll have your eight fifty by noon tomorrow."

It was an aggressive speech by a confidant type-A personality and James was impressed. He understood the success of his foe.

"So do we have a deal Jamie?" said Breg, extending his hand.

"You're not going to stop with the Jamie thing are you?"

"I can't. You're not a James."

"We both belong in jail you know."

"I won't be going to jail anytime soon. Even if that case went to trial, I have incredibly excellent lawyers. The very best. You've made your point. This whole thing can go away now. You can go away. I admire your ingenuity and persistence. Maybe I'll take something from this. Perhaps you've taught me something."

"I highly doubt you'll take anything from this," said James, stepping forward. "Not at your age. I think the old dog learning new tricks adage applies here."

Breg tipped his head. "You've won Jamie. You're going to get back your money. You didn't play nice in the sandbox and look where it got you. Congratulations."

"Not sure I understand your obsession with sandbox references but now that we're done, does somebody always have to win?"

"I don't know if somebody has to win, but somebody definitely always loses. Let's shake like businessmen and get on with it."

James took another step, his right arm swinging past his hip and moving into handshake position, when he stopped. He followed his captive's instructions and looked at Breg's face. He looked at the maroon soaked bandage glued to his cheek and the blood spots stained on his nose. He noticed the bumps protruding from his head and the bald stripe shaved in his hair. His hands were green. Breg's clothes were soiled like a homeless man and his ankle was probably broken. And then he looked not at his eyes, but into them. He didn't see evil or hatred or bigotry. He saw a sparkle. It was an imperious sparkle of contempt that said, "Fuck you. Don't you know who I am? I can't be stopped. Get out of my way. Piss off. I own you."

Breg's eyes were smug and cocky and to him the whole night had been a minor inconvenience, an uncalculated error to be corrected on a balance sheet. It was the price of doing business in the world he lived in, an acceptable loss of collateral damage. Throw money at problems and they disappear forever. Breg relied on it.

James shoved his hand in a pocket and inched backwards until reaching the table. He sat on it, ashamed in his excitement for getting back some of his money, ashamed to be accepting it from a lowlife thief such as Breg. Why had he come to Florida in the first place? Did he secretly hope this would happen all along? He thought of the long bus ride and emptying his savings to buy the used car. He thought of Sun Equity Royal Investments and New York. His New York. Wasn't he supposed to be on a mission? Wasn't he supposed to be a James Bond wannabe? Didn't he declare to set things right?"

A car screeched into the parking lot and locked up its brakes, followed by a door slamming.   "You waited too long," said Breg, pumping his fists. "I warned you about wasting time."

James pointed and said, "Shut up," before picking up the hammer. He turned off the lights and put his back to the wall, sliding towards the window. He looked under the curtains and saw a large man almost as big as himself lumbering up the sidewalk with his arms full. James smiled.

"Are you hungry William?"

A pizza delivery guy knocked on the door next to them, stating he was sorry for the long delay.

"Wow," said James, walking in the bathroom to splash water on his face. "Thank God for free delivery." He leaned on the sink and stared at himself in the mirror. His eyes were dark from exhaustion and he noticed a few broken capillaries on the sides of his nose. "You almost had me William. You almost had my sorry, weak, timid, fat, pathetic ass. I was like a moth to the flame, incapable of flying away. Is that how it is with you William? Is that how it is with everybody? Maybe we can't help ourselves. It's in our DNA."

"What nonsense are you blathering now?"

"I could have left here tonight a rich man. It would have been so easy to get mine and walk away, allowing you to keep your thieving ways. You almost had me under your magical spell."

"Magical spell?"

"It's the all-powerful allure of money that we're hard wired for," said James. "I didn't quit my job and travel thousands of miles to broker a deal with a scumbag like you. A deal I would hate myself for doing the rest of my life and a deal that, whether I believe in any of that karma shit or not, would only lead to something bad. Yet, to my embarrassment, I almost did it."

"We agreed in principal on eight fifty," said Breg. "Are you reneging? I assumed you to be a man of your word."

"I am a man of my word. My own word. That's the reason we're here tonight before I whored myself out. I came here to stop you."

"To stop me? From what?"

"From taking that job in New York."

Breg scrunched his face like he'd sucked on a lemon. "This whole convoluted day has been about the job in New York? What does that have to do with this?"

"Everything," said James. "You're the last person who should be offered that job. You have no right to be in a position of so much power. You fuck people William. You're a fucker. And I almost enabled you."

"I get it," said Breg. "You're angling for more money. You're a quick study Jamie. I'm impressed."

"If I couldn't survive with eight hundred and fifty thousand dollars then what does that say about me? We're not the same breed of animal William. I don't worship money like you do. I'm just scared of never having it. It's a big difference."

"Hand me that phone right now Jamie! Do you hear? We had a deal!"

"We didn't have jack shit. This is a motel room, not a boardroom."

"You think an inbred dolt like you can stop somebody like me from taking that job?" said Breg.

"Yes I do."

"You'd have to kill me first. I've worked my whole life for this kind of opportunity. And I know you aren't a killer."

"You're right, I'm not a killer. If I was, this would be so much easier. But I have no problem killing a man's reputation. Especially a man as twisted as you."

James stood in the center of the room and stretched out his arms, spinning. "You see William, I've been at this luxurious resort for almost two weeks now. It's given me lots of time to think about how to proceed in case I ever had the chance to snatch you."

"So?"

"So, our entire conversation has been recorded tonight. I have cameras hidden everywhere."

Breg whipped his head around, surveying the walls and the ceiling. "I don't see anything. You're bluffing."

"The cameras are hidden. They're very small, like the ones at your estate. In fact, I want to thank you. That's where I got the idea. It's amazing how cheap they were. And if you don't believe me all I can say is...." He paused, adjusting his voice to imitate Breg. "I never fuck around when it comes to video cameras. Look at me son. It's in my blood. I said never." James laughed.

"Even you can't be that dumb. You'd be incriminating yourself if anybody saw what took place here tonight. You'd be going to jail too."

"I've been to jail William, and for what I've done, I deserve to go back. I'm prepared if need be. But who has more to lose?"

"I'll say you coerced me. I'll say you tortured me to fabricate the lies you desired to hear."

"That's a good strategy. It may even work in the legal system. But I wouldn't be sending these tapes to the police. No. I think you need to be judged in the court of public opinion by the sheep and the swine and the masses, who far outnumber your ilk. First, I'd send the video to your new highly prominent and highly conservative company. Maybe even some of their clients. Then, as you probably know, New York is the media capital of the world, the center of the gossip universe. The press would have a feeding frenzy over what they've seen here tonight. Your name and face would be plastered on the front pages and let's not forget about Misty the prostitute. When those photos get out they'd finally be worth the money I spent. How long do you think it is before she's sitting down on the set of *60 Minutes*? How about me? Corporate America does not like controversy William, that I know, and I could go on, but you get the point. To say your reputation would be tarnished beyond repair would be an understatement." He smiled. "You butt fucked the wrong peasant sir."

"You stupid—"

"You stupid what? Are you going to call me more names? I'm not scared of you William. I've got no more scared to give." He flicked Breg on the forehead. "Now here is my deal, the deal I envisioned traveling all the way down here. As of today you're officially retired. You won't be taking that job in New York or any other job for that matter. Do that, and the videos remain hidden."

"You haven't a clue about the ring you're climbing into. This is a bad idea Jamie."

"So was putting my money in your bank."

James opened his suitcase and began packing when Breg said, "One million. One million dollars even."

No response.

"A million five," said Breg, louder.

More silence.

"Two million Jamie. Destroy the video, give me my phone, and walk away. For that I offer you the staggering sum of two million dollars.

"I've got to go William. I have a life to put back together."

"Okay. I get it. You're upset. I'll make you very happy then. Three million. Now that's everything you asked for. That's more than fair."

"You could offer me ten million dollars and it wouldn't matter. As much as I would love to have it, and believe me I would, I don't want it from you. Not like this." He folded a shirt and said, "Oh, one last thing. Don't ever come visit New York. You aren't allowed. Stay here and enjoy yourself. Play golf and shuffleboard and take long walks on the beach. You've got a good life William. Leave the rest of us alone. We don't need you."

Breg's face and neck turned a volcanic red and the bald stripe running through his hair smoldered. He tried standing but fell, hitting his shoulder on the air conditioner. "You're going to regret this in more ways than you can ever imagine!"

"Maybe," said James. "But you'll have to take a number because I'm chock full of regret."

"You're walking away from an amazing future."

"I'm walking away from a horrible past."

"You'll be poor forever, you wretch."

"I've been poor forever, you prick."

"You don't have a clue what—"

"Good-bye William. I pray we never meet again. And I'll have plenty of copies of the tapes in case you get any ideas."

"I'm going to rip—"

"Alright, that's enough out of you for one lifetime," said James, sealing the thief's mouth with an extra tight piece of tape. "Relax, I'll call your pet goons to inform them where their Golden Goose is located."

He wrapped Breg like a mummy until the duct tape ran out and then tied him to the bed with a sheet. James gave the room a final sweep and left a tip for the maid. He collected the three secret cameras, hoping they were hooked up correctly.

It was cool outside, a perfect night for driving, and after hitting a late night fast food joint he headed to a train station in Georgia where he'd remove the license plate and strip the VIN number. He thought about calling Teddy but didn't. The only person he wanted to speak with was Dee. The call went straight to voicemail and considering the time, he counted on it.

He thought about saying something romantic and beautiful, something inspiring. If he'd known any poems he may have recited one. When the message beeped he spoke from the heart, deciding to keep it simple. "I love you hun. I always do." One day, he hoped to hear it back again.

The Pontiac hit a deep pothole getting off the highway and his body jiggled. He vowed to get in better shape and began making a list. First up when he got home was finding a new job. It was also second and third. Fourth was seeing a doctor about his late night urination issue and when he got to number five he stopped. Number five needed to be new, needed to be radical. He said the idea out loud.

"I will no longer worry about money. This I promise myself."

But he knew it wouldn't happen. Almost fifty years had passed and James Horton hadn't known anything else. It's what he did. It's who he was.

CPSIA information can be obtained at www.ICGtesting.com
Printed in the USA
BVOW08s1810090316

439654BV00003B/245/P